Ground Zero

●

Ground

Zero

●

BONNIE RAMTHUN

G. P. PUTNAM'S SONS
NEW YORK

This novel is a work of fiction. Any references to historical
events; to real people, living or dead; or to real locales are
intended only to give the fiction a sense of authenticity.
Names, characters, places, and incidents are the product
of the author's imagination or are used fictitiously, and
their resemblance, if any, to real-life counterparts
is entirely coincidental.

G. P. PUTNAM'S SONS
Publishers Since 1838
a member of
Penguin Putnam Inc.
375 Hudson Street
New York, NY 10014

Library of Congress Cataloging-in-Publication Data

Ramthun, Bonnie.
Ground zero / Bonnie Ramthun.
p.   cm.
ISBN 0-399-14509-5
I. Title.
PS3568.A4744G76   1999   98-48927 CIP
813'.54—dc21

Printed in the United States of America
1   3   5   7   9   10   8   6   4   2

Book design by Julie Duquet

I would like to thank Jerrie Hurd, who teaches fiction writing at the University of Colorado in Boulder. Not only is Jerrie a great teacher and a terrific writer (read *The Lady Pinkerton Gets Her Man*), but she treats every person in her class with respect and dignity, as though we were all best-selling authors.

My friend Megan Silva gave me the services of her English professor father, Dr. John Reardon, as a Christmas present. He critiqued my book meticulously and skillfully. My other editors include my sisters Roxanne, Aimee, and Allison, my mother, Judith, and my father-in-law, Gary Ramthun. This book wouldn't exist without them.

My thanks to the Gamers. My time as a Gamer changed my life. I am still in awe that I had the chance to work within a group of people so brilliant and talented.

At the disk-drive manufacturing firm where I worked after Gaming, I finally admitted that what I really wanted to do was write novels, not program computers. Greg Matheny, Kathy Albrecht, Dean Price, Mark Lutze, Linda Chumbley, Ron Bishop, and my good friend Steve Filips made me realize Gaming was not the only place where brilliant and incredibly funny people worked.

Thanks to my lifelong friends Harold York, Susan Dunn, and Megan Silva; my brothers Nick, Pete, Alex, Dan, and Marc; my fathers Lee John and Dick; and my three beautiful sons Thomas, Ryan, and Jasper. Thanks to Emile Bisson for hiring the newest Gamer, Bill Ramthun, and seating him at the desk right next to mine. Finally, thanks to Bill, my husband and best friend. He's better than fiction.

For my sister,
Roxanne Ailine Tomich

Ground Zero

●

·1

"Hey, Rosen, see those?"

"See what?" Dave Rosen was hunched over his computer. He was typing rapidly with two fingers, but stopped and looked over at Eileen Reed.

"Those flashes up at NORAD," Eileen said. "What're they doing up there?"

Rosen looked, shrugged, turned back to his screen.

"Probably nothing," Eileen said. "But I wanted you to see it. You know, if we both get blasted into hash by The Big One about ten minutes from now. We'll be playing our harps, halos on our heads, and I'll turn to you and say—"

Rosen mistyped, cursed, and rested his forehead with a dull clunk against his computer screen.

"I'm going to kill you," he said. "If you don't shut up."

Eileen grinned.

"I went inside the Mountain once," she said. The North American Air Defense Base, called NORAD, was buried inside Cheyenne Mountain. The cavern had been carved out of solid rock sometime during the 1950s. The only remnants of that huge excavation were a length of road and a tunnel opening. Her office window faced the mountain and she had been looking out the window instead of working on her own report.

"I know you did," Rosen said. He turned his head, his forehead still resting on the screen, and glared at her. "And I'm going to finish this report before Harben puts me back out clocking speeders on I-25."

Eileen pretended to be contrite. Rosen had been in the Special Investigations Division for only three months. He was tall and broad-shouldered, with a firm nose and straight ink-black hair. He was originally from New

York. To a lot of people in Colorado, he looked Navajo. Eileen suspected this was a source of amusement to him, having seen his reaction when people asked about his tribe.

"Okay, I'll shut up," Eileen said brightly, and tried to turn back to her own incomplete report.

But instead Eileen found herself looking at the flashes. There were more of them now, colored blue and red and white. Now she didn't feel like joking any more about The Big One. The pulse of lights from the tunnel that led to NORAD looked ominous. They looked *serious.*

She'd gone inside the Mountain, not on police business, but as a civilian on tour. Once she'd heard about NORAD, she had to go inside. Her mother told her she must be half cat on her father's side; Eileen poked her paws into everything. NORAD had a waiting list three months long for civilians. Eileen signed up and waited impatiently. She did not jiggle and hop from foot to foot when she finally boarded the NORAD bus that would take them down the entrance tunnel and into the base. She'd learned stillness long before. But if she had a tail, it would have been twitching back and forth when the ancient bus lurched and started down the tunnel.

The tour itself had been a bit of a disappointment. The cave was huge and damp and smelly, like old wet clay. The office buildings were sitting on monstrous metal coils, ready to hold steady under nuclear blasts. But they were drably colored and shabby. The buildings looked like old office structures just about anywhere. Then Eileen looked up, and saw the roof of the cavern. Rusty steel nets held back the crumbling rock. This sent a chill through her. There was solid rock over her head, hundreds of feet of it. She wouldn't even be a rust stain if some of that rock decided to come down. The nets looked as frail as cobwebs in the gloom of the cavern's ceiling.

Colorado seemed like such a safe place back in the early fifties, the tour guide explained. Eileen, standing at the back of the group with her hands shoved into her pockets and contemplating the roof, smiled. A mountain was no protection against hydrogen bombs. The tour guide went on to explain that Cheyenne Mountain still operated as the early warning center for any ballistic activity on the planet. The Mountain was not perfectly safe, but it was still the safest place there was. This, too, was chilling.

"Good thing the Cold War is over, right?" The guide laughed, and the tour group obediently laughed with him.

"Now here, these are water caverns. The excavators struck a spring when they were digging, so NORAD has an internal water supply . . ."

Eileen blinked and woke from her reverie as an enormous lightning bolt smashed down from the thunderclouds and danced across the rods at the top of Cheyenne Mountain. The entrance lights continued to flash.

She picked up the phone. She hesitated, wondering whom she could call to ask. She thought of Gary Hillyer. Hillyer was a journalist on the *Gazette Telegraph*. He would rib Eileen unmercifully if those flashes were some kind of standard Air Force drill. But Hillyer would know. He knew everything and everybody in Colorado Springs.

Captain Nick Harben saved her the call.

"Reed!" Harben could have used the phone's paging system, a simple matter of pressing a button, but Harben just liked to yell. Eileen figured Harben would be much happier in a police office from the forties, smoky and grimy and full of atmosphere. Instead, the Investigations Bureau offices were offensively clean and full of sunlight. Plants clustered around large windows that framed a beautiful view of the mountains. Personal computers sat on every desk, linked by a communications network to the rest of the police department and, by special access keys, to the countrywide law-enforcement network. Eileen had a good desk, close to the windows and not too close to Harben. She headed for Harben's glass cube.

Harben looked at her, his narrow face expressionless. He was just hanging up the phone.

"A body was found out at Fort Carson just now. That AWOL soldier, Jerry Pendleton."

"Oh great," Eileen said. "Hey, did you see those lights up at NORAD?"

"I didn't," Harben said with a frown. He looked out his window, squinting a little, then shrugged. "I've seen them once or twice before, Eileen. They might be having some sort of war game."

"Okay," Eileen said, relieved. She'd lived in the Springs for six years. Harben had lived there all his life. "I was beginning to think there was something wrong up there."

"Well, if there was, we wouldn't have to think about it long." Harben didn't smile at his own grim joke. Colorado Springs was one of the first targets for any major nuclear attack, and everybody knew it. The common phrase was "Ground Zero." Colorado Springs was just about as ground zero as Washington, D.C. NORAD was the wartime command center, where the President was supposed to relocate if Washington, D.C., was destroyed. There was supposed to be another huge underground base somewhere in the Russian steppes, similar to NORAD, and undoubtedly targeted by American missiles. None of it made much sense to Eileen, but she had never worried much about it until this morning.

"So let's talk about Pendleton."

"Yeah, right, I know. Why did I get saddled with this assignment?" Eileen dropped into a chair. She was the new Police Liaison for Fort Carson, Peterson, Schriever, NORAD, and the Air Force Academy, the five military establishments in Colorado Springs.

"You're the best person for the job," Harben said dryly. "You were in the Air Force once, as I recall."

"I don't want the Liaison job. I didn't want it. I hated the Air Force. I still hate it."

"You'll have to go talk to the new Air Force Medical Examiner. This is Army, by the way. The Air Force ME handles all the cases."

Eileen sighed. She was sarcastic around military people, and she had a tendency to be rude. Having been in the military, she couldn't help teasing the officers she met, like an unchained dog running outside a kennel. She just couldn't stop herself from barking through the bars.

"This is out at Fort Carson, so you can ask around and see if there are Games going on today," Harben suggested. "I'm sure it's nothing important, but that way you'll stop wondering about it."

Harben glanced at the faint flickerings from the hole in the side of the mountain, and a puzzled crease developed in his forehead.

"Well, I guess it has to be some kind of drill," he said.

North of Bermuda

The Unified German submarine *Edelweiss* dove hard, cutting through layers of cold seawater. She launched chaff, but the Subroc torpedo closed without hesitation. The USS *Guitarro* had been too close when the *Edelweiss* launched her missile. The German sub didn't have a chance.

There was a sound like the ringing of a bell, clearly audible to the frantically scrambling men inside the *Edelweiss*. Some hadn't even made it to their battle station when the bell rang through the hull.

The Subroc's motors stopped. A small flotational pack popped from the stern of the missile and it started to drift slowly to the surface.

"Damn," the German captain said. "We're dead." His crew was more eloquent in their disappointment, and for a few moments the air rang with curses. The crew of the Unified German sub hadn't even known that their own side in the Joint War Games was tracking them. They knew, of course, that they were to be the "rogue" submarine that unexpectedly attacks the United States, but security had been good. The crew hadn't even known their assignment until they'd left port and were in the open sea.

"We avoided her for almost a minute," the Fire Control officer reported quietly when the volume dropped. "Pretty good for this old girl."

"I didn't know a sub was tracking us," the Radar officer said. He was wooden-faced but still clearly upset. "I'm sorry, Captain."

"We got our missiles off before they killed us," the Captain said thoughtfully. "We learn from them. When it is our turn to play the hero and theirs to play the rogue, we'll do better than they did."

The Captain nodded at his first officer. The command was sent. The *Edelweiss* stood down from battle stations. Her part in the Game was over.

Washington, D.C., and NORAD

Washington received the signal while the *Guitarro* was still accelerating. The Secret Service hustled the President to his helicopter in thirty-seven seconds. Since everyone knew the drill was going to happen, the President's schedule was clear and he was sipping coffee in his office when the Secret Service notified him of the alert. Not a particularly realistic drill for the President, but he was, after all, the President. Air Force One was in the air twenty-four minutes later.

NORAD saw the missiles leave the ocean surface. The latest satellite technology sent the information to the computer screens just slightly slower than the speed of light. Air Force Major General Jeremy Kelton didn't change his usual calm expression. He was drinking from a can of soda. He put the can down carefully, reached over, and flicked open a plastic cover. He turned a key.

NORAD buttoned up. The outside lights, flashing for half an hour now in warning of a simulated attack, stopped. Whoever was inside would stay inside. Whoever was outside would not be able to get in until the emergency was over. A quiet tone sounded throughout the cavern. The outside air fans died. There was a faint, almost imperceptible flicker as the power system shunted over to internals. The only door to the gigantic tunnel swung shut with a crash. Air Force personnel raced to their positions. Some still had thick sandwiches clutched in their hands. The cafeteria at NORAD Air Force Base had a reputation for good food, and a number of the shift workers were eating lunch at the time of the alarm.

Colorado Springs Investigations Bureau

"I'm going to try one more time to get out of this, boss," Eileen said earnestly. "I hate the military. I'll be rude. I'll spit in all the wrong places and I'll call colonels by their first names. I'll step on their shiny shoes and get them all muddy. I can't help it."

"I want you to step on shoes, Eileen," Harben said coldly. "That's the general idea. Congress passed the law about civilian police being involved in military investigations just last year, and the military hates it. But there were too many scandals. Like what happened to your friend."

Eileen had told Harben about her friend Bernice when she received her promotion to detective. She figured Harben should know. Harben never showed any emotion, which Eileen thought a relief. She couldn't stand sympathy, particularly about Bernie.

Captain Bernie Ames was flying a standard training flight in Arizona when her A-10 broke away from the formation and headed north. She didn't respond on the radio to the increasingly frantic attempts to contact her. Search planes found the remains of her body and her A-10 two weeks later at the top of a Colorado mountain.

The resulting Air Force investigation concluded "pilot error." Worse, the gossip always added "female" to "pilot error." Eileen, feeling as shredded as Bernie's A-10, could do nothing about the verdict. The records were sealed. No real explanation was ever found for why Bernie decided to fly her plane hundreds of miles north and nose-dive into a mountain. Her friend went into her grave as a bad, possibly suicidal pilot. A bad *woman* pilot.

"I don't want to deal with their garbage," she said heavily. "I doubt I can help. But I'll do it."

Harben regarded her for a moment. She couldn't tell what he was thinking. But then again, she never could. Harben was the definition of a closed book.

"Good. Thank you." Harben picked up a pen and wrote briefly. "Here's the access name for the Pendleton file." He looked up. "What is it?"

"The flashes," Eileen said. "They stopped. I guess it was nothing after all."

•2

From the highway the Air Force base looked like a fenced mile of prairie grass. A few dun-colored buildings dotted the grass. Schriever had been built so quickly there was still a prairie dog town within the fencing. There were no coyotes within the base, and none had yet figured out how to pass the electrified fence. The prairie dogs were very fat. One of the buildings was the Space Command Center, which ran the Ballistic Missile Defense program. The so-called Star Wars program had faded from the public sight, but the funding continued through discretionary, or "black," funds. Few people knew that the Ballistic Missile Defense program was still continuing. Fewer still knew that much of the proposed system was already in place.

Inside the building, the Space Command Center was hooked up to the same satellite feeds as NORAD, although its early warning systems weren't nearly as complex as those of its elder cousin. Space Command's computer screens, however, were greatly superior. Instead of Klaxon and a bright dot north of Bermuda on a black and white map of the earth, a huge screen showed earth's Northern Hemisphere from a lofty altitude. A blue map of the ocean was so precise it looked like a movie shot from the Shuttle. The computer marked concentric rings around the probable launch site. Tiny black lines were already starting to show at the center of the circle. The radars were picking up enough of a track to mark the flight path of the incoming nuclear warheads.

Colonel Olsen, Commander in Chief, Space, picked up the phone that connected him to NORAD. He was at the back of the Center at Space Command, and was a little nearsighted but refused to admit it. Consequently he'd been squinting at the computer map and had a headache.

"Give me validation of that launch!" he barked.

The other phone rang, the Gold Phone. Colonel Olsen scooped it up with his free hand.

"Yes, sir," he said into the Gold Phone. "Copy all," he said into the Blue Phone. "Get me impact," he said to his Space Director, who was sitting elegantly straight and seemingly relaxed at his left side.

"Washington, D.C., and surrounding area," she responded immediately. The glow from her computer terminal lit her expressionless face.

"Oh my God," murmured a member of the audience. He turned to his companion, a Marine colonel. The man was ashy pale. He lived in Washington, D.C., and had come out to Colorado for the Joint War Games. "What happened?"

The Marine looked at him in surprise. Then the officer leaned close to the other man's ear.

"This is a simulation," he said. "Those are unarmed missiles. Duds." The Marine looked at the enormous computer screen. The missiles were climbing skyward in the midst of flames and smoke. "The President is really on Air Force One, but this is his drill with the Secret Service. Those missiles are really aimed toward Washington, but they'll be detonated if the system misses."

"What if they don't detonate?" the other officer hissed.

"Then we'll surprise some fish," the Marine replied impatiently "They're aimed at the bay, and they're tiny. They could splash down next to a rowboat and they wouldn't capsize the boat, though I think whoever was rowing the boat would need to change his shorts. But they won't hit anything. Where were you this morning when the briefing was going on?"

The officer from Washington sat back in his chair in relief.

"Thank God," he whispered to the other officer. "I missed the briefing—I got lost coming out to the base. I thought this was real."

"It could be real," the Marine colonel said grimly. "This time, it isn't."

"Roger, the President is in the air," Colonel Olsen said into the Gold Phone. "Impact area D.C. The missile type is probably SS-N-06, multiple warheads likely. Time to impact"—he glanced over at the Space Director's computer screen—"less than ten minutes. Do I have authority to shoot this down?"

There was silence.

The Colonel stood at attention, one ear to the Gold Phone, the other to the Blue. His face was square and tanned. Laugh wrinkles networked his eyes. A thin line of sweat dropped from his hairline into a wrinkle and disappeared.

"Sir?" Major Torrence, the Ground Director, clenched the tabletop with his left hand. His right finger hovered over the computer key that gave Weapons Response Authority. His finger trembled slightly. He knew this was a game, but it was a deadly serious one. Major Torrence knew about the nightmare War Game three years before, where the blundering and indecisiveness of the command staff caused the complete destruction of most of the American East Coast. Several forced retirements followed the debacle. Even simulated deaths weren't taken lightly, not when they were counted in the millions.

"Less than eight minutes to impact," the Space Director said without inflection.

Colonel Olsen stood like a statue. The phone at his ear was silent.

"We need weapons release to shoot this down," the Atlantic Commander said over the radio communications link.

"There's a manned shuttle launch from Russia today at eleven," a Defense aide said over the same link. "There's a possibility—if we release the Brilliant Pebbles they might shoot it down."

"Are the bombers scrambled?" Olsen asked.

"We have two B-1s in the air, and that's all we have on alert nowadays," Air Command replied from Omaha, Nebraska. During the Cold War hundreds of pilots would be racing to bombers kept ready for just such an event, but not today.

"Seven minutes, thirty seconds," NORAD reported.

"We have to be prepared for a massive follow-on," the Atlantic Commander said. "The President has authorized."

The Colonel didn't say a word. He nodded his head abruptly at Major Torrence.

"Weapons release authorized," the Major roared into his microphone. His finger punched the button that would turn the first "key." There was a faint overload whine from the communications network.

"Brilliant Pebbles released," barked the Space Weapons officer, pressing his console button and turning the second "key."

Far above, in a low earth orbit, hundreds of small bullet-shaped objects received a burst of encrypted computer instructions. The Brilliant Pebbles stopped their lazy orbital spin by squirting out tiny jets of hydrogen peroxide. They deployed their sensing eyes. Circular radar dishes unfolded delicately from shielded housings on top of the Pebbles.

Deployment of the sensing eyes was an expensive operation. The lubrication of the folding joints didn't last forever in the harsh climate of space. The Space Weapons officer, in his excitement, sent the "All Deploy" command to the Pebbles. Every Pebble in orbit around the earth received the instruction and opened its radar eyes. This mistake would earn a sharp reprimand from Olsen for the offending officer.

The Pebbles that opened above the Atlantic had plenty to see. The twin radar dishes on each Pebble caught the bright flare of the burning SS-N-06 rockets. The eyes, now in control, sent commands to the tiny peroxide thrusters. To an astronaut floating a few hundred yards away, the Pebbles would have looked comical. Their big goggle eyes seemed to peer intently earthward, shifting back and forth as they tried to acquire the tracks of the nuclear missiles.

The first two missiles finished boost phase and launched the vehicle that contained the nuclear bombs, called reentry vehicles or RVs. The postboost vehicle started an irregular burn as it launched off the RVs. To the Brilliant Pebbles, the missiles became harder to track. The second set of missiles were still boosting, leaving telltale flare.

Seven Brilliant Pebbles locked on the remaining missiles. One Pebble, achieving an intercept solution, sent a burst of instruction over the communication link. The instruction was a simple one; it was, essentially, "I've got it!" The other Pebbles, still struggling for an intercept on the missile, received the transmission and stopped calculating.

The winning Pebble shed its power packs and support system, called the lifejacket, and leaped toward the missile. Behind it, another Pebble shouted over the communications link and headed for the other missile.

The velocity at impact was nearly incalculable. The Pebble disintegrated into particles. The fragile electrical impulses that were supposed to set off the bomb vaporized along with inert chunks of steel. In a fraction of a second the warhead was no more. The debris dropped toward the ocean below.

"Got 'em!" crowed the Weapons Officer.

"Can that, Captain," snapped Colonel Olsen. "What have you hit?"

"Two boosters, three and four. Two Pebbles launched, two hits, no misses. Two busses are currently deploying RVs."

"Impact time?"

"Two minutes, sir. Impact point is Washington, D.C."

Colorado Springs Investigations Bureau

Eileen sat at her computer, delaying the moment when she would call up the Pendleton file. She was watching the rainstorm and she was thinking about her time in the military. They were not pleasant memories.

Eileen shrugged and turned away from the rain. Time to think of other things. Like teasing the new rookie, perhaps.

"Hey, Rosen," she said. Rosen was editing. His rapid two-finger typing had ended. He was still intent on his computer screen, looking over his report.

"What?"

"The lights up at Cheyenne Mountain ended. Harben told me it wasn't a nuclear bomb."

"Hmm, really," Rosen said dryly. "Like I couldn't tell by now."

"No, but they were tracking something big."

She had his attention now, although he wasn't looking at her. She would win if he looked over at her.

"Something big?"

"Yeah, Harben said for us to go check out the news channels."

Rosen sat up in his chair and looked over at her, and she spoiled the joke with her grin. She couldn't keep it off her face. He knew he'd been had.

"Oh, come *on*," he snapped, and turned back to his screen.

"Ha, I got you to look," she said. "You were about to get up and check out CNN for the big landing of Klaatu and his alien friends."

"Next time if you can keep a straight face I might even go find a TV," Rosen said, and started typing on his keyboard again.

Eileen, having lost the game, still felt cheered. She'd been a rookie her-self, not so long ago. She turned from her computer and looked out the window. There was another thundershower moving in over Cheyenne Mountain. The flashing lights had ended for good, it seemed. The entrance to NORAD was dark and still.

Space Command, Schriever Air Force Base

"Ground Sensor, what are you tracking?"

The ground-based radars on the East Coast were similar to the radar dishes on the Brilliant Pebbles, although the ground radars were much more powerful. Unrestricted by weight or space, the radars had the nuclear weapons along the coast to draw power. They scanned over the Atlantic with muscular pulses of energy, finding and tracking the tiny falling bombs with exact precision. Their job was to take out the missiles that the Brilliant Pebbles missed. They were the last line of defense.

The ground interceptors were a descendant of the Patriot missile system, an advanced smart bullet that could take apart the big city-busting bombs before they had a chance to detonate. The powerful rockets could acceler-ate at high speeds to intercept their targets. They had weak sensors for eyes; the ground-based radars were their eyes, pointing out and aiming them at the incoming bombs.

The interceptors locked onto the incoming RVs.

"Radars are tracking, looks like the ground interceptors are locked on," the Sensor officer said, a puzzled note creeping into her voice.

The interceptors didn't fire.

"Why aren't they firing, Ground Weapons?" Colonel Olsen swung his head like a nervous bull. The narrow black tracks were closing in on Wash-ington with frightening speed.

"Ground Weapons?"

There was no answer from the Ground Weapons station.

Colonel Olsen dropped the Blue Phone from his ear.

"Major Torrence, detonate those missiles," he snapped. Torrence reached out so quickly he knocked over an empty Styrofoam cup that once held coffee. He flipped all four buttons on his console. The missiles abruptly puffed into white smoke and arced toward the ocean.

Colonel Olsen was smiling. Deep laugh lines framed his eyes. It was not a pretty smile.

"Game Director," he said softly. "What the hell is your person doing back there? Sleeping? We have live assets on this Game, goddammit!"

"Debris is down," crackled a voice over the intercom. The chase pilots in the Atlantic had just verified that the scrap metal from the detonated missiles had landed safely in the ocean.

Major Torrence tore the headset from her head and threw it down in exasperation. Colonel Eaton, the Space Director, took the headset gently from her head, not disturbing a hair of her smooth French roll.

The Gaming Center, Space Command, was a long rectangular room with a raised dais at the far end. Built in a series of steps, the room was like a small theater. Twelve audience members, most of them in military uniform, sat in comfortable chairs. At the front of the room was a large-screen projection of the computer simulation. The screen suddenly blossomed with light. The real test missiles had been detonated, but the computer was instructed to continue the simulation if such an event happened. The virtual bombs had just impacted in the virtual city of Washington, D.C.

The audience blinked and muttered at the rising nuclear cloud above Washington. The simulation was detailed enough to be horrifying.

Along each side of the room were the narrow doors that held the operations officers. Directly ahead of Colonel Olsen, at the corner of the room, was the Ground Weapons station door. The other doors opened cautiously. Civilians who ran the different computer consoles peered out with puzzled faces.

The Game Director, a tall balding civilian, paced tightly to the Ground Weapons door and flung it open. The audience, muttering and shifting, grew still in a slow wave as first the front, then the back of the room became aware that there was something wrong.

The Director backed out of the room. He turned away from the door, and the people in the room could see his freckles standing out in a suddenly white face.

Inside the room there was a figure slumped over the console. To Colonel Olsen, without glasses, it appeared as though the woman in the room had a long yellow stick or tube tucked under her armpit. Only as the first muffled screams burst out did Olsen realize the stick was the handle of a screwdriver, and it wasn't tucked under her arm. It was driven deeply into her back, and the sprawled gracelessness of the body could only mean that she was dead.

•3

The time from the discovery of the body behind the narrow door in the Gaming Center to the ringing of Harben's phone was fourteen minutes. Nelson Atkins, Game Director, called Major Jeff Blaine, Chief of Security for Schriever Air Force Base. Major Blaine had dealt with murder before in other positions with the military police. Not at Schriever, though. He wasn't set up for a murder investigation at Schriever and he knew it. He called the base commander, Colonel Willmeth.

Colonel Willmeth had been the base commander for just three months. He hadn't even caught up on his paperwork yet. He put Blaine on hold, cursed briefly and fluently, and opened his intercom.

"Roberta?" he asked. "Can you come in here for a moment, please?"

Roberta came into the room a moment later and shut the door behind her. She was a woman who had been really beautiful thirty years before. She would still be beautiful, Colonel Willmeth thought, if she weren't still trying to look twenty. She had black hair piled high in what was now a trendy do. She wore the latest in high-school fashion and her bright pink nails were almost an inch long. She was the base commander's secretary, and Colonel Willmeth hated her with all his heart.

"What is it, Jake?" she asked. Colonel Willmeth winced at her use of his first name but said nothing. The troops in his last command would have bet their last paycheck that Willmeth could face down a tank or two with his mouth alone, but they had never met Roberta.

"We've had a murder at the Gaming Center," Colonel Willmeth said. Roberta's large black eyes widened.

"A murder?"

Willmeth nodded. He shrugged with his hands outspread, as he'd done a thousand times in the last three months. Only Roberta knew the rules that were specific to Schriever Air Force Base. Only Roberta knew the filing system. Roberta knew where everything was stored. Roberta was the real base commander, and only Roberta and the base commander knew it. Colonel Willmeth had wondered at the sigh of relief Colonel Flaherty had given when he took command, but he'd been too excited at his first base command to care.

"Hang on," Roberta said. She left the office and Colonel Willmeth chewed his lip, looking at the blinking light that meant Major Blaine and thinking black thoughts.

"According to Regs we need to call Air Force OSI, Office of Special Investigations," Roberta said, reentering with a notebook in her hands. "That's Major Stillwell at Peterson Air Force Base." She flipped a few pages carefully with the pads of her nails so as to keep her polish unmarred. "We're also required to notify the Colorado Springs Police Department."

"What?" Colonel Willmeth said, distracted from his contemplation of Roberta's shiny nails. "Civilians?"

"According to Regs this last year, passed by Congress. They've got a military liaison with a security clearance. Detective Eileen Reed. Her captain, that's Harben. I've got all their phone numbers."

Roberta wrote briefly, tore the page from her notebook, and laid it carefully on Colonel Willmeth's desk.

"Amazing," the Colonel said wearily. "Thank you, Roberta. I don't know what I'd do without you."

Roberta smiled her little Mona Lisa smile, the one that made Colonel Willmeth feel like grinding his teeth.

"No problem, Jake," she said. "If you need anything else, let me know." She left the room.

Colonel Willmeth swallowed hard and punched the light on the phone, opening the connection to Major Blaine.

Colorado Springs Investigations Bureau

"Hey, Rosen," Eileen said. She'd typed in the access code to the Pendleton file, and had already read the brief summary. It was time to go out to Peterson and take a look.

Rosen had finished editing and was looking over a printout of his file. He'd propped a foot up on a nearby chair and was sipping from a bottle of purified water. Rosen was a health nut. He never drank coffee or soda, which was a mystery to Eileen. How did he get *going* in the morning?

"Yes?"

"You want to go look at this Pendleton guy? He's a month dead, been lying in the bushes."

"Oh boy," Rosen said. "Is this another one of those so-you-wanna-be-a-detective tests you guys keep coming up with?"

"No, I just want to see if you'll puke," Eileen said innocently.

Peter O'Brien, hanging up his coat on a hook, snorted with laughter. There were damp rings under his armpits and the back of his neck was beaded with sweat.

"Grow up," Rosen said. He didn't smile, but his black eyes glittered. That was his version of a laugh.

"You should go," O'Brien said. "Who knows? Maybe Eileen will puke."

Eileen was opening her mouth for a sizzling reply when Harben yelled her name.

"I don't puke," she said loftily to O'Brien. "And if I do, I'll make sure to puke on you."

"You puke on kiddie rides at the carnival," O'Brien returned automatically. He was already typing his own access code and pulling crumpled notes out of his pockets. O'Brien never managed to remember his notebook, so he ended up writing notes on any piece of paper he could scrounge. This eccentricity was a great source of amusement to Eileen and exasperation to Harben, but O'Brien managed to do a good job with his ATM slips and his grocery receipts.

Harben, on the phone again, was holding the receiver away from his ear.

"I'll have a detective out immediately," he said. Eileen could hear the tiny frantic buzzing from the receiver, the excited tones of the speaker.

"That's fine, she'll sign whatever she needs to, she has a security clearance. Yes, she's our Military Liaison. Yes, she has a lot of experience with these cases." Harben looked soberly at Eileen, who started grinning. "I'll get her out there. Don't disturb the scene, understand? Don't clean up anything, don't touch a thing."

Harben hung up the phone gently and the tiny voice, still squawking, stopped.

"Security clearance, sir?"

"There's been a murder at Schriever Air Force Base," Harben said.

"Schriever?" Eileen asked in surprise. There was never trouble at Schriever. Peterson Air Force Base, sometimes, Fort Carson, all the time, but Schriever, never. It was too small and too distant from everywhere else to be much trouble. Eileen, in fact, had never seen Schriever. It was out on the eastern prairie somewhere.

"Schriever. Some civilian Defense Department woman got herself murdered and that calm, collected voice you just heard was Major Jeff Blaine, Chief of Security." Eileen grinned again. Harben's expression didn't change. Eileen had learned in her first year under Harben that Harben never laughed at his own jokes, or even smiled at them. But he didn't mind if you did.

"She's in some top-secret area with classified information just oozing out of the walls, if the good Major can be believed. He'll be briefing you on the information, you'll have to promise never to tell, et cetera."

"Okay. I guess this takes priority over the Pendleton case?"

"Yes, it does. In fact, the Major tells me the Air Force Office of Special Investigations will not be able to get out there for at least today, so you are on your own. Their Major Stillwell is at some conference in Alabama and they're only one person deep in the OSI at Peterson."

"So he'll show up in a day or so and take this off my hands?"

"Correct, Eileen. But you'll have to write all the new standard Military Liaison reports on the investigation and file them."

"Great, boss," Eileen said, and sighed.

"Get on the road, ma'am," Harben said, and flapped a bony hand. "I hear it's a long drive to Schriever. Oh, and one other thing," he added as Eileen turned for the door.

"Sir?" Eileen asked politely.

"Get their shoes all muddy, Eileen. That's what you're there for."

Space Command, Schriever Air Force Base

"Jake, hello," Colonel Olsen said in tones of relief. He held out a hand, and they shook firmly. They were both the same rank, so military protocol allowed them to call each other by their first names. They knew each other from Germany as well. Their daughters became fast friends in grammar school and were now attending the same high school in the Springs. Willmeth took a look around the Gaming Center. Blaine had them all in their seats. The Civilian Gamers were all sitting at the back of the room. No one looked well. No one was speaking. One was openly sobbing. The room was noisy with the hum of the air-conditioning fans, but that was all. The huge screen still showed the Earth. Willmeth spotted the one closed door. Olsen noticed his glance and nodded slightly.

"Major Blaine is collecting the police detective at the gate," Willmeth said in a low voice. "He'll be here soon, and we can get everyone out of this room."

"We stopped the simulation and shut down the systems outside the base," Olsen spoke quietly in return. "But this is going to fuck us up in Washington, Jake."

"I know, Brad," Willmeth said. "As soon as the police release you from the scene, I've got a secure phone set up. We'll get on the horn and do some damage assessment."

"Good," Olsen said in satisfaction. "Thank you."

There was nothing more to be said. There would be action, later on, and reports to be written and meetings to attend, but for now there was nothing more. The two colonels stood and watched the Earth and the drifting pattern of simulated nuclear fallout.

Manitou Springs, Colorado

George Tabor was taking a walk. With him trotted Fancy, his English spaniel. The spaniel loved her Thursday-morning walks. Meandering up and down the hilly streets of Manitou Springs, they brushed by overgrown lilac bushes and stepped over an occasional cracked piece of pavement.

Tuesdays they walked downtown, which was interesting but not nearly as pleasant to the young dog. The smells weren't as good.

George sat down for a moment or two at his regular stopping point, a low rock wall near Manitou Springs Avenue. It was a pleasant place to sit. The wall was shaded in the summer, sunny in the winter, and had a pretty view of the downtown area. Additionally, there was a crack in the stonework that occasionally contained a small beige cloth bag. George scratched his knee and leaned back and scooped the bag out of the crack and into his pocket.

He didn't always search the stone. If there were no bike chained to a light post downtown, or if it had a flat rear tire, he wouldn't have stopped by the stone at all. But the bike was there, sitting on fat knobby tires, looking cheerful. George felt cheerful, looking at it. Something good, he thought, and absently rubbed his spaniel's ears. Perhaps something very good.

The bag retrieved, he finished his walk briskly, as he always did. The spaniel leaped happily into the backseat of his car and George drove home through the mild summer morning, humming softly along with the radio.

As a child, he'd thought he wanted to be an American. He was a capitalist by birth, it seemed. He'd made pocket change holding places in food lines before he could read a book. He had a thousand ideas about making money. Life would be so easy if he lived in America, he thought. Then in George's adolescence he revised his opinion on America. He could see, even with his limited vision, that the Soviet Union wouldn't hold together much longer. He might be able to live out the uncomfortable years of a Soviet breakup in some nice place like Great Britain or America, working as a spy for his country. Eventually he could come home to a freshly liberated Russia. A man who knew the workings of capitalism might do very well.

George never wavered once he decided what he wanted to do. At twenty-five, to all appearances a dedicated GRU officer, he made the ridiculously easy entry through Canada with papers declaring him to be the American George Tabor. He never looked back.

By the time he had focused on stealing secrets from the Missile Defense program time, his theory about the dissolution of the Soviet Union was proving to be correct. George's contacts started to change. An East German spy took him to a lavish dinner at the Broadmoor. After the first former Soviet satellite started to pay for information, George started probing for more. The new Russian Republic became a customer instead of a master. He expanded, like a good capitalist, to include the new countries that were once satellites of the former Soviet Union. A contact in Japan made a very polite request and delivered a staggering amount of money. George was very good at his job. In the post–Cold War world of espionage, he was in his element. And absolutely *everybody* wanted to steal missile-defense information from the Americans.

Posing as a headhunter for a defense contractor, George had obtained a phone directory from a janitor at the Ballistic Missile Defense Center. The phone listing he received wasn't classified, but it was still a hit. It contained names, phone numbers, and supervisors' names. Eventually, after hours tracing supervisor to supervisor, George figured out each employee's field: operations, administration, engineering, security.

George made discreet phone calls. He interviewed several applicants in his modestly plush office near Garden of the Gods park. He was searching for a person with a grudge. Or a person who needed money. Or even a person who knew someone who needed money.

Six months after the handy little pink directory fell into his hands, he had his contact. George worked on the contact like a fine fly fisherman—a sport he'd recently taken up and found very pleasant. Hooking a trout was like landing a contact into a top-secret installation. He got the same kind of thrill. The contact he found had an immense ego. The contact hadn't been given a promotion in a long time. The contact needed money. George commiserated. George soothed. George asked for some sensitive information—just as a way to get a better idea of the program, so he could steal away good people and put them into better jobs. The contact delivered. The hook was set.

When he asked for classified information, the contact knew who he was. And didn't care. The packet was delivered. It was very good. The contact was in the bag.

George and Fancy entered George's apartment. His spaniel shook free of the leash and raced toward her water bowl as though afraid someone would snatch it away if she didn't get there in moments. Silly dog, George thought fondly. He shut his front door and locked it. He didn't have to draw the shades. He drew them every morning before his walk as a matter of routine. Finally, at last, he drew the savory little bag from his pocket.

The smile, like the Cheshire cat's, was the last to leave. His eyes widened and his face muscles sagged in disbelief. Finally the smile winked out. He crumpled the piece of paper so tightly, he would have a bruised palm later. He said a very American word, with very American inflection. He said it again. Then he picked up the phone and, after a moment, dialed a number from memory.

"Yes?" a voice said briskly.

"Is this 387-7754?"

There was a pause.

"No," the voice said heavily.

"Sorry."

George cradled the phone gently and began to pack.

•4

The Pentagon

"There's been a what?" The Admiral's voice, unbelieving, was nearly shrill.

"A murder, sir. At the War Game Center. That's what stopped the Game."

There was a long pause. The Admiral turned to look out the windows. He had an office at the E level, which gave him one of the prettier views of Washington, D.C. His face was thin and wrinkled. His sharply creased uniform was immaculate.

"Have the ships been notified of the stand-down?"

"Yes, sir, I gave the abort code and we've verified that all the components have received the code. The ships are standing by. We had an All Deploy sent to the Brilliant Pebbles—"

"All Deploy? All of them?" The Admiral's voice climbed toward shrill again.

"Yes, sir. Listen, sir. We knew mistakes like that could happen during the progress of a Game. All Deploy was considered one of the mistakes that could happen. We've sent the stand-down command to the Pebbles, and they're functioning. That's actually quite encouraging, and gives us a lot of data."

"Well, that's something, at least." The Admiral held the phone against his ear and patted his stomach with his free hand. He was rubbing against a network of burn scars, a souvenir of an Iraqi shell that was more accurate than most. The scars no longer hurt, but it was a nervous habit to touch and rub at them. The rubbing soothed him.

"We've had word out to the DIA to find out if they've gotten feedback on this."

"Was this—this was a death? Or was this a murder?"

"A murder, sir. One of the civilian Gamers was stabbed to death, or at least that's what it looked like to me." Olsen didn't like admitting his vision problems.

"All right, then. You aborted the duds in flight. We know the Germans think we were testing our early radar warning against rogue submarines. No one has to know we lost the Game. Everything but the ground interceptors worked perfectly."

"Perfectly, sir," Colonel Olsen said.

"All right. Make sure your OSI team is a bright one. Make sure they know what they're looking for. Who's on the case right now?"

"Civilian police, sir. The Police Liaison."

"Civilian?"

"The Schriever police don't have the resources to investigate a murder. The Peterson investigations officer is in Alabama on a case and couldn't fly into Colorado in less than six hours. Federal law requires we get assistance from the Police Liaison in homicides. There's only one person, and she's ex-military. Air Force pilot."

"Ahh," the Admiral grunted. "Better. I guess it'll have to do. What's this detective's name?"

"Reed, sir. Eileen Reed."

"Check her out."

"Yes, sir. I've already sent the request."

"Thanks, Brad. We'll see you tomorrow here at the Pentagon. We'll have to set up for another Game."

"Yes, sir."

The Admiral pushed the intercom button that connected him to his secretary.

"Get me Mills at the CIA, Delores," he said, and hung up the phone. He turned to contemplate the pretty view, his hand absently patting his stomach. In less than a minute, the phone rang.

"Mills," Kane said into the phone. "There's been another murder."

Schriever Air Force Base

It was a long drive. Eileen fought noon traffic south on Academy Boulevard and turned east on Platte Avenue. The city soon gave way to long stretches of hot, dry open land. She turned off Platte and aimed her Jeep down Highway 94. The open stretches of land became a ranch. Cattle dotted rolling hills, grazing on long brown prairie grass. She thought about Captain Bernie Ames.

They'd met when they'd been forced to bunk together in the overcrowded bachelor quarters in Minot, North Dakota. Bernie loved to talk. Eileen loved to listen. They were fantastically different. Bernie grew up in inner-city Chicago; Eileen was raised on a Wyoming ranch. Bernie, short and round, busty and loud, confessed that she always wanted to look just like Eileen. Eileen, tall and gawky, frozen into silence by any crowd greater than two people, confessed that she always wanted to be just like Bernie.

Bernie would no more have flown her plane into a mountain than she would have put her clothes on backward. Bernie was a fighter. She was not the suicidal type. She loved to fly, she loved to crack jokes, she loved food and men and movies and every delicious part of her life. There had to be a reason she flew her plane into a mountain.

Eileen did everything she could to find out what happened on Bernie's last flight. She went up her chain of command. She found out, astonishingly, that this was the third time a pilot broke away from a formation and disappeared. When her review board came up that year she was passed over for her promotion. The message was clear. Eileen handed in her resignation, and the greatest surprise was the intensity of her relief.

She loved to fly, though it was not a consuming passion. Eileen was a competent pilot without dash, and she knew before she graduated from pilot training that she would never be a great pilot. But she lived while four of her classmates died, so perhaps a lack of dash wasn't so bad. Eileen liked being part of a squadron. She thought it would hurt more to give it all up.

It was only later, as she was waiting for acceptance into the police academy, that she realized how much she'd disliked military life. She'd joined to see more of the world than Wyoming, and because she wanted to be around people. When she was growing up she didn't have many friends. She didn't have any brothers or sisters, and her nearest neighbors were twenty-four miles away over dirt roads.

Eileen found there were pilots from the more thickly settled east who couldn't comprehend that she lived twenty-four miles away from another living being, that there were ranchers who were even more isolated than the Reeds, that a trip to the grocery store was a large and well-planned monthly event. One pilot from New Jersey could not believe there existed a place in the United States where pizza could not be delivered. Eileen laughed for a long time at that. She told him that when she and her high-school friends got a hankering for McDonald's, they would drive three hours into Rapid City, South Dakota. Six hours round-trip for a fast-food hamburger.

Being in a squadron was crowded and never lonely. Delivery pizza was almost always available. Eileen found a real friend in Bernie. Military life should have been exactly what she was looking for.

But something about the Air Force just wasn't right for Eileen, and she knew it long before Bernie flew into a mountain. Being in the Air Force was like eating a meal made of plastic. The food looked delicious, but it didn't taste good at all. The family of the squadron, so enticing when Eileen considered it, turned out to be an insider's circle where the condescension toward nonpilots was childish and cruel. And Eileen always felt like a second-class citizen, no matter how well she flew. She was a girl, a woman, a female. An outsider.

At some point while she was still trying to get Bernie's files reopened, Eileen decided she wanted to try her hand at police work. She wasn't even sure what made her decide that being a cop might be satisfying. Eileen found she loved it. And she was surprisingly good at it. The new Liaison job was going to be difficult, but she was Detective Reed now, not Air Force Captain Reed. Things would be different. She would make sure of it.

Eileen smiled at the cattle. It was a long drive, but a pretty one. Time enough to get her thoughts in order and her temper firmly locked away. Eileen's mother was a true redhead, tall and fiery and very intelligent, with

ice-cream skin and lots of freckles. Eileen's hair was darker and she had no
adorable freckles, but she had her mother's height and her temper. To her
regret, sometimes.

"Step on shoes," she murmured to herself. "But softly, softly now. And
don't forget you're not in the military anymore. You don't have to call anyone 'sir.' "

Eileen found herself missing Jim Erickson fiercely. Jim was her partner,
the senior member of their team. He'd moved to Denver six months before.
Eileen was glad for the opportunity to move up into a senior position, but
she missed Jim's steady and unblinking presence on a case. He made her
laugh. And she'd never handled a really big homicide all on her own before.

"So what?" she said to herself. "I can handle it." Up ahead, she saw a
small sign modestly announcing Schriever Air Force Base and an arrow
pointing to the right.

She made the long curving turn off the highway at a safe and sane cop
speed, about sixty miles an hour, and as she headed down a side road she
could see a group of buildings on the horizon. A cluster of big white golf-
ball shapes, radar dishes, sat beside the buildings. As Eileen approached the
base, she became aware of the enormous size of the dishes. They were
huge, five or six stories tall, looking like puffball mushrooms from an old
horror movie.

"This place is bigger than I thought," Eileen murmured as she took the
final turn onto the base. There was a security patrol Blazer waiting to meet
her, lights flashing. The Blazer was parked in a poor position for Eileen to
speak to the driver. She pulled up to the passenger side, rolled down her
window, and waited as the occupant reached over and cranked down the
passenger-side window.

"Major Blaine?"

"Yes, and you are?"

"Detective Eileen Reed." Eileen flipped open her badge and held it up.

"Follow me," Major Blaine said shortly. He was a trim man with a mustache and a deep widow's peak. His face was pale. Eileen looked at the
sleepy peaceful base and saw a couple of early lunchtime joggers heading
off along broad dirt paths.

She followed the Blazer down a long curving road, lined on each side by
wide green strips of lawn. Sprinklers fought gamely under the hot prairie

sun. Eileen could see brown spots dotting the green. The sprinklers were losing the battle. The Blazer parked by a long, low building and Eileen followed. The base really started here; she could see two sets of sturdy fences with an asphalt strip of no-man's-land between them. At intervals along the fence line she saw posts with cameras mounted at the top. Very serious security. The air was hot and dry and smelled of baking asphalt and prairie sage. Very faintly, Eileen could smell cattle.

"Can I see your badge again, please?" Blaine asked after they both got out of their cars. Eileen gave it to him, and watched as Blaine compared her picture with one in a file he produced from his briefcase.

"I guess you're Eileen Reed, and you have the clearances we require. This is your badge," Blaine said, and sighed heavily. He handed Eileen a square of plastic about as large as the palm of her hand. Where her picture was supposed to be was blank. Blaine held the door open for her, and they entered the building.

Filling the interior was what Eileen took for a moment to be phone booths. She saw a woman standing inside a booth. The woman was facing them and her mouth was set with impatience. There was a loud click and the woman opened the door on the booth. She passed them without a glance, wrapping a neck chain around her badge and stuffing it in a gym bag she carried slung over her shoulder.

"This is the ECF, the Entry Control Facility." Blaine held out his own badge to Eileen. "Those booths are retinal scanners. You enter the portal and it locks behind you. Run your badge through like this"—he demonstrated with a sliding movement of his hand—"and type in your number . . . oh, damn." Blaine dug in his pockets for a moment and came up with a slip of paper. He squinted at it. "Your number is 7893; memorize it. You put your eye to the retinal scanner. This is your first time through, so you'll have to scan twice, once to put your pattern into the system, and once again to establish your entry."

"What is this place, anyway? Why do you have such a fancy setup just to get in this place?" Beyond the other side of the clear glass phone booths and beyond the fencing Eileen could see more green grass, more dun-colored buildings. The whole scene looked ordinary to her.

"I can't answer that yet," Blaine said. Eileen nodded, wondering if her face showed the distaste she felt. The military and its secrets. She hated secrets.

She watched Blaine as the Major went through one of the portals. Eileen felt a brief burst of panic when she entered the booth and the door clicked shut behind her, locking her into a coffin-size glass room. The retinal scanner looked ominous. The booth smelled stale. The eyebrow pad on the one glass eyehole reminded Eileen of surgeon's equipment. She felt distinctly afraid of putting her eye to the small round circle. She took a deep breath, bent down, and pressed the button on the machine. A clear green beam briefly flashed into her eye. She expected pain but there was none, not even the wincing reflex that a bright light causes. She pressed the button a second time, remembering that she had to set her pattern into the system.

There was a sudden honking sound somewhere in the building. Her booth suddenly lit up with red lights. Eileen stood up from the scanner and looked around. She couldn't hear Blaine, but she could see him talking to her. She tried to open the door. It was locked. She tried to open the door she'd entered from. It, too, was locked. Eileen felt a burst of panic and took a deep breath.

"Let me out of here, please," she said through the glass to Blaine.

"Uh, ma'am?" A voice came out of the speaker next to the retinal scanner.

"Let me out of here, please," Eileen repeated through clenched teeth, trying to keep calm. She did not like enclosed places. The booth was getting smaller by the second.

"I'm sorry, ma'am, but you set off our metal detectors," the voice said, sounding bewildered.

"I imagine I did," Eileen said dryly. "I'm carrying a .357 in a shoulder holster." As well as a concealed .38 Ladysmith in an ankle sheath, she did not add. There were some secrets that Eileen didn't mind keeping to herself.

"You're not allowed to carry weapons on base," the voice said, sounding shocked.

"I'm allowed," Eileen said. She glared out at Blaine. "You better talk to your Major Blaine, out there."

Major Blaine walked quickly to an office area at the end of the row of booths. Eileen could see him speaking rapidly to a soldier dressed in camouflage.

"I'm with the Colorado Springs police," Eileen said, hoping her voice sounded patient and wise instead of squeaky and shrill. She felt unsure and out of control. It was a hateful feeling and she felt her temper begin a slow climb to compensate.

Major Blaine waved his arms around. The soldier looked confused.

"Used to be, civilian police held no jurisdiction on federal property, but that's not true anymore," Eileen said conversationally. She was pleased at her calm voice, when what she felt like doing was pulling her gun and shooting the glass.

She wondered if she *could* shoot out the glass in the booth. Eileen felt a quick drop of sweat run down from her armpit and soak into the cotton of her bra. If she didn't get out of this coffin very quickly, Major Blaine was going to spend some time in the smallest jail cell she could find. More sweat ran down her armpits. She felt fury and claustrophobia in a nauseating mix.

The door of the booth suddenly clicked open. Eileen leaned against it and stepped out. The air smelled divinely cool and sweet. She took a deep breath and mentally gripped the reins on her temper.

"That was unpleasant," she said to Major Blaine. He was hurrying back toward her, his forehead wrinkled in anxiety.

"I forgot you'd be carrying a gun," he said, holding his hands out apologetically.

"I will always be carrying a gun," Eileen said calmly. "Is this going to happen again, Major Blaine?"

"No, don't worry," he said. "I had the guard set your pattern into the system. You have a bypass to the metal detector."

"Thank you," Eileen said. She was amazed at her voice. It sounded very steady, when what she really wanted to do was commit all sorts of police atrocities on Major Blaine. "Why don't you show me to the victim now?"

"This way," Major Blaine said, and headed toward the exit. He held the door for her and Eileen accidentally stepped heavily on his shoe as she walked through.

"Sorry," she said sweetly.

Central Intelligence Agency, Langley, Virginia

Lucy Giometti was not having a good day. She'd gotten past the first bout of morning sickness, but the second was coming earlier than she'd hoped. She had a lot of work to do and she couldn't afford to spend her time in the halls at Langley going back and forth from the bathroom. She also had a lot of trouble with her weight. The only way to stop from throwing up was to eat, and she was already well past the weight gain her doctor had set for this month.

She sighed, and opened her desk drawer. It was full of food. She was an attractive woman who'd been absolutely breathtaking in college. Her body had been one flowing curve of female muscle and fitness, and the lines still showed through the soft new padding of fat. Lucy picked up a package of fat-free crackers and opened the twist tie. She eyed the package of fruit pies underneath the crackers, then firmly shut the drawer.

When the phone rang she was immersed in her primary case, a Chinese firm that might or might not be trying to spy on the latest computer-disk technology. Her job was to collect and analyze data for the Central Intelligence Agency. She had a powerful Sun workstation on her desk. Lucy was hooked directly into the TRW credit-check services, as well as some of the other less-well-known credit systems. She had access through her Government Internet channels to all university records, police dispatch files, and medical charts that existed on networked computers. Her snooping was relentless and expert, although she felt she never had enough time to spend on her detective work. Lucy loved the Internet.

Lucy picked up the ringing phone and tucked it on her shoulder, her fingers barely pausing in their rapid typing on the computer keyboard. She was using a "gopher," a computer program that connected to different computer servers across the country, seeking information on her suspected spy, John Chan. What a name. It had to be false.

"Giometti here," she said.

"We have a potential addition to our Missile Defense homicide case, Giometti. This is Mills."

Lucy sat up straight in her chair, her eyes leaving the screen and focusing on the wall behind her desk. Mills was her boss. She couldn't divide her attention between Mills and her computer screen, as she did with most of her callers.

"I have Admiral Kane from the Pentagon on the line. He's the BMD C in C."

"Yes, sir," Lucy said, and resisted saying "I know." Of course, she knew the Missile Defense commander in chief. Who did Mills think she was? She pressed her lips together and drummed her fingers silently against her leg.

"They've had a murder during the War Game they had in progress today. The murder was in Colorado Springs, Schriever Air Force Base. Do you have your file?"

"Yes, sir," Lucy said. Her fingers, resting a half-inch above the keyboard, stabbed toward a key that dumped her two hours' worth of data to disk. She typed rapidly for a moment, and her screen filled with new data. "I have it right here."

"I'll put him through."

Admiral Kane was brisk and to the point. "We might have a problem out at Schriever," he said. "You're the new analyst? What happened to Bob?"

"He retired, sir," Lucy said. "I have the file now. Mr. Mills told me you'd had a murder?"

"Yes. Civilian woman, stabbed. They've got the OSI called in, but he won't be there for three days. They have a civilian Police Liaison man—er, woman—on the job."

Lucy typed quickly, taking notes on one of the windows on her computer screen. As she typed, her eyes were scanning one of the other windows that contained the latest data on the file.

"Civilian detective, sir?"

"Yes, and I don't like it. We don't want any fuss out there. We can't have the press knowing what Schriever really does."

"Of course, sir," Lucy said. Her eyes flickered across the screen. "I know the policy is nonintervention in this particular file. Any investigations that attempt to tie the deaths together are discouraged. We're still investigating at the CIA level, but we're not allowing it anywhere else."

"Good," Admiral Kane said approvingly. Lucy frowned, her forehead wrinkling. My God, had the file been open for that many years? How many deaths had there been with the Missile Defense project? Her mouth dropped open in surprise as she scanned some of the totals in the list.

"I see we've had three incidents at Schriever on this case, none filed as Homicide," she said neutrally. She'd read the file quickly when it had landed on her desk but hadn't given it much thought until now. "All were automobile related."

"We won't be so lucky with this one," Kane said grimly. "Olsen tells me she was stabbed."

"May I have Colonel Olsen's number?"

"I have it here, but you won't be able to reach him until later today. They haven't released the witnesses yet."

Witnesses? Lucy thought blankly. Her hand stole to the desk drawer and pulled out a fruit pie. Kane gave her the number, and she wrote it down.

"I'll get right on it, sir," she said.

"I appreciate it." There was a click, and the buzz of a blank line. Lucy sat with the phone still cradled against her ear, her eyes scanning the data. She bit off a hunk of fruit pie and chewed it thoughtfully. She finally put the phone down and started to work. After ten minutes she opened her desk drawer and pushed aside the fat-free crackers. She pulled out a package of cookies and opened them with her teeth as she typed on her console. This case was going to call for serious snacking.

•5

Schriever Air Force Base

As they walked into the base Eileen figured out what was bothering her about this strange Air Force base.

"Where do the personnel live?" she asked. "I don't see any barracks." There were only about a dozen buildings on the base, and none of them looked like living quarters.

"The housing is at Peterson Air Force Base, about half an hour from here," Blaine said. "This base has no resident barracks, no commissary, no place to buy anything."

Blaine pointed at the farthest building. All the buildings were windowless, with broad lines.

"The Command Center?" Eileen asked. Blaine nodded, and took a deep breath.

"The Ballistic Missile Command Center," he said. "That is the first of many classified facts you are going to find out today."

"Missile defense? But I thought it was—"

"Canceled? It was canceled to the public. It has not been canceled. If this fact gets to the media, we will know whom it came from, Detective."

"I get the picture," Eileen said, sighing. "I have a security clearance, Major." Blaine bit his lip. Blaine was a lip biter, Eileen was discovering.

"Good." He continued to walk briskly toward the building.

After ten minutes, Eileen realized what was fooling her. The lack of windows made the buildings appear smaller than they were. Every building on base was huge, huge like the towering golf-ball radar dishes that were now behind them. It took them ten minutes to walk the length of a building that Eileen thought was an ordinary structure. She felt like an ant next to this bland monolith.

"That's the See-Sock," Blaine said, following Eileen's gaze. "Consolidated Space Operations Center, CSOC. Not quite as large a building as the Missile Defense Command Center."

They reached the building, and Eileen breathed a sigh of relief as they entered the cool interior. The sun had been hot.

"Next badge," Blaine said, handing Eileen one and clipping his own to his shirt. They were standing in an anteroom, alone and indoors. Blaine looked around furtively. It appeared that he was going to give her some more information, she thought in amusement. Major Blaine was acting as paranoid as any military officer she'd ever seen.

"I've already keyed you into the system. This one is simpler, and all you have to have is the badge and the number."

Eileen looked at this badge curiously. It was a pale green and had her name printed neatly on the front below a fancy logo. The plastic was still warm to the touch.

"Enough with the badges," she said with a smile she hoped was charming. "What about the incident?"

"The murder took place today somewhere between eight and ten A.M.," Blaine said reluctantly. "There is—there was—a War Game going on out here today. A full-up, worldwide War Game with what we call hardware-in-the-loop."

"What's that?"

"That means there were ships in the ocean with sailors at battle stations. There were satellite surveillance systems on a state of full alert. It is enormously expensive to put on a full-up War Game."

"Someone just wasted a lot of money by getting murdered, you mean?" Blaine's face flushed a little.

"I didn't mean that. I—Well, the woman who was murdered was a Civilian War Game member, who was supposed to operate her computer a certain way at a certain time. She is still in the room in the War Game Center where she was killed."

"And you're not happy about taking me in there?"

"No, I'm not," Blaine said shortly.

"I left the Air Force as a Captain, Major Blaine. Air Force Captain Eileen Reed. I flew A-10s."

"Oh? A-10s? I didn't know. A— That's great!" Blaine offered his hand again and Eileen shook it, though she knew what he'd bitten back. *A woman, that's right,* she thought. *One of those women fighter pilots.*

"You'll be fine, then," Blaine said. "Being ex-military, I mean."

"I will be just fine," Eileen said firmly. "Shall we go, then?"

"This way," Blaine said. His shoulders rose and he gave a curt little wave at her. His attitude had changed, Eileen realized with a sinking sensation. Before, she was an unknown, a cop, a detective cop. Now he had safely stuffed her into an Air Force captain's box, and that meant she was a subordinate to him. She'd just made her first mistake on the case.

They passed a guard desk after the anteroom. Two men and a woman sat behind a desk, looking bored. The setup was comforting and familiar. Most large office buildings had a similar guard staff, whose primary function was to make sure that only the right people got inside the building. Eileen wondered blankly how many of the wrong people could even get as far as the guard desk. She followed Blaine past the desk and into the building.

Here the atmosphere was very different. The base as a whole did not know about the murder, but in the building worried knots of people gathered here and there, and a sudden hush fell over them as they walked by. Eileen followed Major Blaine to an elevator, which took them slowly to the third floor.

"This is the Gaming floor," Blaine said to Eileen as they walked down another anonymous hallway. Because there were no windows Eileen had no sensation of being on the third floor of a building. It felt more like a basement.

She wondered uneasily if she was going to be out of her depth on this case, and suppressed another longing for Jim Erickson that felt like homesickness. If Jim were here she would be invisible, just the colorless junior partner. She'd solved a lot of homicides that way, but she'd been wanting for several years to be out in the front and on her own. This had the looks of a big case. Blaine stopped at another metal door.

"Last door, you can tailgate on me this time, but watch me. If you go through by yourself you have to know what to do."

Again, his voice was curt. Eileen mentally cursed her big mouth. Blaine swiped the card through yet another odd-looking machine, typed in his number, and pulled on a big steel door as the locking mechanism clicked open.

"My," Eileen said. "Another door?"

"Yes," Blaine said, and stepped up to a huge metal door with a submarine-style wheel on it. As he reached out to touch it, it spun from the other side.

"Someone coming out," Blaine said, and stepped back. The huge door swung toward them noiselessly, and a tiny young woman of Japanese descent stepped briskly through. Her perfume floated along with her, a cloud of Eternity that nearly made Eileen sneeze.

"Oh, good," the woman said. "You'll close it for me?"

Blaine nodded, and they stepped across a doorway lined with flat brass plates.

"What is this for?" Eileen asked, gesturing at the door and the plates. "If this place springs a leak and sinks?"

Blaine didn't smile. "This protects this area from electronic surveillance," he said. "No electronic emissions can escape this quadrant of the building."

A stray thought crossed Eileen's mind and caused her a brief, tense shudder.

"Something wrong?" Blaine asked.

"I just realized that our murderer is probably in this building with us," Eileen said with a mirthless smile. "Be kind of hard to get in and out of here unless you worked here."

Blaine paled at that, and bit his lips to a bloodless line.

"This way," he said, and led the way down the hall.

"Another door." Eileen sighed as they stopped next to a blank steel door. "The last one, I dare not hope?"

"The last one," Blaine said. He put his fingers into a small metal box on the wall and lifted his palm up awkwardly so Eileen could see what he was doing. The box contained a series of buttons, each one numbered sequentially.

"The number is 8030," Blaine said.

"Memorize it?" Eileen offered. Blaine pursed his lips at her disapprovingly and pressed the buttons in the numbered series. The final door clicked open.

"The Gaming Center," Blaine said, and ushered Eileen in.

They walked up a narrow hallway, barely wide enough for Eileen's shoulders, and slanted like a handicapped ramp. There was another door at the end of this oddly tilted hallway, but it was chocked open and through it Eileen could see bright lights, colors, the movement and sound of a crowd.

There was a smell of coffee and donuts and the crowd animal, perfume and aftershave and the rank scent of sweat. People never smelled pretty after they discovered a dead body.

In the crowd, a murderer, and somewhere at the end of the hallway, the murdered. Eileen took a deep breath. However the strangeness of coming here, in the end a murder was a murder. This was going to be her show, and she was going to make it a good one.

They walked through the doorway and movement and noise dwindled and died away. Eileen looked, seeing a blur of faces and trying to see if one stood out with the pale vampire face of the murderer, pale and shiny with guilt. None presented themselves. Eileen became aware that Blaine was speaking.

"Please take a seat and wait. The Springs Police have arrived and we'll get you cleared out of here as soon as possible." This last to a very imposing-looking man with the eagles of a full colonel on his shoulders. A large blond-haired man stood with him. His hair had a fringe of thick bangs, making him look somewhat like a Roman Caesar. He also wore a set of eagles.

"I'm Colonel Willmeth, Miss Reed," the man said, and held out his hand.

"Detective Reed, sir. Just call me Eileen." Eileen smiled and shook his hand, and realized belatedly she'd just called someone "sir."

"I'm the base commander. Major Blaine called me in when he went to contact you. Is there anything I can do to assist you?"

"Has the Medical Examiner arrived? I was told the OSI provides their own."

Willmeth looked at Blaine.

"He's on his way from a case at Fort Carson, he should be here within the hour."

"All right, then. I need to get these people out of here. Can you put them in a conference room somewhere?"

"I'll take care of it," Willmeth said.

"Don't let anyone leave the conference room unless they're escorted. That should be fine."

Eileen stood and watched the crowd slowly work their way from the room, shepherded by Major Blaine and Colonel Willmeth. A rule of investigation already broken. These people had nearly an hour to discuss the murder among themselves. She shrugged, and turned her attention to the room.

It was big, and beautifully proportioned to show to advantage the large-screen displays. The biggest screen showed a view of the East Coast. Eileen looked at this for a moment, puzzled, and realized the swirl of cloud that she had initially taken for some sort of strange hurricane was the spreading mushroom cloud of atomic detonation over Washington, D.C.

"What you are seeing is classified," Blaine said, returning to Eileen's side. He sounded too much like he was giving an order to suit Eileen. "It's a simulation."

Eileen stopped looking at the screen. It looked unbelievably real. The room had rows of seats like an auditorium, with a set of consoles at the end where Blaine and Eileen were standing. The consoles had headsets and microphones, now abandoned. One headset lay dangling over a chair arm, lazily revolving in the chilly breeze of the air-conditioning.

This room was different from a typical auditorium. Along each wall there were doors that led to small rooms. All except one of the doors were open, and although Eileen immediately realized the significance of this, she forced herself to look into the other rooms and note the setup: one console, headsets, microphones, and a comfortable-looking chair. Each of the rooms had a fire extinguisher and a phone along with some other tool-like gadgets that were apparently used on the big computers that nearly filled each room. There were no windows or other exit. The little rooms were barely bigger than phone booths.

Eileen inclined her head toward the closed door, and Blaine nodded.

"I need a list of everyone in this room, names, addresses, phone numbers. Do you have a suspect or have you heard anyone mention a suspect?"

"I thought you knew," Blaine said.

"Knew what?" Eileen asked irritably.

"Terry was murdered in that room, but there's no way in or out of it. These cameras"—and Blaine pointed up toward the ceiling—"record everything. From the moment she walked in there and shut the door, she was on tape. The audience saw her go into the room, and they didn't see anyone else go in. No one could have gotten in or out of that room without the cameras or everyone here seeing them. No one but Terry went in. And nobody came out."

•6

Garden of the Gods, Colorado Springs

George Tabor couldn't do it. No matter how intensive his training had been, he couldn't do it. He looked into his little dog's trusting eyes and put away the pill.

They were in the Garden of the Gods, a city park in Colorado Springs. The Garden was an area with a geologic fault that caused huge rock spires to jut from the ground. The spires reached fantastic heights and were laid edge to edge like knives tumbled in a drawer. The Garden was beautiful in the summertime, with the deep green of the scrub oak setting off the dark red of the rocks. There were bike trails and running trails and horse trails through the park, as well as a few roads for cars. There were plenty of wild spaces in the Garden as well. George had parked his car and walked just a few minutes with Fancy at his side. He stopped in a small clearing that was completely private and hidden.

But he couldn't do it. The sandy soil would be easy to dig to hide the little body of his dog, and he would be free to catch the flight from Denver International Airport he'd booked less than an hour before. The flight left in two hours and it was nonstop to Paris. He couldn't take a dog. What could he do with her? Then he knew.

"Fancy, come on," he said, and they started to walk back to his car. The dog bounded at his side, panting happily, knocking into him so he staggered in the soft soil. "Watch it," he said. He was in his travel suit.

He put her in the car and shut the door.

"You're going to the animal shelter," he told her through the glass, and took a deep breath of the summer air. He opened the door and got in, starting the engine. The interior was still cool from the air-conditioning. "I think someone will adopt you," he said. "At least it's a better chance for you than this."

Even though he knew the risk, George Tabor was smiling as he pulled his car out of the parking space and headed down the road.

Gaming Center, Schriever Air Force Base

"Get me a tape of everything the cameras recorded," Eileen said.

"It's classified."

"I'll look at it here."

Eileen stood still and thought for a moment. Should she view the tapes now, or interview the Gamers now? She desperately wanted to see the videotapes of the Game. She wanted to see how Terry Guzman could have walked into a room and never come out. Someone must have entered that room, and that someone had to be on the tape. But the Gamers were real people, with memories that would fuzz and fade in just a few hours. The murderer, too, if he were one of them, would have more time to knit together a face of innocence. She didn't want to risk that. The tapes would have to wait.

Eileen stepped toward the door. She examined it briefly and could see no signs of forced entry. Eileen pulled open the door by tucking her pencil in the slight crack, careful not to touch the knob.

The stench that met her was palpable, the unmistakable effluvium of death. The body was slumped over the console. The console still showed the nuclear cloud moving slowly out over the Atlantic. The woman—for woman it was, her body curved and lush under what looked like a very expensive linen suit—had one slender hand still outstretched over the computer mouse. In her back, driven deep and puckering the pale green material of her suit, was the bright yellow handle of a screwdriver. There was a wet patch around the puckered place, starting to dry and change colors at the edges. Eileen could not see her face and was glad, not for the first time. She didn't like to see their faces. Never had.

She could easily reconstruct the murder. The woman's headset was hanging from the chair arm, but it was undoubtedly on when the murderer stepped into the room behind her and drove the screwdriver into her back.

Unfortunately, the theory didn't fit. Anyone in the room behind her could see her right now, and if the murderer came through that door every one of them would have seen him. Or her. Eileen looked closely at the walls, seeing only two air vents near the ceiling that were too small for a human being. There was no other door, no window, no duct opening that would allow someone to wiggle through. The only way in or out of that room was through the doorway she was now standing in.

Eileen backed carefully out of the room. The Crime Lab would be here soon, and the Medical Examiner. She hoped the Air Force Crime Lab was competent. She would want their notes. She let the door swing gently closed.

"I've started a list going around the conference room," Blaine said. "Names, ranks, numbers."

"Tell me what went on here," Eileen said abruptly. She realized she'd been waiting for Jim Erickson to ask the question.

"We had a War Game here today. There was an audience, and there were players. The players were in the rooms. The audience members were in their seats. The Commanders were here, behind the audience." Blaine pointed at the dais and the row of consoles. "The audience and the Commanders were all in view of the cameras before the Game started. I was here, too. No one left the room from the time Terry entered that room to the time Nelson opened the door."

"Nelson?"

"Nelson Atkins, the Game Director."

"I see."

"So then there are the Gamers, there are eight of them. I mean, seven of them now. They were in the other rooms."

"Is there any way into Terry's room other than the door?"

"Not that I know of."

"Thank you, Major," Eileen said. "Okay. I'll view the tapes later. I think

I'll release the audience and your high-ranking commanders, once we have their names. Do you have another conference room or somewhere private? I need to interview these people—the Gamers, you said? I'd like to do it one at a time."

"We could use the little one in here," Blaine gestured to an open door, "but the office one is bigger and more private. It's across the hall."

"Sounds good," Eileen said. "Lead me to it. And fill me in on the people I'm going to talk to. I'll let you tell the others they can go for now. I'll contact them later."

Fort Rucker Army Post, Alabama

Major Alan Stillwell did not understand quite what was going on. His orders were to return to Peterson immediately, even though his regular flight was scheduled to depart in less than twenty-four hours. The message had come through a strange channel, as well. His own base commander had phoned him at the officers' quarters. This was odd enough, considering that the Major had seen his own commander perhaps three times in the past two years at Peterson.

However, Major Stillwell was an ambitious officer in a shrinking Defense world. He knew he wasn't a particularly good-looking man. He was short and had a tendency to grow a paunch, and his hair had been gone on top since he was thirty. A drill sergeant told Stillwell in the officer's training course that he'd never make flag rank because of his looks.

"It's a friggin' beauty pageant," the sergeant told Stillwell, at a distance of about a quarter inch. "And you're butt ugly."

But behind Stillwell's ordinary brown eyes was a handsome brain. Alan Stillwell astounded his good-looking friends by capturing an array of beautiful, bright girls during his college years. These girls saw the interior man in the tubby little body and, to his friends' amazement, adored him.

Alan Stillwell was working his way up through the ranks using the same dogged style that won him female hearts wherever he went. So he packed his bags and headed to the flight line.

Waiting for a flight was sometimes a long process, but the orders were clear. He was to return to Peterson on the first available transport and report to his base commander. Stillwell didn't much like to fly. He hadn't minded once, back when he'd finished officer's basic training. He'd even felt regret when he was passed over for flight school because of his lack of perfect vision.

Then came his assignment to the OSI, and investigation. Investigation in the Air Force OSI was primarily aircraft accidents, and they were never pretty. Alan Stillwell threw up until he saw black dots in front of his eyes the first time he assisted in an accident investigation of an Air Force Huey helicopter. The helicopter lay in pieces in a hangar, and young Lieutenant Stillwell was assisting Major Johnston, a veteran OSI investigator. The pieces of the helicopter had been collected carefully and laid out in place. The pieces of the two pilots were mostly cleaned out. Not all. Shreds and splashes of human tissue and blood rotted slowly in the early-summer heat.

Later, a major himself, Stillwell was grimly amused when his own new lieutenant lost his lunch at the last investigation. This one was also a helicopter accident, a catastrophic failure of the rotor mechanism. The reason for the rotor failure had to be determined, and the bodies couldn't be moved until they'd filmed the scene and figured out a potential cause. The bodies were frozen solid in the high Colorado winter, and what sent his young assistant to his knees, vomiting, were the frozen icicles around the mouth of the copilot, a pretty young captain.

Lieutenant Trask abruptly broke into a run and almost made it to the trees before he lost his Air Force cafeteria lunch. Stillwell and the Medical Examiner, Dr. Rowland, nodded at each other sympathetically. You had to be detached. Trask would either learn, or he would find himself in a nice uneventful Military Police job, reading magazines and watching camera shots of windowless buildings.

Now Major Stillwell sat in the flight room at Fort Rucker, Alabama, waiting for a flight to take him to Colorado. He was very detached when at a scene, but he couldn't be quite so detached when he boarded a real plane. He wondered how badly dying in a plane crash felt. Was it really agonizing? Or did the shock make you feel dreamy and uncaring? How long did you have before you realized the plane was crashing? Minutes, seconds, even longer?

"Well, I have one for you, Major," the flight control airman said, setting a piece of paper down on the high flight-line table. "It's not going to be pretty, but it'll get you home. A Chinook, she's brand new and Peterson is where she's being delivered."

Major Stillwell felt a rictus of a smile spread across his face as he took the paper. He hated helicopters.

"I hope they've got a good supply of barf bags," he said. The airman laughed.

"You bet they will. There's some good thunderstorms up near Oklahoma this time of year. Check with Roseburg, he's got extra flight helmets. She takes off at dawn, that's about six hours from now. Better try and get some sleep."

Gaming Center, Schriever Air Force Base

Eileen was catching up on a month's worth of Dilbert cartoons pinned to a nearby cubicle wall when Major Blaine came back. He'd left her at a conference room across the hall and went to select a Gamer for her to talk to. A tall, stooped man with thinning gray hair was with him.

"Nelson Atkins," Blaine said.

"Detective Eileen Reed," Eileen said to the man, and shook his hand.

"Here's the list of names," Blaine said, and handed a clipboard to Eileen. She took the list and looked at it briefly. There were three sets of names, one marked "Observers," one marked "Commanders," and one marked "Gamers." Nelson Atkins headed up the list. Next to his name was written "Game Director."

Eileen waved a hand to the chairs in the conference room. Atkins went in and took a seat immediately.

"I need to talk to Colonel Willmeth about the secure phone line," Blaine said apologetically from the doorway. "You'll stay here until I return."

"That's fine," Eileen said with a glittering false smile, as though he'd asked her a question instead of giving her an order. She closed the door behind Blaine and took a seat. The chairs were comfortable, almost plush, with a dull geometric pattern in heavy fabric. The backs were very high and the arms were padded. The other chairs stood in random positions around the table. After a moment, Eileen realized the chairs were left in the positions they rolled to when the last people to sit in them had gotten up. There was a white board along one wall. It was written and rewritten on so many times, the latest writings were hard to read over the poorly erased ghosts of the old. Eileen studied the board for a moment. She couldn't make heads or tails out of the hieroglyphics. There were circles connected by lines and phrases connected by pluses and brackets, as though someone had tried to do algebra with words instead of X's and Y's.

"Enable Command Authority equals time plus check plus switch?"

Atkins looked bewildered and followed Eileen's gaze to the white board. He smiled faintly. "Data Dictionary Entries," he said.

"Excuse me?"

"It's called structured software design. It's a way of engineering software so you get exactly what you want, every time," Atkins replied patiently. Faint color washed across his forehead, and his shoulders rose a little. "We use it in combination with Object Oriented Design. It works well."

"I see," Eileen said gently, although she didn't. She really wanted to see Atkins get his feet under him a little. This was her territory, the interviews. Jim always had her do the interviews. If he were here, he would be rewinding the Game tapes and watching them, and they would compare notes later.

"Let's talk about what happened. I know you're upset."

"Of course, of course," Atkins said anxiously. "Anything I can do to help. This is terrible, just terrible." He scrubbed at his face with a shaking hand.

"What happened, Mr. Atkins?"

"I don't know, Miss . . . Er?"

"Reed. Call me Eileen."

"Miss Reed. She was fine when she went into the Ground Weapons station. She closed her door, and I went into my room and closed my door. Then I came out when the ground interceptors didn't fire—"

"The what?"

"The ground interceptors. She was supposed to release them to fire at the incoming RVs. Er, reentry vehicles. Nuclear bombs."

"Who opened the door to her room?"

"I did. I went to see why she hadn't—hadn't . . ." Atkins stopped.

"Just take your time, Mr. Atkins," Eileen said.

"I'm okay," Atkins said, and wiped at his upper lip. "I opened the door and saw her."

"What did you see?"

Atkins looked at her blankly. "I saw she had something in her back, that she looked like she was dead."

"Did you touch her?"

"No, I didn't. I turned away, I—I couldn't believe it."

"Was she moving when you opened the door?"

"No," Atkins said after a moment. "No, she was still. She didn't look asleep, even. She looked like a doll. Not alive."

"Did anyone else touch the door or enter the room?"

"I don't think so. I closed it before Major Blaine got there. He didn't open it."

"Okay. Let me ask you some questions about Terry. How long had she worked for you?"

"About a year and a half. I can get her personnel file for you."

Eileen nodded and made a note.

"Please do. Where did she work before this?"

"Digital Equipment Corporation. She was laid off along with about two hundred other people. It had nothing to do with her work performance."

"Why did you hire her?"

Atkins flushed and pressed his lips together. "I think that's obvious."

"Obvious?" Eileen was puzzled.

"Oh, I'm sorry, I thought you knew. Lowell Guzman is our Assistant Game Director. Lowell recommended her highly. We have regulations about hiring relatives, but since she would be reporting to me and not to Lowell, the regulations didn't apply."

Eileen glanced down at his list. "Lowell Guzman, Assistant Game Director." Sure enough.

"Lowell is her brother? Her husband?"

"Husband, I'm sorry."

"Her husband was here? Where is he?"

"He's in the conference room. The base paramedic gave him a shot. He's
pretty woozy right now."

"I'll talk to him when he comes out of it a bit," Eileen said, making
notes. "Were she and Lowell getting along?"

"Lowell loved her," Atkins said angrily. "What are you trying to say?"

"I'm trying to say she was murdered," Eileen said calmly. "Now, did she
and Lowell get along?"

"I think they did," Atkins said, deflated. "They never fought, as far as I
know."

"Okay, then. Did she have any enemies?"

Atkins hesitated too long before answering.

"No, I don't think so."

"Really?" Eileen asked gently. Atkins seemed to huddle back in his chair.
The gray hair seemed darker against the paleness of his face.

"Miss Reed, I don't know how to say this—"

"Just try," Eileen said.

"Okay. Terry was not popular. She wasn't a—an easygoing kind of person. But if you arrest anyone here on suspicion just because they didn't like
her, you're going to ruin their lives."

"Excuse me?"

"I mean it. If you arrest me, I'll lose my clearance. It's doubtful I'll get it
back. The same is true of"—Atkins swept a pale arm from the chair—
"everyone here. I don't want to make you upset, Miss Reed. But if you arrest someone who turns out to be innocent, you'll probably have a lawsuit
on your hands."

"Are you threatening me?" Eileen asked mildly.

"No, no," Atkins said, aghast. "I'm not. I'm just asking you to be—careful, that's all. I'll tell my people to work with you. I just—it's just . . ."

Atkins ran out of steam. He scrubbed at his face again.

"I suppose I can restrict my wild tendency to arrest everyone in sight,

Mr. Atkins," Eileen said dryly. "And in return I assume I'm going to get complete cooperation with everyone?"

"Everyone, I swear it," Atkins said gratefully. He nodded, and nodded again, and kept nodding his head for the rest of the interview as though the nod motor had shorted out somewhere and wouldn't shut off. He told Eileen he'd gone out for coffee once, to the bathroom once, and stayed in the main room for the rest of the Game. He hadn't seen anything or noticed anything.

He plucked at the hairs on his arm while Eileen finished up her notes.

"Bring me Lowell Guzman, please," Eileen said.

"Okay." Atkins shot to his feet and left the room with palpable relief.

Eileen sat and drummed her fingers on the comfortable chair arm, and looked at the queer drawings on the white board. She made a little whistling mouth, but didn't whistle out loud. She looked at the list again. There were seven names:

Nelson Atkins—Game Director
Lowell Guzman—Assistant Game Director
Arthur Bailey—Truth Team Leader
Joe Tanner—Software Engineer
Roberto Espinoza—Software Engineer
Doug Procell—Software Engineer
Sharon Johnson—Software Engineer

"What the hell's a Truth Team?" Eileen said to herself. The door opened. The man who walked in was handsome in a way Eileen liked immediately: strong face, lanky body, big hands. He wore a suit elegantly because he had good lines, but Eileen immediately noticed the color change at the seams and the splotch of mustard along the dark sleeve. His hair was brown and mussed. His eyes were pale green and red-rimmed, as though he'd been crying. He smelled of Dial soap and fresh, anxious sweat.

"Lowell Guzman?" Eileen asked, rising.

"No, I'm Joe Tanner," the man said. "Lowell is really out of it. Whatever the paramedics gave him knocked him right out. Nelson said to come on in, and when Lowell wakes up he'll send him in."

"All right," Eileen said, not meaning it. She sat down and gestured for Tanner to take a seat. "I need to ask you some questions, Mr. Tanner. Can you help me?"

"Joe, please. Yes," Tanner said. He sat down and pressed the back of his hand to his eyes and then his nose. With a complete lack of self-consciousness, he wiped his wet hand on the expensive wool of his suit. He took a deep breath. "Okay."

"When did you know that Terry was dead?"

"The same time everyone did," Tanner said. "When Nelson opened the door and we saw her."

"What did you see?"

"I saw Terry—well, no, I saw Nelson first. He turned away from the door and bent over like he was going to throw up. I saw Terry in her room and she was lying over her keyboard. There was something sticking out of her—her back. Then someone screamed and I realized she was dead. I turned away."

"Did you see Terry after that?"

"Nelson closed the door," Tanner said. "I didn't look anyway."

"Was she moving when the door opened?"

Tanner blinked hard. "No. I didn't see her move. Why do you ask?"

"I want to know when she died," Eileen said.

"Oh," Tanner said in a dazed voice. He was very pale.

"Did you know Terry?"

"Not really. I worked with her, but we weren't friends."

"Do you know someone who would want to kill her?"

Tanner looked down at his own large hands, as though he were trying out the idea on himself. He opened his palms wide and looked at them.

"No," he said finally. "I don't. I really don't."

Eileen nodded. She expected that answer from everyone she questioned. At first, that is. Later, when the heat turned up on all of them, someone would start to talk.

"Okay, then, let me ask you some questions about today. Tell me what you did today."

"I work on the Truth Team during the Game," he replied obediently. "I watch the true picture of the War. We have to—"

"What do you mean, 'Truth Team'? And what's a 'true picture'?"

"Um. Well, we play both teams—Enemy and American. Because our satellite and intelligence operations might screw up, just like in real life, the Simulation tries to duplicate that by rolling the dice."

Tanner smiled at her confused expression, the first smile she'd seen.

"Let me explain. Say you think a submarine is three hundred miles north of Bermuda. What if it's actually one hundred miles south? The American Team sees a little submarine flag north of Bermuda, and the Truth Team sees a little submarine flag south. The Enemy side would have proper coordinates for their own subs and missiles, but they'd have best guesses for ours. The Truth Team knows what we call 'truth,' so we can analyze the Game data later and figure out how the system worked."

"So where's the Enemy Team?" Eileen was confused. Were there Gamers she didn't know about?

"Oh, well, we play the Enemy Team for the Games, mostly. Today it was a full-scale Game with Flag Officers involved. So the Germans played the 'Mad Sub' scenario this time, with real missiles. But they were duds, you know."

"I would hope so," Eileen murmured, feeling even more confused.

"We usually play the Bad Guys in the Truth Room. Sometimes I play the Chinese, the Arabs, the Japanese—"

"The Japanese? You've got to be kidding."

"No," Tanner said. "We play everybody. I mean everybody. I've played a War Game where Great Britain tries to take us back as a colony. I liked that one. I guess you know this is all classified. Major Blaine said to tell you everything we could."

"Yes, I have a clearance. So you play Bad Guys and you know the true state of the Game," Eileen said. She fought another distressing moment of doubt, and cursed Harben for getting her into this mess. "You have your own room in the Center for this?" At his nod, she said, "Did you leave your room during the Game today?"

"No, I didn't," Tanner said. He was starting to look a little better, but now the color drained away from his cheeks again. "Art and I were there the whole time, and we sit in the same room. Doesn't that mean we both have alibis?"

Eileen didn't say anything.

"Yeah, I guess not. We could be in on it together, right? Or maybe I sneaked out while he wasn't looking, or the other way around. It would be tough, though," he added, "'cause we have to talk a lot to keep the Game running smoothly. We also monitor all the computer equipment, and feed the loops in for the President and SAC—Strategic Air Command."

"I see," Eileen said neutrally. Tanner nodded in understanding.

"Sure, you have to have proof."

"Let's talk about Terry again. Why wasn't she liked around here?"

If Tanner was uncomfortable with the rapid change of subject, he didn't show it.

"Did Nelson tell you we didn't like her much?" he asked, then held up his hand. "I'm sorry, I shouldn't ask you that. Don't answer."

"Okay," Eileen said, smiling. "I won't. Tell me why you didn't like her."

Tanner thought this over for a moment.

"I—well, Terry wasn't a very good engineer," he said carefully. "I would have to explain something to her three or four times, and if I didn't write her a memo and date it and keep a copy, she'd come back and say I never told her the information. I don't know how to express this—when you work together as closely as we have to, you have to develop trust. And the Simulation world is a wicked place. You'll be halfway through the development cycle and all of a sudden the whole world will change. When the lab at Lawrence Livermore got that Brilliant Pebble to really work, we had Space Command hammering at our door, wanting to hook up Brilliant Pebbles into our simulation right away.

"A lot of the technology we just have to extrapolate. That means we make it up, on the fly. Lots of stuff is still being tested. Some of the stuff is only theoretical. So we take what we know and make up the rest. What's the flight characteristics of a Patriot Missile? Well, we use data from the Gulf War, take into account the improvements, and simulate nuclear missile impacts instead of Scuds. What happens to a Patriot when the sensors are blinded by a nuclear flash? How do you succeed in target acquisition when you've got sophisticated jamming . . ."

Tanner stopped. He'd been making a speech.

"Sorry."

"It's all right. Go on," Eileen said quietly. She loved people who babbled. Babbling was good. Babbling was great.

"I guess I'm not even talking about Terry. But then again, maybe I am. When you walk into a software engineer's office and you tell them to drop all their work on a space-based laser and start working on Brilliant Pebbles, you need someone who'll shove six months of work onto a back shelf and smile when they do it. And produce a Brilliant Pebble simulation that'll work."

"And Terry wasn't like that."

"No," Tanner said, and his gaze dropped to his hands. "I guess she'll never get any better now."

"What did Terry do when you asked her to simulate Brilliant Pebbles?"

"She complained. That's okay, everybody does. But she would do it in a really mean and ugly sort of way. One time 'Berto forgot about an interface—hmm, an interface is a way for two elements to communicate, okay? 'Berto was working on a communications satellite model, and he forgot about some jamming information that Terry needed to be aware of for her work. So he went to tell her, and I overheard her really giving it to him rough, if you know what I mean."

"What did she say?"

"Oh, something like, 'Thanks for forgetting this, 'Berto, is there anything else you've forgotten?' in that biting Terry sort of way. But when she'd forget something, which was always happening, you know, that's just the way it works, well, she'd pretend that she'd told you and you forgot."

"And you let her get away with it?"

"Well, Miss—er?"

"Reed. Call me Eileen," Eileen said, and couldn't help smiling again.

"Miss Reed, we had a saying here on the War Game Team, just between us little guys. The saying was, 'Whatever Terry wants, Terry gets.'"

There was a little silence. Eileen wrote, knowing Tanner was flushing without looking up, keeping her eyes to her notebook to give him space to recover.

"Because Lowell Guzman is Assistant Game Director."

"Yes," he said.

"Would someone kill her because of that?" Eileen asked. "And why?"

"I don't think so. I don't know," Tanner said. He looked at her with a clear green, anxious gaze, asking for her to somehow understand that he didn't do it, he would never murder Terry Guzman. Eileen had often seen the look before, sometimes on a murderer's face.

"Thanks for your help," she said neutrally. "I'll probably be contacting you again, but if you think of anything, could you call me at this number?" She held out her card.

"Okay," he said, and nodded exactly like Atkins, an eager jerk of the chin. Another suspect glad to escape the clutches of the police, Eileen said to herself. He took the card and stood up.

"Let me walk you out," she said, getting up. "Maybe you could direct me to the john? And maybe the coffee machine?"

Tanner showed her to the bathroom, but he was gone when she came out. Eileen figured she'd missed her chance for coffee, but when she got back to the conference room there was a plain blue mug on the table near the chair where she'd been sitting. A ribbon of steam rose from the cup into the air, and her next suspect was already seated and waiting for her.

·7

Denver Animal Shelter

When the animal shelter woman brought Fancy's collar and leash to him, Tabor almost wept. He could imagine his little darling pacing in confusion, locked in some wretched little concrete box. She could never understand why he had to leave her behind. The shelter woman looked at him with a flat and carefully nonjudgmental face that felt as damning as spittle.

"Here's your collar and leash, sir," she said.

"Thank you," Tabor whispered. He had allowed himself to forget this side of the spy business. He'd become settled in, complacent, and now his dog was going to die and he faced an uncertain future.

He did, however, carry his Bahamas account. His savings were safe. And he had one last piece of information to sell, the last document his contact had smuggled out of Schriever. With that, he'd be able to give up the business and have a real life. Open a restaurant in Georgia. He'd always wanted to do that.

But he'd never, ever have another dog, he promised himself. He carried Fancy's leash and collar to the car. He could hardly see through his tears as he drove out of the parking lot. He turned on the windshield wipers, but that didn't help.

Gaming Center, Schriever Air Force Base

A young man was sitting in the chair opposite Eileen's, liquid Mexican eyes meeting hers without flinching. Eileen settled herself in her chair and took a sip of her coffee. It was excellent, so far removed from police coffee that Eileen almost choked on the first gulp.

"Joe's guest coffee mug," the man said. "He must have decided you were okay. Roberto Espinoza." He reached out and shook Eileen's hand firmly.

"Not Lowell," Eileen said grimly.

"No, he's still passed out," Roberto said.

Eileen knew the accent in Roberto's soft voice. The phrasing was definitely Los Angeles barrio. Roberto carried the bones and skin tones of the nearly pure Mexican Indian, a high narrow forehead and chin with the flat, angled cheekbones that made little pouches below the eyes and kept the face ageless. His nose could be called European, but Eileen had taken several anthropology courses in college and knew the Mexican Pyramids carried profiles like Roberto's. The total effect was one of almost overwhelming male beauty. Eileen supposed Roberto had earned the tough, uncompromising line of his shoulders in more than a few schoolyard fights.

"You're from Los Angeles?"

"Straight from the barrio, *señorita*," Roberto said, and flashed a set of straight white teeth. "I guess you've been there yourself, if you can tell where I'm from."

"Yes," Eileen said, and opened her notebook to a fresh page. Roberto's purely Mexican good looks and the tailored suit made Eileen wonder, for a moment, what the world would have been like if the Aztecs had carried smallpox to the Spanish instead of the other way around. Much was made of the Aztecs' brutal human sacrifices atop the tall temples, but little about the culture that attained a level of civilization that allowed such temples to be built. How would the Aztecs have fared against Nazi Germany? Perhaps the trials at Nuremberg would have ended in a different sort of spectacle than hangings.

"I saw *Stand and Deliver,* can you believe it?" Roberto spoke resignedly and quickly, as though he'd told the story many times. "My elementary school math teacher hauled a TV and a VCR in and made us watch it. I musta beat up a dozen kids that week, 'cause of course I cried. Damn movie. The actor, what's-his-name, teaching a whole class of dumb barrio kids to ace a calculus class. So that's what I did, too. And here I am, and that's my story. Inspired by a dumb movie."

"I saw it, too." Eileen smiled. "How old are you?"

"Twenty-three. This is my first job out of college. I have a computer science degree from UCLA."

"Why did you come here?"

Roberto shrugged his shoulders.

"I was recruited. Government contractors need to fill quotas for minorities, and I had good grades. I had my choice, Miss—Excuse me, I don't know your name?"

"Eileen Reed," Eileen said. "Call me Eileen."

"Eileen, then. Well, I got a lot of offers, and this one paid the most and looked like fun."

"Has it been fun?"

For some reason this struck home. The smooth planes of Roberto's cheeks darkened slightly and the deep black eyes glittered for a moment.

"Until today, yes."

"Did you know Terry well?" Eileen shifted in her chair and took a sip of coffee. The coffee made her think, distractingly, of Joe Tanner.

"I don't know if I knew her," Roberto was saying. "We all work here very closely, but she was—well, she was Terry." He frowned, his brow crinkling in distress. "I can't believe she's dead," he said slowly, as if to himself. "I—"

"Yes?" Eileen asked gently.

"I just can't believe someone would kill her," Roberto said, and Eileen knew that wasn't what he was going to say.

"We've been told she wasn't easy to work with."

"She wasn't." Eileen waited, but the black eyes didn't falter and Roberto offered nothing more. Eileen shifted in her chair and took another gulp of coffee.

"All right," she said finally. "Let's go through the War Game. Everything you did, everything you saw."

When the door finally closed behind Roberto, Eileen flipped to a fresh page of her notebook. She didn't feel particularly bad, though. These Gamers were bright, educated, and totally rattled by the murder. She was getting a lot of good information. It would fall into a picture, eventually, and the murderer would appear from the puzzle pieces.

The person Roberto sent in was a rather short, freckled man with thinning wheat-blond hair and a friendly face.

"Art Bailey, ma'am," the man said, and held out a firm, square hand.

"The Truth Team Commander," Eileen said, shaking the hand and gesturing to a chair. "Still no Lowell."

"Nope, he's still out of it," Art said, and sat in the chair abruptly. Eileen looked at the droop of the shoulders and the cast of the eyes and realized Art was more than distressed—he was completely exhausted. The man should have ruddy skin tones with all those freckles, but he was a shade closer to gray.

"Tell me about the Game, Art. I want to find out who killed Terry, and the best way to do it is to find out what happened."

Art nodded. Eileen had thought that with the blond hair Art would have blue eyes; instead, they were a deep and opaque brown. The color gave a somber expression to the otherwise round and cheerful face.

"All right, where shall I start?"

"Tell me everything that happened today. Just start when you got up and go through everything," Eileen asked. Art shrugged his shoulders and nodded his head. He put a hand to his lips and pinched the lower one. Major Blaine was a lip biter. Art Bailey was a pincher.

"My day started at four-fifteen, I got up and showered and fixed the coffee for Meg and me. She gets up at five to get the kids off to day care at six-thirty, so I always get the coffee made and feed the dogs before I leave at four-thirty."

"You do all that in fifteen minutes?" Eileen asked.

"I'm a time-and-motion kind of person, Miss—"

"Reed. Call me Eileen."

"Eileen. I read this book when I was a kid, it's called *Cheaper by the Dozen,* you ever hear of it?"

"I think I saw the movie," Eileen said, amused.

"Yeah, there was a movie too. Anyway, the dad and mom were time-and-motion-study experts. And the dad would experiment with how quickly he could get dressed in the morning—buttoning up his vest from bottom to top, for instance, because it was faster. I do the same thing—that's one of the reasons I'm in this job."

"Okay."

"So I have everything ready to go, I'm out the door in fifteen minutes flat, the only thing I slow down for is a kiss for Meg. And I'm in here thirty-two minutes later—that includes the drive, parking, going through the retinal scanner, badge check, capsule doors . . ."

"I know, I know," Eileen said, and Art chuckled rustily.

"An amazing amount of work to get in here, isn't it? I hardly notice it anymore, actually.

"So I have to open up the Gaming Center, which means I go through a checklist to see that all doors are closed and locked, all the terminals are shut down, all the printers are empty—"

"You check all the doors?" Eileen asked sharply.

"Yes, there are three. And I sign a document in each door along with the time, to verify that I've checked it. The lists are changed when the sheet of paper gets full—I know where you're going with this," Art said, holding up a hand as Eileen opened her mouth to speak. "There should be lists going back to the time the doors were hung on this Center."

Eileen nodded, and wrote in her notebook. Art waited politely for her to finish.

"I also check the safes where classified information is stored, and sign off those too. Then I log on to the master terminal, and if it's an ordinary day I do whatever needs to be done—test new software, get new machines set up or old ones upgraded. This morning is a Game Day, so Joe and I—"

"When did Joe come in?"

"Oh, I'm sorry, that's right. He got there at five-thirty, so he helped me check the rooms in the center."

"Check them for what?"

"Pop cans, mostly," Art said. "We do our testing in here and it becomes pretty frantic before a game. So before we have a Game, we have to clean up house. The janitors vacuum and carry out the trash, but they never touch papers on the desks. One of the rules. We know exactly what is going to happen in the Game, and the Observers who come here don't."

"Observers?"

"The audience members, sorry. So Joe makes sure there are no telltale notes, like 'Don't forget to release ground weapons when the German sub launches off Bermuda.'" Art's smile died as he remembered that the weapons were not released, and why. His eyes reddened and he blinked rapidly.

"So Joe got here at five-thirty and checked the rooms with you?"

"Yes." Art frowned and pinched his lip. "Miss Reed, I just don't know how anyone could be in there this morning. Joe checked the rooms, and later, so did I. Nelson always checks them too. Then I make a run on the computer systems. I usually choose some scenario that will really wring out the system—"

"Scenario?"

"Yes, um, like a story? I play the Enemy Commander and I launch from four subs, then I play the Blue Commander and I launch back, then I try to shoot down everything in the air, I like doing that one."

"You shoot down our missiles?" Eileen asked in astonishment. She had never heard of such a thing.

"Well, only in my Games, Miss—Eileen. I play the President so I get to say that it's all been a big mistake, and Missile Defense shoots down everything that's flying. It's a lot of work for the computers, and so I know that everything is up and running smoothly for the Game."

"That's what you did this morning?"

"Well, no, actually Joe and I played a different one this morning. He was Enemy and I was Blue and the rules were, the launches had to match size for size. And they had to target the same places the other launch fired from—am I making sense to you?"

"No."

"Like that old game, Battleship, we guessed where the other person had their ships. Except we guess where the other person is going to launch their missiles."

"I think I see. So after that?"

"After that, we sit around and talk until the donuts and the coffee arrive."

"Who brings that over?"

"Oh, one of the cafeteria people—oh." Art's face showed sudden dismayed understanding.

"Who was it today?"

"Clarice. I don't know her last name. She rolled the cart in and unloaded the donuts and the coffee urns, and then she left. I know she left because Joe and I always get the best donuts and the first cups of coffee—it's one of our little perks."

Eileen made a note.

"Clarice wouldn't—" Art began, and stopped. He looked at Eileen with confused and sorrowful eyes. "Somebody did, eh?"

"Yes."

"We got our donuts and poured our coffee and then Nelson came over. He got one too, and we three talked over the schedule for the day."

"Is there a planned schedule?"

"Sure, always. It's in the safe; I could get one for you, but it's classified."

"I'll talk to Major Blaine," Eileen said, and wrote "schedule."

"I think Lowell Guzman came over next, and then, oh, I'm not sure, really, the commanders started arriving, and the audience, and Joe and I had to get the simulation started. I couldn't tell you when people came in what order."

"That's quite all right," Eileen said. "You've been very helpful. Tell me about Terry. Do you remember her coming in?"

"I don't, really," Art said, puzzled.

"I've gotten the impression Terry was kind of unpopular," Eileen said mildly, and watched for Art's reaction. Art shifted in his chair uneasily for a moment.

"I didn't have any problems with her," he said finally. "I got along with Terry just fine, but I never did cater to her either. A lot of the other Gamers did, because of Lowell's position, but I don't report to anyone but Nelson, and I've been here longer than him. If Nelson tried to fire me he would be right behind me in the job line."

"I see," Eileen said. Art was obviously discomfited by this self-promotion, another endearing trait that made Eileen believe Art was everything he did not boast about being: the most valuable member of a very specialized team.

"When did you realize she'd been murdered?"

"When everyone else did, when Nelson opened the door. I couldn't believe it. I still can't."

"I just have one other question, Art," Eileen said, and leaned forward over the polished veneer of the table.

"Yes?"

"How did the murderer get in that room?"

There was silence, and a tiny squeak as Art's chair shifted on the oiled castors.

"I don't know. I really don't know," Art said helplessly, and shrugged once more. "As far as I know, it couldn't have been done."

Eileen leaned back in her own chair and sighed, ignoring the interior voice that kept saying, *Out of your depth, out of your depth.*

"I may be speaking to you later."

"All right, then. I'll get Jeff, he will probably want to take you for some lunch."

Eileen glanced at her watch and noticed with some surprise that it was already noon.

"Cafeteria closes at one, and there aren't any Taco Johns out this way," Art said wryly, and heaved his body out of the chair. "I'll get Jeff for you."

Eileen sat in the silent room, and it was only when Major Blaine opened the door that she realized who Art was talking about. Eileen couldn't imagine anyone calling the stiff Major Blaine something so personal as "Jeff."

"Want some lunch? And what are you laughing at?" Blaine asked, annoyed.

•8

Schriever Air Force Base

Eileen and Major Blaine worked their way out of the first two sets of locking doors, passed through the submarine airlock entrances, and went down a long flight of stairs. There were others in the stairwell, and the smell of food wafted pleasantly from covered Styrofoam dishes held in the hands of some of the people heading up.

"Lots of people eat at their desks," Blaine explained. "I discourage it in my office. We spend enough time inside as it is."

As if to underline his point, the door they were approaching opened and two young women in running clothes walked quickly through and headed down the stairs. Their clothes were damp with sweat and they were gasping.

"Locker room in the basement," Blaine explained, his eyes following the trim figures as they disappeared down the stairs.

"Did Terry ever go running?"

"I don't think so. She kept slim through diet, not exercise. She wasn't athletic."

Eileen nodded. Blaine opened the door and they left the stairwell, entering a glass-walled corridor and an amazing flood of sunlight. The end of the corridor connected to another building, this one a more typical office complex with large expanses of glass.

"It's great, isn't it?" Blaine said, and lifted his head to the bright sky. "That building is like a damn prison."

Eileen was surprised at the intensity of the relief she felt to see the sun again.

"Cafeteria is on the right," Blaine said. They walked into a lovely large dining room with huge windows. The blinds were pulled all the way back, flooding the room with light. The selection of food was sturdy and unimaginative, but looked well prepared. Eileen realized she was quite hungry.

"Have some of the soup," Blaine murmured. "We've got a frustrated chef out here who makes some incredible soups."

They filled their trays—the soup was mushroom; Eileen wasn't too interested but got some out of politeness—and found a seat near the windows. Most of the seats in the sunshine were filled. Hidden speakers played soft country music.

"I got the word before we came down. The ME should be here within about a half hour," Blaine said, and crunched into a salad. Eileen nodded, and dug in.

The soup turned out to be as good as advertised, hot and smoky and thick with fresh mushrooms.

"Very good," Eileen said with a sigh. "I hope I won't be having too many more lunches out here, but this almost makes me change my mind."

"You think you'll close the case that quickly?" Blaine asked, surprised.

"No, I think the Air Force OSI will be here to take this off my hands in a couple of days." Eileen grimaced, thinking of the distant and bureaucratic OSI.

"Well, that's good," Blaine said, with a totally infuriating smile of relief. "I'm sure they'll handle things after that."

"I'm sure they will," Eileen said, balling her napkin and tossing it on her tray.

They stood and brushed their clothes into place, and went to meet the Medical Examiner.

THE GAMING CENTER door was now attended by a single young Army guard. The guard was white-eyed with excitement but standing rigidly at attention. Eileen thought the guard could have been no more than nineteen or twenty.

Blaine nodded at the guard as he clicked the key sequence to open the door. Eileen glanced back as they walked through the door and saw the young shoulders visibly droop with relief.

The big center room was empty now, the clutter of coffee cups and crumpled napkins the only evidence of the former crowd. The room was very cold.

"I've asked Sharon, Lowell, and Doug not to leave the base until they've spoken to you," Blaine continued. "Those are the Gamers you haven't interviewed yet. The Observers have been allowed to leave the base provided they don't leave the city. You'll contact them as you need to."

Eileen nodded, feeling again as though Blaine were giving her orders and finding herself helpless to respond. The only possible response was to be insultingly rude, and Eileen found rudeness difficult. Instead she turned her attention to the video cameras. The video cameras were mounted high against the ceiling. A person would need a stepladder to tamper with them.

"Don't touch the cameras until I can get fingerprints from them," Eileen said as Blaine took out his notepad and pen. "I need the names of the workmen who installed the cameras, whoever repairs them, anyone who might have a legitimate reason to have touched them."

"You'll be able to look at the tapes while we're waiting for Dr. Rowland," Blaine said. He pointed with his pen to a door at the back of the room. "The video center is right here. No one has been in there since the game started. It's all controlled by Art Bailey and Joe Tanner, through the computer."

Eileen was surprised when Blaine opened the door. She had seen television studios before, but this was a surprising sight on a military base. The room was crammed with tall electronics panels. The panels were stuffed with high-resolution television monitors, dubbing equipment, and a soundboard to rival that of a recording studio. There were a couple of comfortable chairs in the same style as the ones in the conference room. Blaine dropped into one and studied the equipment with a frown.

"What do they need this stuff for?"

"To make films about missile defense," Blaine said absently.

"Films?"

"Propaganda," Blaine said shortly, and twisted his mouth. "Beautiful stuff, you should see it. Very exciting. Makes you glad we are building missile defense, all of that. We have to get funding, you know."

"I thought it was all classified."

"The people who see these films all have clearances. These films aren't shown to the Boy Scouts."

"I see," Eileen said, flushing despite herself. How was she to know such a thing? She opened a drawer at random and saw a stack of compact discs. "Your Gamers like their rock and roll too, I guess?"

Blaine turned to see Eileen holding a CD. "I guess they do. At least the thousands they spent on the sound system is being used more than once a month."

Eileen thumbed through the CDs. There was everything there, from classical to heavy metal to Nat King Cole. She opened the Cole CD and saw "Joe Tanner" written within in a large, neat hand. She smiled.

"Er—" Blaine said.

Eileen glanced up, not knowing how much time had passed. Blaine was sitting at the console, his hands busy at a keyboard. It was fascinating to see how much she was learning just from people's taste in music. Arthur Bailey, the earnest Truth Team lead, had a whole collection of hits from the seventies music that Eileen couldn't stand when she heard it the first time. She couldn't imagine someone actually listening to an entire Donna Summer disc. Roberto Espinoza tended toward alternative music. There were no discs with Lowell Guzman's name, but quite a few with Terry's. Terry, whose body was cooling less than fifty feet away, liked Top Forty music. Doug, one of the Gamers he hadn't met yet, was a New Age fan. His CDs were all instrumental Windham Hill artists. Sharon, one of the other unknown Gamers, had only two CDs and the plastic was cloudy and chipped on the cases. She had one Michael Jackson and one Whitney Houston, and although the cases were ancient the CDs inside were clean and shining, with no hair or dust.

Tanner, he of the green eyes and square hands, had nothing classifiable. There were some New Age discs and some classical. There was Nat King Cole, a Replacements disc, one from a local band called the Auto-No, and Aretha Franklin. Eileen knew about the Auto-No. She liked their music a lot. She wondered if Tanner ever went to the local bars where the band liked to play.

"Ahem," Blaine said. Eileen looked up again.

"I don't know how to work this," Blaine said. "We're going to have to get Joe or Art in here. I thought it would be like a VCR, but—" And he spread his hands in front of the bewildering array of equipment in front of him.

"Only one, please," Eileen said. "Only one and we'll both watch."

"That's fine," Blaine said, and picked up a phone. Eileen turned back to the CD drawer, noticing that without even realizing it she had sorted out the music by Gamer. There was a sheet of paper at the bottom of the drawer, and she pulled it out. On it was large type:

TUNES RULES:
1) No more than three CDs in the queue.
2) No stopping the CD in progress. If you hate it, wear earplugs!
3) No volume past the third hash mark. Unless it is after midnight.

Blaine spoke briefly into the phone and replaced it in the cradle. He swiveled around to face Eileen, scrubbing tiredly at his face.

"Joe's coming over."

The phone rang suddenly, startling them both. Blaine picked it up and listened for a moment.

"We'll be right there," he said, getting to his feet. He put down the phone and jerked his head toward the door. "The ME is here. Dr. Rowland. And the whole Air Force Crime Scene crew."

"I'll wait here," Eileen said. Blaine nodded and went to get the door.

Eileen, in her music sorting, noticed there were CDs owned by someone called Sully, a name she hadn't heard in connection with the Gamers. She tapped one of the CDs against her lip gently, finished up her sorting job, put them all back, and shut the drawer as Major Blaine led in a short Air Force captain in a wrinkled, ill-fitting uniform. Behind him were four other people, all in comfortable civilian clothing. The photographer looked upset, clutching his big camera with white fingers.

"Dr. Rowland," the captain in the rumpled uniform said, shaking Eileen's hand. "I don't believe we've met yet, although I know your Captain Harben. A good guy." Dr. Rowland had bright, small brown eyes and a shock of thinning reddish hair. He walked in brisk, abrupt steps and when he cocked his head to the side while shaking hands Eileen almost laughed aloud. Rowland reminded her of a small red fox.

"Nice to meet you," Eileen said. "I'm glad you're here."

"Took me long enough," Rowland said with a quick glance at Blaine. "I've never been through more checks, not even at the Pentagon." Blaine shrugged and spread his hands apart. The photographer blew a strand of black hair off his forehead with a loud snort, but said nothing.

"Where?" Rowland asked, not looking at the screens that had captured

Eileen's attention earlier. The globe was still focused on the eastern sea-board, where streamers of radioactive clouds could be seen flowing north and west. New York City was already covered by a long plume. Blaine pointed at the closed door, and Rowland immediately shifted his grip on his medical bag and strode off in his quick little steps.

"Just got finished on a murder at Fort Carson," Rowland said briskly. "No mystery there, straight overdose. Needle marks still clear. Trouble was," and he gestured for Blaine to open the door, "the soldier was in the bushes for a week. Hot weather is rough on a corpse."

"Pendleton," Eileen said gloomily, and Rowland laughed.

"You'll be working that one too, I imagine? Camera, please. Closed door first."

The camera flashed. The door swung open. Eileen remained impassive. She'd stood watch enough times to know how many terrible odors a dead body emits in the first few hours. After that things get better as rigor mortis sets in, and the smell only becomes awful again after decay really starts to take hold. Eileen didn't envy Dr. Rowland the examination of Pendleton's corpse after weeks in the summer heat.

Dr. Rowland stood for a moment, and to Blaine's amazement and Eileen's approval, took a deep, sampling breath. "Ahh," he said, but it was not an expression of enjoyment. He looked at the shape of the woman, still slumped over her keyboard, looked at the yellow handle of the screwdriver. He gestured for the camera, here, there. The flashes were silent and too bright. Finally he stepped into the room. He crouched down and looked underneath the loosely hanging arm, peering up at the dead face. He stood again, took the wrist of the body, and appeared to be feeling for a pulse. Eileen could see how deeply the fingers were pressing into the skin, feeling the silence. The cameraman took a picture from the same angle, crouching down on limber haunches. One team member took notes in what looked like a notebook. Eileen saw it out of the corner of her eye and glanced at it. As fast as the man was writing notes, the text was turning into typed words on a little computer screen. Eileen turned her attention back to the body.

Dr. Rowland looked at the screwdriver and bent down to his medical bag. He took out a small paper bag and taped it carefully over the screwdriver handle.

"Prints at the autopsy from this," he said in the direction of the fingerprinters, who were patiently waiting their turn. One of them nodded and snapped his gum.

"I need a hand here," Rowland said, looking at Eileen and Blaine.

Eileen stepped into the room before Blaine could move.

"I'll help."

"Okay, then, take her shoulder. We're going to lean her back in the chair. The screwdriver is high enough to miss the back of the chair. She'll be heavy," he warned.

Eileen nodded, and took hold of the slack shoulder.

"On the count of three."

At Dr. Rowland's sharp "Three," both of them pulled the body of the woman up and back in the chair. Her head lolled forward, then tilted back toward Blaine. Trapped gasses gurgled out of her throat. Blaine looked away, grimacing.

Dr. Rowland started examining the chest, the face, the neck, and Eileen met the murder victim. She would see pictures later that would give a better impression of soul and personality than the lifeless clay in front of her. She would get a better idea of what Terry Guzman was like from the interviews she would make. In fact, she already was forming an idea of the personality of the dead woman. Here was the physical thing, however, limp and dead though it was. Terry had rich brown hair and the ring of iris from one dulled eye was blue. Her body was lush and full under the formal green suit. Her skin showed faint marks of sun and wind, and Eileen looked for the character lines. She found a set of lines by the mouth, lines that spoke of self-indulgence and the set of a mouth in bad temper. Already, though, she wondered if she would have characterized those lines as bad temper if she hadn't already known that Terry was not a well-liked person.

The room was too small to hold Eileen, Dr. Rowland, and the photographer comfortably, so Eileen stepped out into the fresher air of the Center. She blinked at the sight of Joe Tanner standing at the doorway, his hands at his sides, his face as pale as chalk.

Eileen cursed under her breath and quickly closed the door. She didn't want Joe to see the body. If he were the murderer, he could use this glimpse of the body to cover up any slipups he might make later. Blaine noticed Joe.

"How long have you been there?" Blaine barked.

"I—I—I just got here," he stammered.

"It's all right," Eileen said, more to Tanner than to Blaine.

"We need to see the videotape," Blaine said to Joe. "I'm sorry to call you over here. I didn't want you to see that."

Tanner shrugged faintly and nodded at Blaine.

"It's okay," he said. "Not something I really wanted to see."

"I need to know how to work the machine," Eileen said. "I'll be going over it quite a bit, and I wouldn't want you to have to stay here while I work."

"Okay," Tanner said.

In the studio, more color came into his face. He obviously felt very much at home. He sat down at a console and logged on to a computer terminal, his fingers striking the keyboard quickly. The screen went dark and then cleared, showing a series of boxes of different colors and sizes.

"Okay," he said to himself, and took a deep breath. "Okay." He turned to Eileen and gestured her closer.

"This is like your VCR, only a little more complicated," Tanner explained. "Ignore the console itself, that won't do anything. It's all hooked into the monitor here." Behind him, Blaine made an *ahhh* sound. "The tapes from monitor A are here," and his finger touched the screen at a large *A*. "To view the tape, press this button with your mouse key," and he moved the mouse so the computer arrow was directly over the View button. "The rest should be obvious; there's Pause, Fast Forward, Rewind, and this one you'll probably like, it's a frame-by-frame option." He pressed the View button, and the TV monitor set into the studio console went dark and then lit up with a scene of the room in front of them, full of people. He pressed the Frame-by-Frame button with his mouse key, and the people froze. Every time he pressed the button, the people made some kind of tiny advance in their movements. The picture was perfectly sharp.

"Good equipment," Eileen murmured.

"The best," Tanner said absently. "Now, there is an audio feature too, you'll want this too. Look."

He moved over to the television picture and picked up another mouse. A cursor appeared on the television screen. Tanner swirled the cursor around in a nervous little gesture, then picked on a tall major with a cup of coffee and a donut in his hand. He held down the first mouse key and drew the mouse sharply downward. Where the cursor was, a box appeared and grew as he moved the mouse. He "drew" a box around the donut-eating major, then let the mouse go and moved his chair back to the other keyboard. He picked up the mouse and clicked on Audio and then pressed a button marked "Listen."

"Resume is the button for when you want to listen to all the conversations again," Tanner said. "Don't forget that, or it's annoying." He pressed the "Play" button on the tape.

"Another show," the major was saying to the person at his side, another major who was wiping his fingers on a napkin. The other major said something, but there was no sound as the lips moved.

"Yeah, they do have some lookers here, don't they? I'd like to hang out in the Ground Weapons room just to look at that babe in the green suit."

Eileen nodded. That was a comment she'd expect about a woman like Terry.

"You can listen to anyone's conversation?" Blaine asked. "What does the whole room sound like?"

Tanner didn't say a word. He turned back to the terminal and pressed the Audio, and then the Resume button. At once, the sound of fifty voices filled the booth, the crowd noise.

"Amazing," Eileen said admiringly. "This may help me quite a bit."

"It's easy," Tanner said. "I'll be at my desk until four o'clock if you have any other questions, and you could call Art or me if you need to."

"That's fine, then," Blaine said. "I'll let you get back now so my team can get to work."

Eileen tried to keep her face expressionless. *My* team?

"There's one other thing," Tanner said, looking anxiously at Eileen. "I need to bring the simulation down. Er, I mean, I need to stop the programs from running." He gestured at the globe in the front of the room. The sun was westering and the lights were coming on in many of the cities.

"Hey, there's lights in the east," Eileen said. "Wouldn't the power be out?"

"Well, I'll be dipped," Tanner said in wonder. "We never let the thing run this far before. 'Berto will love this one!" He snapped his fingers and grinned, and for a moment Eileen saw him as he must have been before Terry's body was discovered: vibrant, alive, full of humor and vinegar. Then as he glanced over at her in amusement, as if to share the knowledge of the computer bug, he remembered the murder. For a moment, he'd obviously forgotten. The light in his eyes died out and he looked miserable.

"What will happen if we just let it run?" Blaine asked.

"You'll crash a Cray supercomputer, is what you'll do," Tanner answered dully. "Every keystroke and mouse movement is stored on the Cray, as well as all the number-crunching to run the simulation. If we just let it run the Cray will fill up like a bathtub. We never run simulations this long, we have to store the data away so it can be processed."

"You can bring it down," Blaine said.

"Please don't get rid of anything," Eileen added. "Not until we know if there's anything on that computer that could help us."

"Okay," Tanner said. "I can bring it down from next door, that okay? Art and I will have to do the cleanup, but we can do that from our desks too, we're linked to the Cray."

"Bring it down, then, Joe," Blaine said, before Eileen could say anything. She blinked hard and thought about whether or not she should challenge him. But she really had no idea what was stored on the computer, or whether or not Joe Tanner or Arthur Bailey would be getting rid of valuable information. Eileen simply could not control everything, and she knew it, so she let it go.

Tanner gave a brief ghost of a smile and got to his feet. He picked a piece of paper from a note board to the side of the console and handed it deliberately to Eileen.

"Our numbers," he said.

"Thanks," Eileen said wryly. A murder suspect, giving her some support against the big bad Major Blaine. This *was* turning out to be some day.

As Blaine escorted him out, Eileen went back to Dr. Rowland. She waited until Tanner was out of sight before opening the door to the little room where Terry was killed. As she did, she realized anew that she had no idea how the murder was committed. The room had only one door, and that was on the monitor. Perhaps the videotape would show something. She froze for a moment, trying to keep her heart from speeding up in her chest. Now was no time for her doubts to show.

"I'm done, you can call the wagon," Rowland said. "She died of the stab wound, I would predict, but I won't know until the autopsy for sure." He was scrubbing at his hands with a disposable wet tissue. Overwhelming the other odors was a smell of baby powder.

"Diaper wipes," Rowland said, winking at Eileen. He dropped the wipe back into his bag. "Greatest stuff ever invented. Take off anything and they smell awful powerful. I've got a little girl, so I steal from our home supply."

Eileen smiled at the little doctor. It was a good smell. In the room the fingerprinters were now going to work. They were done with the door. It was marked with streaks and smears of light brown dust.

"You're the investigating officer, that's right?" Rowland asked.

"That's right."

"This is a hell of a stab wound," Rowland said thoughtfully. "I don't know if the screwdriver was sharpened or not, but even if it was, it still takes a lot of force to drive a screwdriver into someone's back. This person you're looking for is strong. Smart to use a screwdriver. No blood splash like from a knife," Rowland said.

"You can buy one at any store," Eileen added.

"Fingerprints nearly impossible to take from that plastic," Rowland continued grinning.

"And impossible to trace. Who would remember selling someone a screwdriver?"

"Poison is much more difficult. Not sure of the results, or how quick."

"Strangling could be a struggle. It had to be quick, and silent, with no blood."

"Could a woman have the strength to do this?" Eileen asked, abandoning the game. Rowland shrugged, still smiling a little.

"Ordinarily, I'd say no. But the insane have different ways of using power. I've seen a tiny woman who needed two orderlies to hold her down, all because she didn't want her medication. A normal woman, no."

"Insane," Eileen repeated.

"Or full of hate. The person who killed this woman, insane or not, hated her very much."

"I'll remember that," Eileen said.

"See that you do," Rowland said grimly. "I'd hate to be sawing you in two to see what killed you." He winked, and Eileen grinned back, liking him a lot.

"Right."

"Should I call for the stretcher?" Blaine asked at the doorway.

"A stretcher it is," Rowland said cheerfully. "I'll do the autopsy tomorrow. You want a report?"

Blaine and Eileen both nodded.

"Do you have e-mail?"

"I've got it," Eileen said.

"Good."

"I don't have e-mail. We're not allowed to have external computer lines," Blaine said. "Hackers, you know."

"Oh," Rowland said. He put a stubby hand in his medical bag and produced a black address book. "Too bad. Wonderful stuff, e-mail. What's your address?"

"ereed@cxc.siv.gov," Eileen said. She saw the address book was filled with streams of addresses like her own.

"I do all my work on a voice recognition system," Rowland explained to Blaine, writing Eileen's address in a small, neat hand. "I dictate, it produces a pretty packet, all set up just like my old reports. Plus," and he closed the book with a snap, "I can send it to Detective Reed in a few seconds. She reads it, prints what she wants, no problem."

"We have e-mail systems, but they're all internal," Blaine said. "Security."

"I'll send you a packet by regular mail. Can I have your card?" Rowland was brisk and unsympathetic. "I need to get home. I'm not like those TV MEs you see working all hours of the night. I have three little girls."

Blaine produced a card and within a few moments the ME was out the door and gone. His passing seemed to leave a wake like a speedboat engine. Eileen sighed. After the crisp Dr. Rowland, Major Blaine was even harder to face.

"Let's have you view those tapes now," Blaine said.

"I'll interview the other Gamers now," Eileen said firmly. "I'll look at the tapes afterwards."

There was a short silence from Blaine. Eileen looked at him without challenge, waiting to see what he would do.

"That sounds reasonable," he said. "I'll handle the crew in here and you go across the hall. I'll check on you later—" He stopped as there was an almost audible pop. The screen in front of them, now showing lights across the dark half of the world, went black. The lights in the room dimmed slightly, then became brighter. The consoles that Eileen could see had also gone black and still. It was eerie, as though the computer had stopped the simulation all on its own. Eileen knew that Joe and Art must have brought the programs to a halt from their office, as he said they would.

"Fine," Eileen said. "Bathroom break first."

"Right," Blaine said. "I'll get the ambulance crew in here. You know the key sequence to get in next door?"

"Eight zero three zero," Eileen said. Blaine blinked, impressed. Eileen didn't bother to explain that she'd developed her memory for numbers working as a waitress in college, adding up bills for eggs and bacon and chewy truck stop steaks. Let Blaine think she was brilliant. She hoped she would be able to keep at least an image of competence. So far, she felt like she was floundering her way through the day.

"Okay, then, let's get going."

·9

Great Falls, Virginia

Lucy Giometti was home early. She intended to return to work later that evening, but dinner with her husband was not to be denied. She loved to cook and she loved their dinners together.

Her mother lost a baby girl to sudden infant death syndrome before Lucy. She had three younger brothers, so had her sister survived she would have been from the essential cliché, the large Italian family. As it was, her mother gave all her affection to her surviving daughter. Lucy spent a lot of time with her brothers, escaping as much as she could from her mother's smothering femininity. Lucy was the first to try riding her bicycle off the concrete embankment and into the sand pile. She was the first to climb trees, and until adolescence hit was the fastest and strongest of the four of them. Then she fell behind each year, as her brothers became more powerful and she became mysteriously smaller and weaker. She picked up track and excelled at running, but she never quite forgave her body for becoming a woman.

Her father, a policeman, had no interest in his daughter. Even when Lucy graduated in the top ten at her university he had no words of congratulations for her. Lucy was unable to understand her mother and her father had no desire to understand her, and until Ted came into her life she didn't realize how lonely she was. Ted Giometti changed all that. He brought joy. Now they were starting a family. Lucy Giometti fell in love with an English teacher and found she'd learned a lot from her mother after all, when in courtship she tried to please him with her cooking skills.

Her phone rang just as the fettuccine timer went off. Lucy scooped up the phone and held the hot pot one-handed, dumping the noodles into the strainer as she settled the phone into her shoulder.

"Hello," she said.

"We need you in here," Mills said. "Right away."

"I'll be there in forty-five minutes," she said serenely. "You know I don't give up dinner."

"I need you here now, Giometti," Mills said.

Lucy smiled at the phone. "Mr. Mills, I am not involved in any operation that could cause the death of an agent by my presence. Fire me if you wish. Let the gate guards know and I'll give them my badge. Otherwise, I'll be there in forty-five minutes."

Mills hung up the phone and Lucy returned to her dinner task.

"Who was that?" Ted asked, coming out of the bathroom.

"My boss. I have to go back in after dinner," she said, and held her mouth up to him for a kiss.

Gaming Center, Schriever Air Force Base

Sharon of the Whitney and Michael CDs was a solidly built woman in her late thirties, skin the café-au-lait of the Louisiana Creole, eyes a deep and somber black.

"Sharon Johnson?" Eileen asked, standing and offering her hand. "Eileen Reed, Colorado Springs Police, Special Investigations."

"How do you do?" Sharon asked politely. She took the hand and shook it briefly. Her hand was warm and dry.

"Please have a seat," Eileen said. Sharon took a chair quietly, folded her hands on her lap, and waited. Eileen seated herself as well, and studied the other woman for a moment. Sharon's body was thick-figured, big breasted, her legs short and chunky under the soft cream cotton of a dress that was quite obviously new. The shoes were scuffed and well worn, although of good quality, and she wore no jewelry. Her hair, thick and black, curved beautifully to her shoulders and her skin was a miracle, without tonal variation or flaw, a perfect buttered toffee brown.

"Lowell is still not up for an interview?" Eileen asked quietly.

"He asked me to come in first. Doug took him something to eat. He was still feeling pretty bad."

"It has been a terrible day for you folks."

"A terrible day," Sharon repeated.

"Did you know Terry Guzman, Ms. Johnson?"

"Sharon, please, Miss Reed. Yes I did."

"Sharon, then. Please call me Eileen. Were you friends with Terry?"

"No, I wasn't," Sharon said firmly, and stirred in her seat. "But it is a terrible thing, to die that way, a very bad thing."

"Why weren't you friends with her?" Eileen asked gently.

"She felt that I—" Sharon stopped for a moment, a look of bafflement coming over her face. Then her expression fell smooth again. "I don't have a four-year degree, Miss Reed. I am going to night school and they've given me this position while I finish. I—" Here she looked down, her mouth twisting for a moment as though she struggled with some unnamed emotion. "I have been having difficulties. Terry has not been kind to me." There was a pause. "Terry was not kind to me." There was relief in Sharon's voice when she corrected the tense.

"Why wasn't she kind?" Eileen asked.

"I don't know. I wish I knew. She was not kind to me, and I did not speak to her because of it."

"I see," Eileen said. "Was it racial?"

Sharon looked at her without surprise.

"No, I don't think so. You get to know pretty quickly when someone hates you because of your race. She didn't like anyone, I don't think. She never looked at me like I was a human being, but it wasn't because of my race."

"I'm trying to get an idea of what Terry was like, that's all. More importantly I need to know exactly what you did today, everything you can remember. Even if it doesn't seem important. All right?"

"That's fine," Sharon said. She took a deep breath.

"Okay then," Eileen said, smiling. "Tell me everything from when the alarm went off this morning."

Sharon looked surprised, then shrugged.

"I got up at five-forty-five this morning. I have three children and I got them off to school before I came in."

"Where do they go to school?" Eileen asked, hearing "School" instead of "school" in Sharon's voice.

"The Colorado Springs School," Sharon said. Eileen was surprised. That place was private, aimed at the Ivy League. Tuition was horribly expensive.

"It's worth it," Sharon explained. "They pay me a regular engineer's salary, it allows us to pay tuition and eat. They pay for my schooling, the company does, and books. Graham suffers, sometimes—he'd like to be dressed in fancy shoes like the other kids, but I'm bringing him up proud. He knows what it takes and he doesn't whine."

"That is an incredible accomplishment," Eileen said slowly, and meant it. "When did you get to work?"

"I got to my desk about a quarter till eight. I fixed myself some tea and walked over to get a donut, that's our Game Day bonus. When I got into the room I saw Terry talking to Major Travers. There are two donut and coffee tables. Terry was standing by the first one. So I went to the other one."

Sharon focused in on Eileen. "I'm trying to be honest, Miss Reed. I hope this doesn't get anyone in trouble. But you should know how I felt about her."

"I understand," Eileen said quietly.

"All right. I got to the table. 'Berto was there too. I always pick out the blueberry cake donuts if they have them. 'Berto always has those chocolate cream-filled ones? Joe calls them sugar and grease bombs. He eats the chocolate raised ones, though. So we started eating our donuts and we wandered over to Art's console, the Truth Team area. Art and Joe were watching some kind of network monitor on the screen. They—I'm sorry, it was Art—kicked out a couple of chairs and we—'Berto and I—sat down. There was the usual crowd of people in there, all the military types and the Civil Service gray-suits. Everyone was just stuffing their faces with the donuts and drinking coffee out of Styrofoam cups and just talking as fast as their gums could flap. My! Working in the Center, you don't realize how you get used to the quiet. Game Day is always so noisy."

Sharon shifted in her chair. She unfolded and refolded the sensible legs.

"I sat next to Joe and pretty soon we started talking a little bit, about the Brilliant Pebbles. He is pretty stressed on Game Day."

Sharon paused. "Joe and Art were trying to fix a problem on the day of the Game. That's like retooling the motor when you're launching a ship." Sharon shook her head. "I can't stay late, I have the kids, but I was here until six last night finishing up some testing. If I had found a problem, I would have called Marion, my neighbor, and she would have watched the kids until I got the job done. We always make the Game."

"Was everyone that dedicated?" Eileen asked levelly.

"No," Sharon responded slowly. "You know who was not. Her stuff always worked, but I can't see how. Unless—"

"Unless what?"

"I have thought for quite a while that someone else was helping her. I mean, writing her code for her," Sharon said, and bit at her lips. "Software has a fingerprint. You can't write code without leaving your mark on it. Terry wrote sloppy, terrible, confused code. Then it started to get better, right after Sully died and we thought that was it for her—"

"What? Who died?" Eileen interrupted sharply.

"Oh, I'm sorry, you don't know. Sully was another engineer. She wasn't killed or anything like that, it wasn't . . . murder." Her voice died away.

"Tell me about Sully," Eileen said grimly.

"Sully was Harriet Sullivan. She was a Gamer. She was real abrasive, but she was good. Terry and her didn't get along at all. She was—Sully, I mean—she was so fine nobody could touch her, not even Lowell. I know Terry tried to get her fired, she hated her so much. She was so witty, you know? Just that turn of phrase that would sting you bad. If you knew Sully, you would laugh, because she was really a good person. She wrote me a note once when I gave her some terrible code and asked if having three children made me stupid, or was it just a defense mechanism."

"That's rough," Eileen commented.

"Yes. Sully was rough. She made me cry a few times, before I got used to her. Then we were just fine, I understood her. She had no biases, except for stupidity. Then she changed, near the end."

"How did she die?"

"She skidded off the road driving to work. She was broadsided by a truck and killed instantly," Sharon said, her mouth a thin angry line. "She was working a lot of overtime, just like the rest of us, to make up for Terry's mistakes. One person on the team doesn't pull their own weight and everybody suffers. Terry made everybody suffer. None of us liked her before then, but afterwards . . . I don't know how we held together. We had a wake. We never eat the sprinkle donuts during a Game. It's stupid, but they were her favorites. The military guys eat them, usually."

"Why did she change?"

Sharon looked discomfited.

"The girl is long dead, almost two years now," she said. "And it's old news."

"Tell me," Eileen said patiently.

"Sully and Joe were together," Sharon said quietly. "It was very sudden. I expected a wedding within the year. She was so in love she forgot she had rough edges. And then she was killed."

"I see."

"I hope you don't think Joe— Well. Killed Terry, I mean," Sharon said. "I'm sure he wanted to, we all wanted her gone from us. But we put it back together and went on."

She abruptly folded her arms tightly around herself. "I feel like I've told you more than I should, Miss Reed."

Eileen looked at Sharon gravely and sympathetically. Something about Eileen's face, which always appeared to be a rather plain sort of face in her mirror, seemed to open people up like magic. Eileen had three murder confessions to her credit, and none of the murderers could later describe just why they spilled their guts to Eileen.

"I think you listen, Miss Reed," Sharon suddenly added. "You really *listen*. I don't think very many people do that. Anyway, that's what I know. I hope this helps."

"You are helping me a great deal," Eileen said. "Anything you say to me is going to help me find the person who killed Terry. That's what I need. Don't be nervous. The only person this information is going to hurt is the murderer."

"I want that," Sharon said, her eyebrows puckered in distress. "I just don't want it to be someone I know."

"How about we get some coffee and take a break and then we finish up talking about the Game? Sound good?"

Eileen found the coffee machine. She needed time to think, too, to digest the image of the slack dead girl that was forming in her mind. Terry's shadow was beginning to take on the outline of a monster. That was disturbing. She had worked a couple of cases where the victim was an evil person, but both times the murderer was standing ready for the handcuffs when the police arrived. Once, a woman who killed her husband, another a man who killed his sister's boyfriend. Both abuse cases, both straightforward. Terry was different. Instead of a murder of passion, Terry's was more of an execution.

Eileen nearly spilled coffee from Joe's mug. This was confusing, and she was beginning to be tired. There was still much to do, and again there was the whisper in the back of her mind that she was out of her depth, out of her depth. She sipped the hot fragrant coffee and reminded herself firmly that her abilities had nothing to do with Jim Erickson, that they were within herself and dependent upon no one. This was her case. This was her time. No matter how exotic the surroundings, the blood and the death were just the same as any other.

"Just the same," she murmured to herself, squared her shoulders, and headed back to the conference room.

•10

Sharon was waiting for Eileen when she returned with coffee, hands folded in that Madonna quiet pose.

"Where were we?" Eileen said briskly. "No coffee for you? No? I think we left off where you and 'Berto were talking to Joe about those rock things."

"Brilliant Pebbles," Sharon corrected, smiling faintly.

"Tell me about Terry. Tell me when you found out."

"I was in my room. I had my communications gear on, and I played the game. That's all I remember until the ground interceptors didn't go off, and then I heard screams." Sharon shuddered suddenly and intensely, gooseflesh rising on the smooth brown of her arms.

"Did you see anything odd afterwards? Anything different, anything not quite right?"

"I know what you're asking for," Sharon replied, "but everything was odd. Everyone was out of their seats and standing around, and all the doors were open to the rooms. I could see that Terry was dead. I looked over at Joe and he was standing by Art, they were both just as white as sheets, and they were frozen, just frozen. Art's hands were still held over the keyboard like he was going to start typing again.

"And then I saw Lowell, He was looking completely confused, embarrassed really, he couldn't see the room, and he must have been upset that Terry had messed up again. Then he saw the faces, and I think he started to realize that it was worse than he thought. 'Berto came up next to him and put his hand on his arm, and when Lowell tried to start forward he held on to him. I saw 'Berto might need my help and I went to Lowell too. We actually pulled him into his room and shut the door, he was trying to break free of 'Berto and go to Terry, but 'Berto, you know—" Sharon made an arm gesture like a weight lifter, and Eileen nodded. "I held him too, until the first shock was over and he started crying. Then the paramedics came, they gave him some tranquilizers.

"It's funny, really, I think it was 'Berto and I because we've seen death before, we're both from the ghetto. Well, the barrio, in his case. I lost two cousins to the gangs. A girlfriend of mine got killed by a stray bullet. 'Berto, he saw friends go down too. We know death. So we were there for Lowell while people like Joe and Doug were just standing still."

"I'm glad you were there for him," Eileen said quietly. "Is there anything else? Anything you can think of?"

"I don't think so."

"You've been very helpful," Eileen said. "I appreciate it. I might need to speak with you again, but I'll be here tomorrow. I probably won't need to contact you at home. If you think of anything at all, could you call this number?" She flipped out her badge and dug behind it for her business cards. She held one out to Sharon, and the other woman took it in her sturdy fingers.

"Thank you," Eileen said.

"You are welcome," Sharon replied, and got to her feet. "I think you are a good cop, Miss Reed. I've seen bad and I've seen good," she smiled wryly. "And you seem pretty good."

Eileen stood and shook Sharon's hand, feeling absolutely confident that this woman was no murderer. Eileen usually felt this way after an interview. Perhaps that was part of her success as an interviewer. She listened, she believed, she was sympathetic. Sharon could be the murderer.

"I'll get Lowell for you, is that okay? He really needs to go home pretty soon. Nelson called his family in Denver and Lowell's got a brother coming down to stay with him tonight."

"Lowell would be fine," Eileen said. "Thanks."

Eileen glanced at her watch. Four-fifteen in the afternoon. She felt as though it could be midnight. The lack of windows was stifling. She sipped at her good strong coffee and looked through her pages of terrible notes, and wondered if she could talk Bob, the station office manager, into using the page scanner. Then she would have pages of good clean type, with only errors to correct when the scanner couldn't tell what she had written. She'd be at Schriever until late. Perhaps she'd drop by the station after hours. Bob was a notorious tightwad and didn't like Eileen. He kept asking her to type her own stuff, get her own supplies, in general to do all the work Bob was supposed to do for the detectives. Eileen ignored his complaints and made him work for her, which didn't help Bob's temper or his opinion of Eileen Reed.

Lowell Guzman entered the room with another man—it had to be Doug Procell, the only other Gamer Eileen hadn't interviewed. Lowell was shiny pale and sweaty, with blurred and dilated eyes. Sedatives. Doug, the other Gamer, a slender nondescript type in a gray suit, helped Lowell find a seat and vanished with an embarrassed mumble Eileen didn't catch.

Eileen didn't care about Doug Procell at that moment. Her interest was focused on Lowell Guzman, new widower, husband of a murdered woman. Guzman was rather short and gently rounded all over, from pudgy face to square feet in loafers with the seams giving out along the sides. He was not precisely fat, there was no beer belly or rolls around the neck, he was just big. A teddy bear type, a friend of Eileen's had called that kind of man. Huggable.

"I don't want to keep you long," Eileen said gently. "I just need to ask a few questions."

"Okay," Guzman said with an effort, eyes focusing on Eileen for a moment and then sliding away, blurring again. "I—" he said, for a moment struggling to speak, and Eileen noted the strong brown hair, curled like wires on Guzman's head, the healthy tone of the skin under the grayness of shock and medication. Guzman had bushy eyebrows and a firm jaw under a soft padding of fat.

"I—okay," Guzman tried again, then sighed. His eyes teared up. "Okay. Sorry."

"I understand. Just relax for a bit. How old are you?"

"I—oh. Thirty-seven." The voice was rusty but there.

"How old was Terry?"

"Thirty-five." A hoarse whisper.

"How long were you married?"

"Three years."

"Any children?"

"No. I mean, yes. I have two girls from a previous marriage. They visit."

"Okay. How long have you worked here?"

"Four years."

Eileen took him through the standard questions slowly, evenly, without the variations she had thrown the other Gamers. There would be time for that later, when the sedatives and the shock were gone. Terry had come to Gaming barely four months after her marriage. With Eileen's mental sketch of Terry already forming, she found herself wondering if the marriage hadn't been a response to her imminent layoff from Digital Equipment Corporation. Then she frowned at herself. Marriage, to avoid unemployment? Not likely.

"Was Terry married before this?" she asked.

"Yes. She was divorced two years before she met me," Lowell said tiredly.

"Name?"

"Vance somebody. Something real plain. Oh, yes. James. Vance James. Why?"

"We just need to find out everything we can," Eileen said gently. "Where was she born?"

"I don't know."

"Well then, where was she from?"

"I—I don't know that either," Lowell said wonderingly. "I asked once, but she didn't want to talk about it."

"Family? Does she have family?"

"No. She said her mother and father died years ago, when she was in college. No brothers or sisters either, I think."

"You don't know?"

"She didn't like to talk about her past!" Lowell burst out. Fresh tears ran down his swollen and raw-looking skin. "She didn't talk about it. You can find that out by looking at her security paperwork. I never looked at it, she didn't want me to. If there was anything wrong with her past, they would have found it. Okay?"

"Okay," Eileen said evenly. "These are just questions, Mr. Guzman. I'm not trying to accuse you or her of anything."

"Okay," Lowell said with an effort, looking confused and angry, and bewildered. Eileen knew the look. There would be all the stages to go through, the denial and the rage and the bargaining, and the final acceptance. Eileen was often long out of the picture when the last peaceful stage was reached, unless the person appeared at the trial.

"Sharon said that someone would be with you tonight, is that right?" Eileen asked.

"Yes, my brother Jeff."

"Okay, then. Please lock up tonight. I don't mean to alarm you, but whoever it was might threaten you too, Mr. Guzman. And please don't touch any of Terry's things. I'll be by sometime tomorrow to look through them."

"Why would you look through her things?" Lowell asked. He looked exhausted and upset, like a bear being teased in a cage.

"Just a normal part of police procedure, Mr. Guzman. I'll ask you some more questions tomorrow when you're feeling a little better, all right? And if you think of anything, here's my card."

"That's all?" Lowell asked, confused. His fingers trembled on the tiny slip of paper.

"That's all for now. All right, then?"

"All right," Lowell said in relief.

"How about fetching Doug Procell for me."

"All right." He left, and Eileen sighed and worked her shoulders back and forth in her jacket.

"What a day," she murmured. She rose to her feet when Doug Procell entered, the nondescript type in the gray suit, the last of the Gamers. Eileen glanced down at her list, seeing the check marks by every name: Nelson, Joe, 'Berto, and Arthur Bailey before lunch, Sharon and Lowell after lunch. The last check mark was the gray-suited man now extending a hand to her.

"Doug Procell."

"Eileen Reed. Please sit down." Doug sat down, and as he did Eileen took a good look at him, reaching past the expensive suit and the regular features that would make him invisible in any business crowd. Here was actually quite a handsome man, with direct hazel eyes behind wire-rimmed glasses, thick black hair, and a strong chin. His hands and feet were large. There was a good breadth to the shoulders but no real depth, unlike 'Berto. Doug Procell had more of a runner's frame than a weight lifter's. He looked healthy.

"When did you learn about Terry's death?" Eileen asked.

"When Nelson found her, same as everyone else," Doug said. "But I wasn't surprised that she was murdered."

"You weren't?" Eileen asked sharply. "Why?"

"Because I was expecting another murder."

"Another murder?"

"I don't believe Sully—Harriet Sullivan—drove off the road. I think she was driven off the road," Procell said. "I think it was murder. Sully—"

"I know about Sully," Eileen said. "Sharon told me. But she didn't think it was murder."

"I know. No one thinks these deaths are murders. But I do. There have been three deaths here at Schriever in the past four years. Three of them! Two of them were late at night, no witnesses, just the car run off the road and the person inside dead. The third, a person you don't know, John Richmond, he smashed into a garbage truck going sixty-plus in the midst of early-morning traffic. No evidence of foul play."

"You think there was?"

"I'm sure of it," Procell said grimly. "Look, I can get you my file."

"Your file?" Eileen felt completely stunned.

"My file. I've been keeping notes on the murders within the Missile Defense Program since 1987. There were six people killed in Great Britain that year. Their deaths were all strange. All completely mysterious. Why would a young man kill himself by driving his car, loaded with gasoline cans, into an abandoned café in London? That's a death no one wants to die, being burned alive. I don't think he wanted to die."

"Wait, wait." Eileen held up her hand. "Let me get this straight. You think Terry Guzman is one of a number of murder victims? All people who work on the Missile Defense program?"

"Yes, I think so," Doug Procell said. His earnest hazel eyes held Eileen's. "I guess I shouldn't be happy about this. But I've been collecting this information for years, and no one believed me, and now they have to believe me. Terry Guzman wasn't killed. She was executed."

•11

"I'm here," Lucy said at the doorway to Mills's office. "What's up?"

He looked up from his desk and glared at her. He was a thin man with fading blond hair, and if Lucy felt obligated to him in the slightest, she would have hated him as a boss. As it was, she could get a job in the civilian world as a computer engineer within twenty-four hours, and therefore Mills had very little power over her.

Mills knew it, too. Lucy knew he was offended by her. She knew he was offended by her dark Italian beauty, by her intelligence, by her casual attitude toward himself as a boss and her job in general. The worst offense of all to Mills was Lucy's work, which was incredibly good. Mills couldn't *stand* that.

Mills wanted a WASP worker from the 1950s, Lucy often thought, a shrinking white man in a white pressed shirt whose future depended on the good graces of his boss, namely Steven Mills. Mills wore the fifties uniform, perhaps unconsciously. His pants were polyester and his shirts white, and he wore a pocket protector with no sense of irony. His hair was combed back and slightly dusty, and his teeth, though white, were hid behind lips that were always chapped and raw-looking. Lucy thought perhaps he had an ulcer, because sometimes she caught a whiff of his breath and it was chalky and desperate-smelling. She hated when she could smell his breath. She walked into his office and dropped into a comfortable chair without being asked. She smiled at him and rubbed her slightly rounded stomach.

"The baby needed the chow, Steve. So what's up?"

"We had a development in a related case," Mills said.

"The Missile Defense homicides?"

Mills nodded and rubbed his forehead with his small manicured hands. He looked tired.

"The FBI has had a suspect under surveillance for almost two years. The FBI contacted us today. He skipped town. Boarded a plane to Paris at noon and is just clean gone."

Lucy leaned back in her chair. The CIA didn't engage in surveillance in their own country; that was the duty of the Federal Bureau of Investigation. The FBI did the investigation and got the glory in the United States, although the CIA was often the controlling organization. American spies were handled in the press with great fanfare. Foreign spies sometimes made the back-page news as they were deported. It wasn't fair, but that was the way the business worked.

"What kind of suspect?"

"Espionage. NORAD, Peterson, Fort Carson, and Schriever. He posed as a corporate headhunter for engineers. Made quite a living at it, too. His name was George Tabor, and we had positive ID. We almost had him cold. He sold to everybody: the new Russian Republic, the Baltic States, Japan. The only countries he didn't sell to were the Moslem countries in the Middle East, and China. He didn't seem to have any contacts in the Middle East, and he hated the Chinese."

"Schriever," Lucy said. "He was spooked by the murder? Wait a minute. He left at lunch? He must have been tipped off by someone at Schriever."

"Right," Mills said, irritated. Lucy had come to the same conclusion he had, only it took her about three seconds and it had taken him hours.

"So if he was tipped off, that must mean the murdered woman was involved. Maybe she was his contact. Or she smuggled information to someone who gave it to Tabor. What did she do?"

"She was a computer engineer. Software. In the Gaming division. Her name was Terry Guzman, and she'd worked there for almost two years."

"Gaming. She could get a lot of good stuff out the door," Lucy said angrily. Espionage offended her. She hated it. It was vile and disloyal, like cheating a member of your own family.

"Very good stuff," Mills said. "The latest algorithms for the battle managers. The whole Missile Defense program is mostly old technology, you know. Brilliant Pebbles are just fancy rocks. It's the computer programs that make the system happen. She's got—or she had, anyway—connection with all the latest."

"Could she have been killed because she wanted to stop?"

"I don't know. Right now her case is being handled by Detective Eileen Reed, Colorado Springs Police. She's probably still at Schriever. You can speak with her if you want, we can set you up as an employee of the DIA."

"That might be helpful," Lucy said slowly. The DIA was the Defense Intelligence Agency, the organization that handled security clearances. "But first I need to speak to Colonel Olsen. Is he aware of the Missile Defense homicides?"

"He's aware of the need for secrecy," Mills said carefully. "The only military official we brief on this project is the Missile Defense commander in chief. That's Admiral Kane. You'll have to keep this one sealed up. Don't even mention Tabor to Olsen."

Lucy felt a burst of irritation, but controlled it. Why in the world would the CIA want to keep a series of murders so quiet? Why wasn't this case a higher priority within the Agency? There were twelve dead people on that list.

"I'll get on the phone to Olsen. I can contact the FBI on this one?"

"Yes, but don't—"

"I know, I know," Lucy interrupted. She got up from the chair. "They don't know about the missile defense homicides, do they? I won't let it slip."

But as Lucy walked down the hallway to her own office, she made a resolution to herself. She was going to find some answers.

Conference Room, Schriever Air Force Base

Eileen pinched the bridge of her nose, fiercely, the sharp annoying pain bringing her back into focus. She knew she had to quit soon, and leave this place, and get some food.

"Mr. Procell, I want that file," she said, and the slump of relief in Procell's shoulders was almost comical. "I will read it. I will look at it. If Terry is one of your murder victims, then hopefully I can hand off this case to whoever is working the other cases. Right now, they are all supposed to be accidents." She held up her hand as Procell started to speak. "But I will also look at this case as an isolated murder, and I will find that murderer. The best way I can do this is collect your file later. First, I need to find out about you. Is that clear?"

Procell smiled at her peacefully and relaxed back into his chair. "Yes, ma'am," he said. "All I want is for you to read the stuff."

"You got it," Eileen said grimly. She felt a kind of sickness in her stomach. She didn't want to lose this case to the Air Force bureaucracy that had buried Bernie Ames with such careless insult. She didn't want this case, but now it was hers and she intended to finish it, no matter how deep the waters got. If there were multiple murders going on at Schriever Air Force Base, then she was just going to have to solve them all.

She clenched her pen and looked at Procell.

"Now, tell me about you. How long have you been working here?"

"Almost ten years. I worked on another project down in New Mexico before this one."

"Did you know Terry Guzman?"

"Yes, I did. I—I don't want you to find this out later, and think that I'm hiding something, so I'll tell you now. Terry and I went to the same college. Nobody else here knows that."

Eileen didn't hide her surprise. "Why doesn't anyone else know?" It seemed like harmless information.

"Because Terry wanted it that way. She had a bad marriage, I guess, and wanted to leave her past all the way behind her. So when we met again she pretended she didn't know me, and when I asked her later she . . . well, she asked me not to tell anyone."

"What was the university?"

"University of Utah, Salt Lake City. We saw each other in a few computer classes, is all, but you know Terry, she's—"

Abruptly, Doug stopped. Eileen saw the fact of her death strike Doug suddenly, as a reality and not a confirmation of his pet theory. The color washed from his face. For a moment Eileen was sure Doug was going to pass out. Doug reached out and gripped the table edge with one of his big hands, holding so hard the hand washed white and bloodless.

"Okay?" Eileen asked as Doug lowered his head.

"Mlright," Doug slurred. The seconds passed. Doug pulled himself upright. There was sweat on the clear brow, but his eyes were focused.

"Okay?" Eileen asked again.

"I'm okay," Doug said, and sat back in his chair. His face was paper white.

"It hits you like that sometimes," Eileen said gently. Sometimes the fact of murder took a while to sink into the murderer, too. "Just try to relax. You want some water?"

"How about a pop?" Doug still looked faint. "Takes you fifteen minutes to get one. You want to walk out there and back? The pop machines are all the way in the stairwells."

"That sounds like a great idea," Eileen said. "I would like to stretch my legs, actually."

Doug got shakily to his feet and led the way back through the maze of offices, empty now, and down the corridor to the submarine door.

"Why don't they have pop machines in here by the bathrooms?" Eileen asked. There were spaces next to the rest rooms for pop machines, and heavy-duty electrical outlets. The rest rooms were by the submarine doors. There were no machines in the alcoves.

"That's a breach of security, you see," Doug said with a wry smile. "I'm the class crazy, but even I think it's ridiculous that the Russians or the Chinese or whoever would put listening devices in our pop machines. If they can do that, why can't they just put listening devices in our pops, we carry them right back to our desks? I don't understand."

Doug spun the heavy door and stepped through with an ease born of long practice. He gestured Eileen to follow, then spun the door shut with a heavy, final sound.

"What a door," Eileen said.

"Your tax dollars at work." The color was coming back into Doug's face. "I don't mind the doors so much, there are some pretty sophisticated listening devices out there. I was at a Hughes Aircraft facility in Los Angeles once and saw a demonstration. Big Chevy van, not really an odd-looking antenna, not for L.A., and parked outside the Hughes building. Way far away, I mean more than a city block. And they had screens that were printing out what people were typing into their terminals, inside the building. Scary."

"That door stops that?"

"Stops everything. No mice, no insects. I've never seen a spider even. Like a big vacuum jar."

Doug led them to a door marked "Stairwell #3" and opened it. There were huge candy and pop machines humming next to the stairs.

"I've got extra change, let me," Doug said. "You learn to carry change around here. It's a long walk back to your desk."

The pop cans chunked down into the bins below. Eileen opened hers and took a long, grateful swallow.

"This will help," she said. Doug took a long drink of his own pop and opened the door back to the corridor. Eileen did not make it obvious, but Procell ended up going through the doorway first. The corridors were very quiet and very empty.

The conference room seemed even more stifling after the brief walk. Eileen sat down with a sigh. Procell took a chair.

"I feel better."

"Me, too." Procell's fingers trembled faintly on the can of pop, but his mouth had lost its gray, pinched look.

"Tell me about the War Game. Start out with your morning, every little detail. From the time you woke up."

"From the time I woke up?" Procell asked, puzzled. "What does that have to do with your case?"

"I don't know what it has to do with this case," Eileen answered steadily. Procell thought that over for a moment and then nodded.

"Okay," he said. "I got up at five-fifteen and showered . . ."

Gaming Center, Schriever Air Force Base

It was nearly six-thirty when Eileen picked up the conference-room phone to dial Major Blaine. Procell had told her every tiny detail of his day, and she had learned absolutely nothing. Eileen wanted to view the Game tapes, but she knew she was too tired. Harben needed a report as well. She'd seen Blaine lock and tape the entrance to the Gaming Center. Blaine set a security guard at the only entrance to the Center. The tapes were as safe as they could be, and Eileen was hungry.

"Security, Major Blaine speaking."

"This is Eileen Reed, Major Blaine. Can you come guide me out of this place?"

"I certainly can," Blaine said warmly. "I've been catching up on paperwork waiting for your call. I'll come right over and show you the door on our way out, and you can give me your report."

Eileen sat for a moment in silence, feeling her heart pound so loudly that her hand trembled on the phone.

"I report to Captain Harben," she said, much more softly than she wished. She was afraid her voice would crack if she spoke any louder. "But I'll be happy to discuss what I'll need for tomorrow."

There was a small silence. Eileen bared her teeth in a smile. She knew the way the military world worked. Major Blaine thought of Eileen as Captain Reed, a former Air Force pilot and the Major's subordinate. And a *woman* subordinate, to boot. Major Blaine wanted to give Eileen orders. She was not—*not!*—going to let that happen.

"Oh." The voice on the other end of the line showed annoyance. "Well—I'll be right there."

"Thanks."

Eileen set the phone down gently and took a few deep breaths. Her notes lay in an untidy pile in front of her. Now more than ever, she was bound to solve this case. How long did Harben say she had before the Air Force OSI officer arrived? Three days? Not enough time, usually, to close a case. She would just have to work harder on this one.

She flipped through her pad of notes, making an occasional correction or footnote, waiting for Blaine to arrive. The office outside the conference room was totally deserted now. The office lights were on, but the desks were empty. The screensaver patterns that played on the computers gave an eerie kind of motion to the big room, as though right outside of Eileen's peripheral vision the computers were turning, moving, and whispering to each other.

"Creepy," Eileen said to herself. The silence and the motion were oppressive. Undoubtedly the murderer was gone from this building, just as the murdered woman was gone, but the murder itself remained. Eileen shared a solemn belief among police, that the physical location of violence, especially murder sites, retained some kind of malignancy long after the blood and remains were cleared away. Police liked to live in new houses, although they could seldom afford them.

Eileen felt certain she must have spoken to the murderer today. Despite Procell's file, which lay thick and as yet unread by her elbow, she felt certain that Terry Guzman was murdered by one of the people in the Center. She'd probably been murdered by one of the people Eileen had interviewed, though she hadn't the faintest idea who.

She turned to look at the file, bulging with newspaper clippings and paper-clipped reports, and felt an exhausted kind of impatience. She hated this whole military world, had hated it since before Bernie had died so senselessly, and here she was being drawn back into it. Joe Tanner was—

"Well, Detective?" Blaine said from the doorway. "Let's go."

The last of the day's light was fading behind Pikes Peak as Eileen and Major Blaine stepped outside the building. The air was fresh and warm, and smelled of a recent thundershower. Eileen took a deep breath.

"How can they stand to work there?" she murmured to herself. Blaine shrugged and led the way to the sidewalk that would take them to the retinal scanners and Eileen's car.

"The pay is good, the work is good. How often do you really look outside the window?"

"All day long," Eileen said.

"You'll be back tomorrow?" Blaine asked, managing to make it sound like an order. He looked jittery, as though he'd had too much coffee or pop that afternoon. "I spoke to Air Force Special Investigations, the closest time they can have their man out here is in three days."

"I'll return tomorrow morning to review the tapes," Eileen said mildly.

There was silence for a while, as they walked along the flank of the huge building that housed the other space communications center.

"Remember, there isn't anything out here except a weather station, once you leave the base," Major Blaine said stiffly, scratching at his arms as though he had old mosquito bites there. Perhaps she was making him nervous. Eileen liked the thought of that.

"I know. I've had clearances before. Didn't like 'em then, and I don't like it now."

"Tomorrow morning, then. Eight o'clock?" Blaine's light-colored hair looked faintly sweaty where it showed under his cap. The little mustache drooped. He looked tired.

"Sure. All I need is access to the room and paper and pencil. I'll supply the paper and pencil."

"I'll meet you at the gate, to get you through one more time. Then your badge and number and retinal scan will be enough."

"And no more problems with my weapons, I assume?" Eileen asked without a smile.

"No problems," Blaine said.

They came up to the tiny building full of scanners, and Blaine took out his piece of paper again.

"Seven eight nine three," he reminded Eileen. "You just swipe your badge through the slot, like a credit card, and key in the number. You don't need to scan on the way out, only on the way in."

Eileen felt the same claustrophobic feeling as before when the glass door clicked and locked behind her. She swiped her badge through and keyed in the numbers. There was a pause, and a click. She pushed the door open and stepped through. Blaine was already through and waiting for her.

"Everything set? Keep the badge. If I think of anything, I'll call the station." Blaine balanced his briefcase on one knee, opened it, and rummaged around for a moment before pulling out a business card. "I never use these things," he said. He closed the case and put it under his arm, dug in his pocket for a pen, and wrote a number on the card. "My home phone," he said, holding out the card to Eileen.

"Thanks."

"Tomorrow morning, eight o'clock," Blaine said, and turned away. Eileen nodded, and dug into her pocket for her own car keys.

There was a phone in the little retinal-scan building. She called in to the station and told Harben she would be in after she'd gotten some supper. She asked Harben if he wanted anything, and Harben said no. No one ever saw Harben eat. Peter O'Brien swore that Harben was a vampire and drank only human blood. Since there were never blood-drained bodies found in Colorado Springs, O'Brien had come up with the theory that Harben must have a deal with Memorial Hospital. O'Brien had even passed around a rendition of a blood-bank savings account made out in Harben's name. Eileen and O'Brien laughed until they were leaking tears. Harben got a look at it and never cracked a smile, which made O'Brien and Eileen laugh all the harder. A new detective, Stan Jabowski, was too nervous to laugh. He didn't know Harben yet and was afraid that Harben was offended.

"Vampires don't laugh," O'Brien had said, trying and failing to keep a serious face.

Eileen smiled at the memory, and flicked on her lights as she pulled her Jeep out of the parking slot. Then she felt sad, remembering Stan Jabowski hadn't had much of a chance to get dry behind the ears. He'd been killed on Nevada Avenue less than a month later.

Eileen waved to the guard at the gate and accelerated into the curve.

•12

Colorado Springs Investigations Bureau

". . . So that's the wrap," Eileen finished comfortably. She wiped her fingers on a napkin and took a big sip of her soda. The scraps from a sub sandwich lay on waxed paper. A few shreds of lettuce had fallen onto Harben's immaculate desk. Behind Harben the blinds were drawn against the dark.

"Use the scanner, get those notes onto your machine," Harben said. He never referred to a computer as anything but a machine.

"Okay," Eileen said. She picked up the lettuce shreds and ate them slowly. "I didn't get any feel for who the murderer is. This Procell file worries me, too. I'm going to have to call up the traffic-accident reports from those other scientists."

"The ones who were killed commuting to work?" Harben asked.

"Yeah. Harriet Sullivan. Um . . . John Richmond, I think."

"Do you know how many people are killed every year on that stretch of highway, Eileen?" Harben asked coldly. "We scrape up bodies every month from that road. I'm sure Procell—is that his name?—has some interesting statistics, but if the government hasn't taken an interest, I'm not so sure you should waste your time."

"The government doesn't always know what they're doing," Eileen said quietly.

"Bernie crashed in a very expensive plane. There's a greater desire for a cover-up."

Eileen winced.

"A secret murder campaign against scientists in the military would be great tabloid material," Harben continued. "Why wasn't this made public? You said Procell's first notes started years ago."

"I haven't read the whole file."

"I suggest you skim the file. Procell's entire intent may be to divert attention from himself or from someone he's trying to protect."

"Okay," Eileen said, and stretched. "What a day."

"Don't make it too late," Harben said to her. "Oh, and you still have to start on the Pendleton file. I sent Rosen out to do the prelim work, but I want you to check it."

Eileen nodded, and reached out to crumple up the sandwich wrapper and drop it in the trash.

"All right, all right," she said, and hoisted herself to her feet. "You are no fun sometimes, boss."

Harben didn't reply. He had already turned, and was keying in the password to his computer.

"It was a good sandwich," Eileen said to Harben's back. "You shoulda had one."

Central Intelligence Agency, Langley, Virginia

Lucy was deep. She was getting to know George Tabor from a hundred different traces left within the Web. Her office chair squeaked as she stretched, putting her hands to the small of her back. The building was darkened but not quiet. It rustled like a haystack full of mice. Someone had burned a bag of microwave popcorn, and the stench drifted everywhere. Lucy had an open cup of coffee in front of her. For some reason, that killed the burnt popcorn smell. She hated being here at night. She wanted to be home, nestled up to Ted and watching something mindless on the television.

But George Tabor, now. He was an interesting fellow. Lucy saw his face, plain and friendly, as her gopher sent the picture. George made it away clean. His flight landed on schedule in Paris, and from there he could have gone anywhere. Lucy knew his skills would be valuable. Where would he go? Tabor wasn't her problem now, although she thought their paths might cross sometime. She hoped they would.

She picked up the image of the map the FBI surveillance man had created, along with the routes he took when he walked his dog. Those walks were how he made his pickups and dropoffs.

Wait a minute. Lucy paused, trying to focus her thoughts. The drawer of food was empty, and her baby was clamoring for something hot. Something hot and preferably greasy, like a hamburger. But there was something there in the notes, something that snagged at her mind.

That was it. Did he take the dog on the flight? She pulled up the travel records. No, there was no dog checked on the flight. What did he do with the dog? She was an English springer spaniel named Fancy, and he evidently took good care of her, judging by the veterinarian record and the FBI reports.

Lucy thought, her fingers poised over the keyboard. Then she searched animal shelter listings in Colorado. In a few minutes Lucy had a possible listing. He might have dropped her off at a Denver animal shelter before flying out. The shelter listings tried to make the animals as appealing as possible, in hopes of an adoption before the relentless syringe.

"English springer spaniel," the note read. "Female, spayed, three years old. Beautiful dog, very well behaved. Good with children. Please adopt her! Left at 11:25 A.M."

Lucy leaned back in her chair and rubbed at her upset stomach. The baby was too small to be felt, but she imagined the tiny fetus floating inside her, eyes still unformed, with webbed fingers and little gill slits, listening quietly to her and the steady sound of her heart.

"Well, little fish," she said to her stomach. "I think Mr. George Tabor was a very careful person. He was well prepared. And he loved his dog. That's what the FBI report said, anyway. You can tell a happy dog. So if he knew he was going to be leaving town, would he have left his dog at an animal shelter? I don't think he would. He would have found a home for her. I'll call the shelter tomorrow and see if I can find out if that's her."

Lucy paused. Or was she being too sentimental? She sighed, and stretched, and started shutting down her computer links. It was time to go to bed and think this one over. There was a Taco Bell on the way home, too.

Colorado Springs

When Eileen slotted her key into her town-house lock it was nearly eleven o'clock. Her cat was waiting at the door, angrily meowing.

"Oh, Betty, you've got plenty of food," Eileen said, picking up the big orange tabby and stroking her fur. The cat settled in her arms and began to purr loudly, meowing occasionally through her purring as though she were not quite ready to stop being angry. Eileen kicked the door shut behind her and leaned against it, exhausted. "Are you fatter than usual, or am I just tired?"

Eileen had never thought herself a cat kind of person. She was a dog person. Cats were to keep the mice population down on her parents' ranch. Then Betty appeared on her doorstep, a scrawny fluff of orange, furiously hungry. She kept her. She always meant to get a dog, but she was away from home too much to have a dog.

"I'm away too much to have a cat, too," she murmured, rubbing Betty's ears. "Time for a beer and the news and bed."

There was sometimes a man who shared the bed. Two, maybe three, and they hadn't lasted and Eileen wasn't sure why. She liked her solitude too much, perhaps, or she was too used to it. She wanted a man like her cat, self-reliant and self-entertaining. After a few weeks they wanted her to pick up their socks and cook their food and rub their feet after their hard day's work—in short, to turn into a wife. Eileen wasn't ready for that. Not now, maybe not ever.

She set Betty down and the cat stalked over to her dish, looking back at Eileen pointedly. One half of the double dish was full of dry cat food. The other side was licked clean. "And some of that wet stuff for you, too, Bets." Eileen yawned hugely. Maybe she would just forget the beer and the news. She had to be back out to Schriever at eight o'clock. Then she walked over and switched on the TV anyway, just to give herself some company.

Paris, France

When George Tabor opened the door to his modest hotel room, the man standing outside was not familiar to him. That only made sense. George had never seen the face of his major contact. The man was not very reassuring in looks or manner. He had curly black hair and olive skin pitted by acne. He could have been Italian or Spanish or Arab or Eastern European. His clothes were Paris rummage sale, wool turtleneck fraying at the collar and cuffs, sturdy no-color twill pants. He slumped in the doorway, hands shoved in his pockets, and his breath was bad. George immediately mistrusted him.

George mistrusted everything about this horrible adventure. He'd forgotten how clean and empty the American West was. George felt a horrible pang of homesickness.

"You're George?" the man asked.

"Yes, and you are?" George asked politely.

"Mr. Brown," the man said after a pause. "I'm married to Molly. She's unsinkable."

"Come in," George said grimly. This was his contact. He knew the password, specific to Colorado. The unsinkable Molly Brown was a famous Colorado heroine but virtually unknown in Europe. It was a hasty password but a good one.

"I'm to take you with me," the man said. He didn't shift his slumped position from the door frame. "Muallah would like to meet you."

"Muallah?"

"Muallah, the boss," the man said.

"I thought I was going to meet Mr. Wulff," George said in surprise. His major buyer was a polite German, Mr. Wulff. Who was Muallah?

"Wulff is one of his names," the man said impatiently. "But his real name is Fouad Muallah. And he doesn't like to be kept waiting. Let's go."

Colorado Springs

Wednesday morning was breakfast day. Eileen hadn't missed a breakfast with Gary Hillyer in three years. They changed locations occasionally, to sample new restaurants, but they always met at 6:30 A.M., somewhere, on Wednesdays. This month was the Omelet Parlor on Fillmore Street, where Cathy the waitress already knew their favorite breakfast dishes and when to refill their cups of coffee. Eileen pulled into the dirt parking lot, feeling cheerful. The Procell file lay, still unread, on the passenger seat. The notes she took the day before were in a neatly typed stack underneath.

"Morning, Eileen." The waitress showed her to the corner booth she and Gary had decided was the best in the restaurant. The new day's sunlight shone through the windows but left the seat in enough shadow so reading the newspaper wasn't a painful experience. Gary Hillyer was buried behind the morning's *Gazette,* a steaming cup of coffee in front of him.

"Morning, Gary. Thanks, Cathy." Eileen slid into the booth and reached for the sugar.

"Why are you so happy this morning?" Hillyer asked grumpily. He put down the paper, revealing a basset-hound face and tired eyes. Gary Hillyer was tall, with brown hair and eyes and a perpetual stoop to his shoulders. The stoop was more pronounced this morning.

"What kept you up all night?" Eileen asked, stirring sugar into her coffee.

"What makes you so happy?" Hillyer responded. They had met over a case four years earlier. Eileen wanted the information kept confidential. Reporter Gary Hillyer wanted the facts known. The classic confrontation. Casual gossip linked them as lovers, but not to anyone who knew Gary Hillyer very well. Gary lived in a handsome Victorian on the west side of Colorado Springs with Frank, his lover of twenty years. Gary occasionally took Eileen home for dinner, a treat she appreciated. Frank was a gourmet chef, and his dinner parties were legendary.

"New case," Eileen said. She reached for the paper.

"The latest on Nevada Avenue? No? The body at Fort Carson, that

Pendleton boy? Oh, no, that wouldn't put such an interested look on your ravishing face. He's a standard overdose, case already pretty much closed. Must be the death at Schriever? It was a murder, then?"

"Yes," Eileen said.

Hillyer nodded, and Eileen grinned at him. Hillyer would be able to use that.

"What shall it be this morning? Shall I just choose for you? What do you hate the most?"

Hillyer grinned up at Cathy. She smiled, expertly refilling their cups.

"Today's special," Eileen said absently. She'd found the column on Terry Guzman's death.

"Make that two," Hillyer said. "I'm starving."

Paris, France

When George saw Fouad Muallah he felt an immediate sense of recognition. This man, like George, had *style.* He was dressed much the same as his deliveryman, in wool turtleneck and sturdy twill trousers. But Muallah wore them like a king's robes. He would look completely natural with a cloak waving behind his broad shoulders. His skin was olive and flushed with health. His eyes were brown and sparkling with good humor and intelligence. He shook George's hand with a grip that was reassuring and intimate and friendly.

"Mr. Tabor," he said warmly. "At last." His hair was black and tightly curled and he smelled of sandalwood soap. His breath was clean and healthy. George realized with a sense of amusement that he was feeling a little jealous. George had always felt he had a great blend of sophistication and savoir faire. Fouad Muallah made him feel like an awkward adolescent.

"Mr. Wulff?"

"That's one of my names." Muallah laughed. His laugh was terrific, deep and full of delight. George found himself smiling and noticed the deliveryman. The deliveryman had a goofy, infatuated look on his face. Muallah noticed George's glance and turned to the other man. "Ali," he said gently. "We need to be undisturbed. Let no one enter."

Ali's expression was more than infatuation, George realized uneasily. It was adoration. Ali nodded and left. George looked around for the first time. He had been so dazzled by Muallah, he had noticed nothing. The apartment was old and very small, but extremely clean and decorated in a distinctly Arab style. There were small lamps, a length of rich Persian carpet, and pillows arranged around a low coffee table inlaid with mosaic in tile.

"Shall we have some coffee?" Muallah asked, gesturing with his arm toward the coffee table. "We have known each other so long, you and I, and here we are meeting for the first time. We shall relax, and talk."

George settled on the richness of the pillows. Muallah clapped his hands sharply, and a young woman appeared. She was robed and veiled in the traditional Arab way, with kohl-rimmed eyes. She carried a coffee service in silver on a gorgeous tray. Her eyes never glanced at George. She looked only at Muallah, with the same intent adoration as Ali.

"I thought we were going to be alone," George said as the woman poured coffee and settled back on her heels next to the table. The coffee smelled delicious, strong and fragrant and fresh.

"We are alone," Muallah said with a slight frown.

"I have spent long in America," George said, smiling uncomfortably. "American women—"

Muallah waved his hand in dismissal.

"Are rubbish," he said shortly. "As all America is rubbish."

Muallah sipped his strong coffee in the small cup, and George copied him. The coffee was deliciously hot and strong, and George used the moment to try and get his mental feet underneath him. Finding that his German buyer was really an Arab was a shocking discovery.

George, like most Russians, had a deep distrust of all things Islamic. He'd deliberately avoided selling to the Arabs. George's grandmother claimed that she was descended from Batu Khan, grandson of Genghis, who plundered the whole of Russia and Poland in the thirteenth century. Grandmother took care of George when he was small, and some of his fondest memories were of sitting cross-legged on the kitchen table while Grandmother kneaded dark bread dough with her strong arms.

She would tell him story after story handed down through the generations, embellished over time until they had the patina of fairy tales. Their ancestress was a lovely woman, as beautiful as a princess, who willingly became one of Batu's many concubines. She had a *paiza,* a special coin, that allowed her to travel wherever she wished in the conquered lands. Grandmother let George hold the *paiza* once, a strange worn piece of ordinary metal carved with what looked like snakes and swans. It went to his sister, not to George, when Grandmother died. The *paiza* had been handed down through the females of George's family for generations, undoubtedly cherished because it was worthless base metal and could not be sold for food.

So George had Mongolian blood, however diluted, royal blood of the Khans. He'd felt a sense of pride about that. But the Arabs had fared even more poorly than the Russians under the Khans.

Once the most civilized in all the world, the Arabs had great technology, medicine, and literature before Hulagu Khan, another grandson, pillaged and subjugated the Arab world. Hulagu had the last of the caliphs rolled up in carpets and trampled to death by horses, a story that George's grandmother told with relish.

George, remembering his grandmother's stories, had done a little research in the fabulously free libraries of America. The Arabs had nearly risen to conquer again before the Ottoman empire took over. The empire had kept the Arab lands until the British took over the rotting hulk of the Ottomans. Who was to say there would not be another reversal now that the Arabs had technology and education? Oil brought the Islamic world out of the Dark Ages and into the modern world, but their culture was still—George glanced over at the submissive girl and looked away again quickly—barbaric.

Now he found he'd been dealing with Arabs all along. But there was nothing to be done about it. George gave a mental shrug and determined that he would make the best of this situation. Muallah did not know that George was a descendant of Hulagu Khan. And George didn't care whom he dealt with, not really, he told himself. He would make his final sale and disappear. It was long past time to stop playing the game.

"Americans are such rubbish, my friend," Muallah said thoughtfully, sipping his coffee. "And rubbish is meant to be burned, is it not?" He smiled at George, showing dazzling white teeth, and gestured to the girl to serve them more coffee.

•13

Schriever Air Force Base

Eileen was late. The number of cars heading out to Schriever at 8:00 A.M. was astonishing. Eileen sat in bumper-to-bumper traffic and drummed her fingers on the wheel and looked at the cattle moving through the summer grass. There was a big hill at the edge of the horizon, and the sun had risen right through the notch the road made in the hill. The light was blinding even though the sun was well up into the sky. Eileen looked at the streams of cars and thought about Harben's warning. In winter that hill would be treacherous. In winter the sun would be just at eye level at eight o'clock in the morning.

As she approached the bottom of the hill she saw a garbage truck pull out from a dirt side road. The truck accelerated toward her, huge and dirty, and as it passed her she saw another one pull out of the same road. This was the landfill for Colorado Springs, Eileen realized. She hadn't known where it was located. Her own garbage was carried out here each week, to be churned up and buried. She moved forward in the traffic another few car lengths and looked at the truck as it thundered toward her.

"John Richmond," she said to herself. "John Richmond died when he hit a garbage truck." Eileen tapped her fingers impatiently on the wheel and looked over at the Procell file. "I can see it now, a spy getting all dressed up in overalls and a cap, and stealing a Great Western garbage truck." Eileen laughed aloud. "Right," she said to the file. She felt much better.

Eileen parked in the same place she had the day before. She remembered how many of the Gamers had mentioned how long it took to get to their desks.

Major Blaine was waiting.

"Took a while, eh?" he said. "I was late too. Let's process you through."

They entered the security building, and Eileen smiled at the sound of the gates clicking and clacking as people passed through. Most people had bored, impatient expressions on their faces, putting their faces to the retinal scanners as though it were the most natural thing in the world for them to do.

"You can get used to anything, I guess," Eileen commented absently. She was looking in the crowd, looking for someone. She wasn't sure what she was looking for until she realized she was looking for the murderer.

"It's worth it to be safe," Blaine said. He was next in line at the scanner.

They processed through the scanners without comment. Eileen drew a deep breath when she entered and let it out when the door clicked open. Evidently Blaine was right and her guns were not going to cause problems.

"You'll be looking at tapes today," Blaine said. "I'll be tracking the visitors' military clearances. We'll get together for lunch at eleven-thirty or so. I'll call you."

"I'll be in the Gaming Center," Eileen sighed. She still didn't have a handle on Major Blaine. As far as he was concerned, she was a member of his team and he was running the show.

"The Games are canceled, so there won't be anyone in the Center," Blaine said. "I have it all arranged."

They walked along the side of the CSOC building. The early-summer sun was brilliant and already hot, but the shade of the huge building made the sidewalk chilly. Eileen couldn't wait to get rid of Major Blaine.

Paris, France

"It is late, my friend," Muallah said. The coffee was gone, and the tiny sandwiches, and the rich little seed cakes. George was exhausted and humming with caffeine all at the same time. And he was waging a battle to keep from falling under the spell of this remarkable man. To say Fouad Muallah was a gracious host was completely inadequate. He *listened* to George.

When Muallah turned his dark gaze on him George felt as if he were being bathed in a soothing light. Muallah spoke lightly of the documents he'd purchased from George, in an offhand yet flattering way that made George feel good all over. He found himself wanting to like this man. He was vaguely surprised at himself. Whatever mistrust he had toward his ancient enemies seemed to be dissolving in the remarkable personality of this person, this Muallah.

"The hour is late," George admitted.

"You have something for me, my friend? Some last delight that you managed to spirit away from under the noses of the infidels?"

"Yes, I have," George said, smiling foolishly. What was *wrong* with him? "This one is very good. Something you've wanted for a long time."

"You have the locations," Muallah said, leaning forward intently.

"I have the locations," George said. His warmth started to seep away, leaving him feeling chilled and confused. "The locations of every missile silo in the republics of the former Soviet Union. But why would you want them?"

"Does it really matter?" Muallah asked charmingly. "I will pay you handsomely as always, Mr. Tabor. I always keep my promises. Fifty thousand American dollars, in cash. Tonight, if you can deliver the documents."

"I can deliver them," George said slowly. He was so tired. There was something tugging at his mind, but he couldn't seem to clear his head enough to figure out what the tugging meant. He felt the way he did the one time he tried marijuana. For a moment he studied the remains of the seed cakes with a frown, then the thought seemed to float away like a balloon. "I—I'm not used to doing this face-to-face."

"Ah, but I am," Muallah said. "Do not be uneasy, my friend. It is just the same as your drops and safety-deposit boxes. Except here we do our deals in warmth and friendship, with food and drink."

"Of course," George said, feeling ashamed. "I don't mean to be paranoid." Muallah raised an eyebrow at him. "Er, mistrustful. Do you have the money for me?"

Muallah snapped his fingers without looking around. The veiled girl rose to her feet and padded quickly to the door. Ali came in and, at Muallah's nod, went into another room and returned with a cheap plastic briefcase. He set the case by George's feet.

George flicked open the case and glanced at the contents. He'd seen so many piles of money delivered like this, he could make a quick estimate of amounts in a flashing glance. The money was all there, or close enough not to matter.

"Excellent." George smiled. He felt better, looking at the cash. "We can take care of our transaction right now." He unbuckled his belt and pulled it free. The concealed zipper in the back held the developed film: locations, maps, satellite photos, the whole package. Terry Guzman had really delivered. She had no way of knowing it would be her last delivery, but she'd still made it a good one.

"Very nice," Muallah murmured, looking at the film through the light. George replaced his belt and smoothed his shirt. Muallah smiled at George. "Thank you so much. You have no idea what this means to me."

"My pleasure," George said. "If it would not be rude? I am so tired from my flight—"

"Of course, of course," Muallah said, carefully placing the film on the mosaic table. He rose to his feet and clasped George's arm in his own as he escorted him to the door. "You must be very tired, Mr. Tabor. Again, I must thank you. Sleep well."

Muallah took one step back as something impossibly tight snapped around George's throat. It had to be Ali, a garrote, George thought numbly. I should have known, I should have known. . . . The tightness increased around his throat, and George saw a small porcelain lamp go flying into the air as he tried desperately to ease the constriction. Black blossoms started to flower in the air, exploding silently. A spindly little table skidded in front of him and toppled over, one tiny leg broken in two. The flowers grew bigger.

Then George could breathe again, and the relief was incredible. He shook his head and looked around. He was having that old nightmare again, he realized. His restaurant hummed around him. Waiters in spotless white and black hurried by with full platters. The candles shone on the beautiful tables. Georgian ladies, released from their long Soviet peasantry, showed their creamy white shoulders and delicious bosoms in modern gowns. Sturdy Russian men smiled and tilted their wineglasses, good color blooming in their clear cheeks. There was vodka, and the smell of good Russian beef, but suddenly overwhelming was the smell of strong coffee. Arab coffee.

George looked down in horror and saw a slender side table with a shattered leg. He tried to draw a breath and could not. Then he relaxed. He was back in the restaurant with the waiters and the beautiful ladies. He was home, at last.

"He fought like a warrior, Mahdi," Ali said thoughtfully.

"He was rubbish," Muallah said with a shrug. "He served his purpose. Dispose of the body."

Muallah turned without looking back and walked to the mosaic table. The films were there, the lovely priceless films. He picked them up and held them to the light, ignoring the sounds behind him.

Gaming Center, Schriever Air Force Base

The Gaming Center was locked and taped. Blaine had taken care of that chore the night before. The tapes of the Game were left in the video machines. If anyone tried to tamper with the door, the seal would have broken. A tired-looking Air Force soldier stood at the door.

The door to the Center had a spin lock exactly like a safe's. Blaine knew the number but fumbled with the lock before the tumblers finally fell and the door opened and broke the seal. Blaine wrote his initials and the date on a piece of paper that was stuck in a pocket next to the door. On the paper was a long list of initials and dates.

"Every time the Center is opened or closed, it goes on this record." Blaine showed the record to Eileen. Eileen took it and glanced down the list. Most of the initials were AB. Arthur Bailey. She put the sheet with her notes.

"I'll keep this for a while," she said to Blaine. "There might be something here."

"You're dismissed, Airman," Blaine said to the young guard. The guard saluted and sighed and headed down the hallway.

They opened the door and walked up the sloping hallway to the Gaming Center. Only a few lights were on. The screensaver pattern whispered on all the computer screens. Blaine left Eileen at the door and went to turn on the lights.

Eileen looked at the room, feeling as if she was being watched. Probably those damn screensaver patterns again, with their spiderweb images. Or maybe she just knew the Center had a secret.

After five minutes in the television studio, Eileen stopped Blaine.

"Look," she said. "You don't even know how to turn on the power to these boards, much less how to play the tapes back. Just stop messing with it and call one of those Gamers over here."

Blaine looked up from his seat in front of the console. He looked stubborn for a moment, then relented.

"Okay, I guess I don't know how. I swear I've watched it a hundred times, when they have demonstrations in here."

Eileen watched as Blaine picked up the phone, feeling satisfied. Now, why was she wondering if Blaine would call over Joe Tanner? She smiled and dug in her pocket for one of the spare toothpicks she'd swiped from the Omelet Parlor.

"Art? This is Major Blaine." Eileen grinned to herself and peeled the wrapping from the toothpick. Now, this was interesting. What was it about Joe Tanner? Not just that he got her a cup of coffee. Perhaps because the gift was so thoughtful. And his innocence seemed so strong. It couldn't be his looks. If it were just looks, Eileen would be thinking about the gorgeous 'Berto. Joe Tanner intrigued her somehow. He had to be the murderer. He had the best motive: Terry had basically killed his girlfriend.

"What are you smiling at?" Blaine asked. "You look like you're holding a conversation with somebody."

"With myself," Eileen said. "Being a civilian, I can do that. I even talk to myself occasionally." She showed her teeth at the Major and inserted the toothpick in the corner of her mouth.

"Art Bailey is coming over," Blaine said after a moment of frowning at her, which she steadfastly ignored.

"Okay."

There was silence as Eileen looked over the darkened room. She stared at Terry's door. She looked at the cameras. She studied the way the lights were set into the ceilings, the way the doors were hinged. She ignored Major Blaine. She thought, and tried to ignore the little voice that kept asking her how she was going to solve the murder when she didn't even know how it had been done.

Central Intelligence Agency, Langley, Virginia

Lucy Giometti was unloading a grocery bag full of food into her desk drawer when Mills walked into her office.

"Good morning," she said.

"What's the latest?"

Lucy sighed. He couldn't even say good morning. She kept on unpacking food. She'd thrown up twice that morning already and she didn't feel very well. The double beef burrito on the way home last night was pure ambrosia, though. She'd slept soundly all night.

"Well, I don't think the Guzman murder was planned by Tabor or his buddies. And that's my opinion only," she added. She sat down at her desk and started keying into her computer systems. "I'll get you a whole report as soon as I'm finished."

"I appreciate it," Mills said, and without another word he turned and left her office. Lucy sighed and watched her computer software assemble itself on her screen. She pulled open the desk drawer and contemplated the bright packages within. She'd make it through this day too, she thought. When would that baby stop making her sick?

When her computer systems were ready Lucy pulled up the file she'd started on George Tabor. She picked up the phone and dialed the animal shelter in Denver.

"Human Society, this is Debbie," said a cheerful woman's voice.

"Hi, I'm wondering if you could do me a favor," Lucy said. "I'm looking for a dog, a springer spaniel?"

"We have one here," Debbie said. "But she wasn't lost, she was left for adoption."

"Did the person who left her tell you her name?"

"Well, I think so." She sounded eager. "We write them up by the kennel doors. Hang on just a second."

Lucy held the phone to her ear and typed busily, opening connections to the different computer databases that might give her the information she needed. Faintly, she could hear the sound of dogs wailing. She wondered if one of the howls could be Fancy's.

"Hello?"

"I'm here," Lucy said promptly.

"Her name is Fancy," Debbie said, and Lucy felt the rush in her blood. She was right!

"Thanks so much," Lucy said warmly.

"Would you like to adopt her?" Debbie said eagerly. "She's so beautiful, and adult dogs just aren't adopted very much. She's only got three days."

Lucy felt the flush of victory turn to embarrassment.

"Well, er, no, I mean— No."

"Oh," Debbie said. "Then why did you call?"

"I was looking for the person who left her," Lucy said, and winced at the lameness of her explanation. She waited for the questions, but there were none.

"Okay," Debbie said, disappointed.

Lucy hung up the phone after saying her good-bye. She sat for a moment, then turned to her computer screen.

•14

The Center door opened and Art Bailey stepped through. He looked better today. His skin was more ruddy and his shoulders were squared.

"Good morning," he said. "Jeff wanted me to come over and set up the films for you. And I've forgotten your name."

"Eileen Reed. Do you call everybody by their first names?"

"The SecDef was here once. The Secretary of Defense. I didn't call him by his first name."

Eileen looked closely at Art, but the bland face was unreadable.

"I think I'll be okay here, er—Jeff," Eileen said, smiling. "I have your number, so I can call if I have questions?"

"That'll be fine," Blaine said. Eileen expected him to be a little upset, but he looked relieved. "I have a lot of phone calls to make. Feathers are flying from here to D.C. over this."

Art sat down at the studio console and gestured for Eileen to take a seat next to him.

"Joe said he showed you the pick-and-draw capabilities yesterday," Art said. He showed Eileen the tape machines. "Here's the Eject button, just like your VCR. Play, Rewind, Fast Forward—you can do it all from the machines. But you can do it better on the computer console, here." Art flicked a switch. "Joe showed you these buttons? Yes? Here's the key to display time and seconds. We hardly ever use that, but I imagine you might need it. There are four tapes usually made, and we didn't make it to number four yesterday." Art grimaced and stopped for a moment. He looked around him as though lost. Eileen knew the feeling. The fact of a death keeps sneaking up on you at the oddest times, and all you can do is try to turn your head with the blow and keep on going. Eileen watched Art shake his head a little and keep on going.

"Uh, okay, so you have three tapes."

"When did the tapes start?"

"Exactly twenty minutes before Game start. That way we record people as they enter the Gaming Center, as they take their places, and that way we also record the Gamers, that's us, take our places in the rooms. We started taping before Game start when an Air Force colonel accused us of cheating. He thought we 'canned' the simulation. As though we always had to launch weapons at a particular time to make everything work out right. Like a video game instead of a real simulation. We had him play the game any way he wanted to. You launch at six P.M., your Bombers take longer to scramble because more people are eating supper. We really simulate all of that. It was fun to make him accept that this wasn't some big canned demonstration. He thought he was being smart when he played Colonel Olsen's position. He launched a preemptive strike at the Soviet Union, and they responded with subs—"

"The Soviet Union?"

"Oh, this was a while ago. Before we got the Brilliant Pebbles up in orbit and really started wringing this Star Wars stuff out. Anyway, the Soviets—that was me at the time—launched back with subs and a massive follow-on, and we toasted the Earth. Complete lava." Art laughed cheerfully. "He knew he was beat. We couldn't have read his mind and known what he would do. It had to be a real simulation. Now he's in D.C. and he's our biggest salesman out there."

Art sobered abruptly. "Well. Anyway. You'll see everyone enter their rooms. Terry, too."

"You've had overnight to think it over," Eileen said. "How do you think it happened?"

"Aren't I a potential suspect?" Art asked, with a sidelong glance at Eileen. "Should I conjecture? I was worried last night because if I figured it out, you might think I did it."

"If you figure it out, I might think you did it," Eileen said levelly. "I think everyone did it until proven otherwise. I'm not the judge or the jury. All I do is collect evidence and try to make a good arrest. I'll make a good arrest."

Art nodded. "That's good enough for me," he said. "I just don't want to be arrested. I don't want to lose my clearance. I know I'd be proven innocent, because I didn't do it, but I don't want to lose this job. I really love it."

"I'll arrest the murderer, Art, if I can. Not anyone else. Now, how did she die?"

"I don't know," Art said heavily. "I can't figure it out either."

Eileen sighed. Was Art trying to annoy her? Probably not. Art might figure out the way it happened, so he was clearing the avenues of communication to her. He didn't know that Eileen had been holding her breath, willing to promise anything as long as somebody could tell her how the murder had been done.

"Well, if you do, let me know, okay?"

"Sure, Eileen. I'll be thinking about it all day. That's all I've been thinking about all night," Art continued grimly. "I'll be at my desk. Oh, hey, you want music? I can show you how to work the CD player."

"No, thanks, I can't concentrate with music on. But thanks."

When the door closed behind Art, Eileen breathed a big sigh of relief. She turned to the console. After a moment or two of study, she thought she might be able to make it work. She picked up the mouse, swirled the little arrow on the screen around a couple of times, and picked 1 under TAPE. Then she picked Play, and sat back in the big chair to watch.

Central Intelligence Agency, Langley, Virginia

Lucy saw the tiny flashing lights when she returned from a trip to the bathroom. She'd brushed her teeth and bathed her face, but she still felt horribly weak. Tiny beads of perspiration stood in her hairline. The lights caught her eye, and in an instant her wretched stomach was forgotten. The flashing lights were atop a tiny cartoon police car, parked at the bottom of her screen.

She knew what that meant. She'd set a search program, called a search engine, to scan all news reports from Paris for any reference to George Tabor, or any dead bodies found, or any muggings. It was a very wide scan. Lucy had even included a search for any missing dogs or dog-related stories. The cartoon police car had driven across her screen and skidded to a stop, leaving cartoon skid marks on her screen, to alert her that a story containing one of her search elements had been found. She felt a moment of regret she'd missed the little car; she thought it was really pretty hilarious when it skidded across the screen.

Lucy dropped into her chair and clicked on her Paris icon.

Associated Press
POLICE CONFIRM DEATH OF AMERICAN BUSINESSMAN

PARIS (AP)—Police confirmed the death of an American businessman, George Travers, found at the bottom of a rubbish Dumpster in a Paris alley. A transient searching for aluminum cans found the body at approximately 10:30 local time. Travers' body had been robbed and he was apparently the victim of strangulation. He was identified through the hotel staff where he was staying. His room was undisturbed.

Lucy had her fingers at her temples and realized vaguely that the tips of her fingers were wet with sweat. George Tabor was dead. Travers was his alternate set of identification. He'd been murdered so quickly, it was chilling. Lucy knew he'd carried something out of the country and it had to be something from the Missile Defense program. How sensitive was it? Why had George been murdered? He was a valuable agent, a spy with a lot of successes under his belt. Most large organizations would be happy to welcome George into their ring. He would be an asset.

Unless the organization George dealt with didn't like him. Or didn't like what George *was*. Lucy massaged her temples. Perhaps there was something in the CIA files on George's contacts. She had to get access through Mills to see those files, though. Lucy sighed heavily. She dug a package of crackers out of her desk and forced herself to eat five of them before she went to see Mills.

Gaming Center, Schriever Air Force Base

The room was crowded and noisy. Eileen could not see Terry Guzman. Joe Tanner stood in his rumpled navy suit, talking to a colonel; Eaton, wasn't she? Arthur Bailey was already in the little room that he shared with Joe, the Truth Team room. Eileen noticed a poster of national flags hung on one wall, and smiled, thinking of Joe playing a War Game where England was the enemy. Art was sitting in front of his console, looking intently at the screen. Nelson Atkins stood with Colonel Olsen and Major Blaine. The premurder Blaine was relaxed and confident. He slowly ate a chocolate donut and licked his fingers clean afterward. Nelson looked nervous. He picked at the hairs on his arm and kept looking around with darting, bird-like movements. Lowell Guzman was in his tiny room. His headphones were on and he was flicking switches on his communications set, a square wooden box lined with brightly lit buttons. He kept tapping at his mike, as though it weren't working. Eileen looked into the next room. It was empty.

Terry Guzman walked into the Center. From Sharon's story, Eileen expected her to be there already. Perhaps she'd been to the bathroom. Her lipstick was fresh and peach-colored. Her suit was pale green. She was stunning. Eileen fumbled for a moment before she managed the Pause button on the tape. Terry stood, vibrantly alive, frozen on the screen. The lines of discontent were there, but the way she held herself made such tiny details irrelevant. Eileen pressed the Play button. Terry walked to Major Torrence, the Ground Weapons commander, and started speaking. Her voice was lost in a dozen different conversations. Eileen would capture her conversation later, as Tanner showed her. Right now she wanted to absorb the whole scene. The murder scene. These were the last minutes of Terry Guzman's life.

Terry smiled and spoke to Major Torrence. She touched her brown hair, shifted from one round hip to the other, threw her head back, and laughed. She was holding a notebook in one hand. She held herself like a young girl, light on her feet, her chin proudly level on the slender neck that was only just beginning to show the signs of age. The lights dimmed, and Terry made a smiling farewell to the Major. She strode toward the room in measured, even strides, swinging the pretty fanny just a little. As she entered, she did not look back. She examined her console, picked up her headset, and sat down in the chair. Eileen could see every inch of the tiny cube. The door swung outward, not in. No one could be hiding behind the door. The console table was a spindly affair, a platform on a single stalk of a leg. No one could be hiding behind the console table. Besides, even if they were, how would they then get out? Terry checked her microphone. A person walked in front of the cube, blocking Eileen's view for a moment. Terry was now taking off her headset. She came to the door. Nelson Atkins walked to her and spoke to her for a moment. She nodded, and Nelson swung the door shut.

Eileen leaned back and breathed. She hadn't realized she'd been holding her breath until now. She rubbed a cold hand on her forehead. Terry would not come out of that room alive.

She found the mouse key and pressed Rewind. The rest of the audience had been a blur. It was time to see what everyone else was doing. Eileen opened her notebook and read down the list of names. Besides the Gamers, there were twelve audience members and the Command Team, Major Torrence, Colonel Olsen, and Colonel Eaton. Major Blaine told her the audience was in full sight of the cameras for the full hour and a half of the Game. She would check on that. Right now, Eileen added a name to the list. Terry Guzman. She put a check mark next to the name. She had watched her on the tape. After a moment, she made two columns on the paper. The first column she titled "Watched on Tape." The second column she titled "Listened on Tape."

The machine made a whirring noise and stopped. Eileen pressed Play.

Paris, France

Muallah stood on his apartment balcony, breathing the muggy air of Paris as though it were the finest morning breeze from the desert. He looked at the teeming city around him as though he already stood on the balcony of a palace, looking at his subjects. They *would* be his subjects.

> *"Prophecy is the Lamp of the world's light;*
> *But ecstasy in the same Niche has room.*
> *The Spirit's is the breath which sighs through me;*
> *And mine the thought which blows the Trumpet of Doom."*

Muallah savored the words, repeating them slowly. Al-Hallaj had said those words in Baghdad in 922, before he was executed. Some said it was a prophecy fulfilled when the Ottoman Empire collapsed. Muallah knew differently. The prophecy was yet to be fulfilled. The prophecy was speaking about *him*.

"Mahdi," Ali said quietly behind him.

Muallah waited a moment and then turned to see Ali waiting patiently. Ali would wait until darkness fell, until Ali shriveled and died from lack of water, until Muallah was ready for Ali to speak. All Muallah's people felt this way about him. This was one of the reasons Muallah knew he was touched by Allah. This was one of the reasons Muallah knew he was the One of the Prophecies.

"Yes, my Ali?" Muallah said gently.

"Achmed has a transport, Mahdi. A four-wheel-drive Mercedes, but old and battered as you requested. They await us in Mashhad. I have purchased our plane tickets. Will you see them?"

"I trust they are good," Muallah said with a wave. Ali's face flushed with pleasure. "Have Sufi pack our things. We shall not return here."

Muallah turned away and contemplated the city again. The Trumpet of Doom was a prophecy not for the fall of the Ottoman Empire, but for the fall of the Western Empire. It was time for the rebirth of the Arab Empire.

Muallah had worked and waited many patient years, waiting for the right information to fall into his hands. At last the foolish American-Russian had given him what he had to have. The dead spy had delivered to him the location of the Trumpet.

Fouad Muallah would blow the Trumpet of Doom, as the prophecy had said. Out of the ashes of the Western Empire the Arab Empire would be reborn. Muallah would be the One of the Prophecy, the Emperor. He drew a deep, satisfied breath and recited the poem again, savoring the words as they flowed off his tongue in gorgeous Arabic.

•15

The tape was in the pre-Game stage. Eileen was watching Lowell Guzman, who casually took a sprinkle donut and ate it. Weren't the sprinkle donuts reserved for the memory of Sully? Eileen knew they were. An eccentric memorial like that was unforgettable. Yet there was Lowell, eating the Holy Donuts. Odd.

The door to the Center opened. The real door, not the one on the tape. Someone was coming into the Center. Eileen fumbled for a moment before pressing Pause on the recording. She turned.

The person who stepped through the door was the tall, gray-haired Game Director. Eileen thought for a moment and then came up with the name.

"Nelson Atkins?"

"Yes, you remembered," Atkins said. He was more composed than he had been the day before, although the skin around his eyes was pouched and webbed with stress. He was wearing slacks and shirt and a Western-style string tie. The tie clip was silver and turquoise and looked Navajo. It was a handsome piece of jewelry.

"That's my job," Eileen said. She stood up to shake Atkins's hand.

"I don't want to bother you, I just wanted to make sure you have everything you need," Atkins said. His grasp was firm and dry.

"Art helped me set up the videotapes," Eileen said, and gestured to the control panel behind her. Atkins nodded.

"Good. I figured he would. I brought the personnel files you wanted." Atkins held out a bulky accordion folder. "These aren't classified, but they are very personal, so if you'd be careful with them—"

"I will, thank you," Eileen said.

"Can I do anything else?" Atkins asked. "I know we're all suspects, even me. I want to help if I can." He held out his hands in an open gesture. Eileen noticed they were big hands, and they looked familiar. Eileen recognized after a moment the calluses that could only come from horseback riding. Atkins's hands looked like her father's hands.

"No, I don't think so." As Atkins nodded and turned to go, Eileen said, "Wait. There is something."

"Sure," Atkins said. "What?" There was no hesitation, no furtive guilt or telltale dampness around the forehead or upper lip. If this plain, sturdy man was a murderer, he was hiding it very well.

"Why is a clearance so hard to keep? Art just mentioned it to me a few minutes ago, and you told me yesterday if I arrested someone they'd lose their clearance."

"Jeff Blaine told me you were in the military," Atkins said. "Didn't you have to worry about them there?"

"Not really," Eileen said wryly. "You really had to screw up big time to lose your clearance in the Air Force. Drugs, conviction. Arrest wouldn't do it, or every Saturday night a dozen airmen would lose their clearances."

"Not in the civilian world," Atkins said. He put his hands in his pockets and leaned a big shoulder against the door frame. "If you get too deep into debt, you're out. They run a credit-card check yearly."

"Who does?"

"The DIA. Defense Intelligence Agency. They do civilian clearances. If you have too much drinking, any drugs, any arrests, any big financial problems, you're out. Still, though, we have those spies like the Walker Ring, or Aldrich Ames. They do a lot of damage, selling secrets."

"I know they do," Eileen said. The hatred against spies ran deep in any pilot or soldier. Eileen knew if she'd had to fight in her plane she'd be going up against technology that was stolen from her own country. There was nothing worse than a spy. Eileen felt that they were the worst of thieves, stealing from a whole country instead of just one person.

"We hate them too, here," Atkins said. He jingled the change thoughtfully in his pocket. "After you play a few War Games and lose, you don't mind the background checks so much. I don't think anyone minded."

"Are those background checks in these folders?" Eileen asked.

Atkins shook his head. "Those are kept at DIA. I suppose you could get them from DIA. I've never seen them, myself, not even my own. I wouldn't want to see them. They get really personal." Atkins looked away, into the Gaming Center, where the screens whispered with their spiderweb pattern, repeating and repeating. His eyes looked sad. "I wonder what happened to her," he said, and Eileen realized Atkins was looking at Terry's door. "I wish I knew."

"Me too," Eileen said. "I appreciate the files."

"Okay," Atkins said. "If you need anything, let me know. I'd appreciate if you'd keep the files with you until you can give them back to me personally. I wouldn't want anyone else seeing them."

"No problem," Eileen said.

After the door swung shut, Eileen sat down with a huge sigh, the folder in her hands. Nothing about Nelson Atkins betrayed anything but the most profound innocence.

She looked at the folder. She could go over that later. Right now, the tape had barely begun. Eileen found the proper button and pressed Play.

Joe Tanner: "Art, pal, we better not hit that packet problem during the big follow-on."

Art Bailey: "We won't. Don't worry. You better worry about that racquetball tournament you and Meg are playing next weekend. I'm not looking after the kids all day to have you guys lose, you know."

Joe Tanner: "Win or lose, we're still expecting supper. It better be good, too."

Art Bailey: "Pizza is always good. Close the door, it's time."

The door closes upon them.

Roberto Espinoza: "So we have the church retreat in two weeks, and I don't care what happens here, I'm going to make it this summer. A week of fishing and praying and hiking—"

Doug Procell: "That sounds great. I don't know about the praying, but the fishing and hiking parts sound good."

Roberto Espinoza: "You'd like that too, I bet. It's very spiritual. Plus, the North Fork runs right through the retreat grounds and it's private fishing."

Doug Procell: "Ah, man. You dog. Wouldn't you know it, private fishing. I'd be taking a retreat about once a week in the summer, eh?"

Roberto Espinoza: "Prayers and the right fly, works every time. Hey, let's go. It's show time."

They go into their rooms, and the doors close upon them.

Sharon Johnson: "Yes, I'll be done with my class in another week."

Nelson Atkins: "So how is it going?"

Sharon Johnson: "It's a tough course, but I think I'll do okay on the final. It seems to take so long, but I'm getting there. I have to go now, I need to check out my headset."

Nelson Atkins: "All right."

The door closes upon her.

Lowell Guzman, on the sound system: "Art, can you hear me?"

Arthur Bailey, on the sound system: "Loud and clear, Lowell. What's up?"

Lowell Guzman: "I was having trouble with my headset, but it seems to be okay now."

Arthur Bailey: "Sounds good now."

Lowell Guzman: "All right, then. I'm almost ready."

The door closes upon him.

Nelson Atkins: "We'll be starting in a few minutes."

Terry Guzman: "I know that. Thank you."

Nelson Atkins: "I just wanted to make sure you were comfortable."

Terry Guzman: "I'm fine and I won't screw up. Is that what you were trying to say, Nelson?"

Nelson Atkins: "Terry, now—"

Terry Guzman: "Don't worry, Nelson, you'll give me a complex. You know I'll do great, I always do, don't I? Now, quit hovering and get on with it."

The door closes upon her.

Fort Rucker Army Base, Alabama

"What do you mean, canceled?" Stillwell asked. He'd been waiting for so many hours in the plastic chair, his butt was beyond numb. Nobody told him anything, just asked him to wait, please, sir.

Now it was past lunch and the flight sergeant finally let him know the Chinook was not leaving today, in an absentminded manner that left Stillwell wanting to choke him senseless.

"What about another transport?" Stillwell asked, gritting his teeth.

"No available spaces, sir," the sergeant said. "You'll just have to come back at dawn tomorrow, sir. I'm sure she'll be ready for takeoff then."

Stillwell gave up. He'd been in the Air Force long enough to know when to surrender to bureaucracy. Whatever was out in Colorado Springs would just have to wait another day for Major Alan Stillwell.

Gaming Center, Schriever Air Force Base

Eileen stretched and sighed. Terry's voice was husky and teasing and very cold. She looked at her list of check marks. All the Gamers were covered. Now it was time to see who left the room during the game. She leaned forward to pick up the mouse again and the phone rang, startling her. It rang again, and she shrugged and picked it up.

"Miss Reed?"

"I thought you called everyone by their first names."

"You and the SecDef, I guess." Art laughed. "I was wondering if you wanted some coffee. Joe mentioned it. So we tried to figure out if offering you coffee would mean we were sucking up to you. Then we decided, screw it. Want some coffee?"

"I would love some," Eileen said gratefully. "If you poison it, then I'll know you're the ones, right?"

"Well, your replacement would," Art replied cheerfully. "I'll be right over with a cup."

Eileen put the phone back in the cradle and grinned at it. "Send Joe," she said to the dead line.

Art brought the blue mug and a white carafe.

"Only the best for our women in blue," Arthur said. He put down the carafe and expertly poured a cup. He handed it to Eileen and perched a hip on the edge of the table.

"I know how it could be done, if I weren't here and didn't know it didn't happen that way. Does that make sense?"

"Sure," Eileen said, and sipped the coffee. As excellent as yesterday's.

"Someone hides in the room. Somehow. Okay, the room is too small. But let's say. The door shuts, murderer kills her as soon as she puts on the headset."

"How does murderer exit?"

"In the confusion surrounding the body, the murderer steps from his hiding place and becomes one of the horrified crowd."

"Nice. I saw it on late-night TV last week," Eileen said dryly.

"Me too," Art said, and his shoulders slumped. "Besides, I was there. There wasn't anyone in the room."

"I've been watching the tapes. I've zoomed in so close, I can see a stray hair fall from Terry's back and land on the carpet behind her. Nothing."

"I could explain it in a *Star Trek* episode," Art said glumly. "A mysterious creature that could blend into the walls. I don't know."

"I want to know too. There's got to be a way. There *was* a way. Thank you for the coffee."

"I wish I weren't a suspect," Art said quietly. "If I could be here, watching the tapes, I might see something—"

Eileen shook her head no. Art pinched his lip between two fingers.

"Smart. I'd do the same. Wish I had an alibi, though."

"Believe me, so do I," Eileen said. "So do I." As the door closed behind Art, Eileen turned back to the machine. It was time to move beyond the Game start and see the discovery of the body. She wrote the time of Game start in her notebook: 7:57 A.M.

"They started early," Eileen murmured to herself. She poured another cup of coffee, and pressed Play.

NELSON ATKINS SWUNG away from the door, his hand to his mouth. He swung away from the door, his hand to his mouth. He swung away a hundred times, obeying Eileen's hand on the mouse key, until Eileen knew beyond a doubt Terry Guzman was not being murdered as the door opened. Her body was still and lifeless from the moment the door started its swing. Nelson could not have stabbed her or shot the screwdriver from some hidden device at the moment he opened the door. She would be twitching. She would be hitching, breathing a last breath, the headset falling from her head. Terry was absolutely still.

"Damn," Eileen said. She rubbed her eyes. Was there any way to view the tapes that she'd missed? She hadn't played them backward yet, but other than that she couldn't think of another way to look at them. The phone rang.

"Lunch? Shrimp bisque is our soup today. I never miss shrimp bisque."

"Sure, Jeff," Eileen said, feeling a ridiculous sense of guilt over calling a major by his first name. "Lunchtime already?"

"Lunch already. I'll be right over. I'll bring a guard so we don't have to lock up the Center."

"Okay."

Eileen hung up the phone and turned back to the screen. Lowell was being dragged into his cube by Sharon Johnson and Roberto Espinoza, his mouth a wide O of confusion and despair. Art Bailey and Joe Tanner stood side by side in their Truth Team doorway, looking with blank shock at Terry's back. Colonel Eaton, the smooth and elegant Air Force officer, stood with eyes round and wide, hands braced on the table in front of her. The audience members, seven military and five government civilians, sat in their chairs and held their hands over their mouths like little children watching a scary movie.

Doug Procell looked frightened. He looked behind his own back. He was the only one who realized or thought there might be danger. He sat down carefully against the wall of the Center and folded his trembling arms.

"Good acting, whoever you are," Eileen said to herself. She realized she was tapping a pencil against her teeth, and stopped. "Damn fine acting."

The door to the Center opened. "Shrimp bisque," Blaine said cheerfully. "Lunch break. Have you got anything?"

"No," Eileen said shortly.

"Oh. Well. Let's go get some food. Things always look better after lunch."

Eileen gathered her notes.

Paris, France

Muallah closed Sufi's staring eyes with one gentle hand. She was a beautiful creature, or had been. Her skin was still warm and soft, still fragrant with the soap she liked to use. He was sorry to have to dispose of her, but there was no way to bring her with them. He'd honored her with one last visit from him, a last touch of his body to hers, before he had Ali strangle her. She had fulfilled her destiny and deserved that final gift.

Muallah turned away. Ali was just finishing up at the sink. He'd washed the blood from his hands and his garrote, and was coiling it. His face was blank and smooth, as always.

"It is time," Muallah said. Ali nodded, and Muallah gave a last glance around the apartment. All was ready. The only things left were rubbish they did not want to bring with them. Muallah squared his shoulders, feeling a dizzying sense of excitement. The waiting was over. It was time.

•16

The shrimp bisque was as incredible as advertised. Eileen went back for another bowl. The cook, a tall cheerful-looking young man, smiled over the steam table at her. His hair was black as a crow's wing and fell over his forehead.

"Nice, eh? One of my best."

"Delicious," Eileen said. "What are you doing out here? You should be a chef somewhere."

"I'm working regular hours," the man said. He wiped enormous hands on his apron and walked over. "You the detective, eh? Going to tell us who murdered Terry? Nice to meet you."

They shook hands.

"I work here because they pay me as well as a fancy restaurant. I get to cook for all the uppity-up military types that come out for the games. And I go home at five o'clock, instead of going to work at five o'clock. Can't beat it. John Wells, by the way."

"Eileen Reed. Thanks for the soup."

"Find that bad guy. I don't like thinking this place has a bad guy, eh?"

"I'll do my best, John," Eileen said, and found her way back to her table. She noticed Art Bailey and Joe Tanner sitting a few tables away. 'Berto joined them with a full plate of food. Joe's tray contained the remains of a salad. Eileen smiled. Art glanced over and waved a bit nervously. 'Berto and Joe also nodded, 'Berto with his shy pretty smile and Joe grave and unsmiling.

"The great detective contemplates the suspects," Eileen said gloomily, crumbling her crackers into the soup. "I'm probably ruining their lunch, looking over at them."

"Maybe," Blaine said, wiping his mouth. "We've never had a murder out here before. No one knows what to do or how to act. I think—"

Eileen never did find out what Blaine thought. There was a gasp and a half-smothered shriek from the tables by the windows. Eileen was out of her seat without thinking, her hand reaching for her gun, and because she was standing she got the best view out the window of an eagle sweeping down for a second blow on a prairie dog. The fluttering shadow of the first, missed strike was what brought gasps from the tables nearest the windows.

The eagle stood on the grass with wings extended, less than ten yards from the windows. The cafeteria was set at the edge of the developed portion of the base. Wild grasses grew to the distant fences beyond the glass.

"Is that a hawk?" someone said in a wondering voice. Eileen crowded to the windows with everyone else in the cafeteria. They stood watching the huge bird as it looked around, mouth open, fierce eyes blinking.

"That's a golden eagle," Eileen said. "What's it doing out here?"

"It can't see us," Joe Tanner said at Eileen's side. She looked up at him. He was quite a bit taller than she was. His face was rapt. His eyes were shining like a child's. He was crowded close to her in the press of people at the glass, and she got a clear whiff of aftershave.

"An eagle," someone else said softly. "Wow."

"The glass is polarized. It can't see us through the glass," Art Bailey said.

The eagle glanced down at the tan body half-hidden in the grasses, and shifted its talons back and forth.

Twenty people stood watching, silent and delighted.

"I thought eagles had white heads?"

"That's a golden eagle. They're larger than bald eagles," Eileen said. "We have them back home. They love those prairie dogs."

"They've been getting mighty fat without any coyotes in here to eat on them," John Wells said. The cook was standing at the back of the small crowd, wiping his hands on his white apron. He looked as excited as everyone else, like a child who has been given an unexpected present. "I bet that bird decided those critters were just too fat to pass by."

"I wonder if it will nest here?" Joe asked no one in particular. A half-dozen murmurs answered him, and sighs.

"When the prairie dog is dead, she'll carry it off," Eileen said. "Sometimes they have to wait, because the strike doesn't kill right away."

As if the eagle heard Eileen, she raised her wings sharply and looked around. The talons shifted, found another grip, and with a powerful spring the eagle rose into the air with the prairie dog dangling below.

The crowd at the windows said "Aaah" in unison. The eagle dwindled, became a speck, and disappeared into the sky. Excited chatter burst out as people turned away from the window.

"Show's over," Blaine said.

"Wasn't that incredible?" Joe Tanner said to Eileen. "Wasn't she beautiful? Do you think she was a she?"

"Yes, I think she was a she," Eileen said. "Males are smaller. Maybe she'll hunt here more, if those prairie dogs are as fat as John says."

"I hope so. I was going to ask the boss what he was going to do about them. Those prairie dogs'll move right into the storeroom if we don't slow 'em down," John said. "We can't poison 'em, they're on federal property. Protected. Wasn't that pretty?"

"Let's go, Joe," Art said fondly. "You freak. We're going to be late for the meeting."

"'Bye," Joe said to Eileen. He looked embarrassed, as though he had just remembered who she was. "Thanks."

"Sure," Eileen said.

For a moment she and Joe Tanner and the others had been simply people watching something extraordinary together. She wished the moment had lasted longer. She wished the prairie dog had put up more of a fight. She smiled at herself in mockery.

"You ready?" Blaine said.

"I need to find a phone," Eileen replied. "I have to call my boss."

Harben's voice on the phone line was chilly.

"You going to spend all day out there? You haven't started the Pendleton case yet."

"I've got a lot to do here."

"I'm sure you do. Try and make it back before six o'clock. I want to discuss the case with you."

"Shall I bring dinner?"

"Very funny. No, I brought my own supper today." Was there the ghost of a smile in Harben's voice? "Bring whatever greasy concoction you wish, but be here by six, please."

"I expected candles and music," Eileen said, and hung up before Harben could respond. That was the only way to win.

"Ready to go back up? You know the numbers now?" Blaine asked as Eileen turned away from the phones.

"Yeah, I'm ready. I'll be leaving about five-thirty or so. I have a meeting with the Captain at six."

"Leave at five or you'll be late," Blaine advised. "It's a longer drive than you think."

"Okay," Eileen said absently. "Thanks."

Central Intelligence Agency, Langley, Virginia

Lucy munched thoughtfully on a Hostess Twinkie. She licked whipped cream from her upper lip. The files were all on-line, including the pictures and the maps. George Tabor was terrific. He'd been trained and installed by the GRU, the military branch of the KGB, and at the fall of the Soviet Union had somehow managed to position himself as a freelance spy.

One of the FBI agents had even ended up going to bed with him, and her report was unblushingly specific. She hadn't been ordered to sleep with him, she'd just ended up there. George was so darn *American*. He was romantic and full of laughter. The FBI agent had been reassigned immediately after the report.

"Yeah, no shit," Lucy said to herself. She grinned around the Twinkie. The female agent had not been able to find any proof that George Tabor was the spy they all knew he had to be. George was so deeply under cover there was nothing the CIA or FBI could do but watch him and hope he made a mistake.

Lucy moved on to the foreign files, the CIA-gathered intelligence on the buyers. There were a surprising number from half a dozen countries. Missile Defense information was hot. Lucy clicked her tongue. The *Germans*? That seemed odd. The Americans were so tightly allied to the Germans, they would probably *give* the Germans defensive systems once they were made public.

Lucy looked up Mr. Johann Wulff. No picture. His profile was sparse. *Wait a minute.*

Lucy leaned forward. The last known location of Mr. Wulff was Paris, France. Paris.

"I think we have our last contact," Lucy murmured. "Who are you, Mr. Wulff? Inquiring minds want to know."

She reached for the phone.

Gaming Center, Schriever Air Force Base

Eileen figured out a way to follow a person through the course of the Game. She drew a blue colored box around them with the computer keys and pushed the Fast Forward key. Eileen could then lean back and watch the box as it followed the movements of the person. She played the tape quickly for all twelve audience members. That didn't take much time. None of them got up during the Game. Eileen checked off their names as she watched. Every audience member, the seven military and five civilian, were seated safely in a chair from the moment Nelson closed Terry's door to the moment he opened it.

The Commanders, Eaton, Torrence, and Olsen, were clean as well. Olsen paced nervously back and forth, which made the blue box hop and jerk along with him as the tape ran on fast forward. He never left the Commander's area. Eaton and Torrence didn't get up from their chairs.

Nelson Atkins left his room, presumably on a bathroom break. He monitored the communications equipment and the links to the other military centers from his room, or so Eileen gathered from listening to his conversation with Art Bailey. Eileen noted the time when Nelson left and the time he returned. Six minutes, forty seconds. Time enough.

Major Blaine, who wasn't assigned a position during the game, was in and out of the Center a half-dozen times. Either man, Atkins or Blaine, could have committed the crime when they were absent from the Center. But how could either one of them have killed Terry Guzman when they were off camera? The only way in or out of Terry's room was through the door that was on film. The other Gamers were off camera too, locked in their small rooms.

Eileen felt a lifting of her heart as she thought of Joe Tanner and Art Bailey. They would have to be in on the murder together, or both be innocent. Even though they were both unseen by the cameras, they were together in their small room until the murder was discovered. Eileen didn't want either one to be the murderer.

But how did the murderer get into the little room? If the murderer was one of the Gamers, how did the Gamers get out of their little rooms?

Eileen stood up. What was it? There was something—

The phone rang. The hovering idea vanished. Eileen cursed under her breath and picked up the phone.

"Hi, Eileen, this is Art Bailey. I was wondering if you would mind me coming over for a few minutes."

"Why?"

"Well, Joe and I both, actually. We have to pull tapes from each of the Silicon Graphics drives. It's part of the routine. They contain classified information, and they were left there the day before yesterday. We really need to get them in the safe."

"All right." Eileen hung up the phone and dropped into her chair. She started the tape again.

Art and Joe Tanner entered a few moments later. Art lifted a hand, and Joe nodded gravely at Eileen. She nodded back. In jeans and a sweatshirt, he looked just right. He was fascinating. He was puzzling. Eileen watched as Art moved toward the row of doors along one side of the room and Joe started toward the doors on the other side. Terry's room was taped shut. They looked over at the door and then looked away. Joe glanced back at Eileen, perhaps feeling her gaze on him.

I'm the policeman, Eileen thought as Joe turned away hurriedly. He isn't embarrassed because a woman is looking at him. He's afraid because the detective might think he's a murderer. Or he's afraid because he *is* the murderer.

She turned her eyes back to the screen and set the button to Listen mode. *"Did you and Art fix the BP flare problem?"*

"We think so, Terry. There was a network packet problem—"

"I don't care what it was, I just wanted to know if I had to come up with some sort of explanation. I think I'll have one just in case, don't you think?"

Joe looked at Terry in a calm, friendly way, as though he didn't understand the poison in the woman's words.

"Okay, that would be a good idea. Just in case."

Terry walked away, and Joe betrayed himself with one tiny, telltale swallow, as though he were trying to clear his mouth of something bitter. His face didn't change. He turned back to Art, who was speaking to Colonel Eaton.

"Miss Reed?" Eileen jumped in surprise. Joe stood at the door of the studio, looking nervous. Eileen had a queer doubling feeling for a moment, seeing Joe in front of her and on the screen at the same time.

"Yes?" She pushed the Pause button on the monitor screen.

"I brought you a pop. Doug told me what kind you got yesterday, so . . ." He held out a pop can to her. It was beaded with moisture and looked wonderful.

"You and Art sure take care of me," Eileen said. "Thank you." She took the can from him and popped the tab. "And thank you for the coffee yesterday. I really appreciate it."

"You're welcome. I sure hope you find out who did it," Joe said. He leaned against the doorway more confidently and brought his other hand into Eileen's view. He had an open pop can in it, and took a sip. The sweatshirt he wore was thick and green and had a wolf on the front. "Ski Banff," the shirt suggested.

"I hope so too. Did you think of anything more since we talked yesterday?" Eileen asked. She wanted to ask Joe if he'd ever skied Banff. She wanted to ask him if he had had anyone special since Harriet Sullivan. She didn't ask. What was wrong with her? If Terry had caused Sully's death, Joe had the best motive she'd seen for the murder. The only motive she could think of, as yet.

"No," Joe said, and looked down at his pop can.

"Sharon said she thought someone was writing Terry's code for her," Eileen said. She took a sip. Joe looked up in surprise.

"She told you that?" Joe said. "I'm—well, I'm amazed. We've talked about it, you know, because it just seemed like all of a sudden her code got really good, but—"

"She wanted to help. She knows the little things can be important."

Joe looked at the floor again.

"She told you about Sully, didn't she?" he said in a low voice.

"Yes," Eileen said. "Do you want to tell me about her?"

"No."

"Did you kill Terry Guzman, Joe?"

"I did not," he said hotly. "I did not. I hated her, but I wouldn't. I could never."

"I just want to know who did," Eileen said.

"That all the tapes, Joe?" Art asked from behind Joe. "Can you bring them across for me? I want my turn with the detective, here."

"Your turn?" Eileen said. She finished her pop.

Art handed his tapes to Joe. He took them and left with a brief, anxious glance toward Eileen. Eileen raised the pop can to him in a small salute, then pitched it into the corner wastebasket with perfect accuracy. A small symbolic message for Joe Tanner.

"Two points," Art said admiringly, not understanding. That was all right with Eileen; she was sure Joe *did* understand.

"So what do you want, Art? You figured out the murderer yet? I have to go in"—Eileen checked her watch—"forty-five minutes. Gotta date with the boss."

"No, I haven't figured out the murderer," Art said. "But I thought I would show you the Gaming computer system and how it works before you go. Don't know if it'll help or not."

"Worth a try. I'm sick of these damned tapes."

Berlin, Germany

Muallah looked out the small window of the airplane and watched the refueling trucks. He schooled himself to patience. A private jet was out of the question, however much it would have made the journey easier. The helicopter that awaited them in Mashhad would satisfy his desire for speed once they reached the northern Iranian city. From there the helicopter would bring them into Uzbekistan, former subject state of the USSR.

Muallah had targeted Uzbekistan more than two years before. He knew there were missile silos somewhere there, and he knew the Uzbekistanis were more Islamic than Russian in their loyalties. He'd thought that Uzbekistan would be a fine place if he only had the exact location of a missile silo. Uzbekistan was close to Iran, one of the countries where Muallah was held in a certain . . . affection. He'd found plenty of help there for what the Iranians believed was just another terrorist group.

Muallah smiled, his fingers resting lightly on his copy of the Koran. The Iranians meant to use him. As did the Libyans and the Iraqis. None of the governments were aware that Muallah was using *them*. When they discovered their mistake, their own people would already be Muallah's fanatic subjects, loyal to the death to the One of the Prophecies. The one who blew the Trumpet of Doom would topple governments before him like straws in the wind.

"Allah akhbar," Muallah murmured, and opened his Koran. He ruthlessly suppressed his excitement. The time was coming, but it was not yet upon him.

•17

They stood in the Truth Team room. Art showed Eileen a screen full of little windows, each one flashing and clicking.

"I'm backing up the data from the Cray to the Digital storage devices, basically just a bunch of big machines with tape drives. The Silicon Graphics computers are hooked into the network, but it would take too much time to transmit all their data, so we just push it onto tapes and store it. The whole system, the whole Game, is started off from my console, right here."

Art touched the mouse key and brought a window to the front of the others.

"This window would start a program, which would call other programs on the Silicon Graphics machines. These programs all talk to each other via messages, across the network. So these computer programs are like people on a party phone line, each talking away at each other. Say, you have a battle manager who wants to fire a Brilliant Pebble? He calls up the Environment guy and says 'Hey, what's the weather like?' Or sort of like that."

"Okay," Eileen said.

"The Crays are our big machines, they run most of the processing to figure out intercepts, the weather, the time of day, everything else you can think of. I'd like to show you one, if you would like."

Eileen had heard of Crays. She didn't think the enormous supercomputer would have anything to do with the murder, but she was curious to see one.

"Sure," she said to Art.

"Okay, we have to leave the Center for a few minutes. You want me to lock the door?"

"Yes, please." Eileen was immediately suspicious.

"Don't worry, Jeff changed the combination yesterday. You want to leave for good, right now? I'm not doing this well, am I? I mean, Jeff Blaine has the only combination to this room. Nobody could come in here while we're gone. But in order to get back in, we'll have to have the Major back here."

"No, you're not doing this well." Eileen couldn't help but laugh. Art looked so crestfallen. "But I'll tell you what. I will leave for good. That'll give me a chance to pick up some supper." She bent and gathered her notes into a pile. "That's all I need."

"Okay, then," Art said cheerfully, good humor restored. "Let's go see the Cray."

They walked down the sloped hallway to the door. "Notice the slight slope to the hallway," Art said.

"I did notice that. Why is that?"

"The floors throughout the Gaming Center are raised a little bit, to allow the network communications cables to run underneath the floor," Art said. "The Cray has enormous cables, and the power cables to each of those Silicon Graphics are also huge. In addition, the space underneath is chilled and vents are put in underneath each SG, to make sure they don't overheat. They—"

He stopped. Eileen stopped.

"The floors are raised," Eileen said. "How do you get underneath the floors?"

"The floors come up in big metal squares," Art said. "You can raise the floors everywhere in the Center. The carpets are designed to raise in big flaps, but they're interlocked so you can't see how they come apart. But I don't think there's room—"

Eileen turned and ran back into the Gaming Center. Art followed. Eileen stopped at Terry's door, looking at the floor. Streaks of dust lay everywhere. The chalk outline was oddly shaped, drawn around the chair where she'd died. It didn't look like a human, just an irregular blob.

"The floor," Eileen said. The carpeting looked solid and plush.

"The carpet is cut into interlocking squares. If you look at the pattern, you can almost see it. The squares can be lifted up," Art said. "Then the floor tiles can be raised. But I don't think you could crawl around down there."

"Could you enter this Center from across the hall? From downstairs?"

"No. The Center is sealed. The vents are only so big," Art said, holding his hands a few inches apart. "Let me get a suction tool, that's the way to lift up the floor tiles. You want to go underneath the floor? I really don't think you'll fit."

"Yes, I do. But not from Terry's room. I'm going to want prints from underneath that tile."

"He left prints on the underside?" Art said doubtfully.

"Maybe so," Eileen said grimly. "I want to check out those vents. If no one can get in or out of this Center, then . . ."

"Then what?" Art said. He walked back to the television studio and returned with a metal bar with two suction cups attached at either end. "This will bring up the tiles. And here's a flashlight."

"Then the person who killed Terry Guzman was one of the Gamers," Eileen said. Art stopped, and the suction tool drooped in his hand. The color drained from his face.

"No one else could have done it. Every other person was in sight of the cameras. Unless the film has been tampered with. I won't rule that out entirely.

"Whoever it was was sitting in their own cube, one of the little rooms in the Center. They lifted their own floor tile, crawled underneath the floor to Terry's room, killed her, and crawled back. Then they pretended great shock and amazement when her body was found. No one else could have done it. It has to be one of the Gamers who were in those rooms."

"Oh, no," Art said softly. "Oh, please, no."

"You are still on my suspect list, Mr. Bailey. Although you and Joe would have to be together on this."

"We could have done it, but we didn't," Art said steadily. He held out the suction tool and the flashlight. "But you shouldn't believe me, of course."

"I don't," Eileen said. "I'm going to give Major Blaine a call, then I'll go under the floor. I'd like to have you leave the area before I do this."

"I understand," Art said. Eileen took the metal tool and the flashlight from him. "You pull the lever in the middle and that breaks the suction," Art explained. "Those tiles are heavy, so be careful."

"I'll be careful," Eileen said grimly.

Art turned and left the room without another word, and Eileen sighed and scrubbed at her forehead with her free hand. She could see Art in the witness stand, with the same mournful innocent look on his face. She could see Art in the electric chair. Art could be a murderer. But it felt bad to mistrust him, just the same.

"Major Blaine speaking."

"This is Eileen Reed, Jeff. I need you to get the SID people back here. I need you to come up here, too."

"What did you find?" Blaine said immediately.

"I found out how it was done. I need the print people. Get up here." Eileen hung up the phone and clicked the locking mechanism on the suction tool.

"Here we go," she said to herself.

The carpet flap came up like a jigsaw puzzle piece. The sturdy carpet pieces were laid across a metal checkerboard of tiles. The tool sucked up against a metal tile firmly, but it took Eileen a couple of tries to get the heavy tile up and out of its metal frame. When the tile moved aside, a blast of cold air hit Eileen in the face. The opening was pitch black, and cold.

Eileen made a little whistling mouth but didn't whistle. She had never liked dark places very much. The flashlight was powerful and the batteries were fresh. The floor looked as if it was a good distance beneath the layer of tiles. Huge gray cables snaked across the floor. Bright red and blue lines twisted through the cables. The gray cables looked like enormous snakes.

"Snakes, why'd it have to be snakes," Eileen quoted to herself. She checked her gun and looked around the room. Blaine would figure out where Eileen had gone when he came in. Eileen had pulled up the floor tile directly in front of the Center door. If Blaine didn't look down, he'd fall right into the hole when he walked in.

Eileen dropped into the darkness. She crouched down, and only then thought perhaps the murderer was waiting in the dark for her. That perhaps she should have drawn her gun. She peered around in all directions and felt her body prickle with sudden sweat.

There was nothing but cables, and thin metal columns that supported the frame that held the tiles. Eileen swept the flashlight around in a circle. She could see to the walls in every direction. The walls were concrete, solid, pierced by cables and vents that were only big enough to let a good-size rabbit through, if that. Eileen swept again, more slowly, looking. There was no dust. The chilled air started to cool the sweat, and Eileen began to feel the cold. There were cables dangling from the metal framework, attached to the Silicon Graphics machines above her. Eileen crawled forward a few paces. The fit was fairly tight, but she could move around. She'd found her murderer's pathway.

"Miss Reed," said a voice, and Eileen backed up. She looked up out of the hole to see Major Blaine. "What are you doing?"

Eileen stood up.

"I found out how the murder was done," she said. "And I found out it had to be one of your Gamers. Unless—" Eileen looked around. "What if the murderer were hiding in the floor? They could have gotten out sometime yesterday, when no one was looking. You said all doors weren't guarded? They were dead-bolted?"

"Wait, wait, what's going on? I don't understand. Explain."

Eileen sighed and stepped out of the chilly hole. She clicked off the flashlight.

"This is how the murder was done. The murderer was either one of your Gamers, or someone already here, hiding underneath the floor. Unless there was someone here before the Game began, it has to be one of the Gamers. They pulled up the floor tile in their cube, dropped underneath the floor, and crawled to Terry's room. They came up through a floor tile behind Terry, stabbed her, and then went back underneath the floor. Get it?"

"Got it," Blaine breathed. "I got it."

"Okay. If the killer was a Gamer, they went back to their room, put on their gear, and pretended everything was okay. If this murderer was another person, when did they leave? Could they have left the room last night, after everyone had gone?"

"I understand now. But they couldn't have. All the doors except one were dead-bolted from the inside. The other one was locked and guarded. They were still all dead-bolted this morning when I checked."

Eileen stood looking at the hole in the floor. She shut out Major Blaine and thought about the possibilities of what she'd just discovered. She'd had this ability since she was a child. Perhaps it had been born in her. She could turn off all input and stand in a clean white room in her head, arranging puzzle pieces.

So she stood with a blank face, looking toward the hole in the floor but seeing a white room and a white table. Some of the pieces went together. Terry Guzman's piece lay neatly surrounded by interlocking Gamers. A pile of white pieces lay off to one side. The Procell file. Now a new puzzle piece appeared. It had a familiar shape.

Bernie Ames, the best friend of her Air Force days, was killed and classified a "pilot error" death. Bernie would not fly into a mountain. Bernie would not make such a mistake. Eileen tried to get the documents about the A-10 crash. The documents were sealed. Other documents were mysteriously missing. Was Bernie shut up because she knew something? Was the plane crash the result of some scandal, some error, that the Air Force didn't want brought to the light of day?

The puzzle piece that refused to be solved had existed in Eileen's white room for seven years. Now it suddenly joined the Gamers that surrounded Terry Guzman. There was another possibility for Terry's death, the same sort of piece that fit in with Bernie's unadmitted murder. The piece was titled "Cover up." It could fit.

Eileen blinked and looked at Major Blaine, who was speaking to her. Eileen hadn't heard a word he had been saying.

". . . one of the Gamers? It must be? Miss Reed?"

"Or maybe that's what I'm supposed to think, Major," Eileen said coldly. "Maybe. I want the names of the guards who were at this door last night."

"Surely you don't think someone else was here—"

"I think I'm going to keep my mind open," Eileen said. "I need the names of those guards. And your OSI crime scene team needs to get prints from this floor." Eileen glanced at her watch. "I've got to go, I'm going to be late."

"Will you be back tomorrow?" Blaine asked, for the first time looking lost.

"I'll be back," Eileen said. "I've got some other work I need to do. I'll be back at eight."

"I'll expect you," Blaine said. "You—"

But Eileen was already walking away.

She passed Roberto in the hallway as she headed out. Roberto was coming through the doors with a can of pop in his hand, and he gave Eileen a cautious smile. Eileen lifted a hand to him. Her other arm was full of her notes and the personal files of the Gamers. Along with the notes, she carried the Procell file.

•18

Colorado Springs Investigations Bureau

Associated Press 5-April
POLICE CONFIRM DEATH OF FIFTH SCIENTIST
UNDER UNUSUAL CIRCUMSTANCES

LONDON (AP)—Police on Sunday confirmed the death of a metallurgist involved in secret defense work—the fifth such case in the past eight months in which authorities have been unable to establish the cause of death.

A sixth scientist, a research expert on submarine warfare equipment at the University of Loughborough, vanished in January.

Eileen took a bite of her third taco and wiped some shreds of lettuce off the file. The file was extremely neat. The newspaper articles were folded and slipped into envelopes, stapled to a photocopy of the article. The name and date of the newspaper had also been included when Doug Procell clipped his articles. There were pictures, too, one of them of a spectacular wreck. One glance and Eileen knew it was a nonsurvivable wreck. There was nothing that the paramedics called "living space," the bubble formed of twisted metal and glass that could hold a human being. Sometimes people died when there was a living space in the vehicle, because their seat belts weren't on or they didn't have the ancient animal cunning to hunker down when the accident started to happen. Sometimes, though, nothing would help because the living space was destroyed. The car in the newspaper photograph was one of those. The only recognizable thing were the wheels.

Harriet Sullivan, 26, was pronounced dead on arrival at Memorial Hospital after this single-car rollover on Highway 94.

Eileen looked at the picture again. Then she turned it over and read the next article. It was another article from England, but it was a completely different murder.

Associated Press Fri 10-April 00:41
DEAD SCIENTISTS MYSTERY BAFFLES BRITAIN

LONDON (AP)—On March 30 scientist David Sands climbed into his car, the trunk packed with tanks of gasoline, and drove into the front of a vacant restaurant. He died in a fireball that incinerated him almost beyond recognition, the fifth British scientist involved in security-related research to die in mysterious circumstances since August. A sixth scientist has been missing since January. Together the cases add up either to a series of bizarre coincidences or to a cloak-and-dagger conspiracy.

Eileen stretched. She finished her taco and took a big swig of her pop. The murders were fascinating, but there didn't seem to be much connection to Terry Guzman. She bent to the article.

"Eileen, what are you reading?" Harben asked from behind her shoulder. "Oh. I see."

"Procell's stuff is interesting, but still." Eileen snorted.

"How much is there?" Harben asked.

Eileen measured the remaining papers with her fingers. "An inch and a half, boss," she said gloomily. "I'll be here all night."

"Don't be here all night. You've got some work to do tomorrow. They might come up with some prints from your discovery, or perhaps not. You need to talk to those Gamers again. Someone will crack."

Harben tapped a finger on the file. "Good work, by the way. In most mystery novels, however, once the good detective figures out the locked-room mystery, he knows immediately who has committed the murder."

Eileen grinned at Harben. Harben's congratulations always made her feel good.

"I'll get there."

"See that you do."

Harben turned and went back to his office. Eileen crumpled up the taco papers and tossed them into the wastebasket. She turned to the next article and began to read.

HOURS LATER, Eileen glanced up at the clock and winced. Eleven. Betty would be hungry. She'd missed the local news again. She rubbed her forehead and stacked Doug Procell's papers. John Richmond's article was not accompanied by a picture, mercifully. He must have died instantly when the garbage truck slammed into his little commuter car. The other deaths were all at other military bases, sometimes mysterious but mostly just common accidents. Eileen lingered over a picture of an unsmiling, curly-haired woman with dark eyes. Harriet Sullivan. Sully. The notice was her memorial service, and Joe Tanner was not mentioned in the survivors list. They probably weren't officially engaged. Eileen put the picture in the file and shut the cover. She sighed.

"Done?" Harben's voice startled her.

"I'm done. I don't think I learned a damn thing."

"Could she have been executed?" Harben asked quietly.

"Yes, I think so," Eileen said, and looked up. Harben was sitting at the desk next to her own, a cup of coffee in one relaxed hand. The man was uncanny, he was so silent. Eileen should have heard him walk up and sit down, but she hadn't. "Major Blaine would have to be involved, I think. I saw him tape the door shut. But who's to say he couldn't have smuggled the murderer out before he sealed the door?"

"More important, who was brought in to commit the murder?" Harben asked quietly. "Where do you hire a killer with a security clearance?"

"You're right," Eileen said. "They'd have to bring someone new on base to do that. A mole. A spy. Maybe there's a trail there."

"I find the scenario unlikely, Eileen," Harben said. "A killer who has a clearance, who is brought onto the base to kill someone, who is hidden in the dark and the cold for hours . . . with no guarantee he won't be discovered and shot to cover the whole mess up. Then the killer is smuggled out of the area with no one spotting him?"

"Accidents are much easier to arrange," Eileen said grimly.

"Which is why I don't believe this is an execution," Harben responded. He leaned back in his chair and sipped from his coffee. "I think you've met your murderer already, Eileen. You just have to find out which of your Gamers it is."

Eileen was opening her mouth to speak when the on-duty phone rang.

The Investigations office was quietly busy with the nighttime shift, but just the same the phone cut through the air. Harben took a small measured sip of his coffee as the on-duty officer picked up the phone. The officer was Rosen. New detectives always pulled the worst shifts. Eileen hadn't even noticed he was there, she'd been so absorbed in the case. Rosen spoke for a moment and then glanced over at Eileen and Harben. He nodded his head at them and waved for them to come over.

"Oh, no," Eileen said, and got to her feet. She knew, she always knew. She saw the shy smile of Joe Tanner as he handed her a can of pop, and swallowed past a lump in her throat.

She took the phone.

"Detective Reed here."

"Oh, Miss Reed, thank God," Major Blaine said in a hoarse voice. "Thank God. Can you get out here?"

"What happened?" Eileen said tightly.

"It's Art. Oh, God, it's Art. Art Bailey," Blaine choked.

Eileen had spoken to Art just a few hours before, when she'd told the sad-eyed Truth Team leader to clear out of the Gaming Center.

"What about Art?" Eileen asked.

"It's—I—He's been murdered," said Blaine.

Colorado Springs Investigations Bureau

"I'll be right there," Eileen said. She hung up the phone. She stood there for a moment and then turned to Harben.

"It's Art Bailey. He's been murdered too. I didn't let him help me with the floors," Eileen said. "I didn't let him look at the tapes with me. He must have thought of something. He must have figured it out."

Harben looked down at his coffee cup, his mouth tight.

"This will not be an unsolved case," Harben said coldly. "I'll send officers out to the other Gamers' houses. You have the names and addresses in your file? What's your file and code name access?"

"The file is TGUZMAN," Eileen said, reaching for a scrap of paper and writing it down. "And the code name access is MEDEA." The software system picked the code names and assigned them to case files. Eileen had felt a chill when she first saw the code name. Medea was the mythological queen who murdered her own children.

"Dave," Harben said. Rosen looked up from his desk and got to his feet at Harben's nod. Eileen had thought over the past few weeks that perhaps Harben was going to assign Rosen as her partner. She'd worked without a partner for nearly six months, ever since Jim Erickson moved to Denver. Eileen liked working without a partner, but that couldn't go on much longer. There was too much to do, working alone. Harben had given her a chance to get her hands on the Senior Detective position, and now it was time to see if she could keep it with a new partner. Dave Rosen looked like a good choice. He was smart, and he was green. This was a test, for both Rosen and herself.

"Yes, sir," he said.

"Eileen's file on the Guzman case. Get the other Gamers listed here on the phone. Find out who they are. Read the file. You'll be assisting Eileen on this case. Understood?"

"Understood, sir," he said quietly, and took the scrap of paper. His eyes glittered, and Eileen remembered that was Rosen's way of smiling. He was a rookie, but he was going to be good.

"I've got to go," Eileen said. She had to get to Schriever. "I'll contact you by radio."

"All right," Rosen said, as evenly as before.

"Keep in contact," Harben said. "Watch your back, Eileen."

"I will," Eileen said, and headed for the door.

THE DRIVE OUT was one of the longer ones in Eileen's life. She wished she'd trusted Art. Why had she told him to clear out of the Gaming Center? How often had she wished she'd made Bernie tell her what was going on? Or that young detective, Stan Jabowski, the one who'd been killed so quickly on Nevada Avenue, how often had she wished she'd been nicer, shown the boy the ropes a little better? Eileen made the last turn onto the long stretch of Highway 94 and thought about Art's hurt expression when she made him leave the Gaming Center.

"What did you think of, Art?" Eileen said to herself, and struck the wheel with the palm of her hand. "What did you do? Who did you call?"

Or was Art a suicide? Did he kill Terry and then kill himself out of remorse? Major Blaine said Art was dead, didn't he? Or did he say he was murdered?

Eileen chewed on her lip. She was driving as fast as the Jeep could go.

"Nine seven oh four, this is CXO, please come in."

Eileen took the phone from its hook. "This is Reed."

"This is Rosen. I've contacted Sharon Johnson at her home. She was apparently asleep. I've instructed her to remain in her home and ask a neighbor to come over, since she is alone except for her children. I've also contacted Doug Procell, also apparently asleep, also at his home. He will stay at home as well."

"Thank you."

"I'll let you know as I contact more. Out."

Schriever loomed in the distance, brilliantly lit in the dark plain. Eileen spun the wheel and took the exit off Highway 94 with a long squeal of her tires.

"Nine seven oh four, this is CXO."

"Reed here."

"I've contacted Roberto Espinoza, also at his home. He claims he was in a class this evening, until nine or so. He's given me the names. Evidently it was a church meeting. I'll verify."

"Nelson Atkins? Lowell Guzman? Joe Tanner?"

"No response."

"Call Sharon Johnson. Ask her if she knows where they are." Suddenly that heavy feeling was back in Eileen's throat.

"Affirmative. Out."

Eileen pulled up to the guard gate and showed her badge. The guard waved her through and she drove toward the lighted building of the retinal scanners. There was a flashing military police vehicle waiting on the other side of the scanners. Blaine sat inside, head lowered and forehead resting in one hand.

Eileen scanned her way through the glass booth and walked up to Blaine. She carried her police phone with her.

"Nine seven oh four, this is CXO."

"This is Reed." Blaine sat up and looked at Eileen, his eyes bloodshot. Eileen held up a hand as Blaine opened his mouth to speak.

"Sharon Johnson said that Joe Tanner's class didn't get out until nine-thirty. He is possibly on the UCCS campus in the computer lab. It stays open all night. I've sent a patrol car to check."

"Copy," Eileen said. The heavy thing wouldn't let go of the back of her throat.

"Nelson Atkins is not responding to phone. I've sent a car to check his home. I have contacted Lowell Guzman. He is disoriented and said he didn't hear the phone because of medication."

"He's the husband of the first murder victim," Eileen said.

"Okay. He is at home and says he has been there all evening. No witnesses. Maybe neighbors, but he's not sure. We'll verify. Out."

"We're checking on the Gamers," Eileen said to Blaine. "We've contacted almost all of them."

"Art's in the Center," Blaine said. "The night guard thought he heard something but didn't have the key combination to get in the door. Loud voices, he said. Then a shout, like a scream." Blaine gestured for Eileen to get in the police car. Eileen held on as Blaine turned the car on the soft sod of the lawn and headed toward the Space Command center.

"They called me at home. I'm the only one with the combination besides the Gaming staff." Blaine's voice was flat.

"Why doesn't anyone but you have the combination? What if there were a fire?"

"Anyone *in* that room would have the combination," Blaine said dully. "Anyone else couldn't get in. This is a compartmentalized base. That means nobody has access to particular rooms unless they have the right need to know."

"Did you touch anything?"

"No. I saw it was Art and I saw he was dead, and I got out."

"Are you sure he was dead?"

"I'm sure," Blaine said, and swallowed hard. He stopped the car in front of the building, and they got out.

"CXO, this is nine seven oh four," Eileen said before she entered the building. She remembered Procell's speech on the building's construction, how it was made to block out electronic signals.

"This is CXO."

"I am entering a shielded building. You can reach me at—" Eileen looked at Blaine.

"Oh, uh, the center number is 344-8814."

"344-8814, got that?"

"Copy."

"Anything on Atkins or Tanner?"

"Negative."

"Copy," Eileen said, and turned off her phone.

"Let's go," she said, and thought of Joe Tanner. She wondered if Art had asked him to help do whatever he had done to get himself killed. She wondered if Joe Tanner had killed Art. Or if he was lying in some darkened corner of the Center, as dead and still as Terry.

•19

Great Falls, Virginia

The phone rang in the darkness. Ted Giometti sat up, instantly awake, instantly afraid. Who was dead? He picked up the phone.

"Hello?"

"I need to speak to Lucy Giometti, please," Steve Mills said crisply. Ted sighed, and his shoulders slumped. He'd completely forgotten his wife, the warm hump of covers at his side. His aunt and his cousin had been in a car wreck when Ted was thirteen, and the doctors hadn't known if they were going to live or die. His aunt Mary did die, after the first long week. The phone became the family's enemy. The phone was still the enemy, even though Wilson recovered completely. He was happily married now and had a child of his own. Still, Ted never forgot the feeling when the phone rang, and he never forgot his mother's face when they told her about her sister.

"Sure, Steve," he said. "Hang on." Ted shook his wife's shoulder gently. Mills was such an asshole. Couldn't he just ask to speak to Lucy? What, did he think there were two Lucy Giomettis at this address at three o'clock in the morning?

"Wha—?" Lucy said. She didn't wake easily.

"It's Mills," Ted said. Lucy brushed a sheaf of her silky dark hair away from her face and took the phone.

"Lucy here," she said. "What? Okay. Yeah, okay. I'll be in at eight A.M., Mills." There was a silence, and Ted could hear the tiny buzzing of Mills's voice.

"Steve, I don't know why you would want me in at—" she paused and glanced at her clock—"three A.M. I'd be a useless wreck by two o'clock in the afternoon. I'll be in at eight and I'll get right on it. Bye." She hung up the phone and lay back in the bed.

"What an asshole," she said to her husband. He leaned over and kissed her.

"Hmm, three A.M. until eight A.M. Just enough time," he said.

"What?" she protested, laughing. "That's what got me fat and sick in the first place, you brute." She fought against his hands, giggling, then relaxed under him. Her face grew serious as she looked into his eyes.

"Kiss me," she said as his hands caressed her. "It's the middle of the night and I think I hate my boss. Kiss me and make me forget what he just told me."

Gaming Center, Schriever Air Force Base

The Gaming Center door was attended by a familiar-looking guard. After a moment, Eileen realized it was the same guard who'd been there the previous morning. It seemed like days ago. This must be the night guard.

"At ease, Airman," Blaine said.

"Where's the SID unit?" Eileen asked. Blaine looked at her blankly for a moment, as though Eileen were speaking in a different language and he was translating in his head. "The Special Investigations Division guys. Crime Scene. Dr. Rowland. Photographer. You know?"

"They're on their way," he said. "Dr. Rowland didn't want to get out of bed."

"Are you all right, Major?" Eileen asked.

"I'm fine," Blaine said. "Let's go inside."

Eileen didn't feel that Blaine was fine. Blaine looked like a man who'd just been woken up. Or he was stoned. Or he hadn't slept in days. Anything was possible.

"Okay, let's go," Eileen said heavily. They walked up the sloping hallway, and she felt the tightness in her chest she always felt when she knew the victim personally. Most times it was another cop. Once a neighbor, an older woman Eileen used to speak to occasionally when she brought in her mail. Seeing a body like that was the ultimate indignity. In most cultures the family members would bathe and prepare a body before visitors were allowed to see. Eileen knew why, after the first time she'd seen the sad sprawled form of a person she knew. Her instincts were to cover the poor person, to arrange their clothing, to give them some dignity that murder robbed. She wanted to close their eyes, and say good-bye, and she had to leave their bodies in disarray, in their own blood and wastes. She hated to see the body of someone she knew.

Art was lying on his side near the door. It had been a hard death. The wheat-colored hair was matted and dark with sweat and blood. He'd been trying to crawl to the doorway after the murderer had stabbed him. The murder weapon was lying on a table, set carefully there, almost contemptuously left out in the open. It was wiped clean. A sharpened screwdriver. Eileen took a handkerchief from her pocket and flicked the main banks of lights to brightness, using the handkerchief so she wouldn't disturb prints. A useless exercise. Blaine, standing in her shadow in the doorway, winced at the light and looked away from Art.

"There's no one else here," Eileen said. "Check anyway, behind these desks, look around."

"Okay," Blaine said.

"Don't touch anything. You see something, you call me."

"Okay," Blaine said again.

Eileen looked down at Art.

"I'm sorry, Art," she said softly. She started to bend down when the phone rang. Eileen spent an endless minute searching before she found the phone in the television studio room.

"I need to speak to Detective Reed," a voice said crisply.

"This is Eileen, Rosen," Eileen said.

"We've located Joe Tanner. He was in the UCCS computer lab with several members of his class. They had some assignment due that they were all working on. He didn't leave the lab."

Eileen had to swallow twice before she spoke.

"Nelson?"

"No contact. We have verified with Roberto Espinoza's church group that he was attending a Catholic Youth Organization meeting until nine-thirty. He teaches eighth-graders. He was there since six o'clock this evening. He said he went straight home, fixed a microwave dinner, and went to bed. We have verified with Lowell Guzman's neighbors that he was in his family room watching television. They could see him through their living-room windows."

"After you contact Atkins, when you do, I want you to visit each Gamer's house. You shouldn't need a search warrant; they are all willing to cooperate. Or at least, they're supposed to cooperate. I want you to look for one thing. Look in the trash, on the floors, in the backyard."

"What do you want me to look for?"

"Metal shavings. He—or she—had to sharpen that screwdriver somewhere."

"I understand."

"Watch yourself, Dave," Eileen said, and looked over at Art's body. "Whoever this is, he's getting very desperate. And he's getting very good at killing people."

"Understood. Out."

Eileen hung up the phone and turned again to Art Bailey's body. There were two stab wounds, one in the back and one in the neck. The neck was the fatal injury. Eileen could see how the murderer struck once, pulled the screwdriver free, and slashed at Art as he struggled to rise from his chair. The slashing, second strike was the one that tore open Art's neck and finished him. Art saw the murderer before he died. The wound was in the front.

Eileen felt tired. Had Art seen a friend? His surprise was his undoing. He didn't expect the second blow. There were no marks on his hands from warding off strikes. There were no other signs of a struggle. Art stood in amazement, and let himself be killed. Eileen remembered Tanner mentioning Art's gentle nature, and for a moment she had to struggle with a choking feeling of rage and frustration. Art was dead. Eileen Reed hadn't been able to stop it from happening. She felt sick.

"There's nothing else here."

"Any clothing? The blood would have spattered this time."

"No clothing."

"Anyone see someone leave this room?" Eileen knew the answer before Blaine shook his head no.

"Damn it!" Eileen said explosively. "How about the base? You keep a record in those scan things?"

"No record, and no guards. We could ask the guard at the gate if he saw any particular car that was driving too fast."

"Call him. Not that phone," Eileen added as Blaine headed toward the television room. "I'm in contact with my assisting officer on that line."

"Someone else?" Blaine said.

"Detective Rosen. He's tracking down each of the Gamers to see if they have alibis."

"I was thinking," Blaine said slowly. "The murder was done at change of shift. Eleven is when the night shift arrives and the swing shift leaves. That's why he killed Art at eleven. He drove out of here with a hundred other cars. He went through those scanners with hundreds of people."

"Clever," Eileen said grimly. "He or she."

"Yes," Blaine said. "I'll call the guard anyway, just to check. Do you want coffee or a pop?"

"Coffee," Eileen said.

"Yes, I'm going to get some. I'll get a cup for you too." As Blaine left, the phone rang again.

"Reed speaking."

"This is Rosen. I'm mobile. No contact with Nelson Atkins. I'll be trying his house first to see if he's home."

"You got assistance?"

"I'm with Officer Hetrick."

"Would Shelly turn me in if I said, 'Be very careful'?"

"You mean because I'm a girl, girl?" Shelly Hetrick came over the line, her voice bright and sarcastic.

"Well, yes."

"I'm turning you in," Hetrick said.

"Look for fresh blood. I think the perp got splashed. Okay?"

"Clear. I'll carry my parasol, dear."

"Thanks. Out."

Eileen hung up the phone, smiling. Shelly Hetrick was deadly. Eileen would worry less about Shelly than she would about Rookie Rosen. The door beeped, and Eileen heard the familiar voice of Dr. Rowland.

"At least this time I knew it would take forever to get here," he grumbled as he entered the room. Rowland was dressed in his uniform, but his hair was flattened on one side and hastily combed. The SID unit followed. The fingerprint people were different, but the photographer was the same. The photographer looked fresh and alert with the bright energy of a night owl. Eileen envied him.

Rowland looked at Art, looked at Eileen.

"Didn't catch him quick enough, eh?" he said, then grimaced. "Sorry. Not your fault. No clues. Any motive for this one?"

"Maybe he found out who it was," Eileen said. Rowland nodded, and put down his bag.

"I sent the autopsy report to you this evening," he said, bending down and examining Art. "I'll try to be quicker on this one."

Eileen walked away from the camera flash and the bustle of activity. She followed the blood trail that went back to Art's console. The blood spray on the carpet was consistent with a blow to the throat after Art rose from his chair. The chair was tipped on its back. The console was still logged on to the system. There were windows open and flashing with lights and color. Eileen looked at the big screens. They were dark and empty. The windows on the console looked like the War Game simulation Art had showed Eileen that afternoon.

Eileen stood in front of Art's console. What was Art doing on the computer? He was obviously running some kind of simulation, but there were no graphic displays. The big screens were dark. Art's console was doing something, though.

"Detective," Rowland called. Eileen looked over at Rowland, who was squatting by the body and beckoning with one gloved hand.

Eileen started to walk over, and the console beeped shrilly behind her. She turned to see one of the little screens flashing the word "Found" over and over in red letters.

"Found?" Eileen said. "Found what?" She crouched over the console, trying to see if there was a name in any of the windows. Suddenly the whole console flashed and went white. Eileen jerked her hands back and away, but she was sure she hadn't touched anything.

"Time Limit Exceeded." The words scrolled across the screen. "No Interaction. Logging out ABAILEY at 0123 hours."

The screen went dark, taking whatever Art found with it into blackness.

•20

Central Intelligence Agency, Langley, Virginia

"The Medical Examiner's notes are on-line now," Lucy Giometti said tersely. She'd finished reading Terry Guzman's autopsy earlier that morning, a report that had been typed in half a continent away by the concise Dr. Rowland. The autopsy report had briefly pushed aside her inquiry about Johann Wulff. Lucy intended to get back to Wulff as soon as she could. Wulff had a taste about him that made Lucy feel certain he was the key to Tabor's death.

The FBI special agent in Colorado Springs, Fred Nguyen, was on the phone that was socked against her left ear. Nguyen was a second-generation Vietnamese, child of a large family that made it out before the fall of Saigon. He spoke perfect English accented with more than a touch of California. Lucy had called up his picture from the FBI files, and the mental image of the blond football player that went along with the voice disappeared when she saw the thin Asian face. His eyes in the picture were black and small and expressionless.

"So, hey, I'm not saying these are related to this George Tabor dude," the cheerful voice sounded in her ear, "but I don't know why they're happening at the same time. It's weird, man."

"Fred, my friend, I don't know either. I know we've got nothing on Arthur Bailey. He's salt of the earth. Clear all the way back to grade school. Never even been out of the country."

"Yeah, that's what my reports say too. I think maybe Tabor just got spooked and ran, is all. Damn. It would've been great if we'd been able to grab him alive. We'd been tracking this guy for a long time."

"Well, if anything more comes up, I'll let you know," Lucy said. "Thanks."

"Thanks, Lucy. I'll get in touch if I find something juicy."

Lucy hung up the phone and pulled open her desk drawer for the fortieth time that morning.

"No, no, no," she said to herself.

The phone rang. It was Mills.

"What's up?" Lucy said, her eyes still wandering over the stacked cookies and pastries in the drawer.

"We've got an appointment at the Pentagon," Mills said, and the bafflement and fear were plain in his voice.

"At the *Pentagon*?" Lucy said.

"I don't know what's going on. The Deputy Chief called me personally. This is getting pretty damn hot, Lucy. Be in my office at one o'clock."

Lucy didn't realize for a moment he'd called her by her first name. Then it struck her. Mills must be really upset. And she still hadn't nailed Johann Wulff.

Lucy pulled a fruit pie out of the drawer and picked up the phone. She had a few hours. She'd have to use them well.

Colorado Springs

"I have witnesses. I was in church."

'Berto sat on the couch in his apartment. His thick black hair was uncombed. He was wearing gray sweats and a black tank. He didn't look as if he'd slept much.

"I know you were in church," Eileen said. She didn't feel much better than 'Berto looked. The morning sun was just touching through 'Berto's blinds.

'Berto's apartment was small. Two or three days' worth of dishes were piled in the sink. The carpet was clean, although it was old. There were gym clothes on the floor and a few brightly colored ties hung over some chairs. The overstuffed armchair in front of the television was piled with newspaper. The table next to the chair was loaded with old pop cans and magazines. Eileen could see the corner of the bed at the end of the short hallway. The bed was unmade, but the room looked clean.

"Pretty small place."

"Small is all I need," 'Berto said. He got to his feet. "Coffee? How about some orange juice?"

"Coffee would be nice," Eileen said, and followed 'Berto into the kitchen. 'Berto pulled out some filters and a grinder and started to make coffee.

"I haven't been shopping, but I could make you something. You want breakfast? You going to haul me in?" 'Berto ran the words together and tossed the last line off lightly, but there was nothing light in his dark and miserable eyes.

"No."

The tough line of the shoulders slumped. For a moment 'Berto looked like a relieved, frightened little boy. Then he turned his face away and began rinsing the filter holder.

"So why are you here?"

"I want to talk some more. You can afford better than this, can't you?"

"Maybe," 'Berto said.

"You can afford a maid, though?" Eileen asked.

"I don't have a maid," 'Berto said, and finished assembling the coffee. He turned the switch to start the brew.

"Looks like you have a maid."

"Okay, my cousin," 'Berto said. "She comes by once a week. She works as a maid, okay?"

"I'm not trying to say anything," Eileen said mildly. "I just thought you had a maid for a place like this, that was funny. A girlfriend would treat a place differently."

'Berto leaned back against the counter and folded his arms. He smiled faintly.

"You notice stuff, I guess. No girlfriend. Estelle, she comes by for a favor."

"A favor?" Eileen said, and eyed 'Berto. 'Berto shifted nervously. " 'Berto, look. You don't drive a hot car. You live in a dump. You don't have great clothes. But I've seen your salary. Why don't you live better? Are you being blackmailed?"

"I'm not being blackmailed!" 'Berto's shoulders rose. He seemed unsure whether to laugh or get angry. "I'm—look. Well, hey. I'll show you."

'Berto walked over to his cluttered coffee table. He rummaged around the newspapers and magazines stacked on top. He pulled out a photo album.

"Ready for the sob story, eh?"

Eileen glanced at the coffeepot. It was nearly done. She opened the cabinet above the coffeemaker and the coffee cups were there, in the most logical place for them to be. She looked inside before she poured, but they were clean.

"So give me the sob story. You take milk?"

"Black is fine for me," 'Berto said. "I couldn't sleep last night. Nelson called me and told me about Art. I was thinking about Art. Terry too."

'Berto put his photo album on the kitchen counter. He opened it. Eileen took a sip of his coffee and looked.

"This is my brother Luis. College. Tuition. Books. This, my sister Isabelle. Okay, no college for her. Two little ones, boy and girl. College for them. Eh?"

Eileen looked at Luis, a younger, thinner version of 'Berto. The slate-black eyes were smiling. The UCLA sweatshirt was fresh and white. The sister Isabelle, chunky and plain, had two happy children in the circle of her arms. There were more pictures. Eileen flipped through the album, sipping her coffee, seeing the signs of prosperity appear as the children grew. The bright spots of new lamps, a new carpet, new clothing. There were pictures of another woman, a thin beautiful girl with an angular, Spanish look to her face. She wasn't smiling in any of the pictures. She wore a lovely red dress, and looked almost embarrassed, as though she knew she looked spectacular.

"Another sister?" Eileen asked. 'Berto smiled.

"Mi madre," he said proudly. "My mom. My dad was a cop, got killed a long time ago. She's beautiful?"

"Wow," Eileen said. "She sure is."

The sun, rising, laid a strip of brightness across the kitchen and picked up the glare of the picture film. Eileen closed the album and refilled her cup.

"You support them all," she said. 'Berto shrugged.

"They know it, they knew it before I got all my clearances through. The government didn't mind that I send my money to my family. I don't think my investigating officer liked it, though."

"Your investigating officer?"

"Yeah, they send one out to interview the family, your friends, your professors. People from your last jobs. Sometimes they interview you, too. This one did. When you get this kind of clearance, they do a background check on you. This guy was a young white guy. Didn't like visiting the barrio. Didn't think I should be wasting money. A man with no family." 'Berto grimaced in disgust. "He doesn't understand."

"I know you have an alibi for last night," Eileen said quietly.

"I teach classes, sure. My cousin is a priest. My father's sister, she's a nun. The Church is important to us. I'll have my cousin say a prayer for Art."

There was a little silence. Eileen looked at the slight steam that rose from her cup, then looked up at 'Berto. She knew there was more to 'Berto's story than he was telling her. Something about 'Berto's good looks, the misery in his eyes, urged her on.

"But no prayers for Terry."

'Berto was standing with an elbow on the kitchen counter, his other hand on the cover of the photo album. He stood frozen.

"Oops," Eileen said.

'Berto opened his mouth. Closed it again.

"'Berto," Eileen said softly. "Come on."

Incredibly, 'Berto's eyes filled with tears. He hung his head, his hand pressed to the album as though it were holding him up. Eileen didn't move. She hardly breathed.

"Please," Eileen whispered to herself. She needed just one little break, that's all. Just one break. 'Berto lifted his head and wiped his eyes. He looked very young.

"I'll tell you," he said. "Can we sit down?"

Central Intelligence Agency, Langley, Virginia

"An efficient job," Lucy mused, looking at the autopsy photographs of George Tabor. She was on the phone to Charles D'Arnot, a Paris police detective who supplemented his income by helping out the American CIA.

D'Arnot spoke perfect English with a slight Scottish accent, which Lucy found hilarious. They were looking at pictures together, half a world apart, on the Internet. Lucy patted her computer monitor affectionately.

"Go to the next one," D'Arnot said. A red arrow appeared on Lucy's screen, showing the ligature marks on the neck. "He was a professional. Only one mark. He never had to shift positions, and the bruising is slight. There is bruising, though." The arrow disappeared and reappeared at another place on the screen. "Your Mr. Tabor fought well, Lucy."

"He was surprised," Lucy murmured. "You can tell."

"We have another set of pictures for you, *chérie*," D'Arnot said cheerfully.

"Another set?" Lucy asked, sneaking a glance at her watch.

"Not of Tabor," D'Arnot said. "I'm uploading now."

Lucy watched with amazement as a new set of autopsy pictures appeared. The victim was a female, Arab, and young. She had the same markings on her neck as George Tabor. Even to Lucy's untrained eye, she thought the marks looked similar.

"Eh?" D'Arnot said with satisfaction.

"Who is she?" Lucy breathed.

"Sufi Ad-Din," D'Arnot said. "Found in her apartment less than five blocks from Tabor's rubbish heap."

"She's Arabic?"

"Jordanian, formerly Palestinian," D'Arnot said. "She had a lover. She told her neighbor what his name was, and the name he used when he traveled. Her neighbor was a—how do you say it in English?—"

"A girlfriend? A chum?" Lucy said.

"A chum," D'Arnot said. "Evidently the lover didn't know about the chum, or doubtless Sara would be as dead as Sufi."

"What was his name?" Lucy asked. Her fingers tingled and her heart pounded. She knew what D'Arnot was going to say before he said it.

"Johann Wulff. But his name was really Fouad Muallah. He is Jordanian as well, according to the chum, but we don't have any further information. We put a warrant out, but he has probably flown the coop, as you say."

"Fouad Muallah," Lucy said. She bit her lips to keep from laughing out loud. "I'll see what we can find out, Charles."

"You do have some good resources," D'Arnot said wryly. "If you track this man down, I'd appreciate a call, *chérie*."

"You shall have it," Lucy said. "Thank you very much. You've given me a lot to work with."

"Of course," D'Arnot said with a Frenchman's modesty. "And now I must go. My companions, they grow suspicious if I spend too long on the phone."

"I understand," Lucy said. "Thanks so much."

"I told them you were my lover," D'Arnot said with a laugh. "So if you ever come to Paris, I hope you are as beautiful as your voice. I do have a reputation to keep."

Lucy chuckled for a long time even after she hung up the phone, even as she set up her search engine to seek out Fouad Muallah. After three months of feeling like a bloated horror, it was wonderful to hear flattery. French flattery, no less. *Parisian* flattery. Ted would pretend to be jealous and cover her in kisses tonight.

But before tonight, she had to meet with someone at the Pentagon, an Admiral Kane. There were monsters to defeat before she could return to her castle and her prince.

"And a monster to find," Lucy murmured, leaning over her keyboard. "A monster named Fouad Muallah."

Fort Rucker Army Base, Alabama

"You know what they call a Chinook?" Roseburg asked him as Stillwell signed for his flight helmet.

"What?" Stillwell asked apprehensively.

"A loose collection of nuts and bolts flying in formation," Roseburg laughed.

"Why, thank you," Stillwell said. "I really needed to hear that."

"Have fun," Roseburg said. "You've got two damn good pilots, I'll tell you that much. Anything goes wrong with that bucket of bolts and they'll bring you through it."

"I'm comforted," Stillwell murmured, and headed in the direction Roseburg pointed. He ducked out of the hangar into the wet and the heat of an Alabama morning. The hills and forest—well, jungle really; Alabama woods were more like a jungle to Stillwell and always would be—were faded by the humidity into a soft palette of green and blue. The jungle started at the end of the runway, and on the runway was his ride.

The Chinook was an ungainly-looking aircraft with two rotors, one at the head and one at the tail. She stank of jet fuel, even at a distance. The air shimmered above her engines. Her rotors were turning lazily. Chinooks looked like a joke, Stillwell had always thought. But he had presided at only two fatal crashes of the ridiculous-looking birds. The statistics were with him. Or so he hoped.

He hopped on board, clutching his flight bag. At last, it looked like he was heading for Colorado.

Colorado Springs

"I started at Schriever out of college," 'Berto said to Eileen. "I wanted money, to help my family, and I wanted to do graphics simulation. That's what I love. When I interviewed, they showed me a globe of the earth on a Silicon Graphics Indy. It was so beautiful. I could see the sunrise line. I could see the city lights in Europe. That's what I wanted to do.

"So I start, and there's Art to help me. Ahh, I miss him. I'm going to miss him forever. I didn't know how to set up my workstation, and Nelson isn't around. I'm too nervous to talk to Joe or Sharon or Doug, and Lowell is busy. So I see this guy who looks friendly, and it turns out he's Art, the genius. I ask him to help me, he gets up from his desk like he's been waiting all day just for me. Turns out he stays late that night to make up for the time he spends with me. But that's Art.

"He comes over and sets me up. Soon we're talking graphics and morphing and the latest Hollywood pictures. I'm kind of arrogant, you know, stupid, because I've just graduated and I know everything, I think. Art, he never slaps me around like he should. Sully, oh boy. First time I pull that shit with her, she takes me down."

'Berto stopped for a moment. He looked blankly into the distance.

"Sully first. Now Art. I knew when she got together with Joe. He was on fire. He blew out like a candle when she died. Art got him through it, I think. Art and Meg, that's his wife. Now Art, he's gone too. Joe, he's going to be hurting so bad. I want to call him, but I don't. Too scared of what's going to happen. I think everyone thinks I'm the murderer. I think you knock on the door this morning, this is the end."

"Why?" Eileen asked.

"Because of me and Terry," 'Berto said. He swallowed hard and rubbed his palms against his sweats. "I'm getting there. It's hard.

"So my second year there, I'm graphics king with Art's help, and I'm getting along with my new friends, and my family is happy. They find me Elena and her family, they're cousins away, but so I have family."

"But nobody special," Eileen said.

"Nobody special," 'Berto repeated. He didn't meet Eileen's eyes. "Terry and I never talked much. She was *muy guapa,* yes? She and Sully were different sides of the same coin. Sully, she was strong, but she was a woman. Full of heart. Terry, she's strong but full of hate. Hard to see that at first. You look at her, you think, I know what would make her happy. Get her in bed, get past all that armor, fuck her, she'll be happy. She just looks like that's what she needs.

"Lowell didn't know how to handle her, that's for sure. Always looking a little bit puzzled. And her holding out that body like a piece of fruit. Lowell doesn't know what to do with it, that's for sure."

"She decided she wanted you?"

"She wanted me, sure. Not that I knew it for a while. She made me want her. I never knew until a lot later how I'd been set up."

"Set up?"

"Set up like old style, woman style. She knows—knew—tricks they wrote in the book years ago. Centuries. I don't know. A woman like that, you burn for her. You want to conquer, to break her down, make her soft. You don't know you go to bed with her, you give her what she wants. Then she eats you afterwards, like a spider. No use for you after it's done."

'Berto sighed and shifted on the couch.

"Why is it so easy for me to tell you this? They sent four of us to a con-ference, we had to attend some seminars on graphics. It was fun, the semi-nar part. Terry, me, Joe, and Sully. They didn't much like each other then. Or maybe they already liked each other but didn't know it. We all went to dinner, and they both disappeared to their hotel rooms every night. Not with each other. Sully probably set up her laptop and played. You can't log into the system long distance—it's secure. But she liked those computer games. Joe, he read, I think, or went and swam in the pool. He's always working out. He didn't like Terry and maybe he had a crush on Sully, and I think he would have liked to spend time with me, but the only way to do that would be to say, I'm a guy, I want to hit the bars with 'Berto, okay?" 'Berto laughed. "Joe was too nice for that. So he disappeared, and Sully, so there was Terry and me."

"We went to the bar that first night, and somehow it was me asking her, I don't know how she did it. I thought I was in control."

"Did it happen the first night?"

"Oh yeah, and the second too. That first night, I was so drunk. Don't know how that happened either. But there she was in my room, and all I wanted to do was get her out of her clothes, get her under me."

'Berto put his head in his hands, and his shoulders rose. "I am so ashamed the next day. Married! I break a solemn vow, me, Roberto. I wanted to be a priest when I was a little boy, an altar boy. And this is what I did."

"She used that, didn't she?" Eileen asked. Now she felt she understood all the references to Terry's sharp tongue. Joe hadn't understood when Terry asked 'Berto if he'd "forgotten anything else." 'Berto knew what Terry meant.

"She used it. I was ashamed and hungover, and the next night I was back in her bed like I had a ring through my nose. Then we flew home, and I took a shower forever. I didn't want to go to work the next day. But everything was fine. At first. Then she would make references, in front of Lowell even, with that little kitten smile on her mouth and her eyes, so wide. Ahh, I blamed myself at first. But after a few months, I knew what she wanted. She had me on a string like a puppet, and she knew it. I didn't want to hurt anyone. I didn't want to see disgust in Joe's eyes. Or Art's. She knew that."

"Did she ever ask you for any favors?" Eileen asked. She was thinking of Sharon's suspicion that someone was writing Terry's code.

"I helped integrate her code," 'Berto said. "That means I helped make her part fit into the simulation. I never complained about her stuff. After a while, it got a lot better. She didn't ask for anything, she just had it. She had it there and we both knew it."

"Did you hate her?"

"I hated her enough to kill her," 'Berto said. "I could have killed her. But I didn't. I don't know how to make anyone believe that. I didn't kill her. She could have pushed me over the edge, I could have killed her. But I know I would have been sobbing for the priest the moment it was over. I got dispensation from my priest for adultery. I would have volunteered for the classes anyway, but they're part of my penance. He absolved me, and I'm washed clean. Terry knew that, I think. She knew she had me through embarrassment, and shame, but not through shame of my immortal soul. She hated that, I think. She ate people. She liked to have their souls."

Eileen shivered involuntarily.

"Someone hated her. I think anyone who knew Terry would hate her. But it wasn't me. *It wasn't me.*"

Mashhad, Iran

"Mahdi," the man said in reverent tones. The Mercedes was as dented as advertised, but gave a reassuring rumble of power. Muallah was aware of the deadening weight of exhaustion beneath his excitement. He needed sleep.

"Allah be with you, Haadin," Muallah said, smiling at the look of joy on the man's face. Ali silently loaded the baggage into the back of the Mercedes, his face reflecting nothing, not even weariness.

"I need to rest," Muallah added shortly. Haadin seated him immediately in the Mercedes and drove with a reckless dash through the dusty streets of

Mashhad. Haadin had rooms, of course, the best of which remained empty for Muallah. The rest of the rooms were occupied by Muallah's Chosen Ones, ready at last to serve him as they knew they were born to do.

Muallah rested his head against the back of the seat, trying to ignore the bumps and swerves. He needed to conserve his strength. He would allow himself only a few hours of rest before they began.

•21

Central Intelligence Agency, Langley, Virginia

"Charles!" Lucy said with delight. She had a substantial CIA file she'd found on Fouad Muallah. Paper pages were spread on her lap and electronic ones covered her computer screen.

"Lucy, *ma chérie*," D'Arnot said. "I have an interesting tidbit for you."

"I'm ready," Lucy said. She clicked on her notes screen and made an entry for D'Arnot's information.

"I spoke again to Sara, the chum," D'Arnot said. "And something she said matches with what we found with Sufi."

"Okay, I'm ready," Lucy said, typing.

"Sufi had intercourse minutes before she died. Not rape; there was no trauma. But she was killed immediately afterward."

Lucy paused, her fingers poised over the keyboard.

"He's an egotistical bastard, isn't he?" she said.

"Yes! You're beautiful *and* intelligent," D'Arnot said admiringly. "Yes, Sara spoke of Muallah as a man who treated Sufi as a toy. Sufi loved him. She worshiped him."

"Muallah worships himself," Lucy said slowly. She typed quickly. "He had sex with her as a gift to her before killing her, didn't he?"

"Looks like it to me," D'Arnot said. "This is a very dangerous man, I think."

"I think so too," Lucy said. She looked with new eyes at the file on Fouad Muallah. "I think so too."

Colorado Springs

"Detective," Doug Procell said in tones of relief. His face was thin and white and miserable. He looked like a handsome vampire two kills short of a full meal. He stood in his doorway and regarded Eileen. He was wearing sweats, the Gamer off-duty uniform, it seemed. His were gray, and looked old.

"Can I come in and talk?" Eileen said. "I'm too damn tired to haul you in."

"Yes, of course, I'm sorry," Procell said, still looking at Eileen with a relieved expression. He swung open the door and nudged a golden retriever back with his bare foot.

"Back, Cherry," he said. "Go lie down." The dog pressed against his foot and wagged its tail, looking at Eileen with shining happy-dog eyes.

"I like dogs," Eileen said mildly. "It's all right."

Cherry didn't jump on Eileen as she entered. The dog sat in her path and put up a paw, wagging its tail. Then it switched paws. Eileen gravely put out a hand and shook the paw.

"Nelson called me last night, after the police called. He said to stay home today. I don't think I could have gone to work anyway," Procell said. "Do you want some coffee?"

"No coffee," Eileen said, and patted Cherry on the head. She followed Procell down a hallway and into a sunny living room. The newspaper spread over the floor in untidy piles. Cherry immediately headed for a bright band of sunlight, her tail wagging. She flopped down in the sunlit section and gazed back at Eileen.

"She's happy I'm home," Procell said.

"How about your wife? Kids? Are they home?" Eileen knew they weren't, just by the empty-house feel of the place.

"Janet, she's at work. She's an attorney. And Martha is in day care. I had Jan take her to school anyway; I wouldn't be able to think about taking care of her today. You sure you don't want coffee? How about some breakfast?"

"Well, breakfast you could interest me in," Eileen said, and shrugged off her jacket. Her shoulder holster was clearly visible, but Procell seemed more relieved at the sight than discomfited.

"Okay," Procell said. Unexpectedly, he grinned. "I'll fix you a good breakfast and then you won't arrest me. Isn't that how it works?"

"Depends on the breakfast," Eileen said. Procell went into the kitchen and Eileen took a seat at the bar. Cherry abandoned her place in the sunlight and walked over to Eileen. She nudged Eileen's hip with her nose until she reached down and started to pet her.

"Cherry's a big baby," Procell said, opening the refrigerator. "She loves being petted. I think I could eat something now." He set out eggs, cheese, and a package of what were obviously homemade tortillas. "Huevos be okay? I make them spicy."

"Good huevos rancheros might keep you out of jail," Eileen said, and turned so she could rest her back against the wall. She closed her eyes, her hand smoothing the dog's silky head, enjoying the sunshine.

"You don't think I did it, do you?" Procell asked, cracking eggs into a bowl. His voice was sounding less pinched. Eileen suddenly realized why Procell was happy that she was here. Procell felt safe. Procell wasn't afraid of being arrested. He was afraid of being murdered.

"No, I don't," Eileen said. "But I don't think it was your conspiracy, either."

"You don't?" Procell asked in surprise. "I would think that would be certain now."

"Why?"

"Well, because Art was murdered. Why Terry and Art both?"

"Why don't you tell me?"

"I don't know." Procell was honestly bewildered. He started beating the eggs again. He added some spices and milk, and poured the mixture into a skillet. He got a bowl of refried beans from the refrigerator and set them in the microwave to warm, then opened a can of green chili sauce. He handed a block of cheese and a grater to Eileen, who took them and started working on the cheese. The kitchen began to smell delicious.

"All right, then, answer me this. How did a hired killer get clearance to come onto the base?"

Procell, stirring the eggs, stared over at her blankly.

"He'd have to have help."

"Exactly. How did the killer get under the floors?"

"Someone had to put him there," Procell said slowly. "I never really thought about it. If that's the case, then—Major Blaine!" He looked at Eileen with amazement. "It's Major Blaine! It has to be! He—he—"

"Hold your horses," Eileen said. "Major Blaine would be suspect number one in a conspiracy. But even Major Blaine couldn't get a new person on base without leaving a trail a mile wide. There is no trail. No one new came onto the base in the last two weeks, not anyone with a permanent badge. We checked on all the temporary types too, and they're all accounted for during the time of the murder. And what about getting Mr. Hired Killer out of the floor?"

Procell stirred the eggs and shook some chili powder into the skillet. His attention remained focused on the food. Eileen couldn't see his expression.

"I think I just figured whoever it was could do anything. But killing Terry like that . . . you know, it's not their style."

Eileen, still grating cheese, felt a chill. There was a pattern in the Procell file, and she'd completely missed it until now. The deaths were all automobile related. Not a single scientist whose obituary filled Procell's file had died of any other cause. Some were more bizarre, like the young Briton who had driven his car into a stack of gasoline canisters. Some were completely normal, like Harriet Sullivan's single-car accident on the highway. Procell, the author of the file, saw the pattern. Eileen hadn't.

Terry's murder, and now Art's, were completely out of pattern. What troubled Eileen was the feeling she was seeing the shadowy edge of something much larger than Terry or Art. If there was a relationship, it was too subtle to be seen. She still couldn't believe in Procell's conspiracy. But there seemed to be *something* going on.

"If they are separate, if they were murdered by another person, what will that do to my conspiracy members? That's what I'm thinking now," Procell said. He spread the refried beans over the tortillas and folded the eggs inside. He took the cheese from Eileen and filled the tortillas with the shredded cheese. Then he poured the green chili sauce on top and put the huevos into the oven to warm.

"This is going to be good," Procell said. "I mean, let's say we have Person X, who murdered Terry and Art. Then we have Organization Y, which has murdered a bunch of scientists on missile defense. What is Organization

Y doing right now? If Person X is some clumsy amateur, Organization Y may be revealed simply because X is out there. I hope this happens. You know that somebody is killing us."

"Maybe two somebodies. Maybe two groups of somebodies."

"So maybe Organization Y panics? Maybe they make a mistake. Like killing Art."

"So you're saying Terry was killed by Person X, for reasons unknown, so Y responds by taking out their next victim early."

"Right. Art Bailey. Smartest man in defense simulations. Breakfast is done. Want some juice? Milk?"

"Milk would be fine," Eileen said. She smiled wryly at Procell. "You get this detachment from your job, don't you?"

Procell looked at her in surprise. He was carrying the hot plates with two oven mittens. They were shaped like cartoon sharks.

"Detachment?"

"Yes. We're talking about murder, you know."

Procell put the plates down and went back for the milk. He flushed a little.

"Well, we're all used to talking about death. In the large sense. Casualties, millions of them. We put together this one briefing for a senator from a state I won't name. The bastard wanted to cut out our black funding. We showed him a War Game where a submarine from—" Procell paused. "Well, from a place. This sub launched a missile and took out one city. Los Angeles. We calculated the casualties. Deaths from the blast wave at ground zero. The overpressure drops exponentially as you move outward from ground zero. So some people survive, the ones quite a way from the blast and behind big buildings. You have hundreds of thousands who won't survive, blinded and burned. We showed him the graphs. Came up with a dollar figure. Every burn unit in the country would be filled by the ones who just might make it. Damn, we even calculated burial costs for the dead. Added up to our funding for five years. If we stopped one bomb, that would equal our funding for five fiscal years. Talk about cheap insurance. Bastard still voted to cut funding."

"You're used to death, in other words."

"Yeah, I am. Not so much my own, though. I'm not very brave. I've been sitting here all morning waiting for some Bond assassin to come through my door and tell me we're taking a ride." He gestured to the table. "Let's eat."

The meal was as good as it looked. Eileen dug in, relishing the taste of homemade food. She was an indifferent cook and didn't spend much time at home as it was. Procell was neat and quick.

"This is very good," Eileen said after half her tortilla was gone. She felt more tired but better able to handle it. A quick nap in the early afternoon and she could go all night. She would have to.

"Thanks. I'm glad you came over. Not just because I feel safe. But because I want to help."

Eileen straightened in her chair at that. "Art wanted to help, too," she said grimly. "I think he figured out something. And I think that may be what got him killed." She told Procell about seeing the lines "Found" before the screen went dark. She did not tell Procell any other details.

"Found," Procell said slowly. "Art must have thought about something. I don't know what he did. It was the computer, you said, not the video-tapes?"

"The computer terminal. That's what said 'Found.'"

"Well, maybe he did," Procell said. "If so, then perhaps my Organization Y is sitting tight, maybe even going underground."

Eileen kept from sighing by taking a mouthful of tortilla. Procell was on a single track about his pet theory.

"That means we have Murderer X who has killed twice. Why? I can come up with all sorts of reasons why Organization Y would kill scientists. Money from powerful governments, political goals, even environmental extremists who want to keep mankind out of space. But why one murder? Why Terry?"

"Terry was a girl that made people hate her," Eileen said. She glanced at Procell, who was finishing his milk. Procell looked mild and innocent. "Why did you want to murder her?"

The shot went home so easily, Eileen felt ashamed. Procell paled instantly.

"Me? I didn't. You know I didn't!"

"I didn't say you murdered Terry. I just want to know why you wrote her code for her."

Eileen trusted her instincts. They weren't wrong this time. Procell looked as though he'd been punched in the stomach.

"Why—how did you know?" he said finally, after swallowing a few times. There was a green tint to his face. Eileen hoped Procell wasn't going to lose the excellent breakfast he'd just eaten.

"I found out. Terry couldn't have written good code. Not the stuff she magically started turning out. Why did you do it?"

Procell slumped in his chair. He put a hand over his eyes. Eileen leaned forward intently. What did Terry do to this man? She could still see the image of the young, defeated 'Berto in her mind. She could still hear the baffled hurt in his voice.

"She was blackmailing me," Procell said quietly behind the hand. "We went to the same college together. She knew she couldn't keep up on the project, but she wanted to stay on. I don't know why. Maybe because Game Days are so fun. Maybe she liked to walk around with all the military officers looking at her. I don't know why."

"What did she have on you?"

"I had a love affair with the wrong person," Procell said. He didn't meet Eileen's eyes. "She knew about it."

"A love affair? How could she blackmail you with that?"

"Security clearances are touchy things," Procell said wearily. "You have financial problems, you're out. You have relatives in some foreign country the government doesn't like this year, you're out. Anything in your past that could be a blackmail risk, and you're out."

Cherry wandered over to her master and nudged at his hip with her nose, hoping for a treat. Procell caressed her head absently.

"So what was her blackmail?"

"An affair with the wrong person."

"Stop stonewalling," Eileen said. Procell looked at Eileen's face and paled even more.

"You going to write this down? Could you not write this down?" There was naked appeal in Procell's voice. "This is my life you can ruin. Terry was the last one who knew. I thought I was okay once she was dead—"

He stopped. Eileen looked at him.

"I didn't, though! I would never. I'm—"

"So what was the blackmail?"

"I did her code for her," Procell said, looking at the carpet, "so she wouldn't let slip that I had an affair with a professor at college."

"A prof—"

"A male professor," Procell said, and looked at Eileen.

There was a silence.

"Oh," Eileen said. There didn't seem to be much else to say.

"I'm not even bisexual now," Procell said. "I think I got fooled into it for a while. I'm not one of those closet gays who marry and raise a family. I wasn't sure of my identity and so I experimented, and then I met Janet right after I graduated. That was it for me. I love her more than my life, Miss Reed. She's everything." Procell looked down at his hands as his voice broke. "She's everything. And we have Martha. If I were an attorney too, then it wouldn't be a big deal, maybe. But I'm in Defense. I'd lose my job in a snap. I will lose my job. They don't give gays security clearances, even if they aren't gay."

"That's a damn good motive for murder," Eileen said. She felt fresh outrage at the military, at the whole clearance system. Eileen supposed you could murder to keep your clearance, if it was that hard to keep. Although she wasn't quite sure. Murdering someone over a piece of paper? But Procell was the proof, sitting in a devastated silence at his own dining-room table. Nelson Atkins, with his pale freckled face. Major Blaine, with his endless report writing. The security clearance was the means of earning a living. Without the paper, the good life would be lost. Would someone do murder to keep from losing their livelihood, their job, their self-respect? Eileen didn't have to think about that one for long. And Terry knew the weaknesses of the people she worked with. What was Joe Tanner's Achilles' heel? How about Sharon Johnson? Nelson Atkins?

"If I was going to murder her I would have done it a year and a half ago," Procell said bitterly. "I haven't spent an entire weekend at home for almost two years because I've been doing two jobs. Terry never leaves late, she takes weekends and holidays, and she would smirk at me and flip her narrow little hand at me as she got into her coat and left, while my two-year-old daughter is being fed at home and I'm working on Terry's code. Writing her name instead of my own into the computer code! I wish you knew how that felt. Like painting a picture and having someone else sign their name to it. I would have done it long ago, if I was going to do it."

"She wasn't a good person, was she?" Eileen said gently.

"She was a monster. She's owned my life for the past two years, and now she's going to ruin me forever after she's dead."

"No, she won't," Eileen said impatiently. "What do you think I am?"

Procell looked up, and Eileen had to look away from the expression in his eyes.

"There's no reason to take any of this down unless you turn up as the murderer," Eileen said. "Sure you've got a motive, and you're still a suspect, but I don't compare notes with Major Blaine."

Procell put his head in his hands for a moment, his long fingers squeezing his skull through the thick handsome hair. Then he took a deep breath and sat up straight.

"Thank you," he said quietly. "I don't know how else to say it. Thank you."

"Don't thank me," Eileen said. "This was another lead that I've followed down to the proverbial blank wall. Should something break on this case, however, that points your direction, all the huevos in the world won't keep you out of jail."

"Yes, ma'am," Procell said, his voice light and dizzy with relief. "You won't. I mean, it won't. I promise. I swear it."

"I'm going to have to be going," Eileen said. She balled up her napkin and tossed it on the table. "I really appreciate the breakfast. If you think of anything—"

"I'll call," Procell said eagerly.

"Don't try anything, all right?" Eileen said sternly. "If your conspiracy group Y isn't out there, you know we have Mr. X. Or Miss X. Whoever it was, they killed Art."

"Yes, ma'am," Procell said, trying to look sober but failing. He was euphoric. Eileen felt chilled again as she walked to the door. Procell looked like a victim. The Gamers looked as if they were all marked for death.

•22

The Pentagon

"What's going on?" Lucy asked Mills. They were in one of the briefing rooms at the Pentagon, the one that was set up like a small movie theater. They'd been escorted there by a Navy lieutenant and asked to wait. That was an hour before. Lucy itched to be back at her computer, finding out more about Muallah.

"I don't know. The Chief told me I had to come over here, and bring you. He said he'd be with us but he's got something too hot to leave. I hope I'm not in trouble."

Lucy smiled wryly. What a total asshole Mills was.

"You want some cookies? I have to eat or I'm going to be sick again."

"No," Mills said nervously. Then he glanced over at her as she opened a package of chocolate-chip cookies. "Well, maybe one," he said.

The cookies made them both feel better, but the sugar increased Mills's nervousness. Lucy stretched out in the comfortable chair and closed her eyes so she wouldn't have to look at him.

"This has to do with the Missile Defense homicides, I'm sure of it," he said.

"You've been pushing me pretty hard on it," Lucy said, her eyes still closed. "Did you know Fouad Muallah has a master's degree?"

"The guy you think killed Tabor in Paris?"

"Yes," Lucy said, pressing her lips together to keep back a sigh. "He did his thesis on an eighth-century Islamic poet, who was supposed to be some sort of Arab Nostradamus or something."

"I wonder why they wanted to see us here at the Pentagon," Mills said worriedly.

"So this terrorist was interested in the Missile Defense system," Lucy continued, wishing she were talking to anyone but Mills. "Why? Why would anyone at less than a governmental level want access to that information? Missile defense isn't a terrorist kind of thing. You can't use it to bomb someone, or threaten someone. So why was he so interested?"

"I haven't done anything wrong," Mills said.

"I'm sure you haven't," Lucy said soothingly, suppressing another sigh.

"I decided to give you the homicide project," Mills said thoughtfully, his knees bouncing to the nervous tapping of his feet. "The DDCIA wanted me to give it to Felix, but I thought you'd be a better man—er, analyst for the job."

"Thanks," Lucy said, and looked over at him in surprise. Felix was only slightly younger than her retired fellow analyst, Bob. "So did you tell the DDCIA you gave the file to me instead of Felix?"

"I did yesterday. He didn't like it, and I don't know why."

"Maybe that's what we're about to find out," Lucy said. Mills stilled his feet with an obvious effort when the door opened.

"Admiral Kane," Mills said, leaping to his feet. "Steven Mills. This is Lucy Giometti."

"Hello," the Admiral said. There were lines in his face that were sagging with weariness, but the uniform was sharply creased. "This is my aide, Lieutenant Jefferson." Lucy and Mills nodded at Jefferson, whose face was impassive above the white of his uniform.

"So you're the girl who has the BMD homicide file," the Admiral said with a charming, grandfatherly smile.

Lucy, who was looking at his eyes, was not fooled by the smile.

"Yes, sir," she said politely.

"Any new developments on the case?"

"Not so far," Steven Mills said as Lucy opened her mouth. She looked over at Mills in amazement. Mills gave her a warning glance, as though to tell her to keep quiet and let him do the talking. Did he think she would suddenly turn into his little fifties mouse *now*?

"Except for the Fouad Muallah connection," she said smoothly, watching Mills's face flush out of the corner of her eye. "We believe he is the contact for Tabor's information, and probably his murderer."

"But we don't have proof for that, yet," Mills broke in quickly.

"And we're not sure why," Lucy said. "I'm working on some information right now, but that's as far as I've gotten."

"What about the local murders, then?" the Admiral asked.

"The local detective hasn't made any breaks in the case," Lucy admitted. "I don't have any information other than the police and autopsy reports."

"I hear you're quite an arrogant analyst," the Admiral said pleasantly, and for a moment Lucy thought she must have heard him incorrectly. Then she saw the glitter of his eyes.

"You hear right, I suppose," she said, and kept her face pleasant and inquiring. It took an effort. Behind Admiral Kane's shoulder she could see Jefferson, standing quietly. Her heart felt as if someone had just dumped a gallon of adrenaline into her system. She felt the beginnings of a completely unexpected attack.

"You're arrogant, opinionated, and I question your commitment to your job. You leave early, you always take lunch, and you never come in on the weekends."

"And I always get my work done," Lucy said, still calmly.

"I find that astonishing, considering the amount of hours you put in on the job."

"I find it astonishing that some people stretch an eight-hour day into a twelve-hour day without getting anything done," Lucy said. But she could feel her face flushing with emotion. She was itching to track down Muallah and figure out what he was doing, and her time was being wasted with *this*?

"Did you bring me all the way over here to chew me out? Don't tell me about commitment to a job, Mr. Admiral, *sir*." She tried to keep from spitting out the words, noticing Mills's white and desperate face and ignoring it. "Commitment doesn't mean spending time at work or brownnosing the boss. Commitment means applying your mind to your work, which I do. I can get my job done in forty hours, and I do. I love my job. But you can't destroy my life just because I love my job. You can't ransom my brain and my skills. You don't like my work, tell Steve to fire me. It won't even disturb my sleep." There was a silence in the tiny room. Lucy could see Jefferson's broad and delighted grin behind the shoulder of his boss. She tried to calm her racing heart. She sat down without permission and crossed her legs deliberately. She'd learned in a thousand family arguments that the most infuriating position to take was one of calm superiority. It worked on her brothers, anyway.

"You question *my* commitment?" she said, and closed her eyes as though she were bored with the conversation. She clenched her hands against the armrests of her chair to keep them from trembling. "You're the Missile Defense commander in chief and you've got fourteen dead scientists. Now you've got a dead spy. What are you doing about that? The same nothing you've been doing for years?"

The Admiral laughed aloud.

"Just checking, Mrs. Giometti," he said. "You're about to become one of a few dozen people in the world to know this particular part of history, and I wanted to make sure you were up to the task."

Lucy opened her eyes and saw the changed face of the Admiral smiling tiredly at her. He looked grandfatherly and kindly. Mills, at her other side, was still pale and shocked.

"What the hell?" she started, and Admiral Kane held up a hand.

"Let me explain. Steve Mills here is CIA to the core. He'll never leave. You might. You might walk out the door tomorrow, as you put it so succinctly. That's why we wanted Felix to have this file. You ended up with it." The Admiral threw a steely glance at Mills, who paled even further, although it didn't seem possible. "But what's done is done.

"I wanted to see what you were made of, Lucy," Kane said. "You aren't going to like what I'm going to say. You could damage national security by knowing this information, but you could damage national security by not knowing this information. So I had to decide."

He grinned at her, and she felt a reluctant and helpless liking for him.

"That's why they put me in this getup, to make these decisions. I'm going to show you something, and let you make your own decision."

"About what?" Lucy asked evenly.

"I've sent word to an Air Force captain named Stillwell. Alan Stillwell. He's the OSI officer that should have taken on this Schriever investigation. He'll be at Schriever tomorrow night, and he's going to take over the investigation from the civilian detective."

The Admiral looked calmly at Lucy. "He will be told to cover up the entire incident. No more waves. No news. He'll bury it as deep as every other homicide on this case. As of tomorrow night, the Schriever incident will be closed."

Colorado Springs

"Mrs. Bailey?" Eileen asked.

"No, I'm Susan. I'm her neighbor. Who are you?"

"Detective Eileen Reed, ma'am, Colorado Springs Police. I'm investigating the murder of Terry Guzman and Arthur Bailey." She held up her badge.

The one eye she could see through the chain on the door regarded her doubtfully. The eye looked at her badge, back at her face, then crinkled in what could be a smile or a grimace of worry.

"Come on in, then, Detective. Meg is here, and I think she's up. I fixed her some soup an hour or so ago, and she ate some of it."

The woman fumbled with the chain for a moment. The door swung open and a slender, lovely girl looked at her. Eileen blinked in surprise, then looked at the eyes again. The woman was in her forties around her eyes, and in her twenties everywhere else, from the boyish curve of hips to the curly black hair.

"I'm Susan Lazecki. I've been taking care of Meg since we found out. Come on in."

Eileen followed the girl—woman, she corrected herself—down a dark hallway and into another sunny family area. This one was scattered with toys and papers and magazines in an untidy mess. A huge gray cat was sleeping on a pile of laundry in a basket. Eileen looked at the clean clothes in the basket and got an uncomfortable image of Meg Bailey, worried, getting ready to fold laundry, setting down the basket to answer the phone call that would destroy her life.

Susan Lazecki turned around in the family room and regarded Eileen nervously.

"Please don't treat her badly."

"I just want to ask her some questions. I knew Art Bailey, Mrs. Lazecki. I was working on the murder of Terry Guzman when this happened."

That was the wrong thing to say. The young face with the old eyes sparkled with tears.

"Why couldn't you stop it?"

"I've been asking myself that question since last night at eleven-thirty, Mrs. Lazecki. I haven't had any sleep since the news came in. I still haven't caught the murderer." Eileen didn't like the taste of the words in her own mouth. She was tired and upset. She wanted to be Harben, seemingly capable of dismissing emotion when it interfered with her thought process. She sighed, and held out her hand.

Mrs. Lazecki regarded it, and her, and then shook Eileen's hand. Her hand was small, but her handshake was very firm.

"I'm sorry," she said. "I just—please don't hurt her. She didn't want to cry, and didn't want to cry, and then she let it go all at once. I haven't slept either, Miss—er—"

"Eileen Reed. Call me Eileen."

"Eileen. She got up an hour or so ago, and I fixed her lunch. And I—"

"Susan tries to protect me, I think," said a soft voice from the stairs. Eileen and Susan Lazecki turned to look. Meg Bailey stood at the foot of the stairs, dressed in dark sweatpants and a sweatshirt. Meg had brown hair and soft brown eyes and fair skin that was gray and lined with grief. She would be pretty, perhaps, with love and happiness in her face.

"I'll be okay to talk for a little while," she said, and let go of the banister to walk to the dining-room table. It looked like an effort. She sat down and gazed at Eileen. "I'll just sit here, is that all right?"

"Will you be okay?" Susan said.

"I'll be okay. Art talked about you, Miss Reed. He said you were working very hard on solving Terry's murder."

"Did he tell you why he went out to Schriever last night?" Eileen asked, taking a seat at the table. Meg's hands clenched on the tabletop.

"No, he didn't. He's the kind of man who gets up in the middle of the night when he thinks—thought—of something, and then off he'd go to work. He'd catch up on his sleep later. He—" Here Meg's voice scaled down to a harsh whisper. "We were reading, we'd put the kids to bed, and he stopped reading and looked at the wall. Then he got up and got dressed and kissed me good-bye, and then he went. That was it. Your other officer, Detective Rosen, he asked me this too."

"I'm sorry I'm covering the same ground," Eileen said. "I don't want to waste your time, but I wanted to speak to you personally. Also, I wanted to look at Art's office, if he has one."

Meg was already shaking her head.

"We don't have one. What could he bring home? We have the kitchen organizer, that's where we sit and do bills. Would you like to look through that?"

"I'd like to, please," Eileen said. "Detective Rosen already looked, though, didn't he?"

Both women nodded their heads at the same time. Eileen sighed. Well, she had expected that.

"Detective Rosen was just assigned to the case," Eileen explained. "He's good, and he'll give me a thorough report, but he might have missed something. At least, that's what I'm hoping."

"What are you looking for, Detective?" Meg asked.

"Something to tell me why he went out there. Can you remember anything different about what he did last night? Did he make a phone call, or did anyone call here? Someone had to know he went out there."

"He did make a call," Meg said, and scrubbed her hands across her face. She started crying but didn't seem to realize it. "I told the policeman that, too. He made it from the kitchen. Sometimes he calls Nelson to tell him he'll be going in. Sometimes he calls Joe, if he needs Joe to meet him there."

"Joe wasn't home," Susan said quickly.

"You know him?"

"He's a friend of the family," Meg answered for Susan. "Don't get defensive, Joe's been cleared. That's what the other detective said. Isn't that right?"

Eileen nodded. "I know he was in class. I'll be calling on him later to ask him about the case. Art made a phone call? Do you remember what he said?"

"I don't. I heard his voice in the kitchen, then he hung up the phone. Then he left."

"Was there something about the conversation that was different?" Eileen asked. "Think about every second. I know it's hard. But think. Did he talk for a long time? Were the tones of his voice angry, upset? Did he laugh at all?"

"Please," Susan began, but Megan Bailey held up her hand.

"Yes. I remember." She looked up at Eileen, and her expression was dazed, almost hypnotized. "He didn't laugh, and he wasn't upset. He spoke for a moment, then he hung up the phone. Even, measured tones. No life to them at all. Like—"

"Like he was leaving a message," Eileen said. "That was it?"

"Yes. Yes! He left a message. It must have been Nelson he left the message for. Or Joe."

"A message," Susan Lazecki breathed.

"The message might still be there," Eileen said. The tiredness was gone as though she'd received an electric jolt. "Wherever he left it. Did he dial more than one number?"

"No, just one," Meg said. "Just one." Her voice broke unexpectedly, and she bent her head down so Eileen couldn't see her expression. She felt a terrible pity for her, and a terrible anger. It was a hateful feeling, but she didn't think about it. There was no time.

•23

Black Forest, Colorado

Nelson Atkins lived in the Black Forest, a sprawling stretch of dense forest east of Colorado Springs. Sheltered from the prairie winds and set to catch the moisture sweeping from the Front Range, the Black Forest is a place of towering, thick pines. Eileen had been out to the Forest occasionally, and found Atkins's house without much trouble. The house was large but not pretentious, built to sit in the sun along a stretch of meadow. There were some pretty horses in the shade at the edge of the meadow, grazing contentedly.

Atkins opened the door when Eileen pulled up. He was in jeans and a T-shirt, the first of the off-duty Gamers to break the pattern of sweat clothing. Eileen caught an immediate strong odor of horses as Atkins shook her hand.

"Just got in from grooming. I asked Caleb to stay out and finish up."

"Your son?"

"Yes. He runs the horse business with me," Nelson said, and gestured for Eileen to enter the house. "We sell Appaloosas. My wife died three years ago. Cancer."

"I'm sorry," Eileen said automatically.

"It was quick. Caleb took over the business. I was planning to sell after Cassie died, but he convinced me to stay with it."

Atkins showed Eileen into a sitting room. There was dust on the cabinets and dead flies on the sills of the quiet room. Caleb loved the horses, but he didn't much bother with dusting or cleaning. Atkins was oblivious. He looked stronger in his own home, more in control of his environment. Eileen, watching the Game Day tapes over and over, developed an impression of the Game Director as a man uncomfortable with authority. A man who didn't want to lead. His handling of Terry Guzman's poisonous personality was inept. He was probably as oblivious to Terry's effect on his team as he was to the tiny dry carcasses of the flies on the sills of his home.

"Do you want something to drink?"

"Thanks, but no. I would like to look at your answering machine, if I could."

There was no reaction from Atkins except puzzlement. Eileen, who was braced for the guilty reaction she craved, relaxed in disappointment. She didn't see the other indication she was looking for either. She wanted to see Atkins going through the mental check—"Did I do everything right? Did I wipe the prints? Did I get rid of the tape?"—that Eileen had seen in a few people who'd later been found guilty of murder. There was nothing but puzzlement in the freckled face.

"My answering machine? I have voice mail, if that's what you mean. I don't have an answering machine."

"Did Art Bailey leave you a message, Mr. Atkins?" Eileen asked, leaning forward. Would every lead turn into this frustrating blank? "I have reason to believe he left a message for you, or for someone on the Gaming Team."

"I didn't get a message from Art," Atkins said. He grimaced and shook his head. "I checked this morning, I use the same voice mail for the horses as I do for work. There was nothing from Art. Why would he leave me a message?"

"Didn't he usually leave a message when he went into work for a late night?"

"Oh. Well, yes," Atkins said, his expression so lost and wandering that he looked stupid. Eileen remembered the veiled contempt that Art held for Atkins, and the way the Gamers looked to Art or Lowell instead of Atkins when they needed help.

"Why are you the Game Director?" Eileen asked neutrally.

"I was the Assistant Game Director when Paul Wiessman won the lotto," Atkins said promptly, and looked so unhappy Eileen nearly burst into laughter.

"He won the *lotto*?"

"Yes, can you believe it? I was supposed to be the assistant just for the last three years before I retired. I didn't want to lead the Gamers. That wasn't what I was supposed to do."

"Why didn't you turn down the job?"

"I was only supposed to have it for a few months. But the productivity was so high they wanted to keep me. I didn't do anything, or at least that's what I thought."

And that's why the Gamers wanted you, Eileen thought. You didn't do a thing and you didn't get in the way. A perfect manager.

"So the person before you retired when he won?"

"He was only thirty-three. I guess you could say he retired," Atkins said grimly. "He fishes a lot now, and rides dirt bikes for fun. The funny thing is, he got the job by default too. The Game Director before Paul was Karen. Karen somebody, I don't know. She was up and coming in the Defense Simulations world, built the team, hired Joe and Art and Doug."

"Then?" Eileen prompted. She was having a hard time keeping a grin from her face.

"Then she took a diving trip to the Bahamas," Atkins said. "She met a guy and fell in love and never came back. She sent her badges by mail. Can you believe it? Like a really dumb romance novel. Cassie used to read them all the time."

"Was he rich and handsome and French?" Eileen asked, seriously close to collapsing with laughter. She knew she was exhausted and that was affecting her judgment, but this was hilarious. Her mother liked to read those novels too.

"Well, rich and handsome. American. They run a dive shop. Joe's been down there for a vacation. Karen was supposed to be the first woman on the board of directors, she was that hot. And she threw it all away." Atkins shook his head, but there was no censure in his voice. He sounded glum and admiring at the same time.

"So you ended up with the job."

"I did," Atkins said, looking with a lost expression at Eileen. "I never wanted this. I thought we were doing all right, and then Terry was killed. Now Art. I'm going to resign. I'll lose some of my retirement benefits, but not all of them. It doesn't matter anymore."

Eileen thought Atkins looked like an old janitor who'd somehow ended up in the president's chair. He really wasn't management material.

"Can I check your voice mail, just to make sure?" Eileen asked. "I'll call Joe from here. I need to talk to him."

"He'll be at the health club," Atkins said immediately. "If he's not home. He works out when he feels bad. I've got the number. I've called him there before."

"Okay," Eileen said. "Thanks. You know, I think I'll change my mind about that offer of a drink. Do you have a pop?"

Atkins went to the kitchen to get Eileen a cold drink, and she shook her head. She'd check Atkins's voice mail and call Rosen to check on his progress, then she'd meet Joe. She scratched at her cheekbone and refused to think about how glad she was that Joe had an alibi for Art. She also thought about how Joe didn't have an alibi for Terry. Joe Tanner had one of the best motives for killing Terry Guzman, and that lead hadn't ended yet.

The Pentagon

"I think you'll agree with me after I've finished," the Admiral said.

"Agree with you?" Lucy said in a hoarse whisper.

"Agree with me. I'm going to have Jefferson here get us some supper. Lucy," Kane said, and his face became a grandfather's again. "Trust me. Eat something and calm yourself. It's bad for the baby."

Jefferson spoke up then, surprising both Lucy and Mills. "You better eat something. This is going to be hard enough as it is." Lucy saw Mills look at Jefferson with a frown, as though a servant had spoken up, and her rage came under her control as she felt the familiar wash of contempt for her boss.

"That would be just fine, Mr. Jefferson," she said. "I would like some supper. I didn't realize we'd be here so late."

Jefferson smiled at her with an echo of his boss's kindly twinkle. "I've got an order already in. Chicken and mashed potatoes. That's what I fed my wife when she was pregnant and feeling peckish. It will only take me a minute to get it."

The Lieutenant left the room, and Lucy turned to look at Admiral Kane. Her opinion of the old man inched higher.

"Young Jefferson will be taking my place someday, I hope," the Admiral said thoughtfully. "He's quite a brilliant young man."

Lucy knew the position of aide to a high-ranking officer in the Pentagon was highly sought. Even though the job was basically that of a servant, the mantle of command was almost inevitable. She wondered if Mills knew that, or if he thought Jefferson was merely a servant.

"What are you going to tell us?" she said. "Can't you just summarize it in twenty-five words or less so I can get home at a reasonable hour? After I've eaten your food, of course."

Kane smiled with his eyes. He understood she was offering a little olive branch, and he took it. Lucy felt a little better. Kane might be the kind of person she could deal with. But why would he bury the investigation?

"I'm going to show you a film," Admiral Kane said. "Ahh, Samuel. Supper."

The chicken dinner was in small bags, packed like lunch. But the paper bags were hot and smelled delicious.

"Let's get the film started," the Lieutenant said, passing out the bags to Lucy, the Admiral, and Mills. "I suggest you eat quickly. The first part isn't so bad. You won't be eating much later on."

"Are you feeling okay, Miss Giometti?" the Admiral asked, and this time the solicitude was real. Lucy felt sick with the swings of emotion in the room, but she wouldn't admit that. And the food did smell delicious.

"I'm feeling all right," she said. "I'll be all right."

"Good girl," he said warmly.

Lucy opened her divinely smelling bag of food. Lieutenant Jefferson started the film. He didn't dim the lights all the way, so she could see her chicken. She dug in.

Garden of the Gods, Colorado Springs

Eileen found Joe Tanner's car where he'd agreed to meet her. Garden of the Gods was quiet and still in the late-afternoon heat. The deep red of the rocks was paled by the sun. Eileen saw him as she parked her car next to his. He was sitting halfway up the slope of a rock, in the shade, in a white T-shirt and black sweatpants.

Eileen chunked the door shut and climbed the rock, the soles of her shoes gripping firmly. They looked like women's dress loafers, but they had the structure of running shoes, a recent invention that police were finding very useful. She found a flat place next to Joe and sat down. The shade was cool and good after the heat of the car and the sun. The rock gave a good view of the spires of the Garden, and the sprawl of the city beyond.

"This is a pretty spot," Eileen said mildly. Tanner turned his attention away from the view and looked at her. His eyes were red-rimmed. Lack of sleep? Tears? Eileen didn't know.

"Thanks for meeting me here," Joe said finally. "I don't think I could be inside right now. I didn't even go running. I've just been sitting here."

"I'm sorry about Art," Eileen said, and waited for the accusation. She should have found the murderer before now. She should have stopped this from happening. She turned her view to the drowsing city beyond the red-gold spires of the Garden and waited.

"He should have called you," Joe said surprisingly. "Art was all heart and brain and no common sense. He figured out who the murderer was, and the murderer found out."

"How do you figure that?" Eileen asked casually.

"Because he was killed at the Center," Joe said. "He was there at midnight and he was doing something. He told me about the tiles, by the way. I never thought of them either. Then Art must have remembered something else. I've been awake all night trying to think of what it could be. Whatever it was, he was on the right trail."

"I wonder," Eileen murmured.

"Oh, come on," Joe said harshly. "Don't try that Detective Columbo bullshit on me. Who do you think you're dealing with, a bunch of idiots?"

"I don't think I'm dealing with idiots," Eileen said steadily. "I haven't found the murderer yet, now have I?"

Joe surprised her with a deep and husky laugh, then turned his head away and coughed. He kept his head averted for a few moments.

"God, I miss Art," he said finally, turning back to her. "Do you think I did it? Killed them?"

"I know you didn't kill Art," Eileen said. "Unless you're not acting alone."

"Sure, one of Doug's conspiracy gang," Joe said. He blinked firmly a couple of times to clear his eyes. "Tell me. Why is it easier now?"

"For some, there's no feeling at all after a while," Eileen said.

"But not for you."

"No, not for me."

There was silence between them. Joe was looking at her curiously, and for the first time Eileen felt uncomfortable. He was really *looking* at her.

"Do you think there's a conspiracy?"

"I don't know," Eileen said, and shrugged her shoulders. This was getting nowhere, and she was finding herself increasingly aware of losing her grip on the conversation.

"Hey, I'm really hungry," Joe said. "Do you want to get something to eat?"

Eileen's stomach responded before she did; her last meal was the huevos rancheros at Doug Procell's house that morning. The growl was audible to both of them. Joe grinned, then laughed, and Eileen laughed with him. Nobody who laughed like that could be a vicious murderer, her heart insisted. What the hell was *wrong* with her?

"Come on," Joe said, getting to his feet and holding out his hand to her. "Let's get some food."

"I know a place near here called Joni's," Eileen said, getting to her feet and brushing off the seat of her slacks.

"Oh, yeah. Old Victorian House. I've never been there. I'll treat."

"That would be a bribe, Joe," Eileen said severely, feeling like bursting into very undetectivelike laughter. "It will have to be my treat."

"Okay," Joe said immediately. She had not taken his hand, so he dropped it reluctantly to his side.

"You first," Eileen said, and Joe immediately understood. He grinned sarcastically.

"Of course, Detective," he said, and turned to go down the rock. Then he turned back, and his face was so serious Eileen nearly took a step back.

"Don't trust anyone," he said. "I'm glad you don't trust me either. You shouldn't trust *anyone* until you find out who this is."

"That's what they pay me for," Eileen said with a confidence she did not feel.

"Okay," Joe said, and turned to make his way down the rock. "Let's take my car, so you can hold your gun on me while I drive."

Eileen didn't have to see his face to know that he was smiling again.

Mashhad, Iran

Muallah felt reborn as he bathed in the warm Arab water. The few hours of sleep had been deep and restful, and he woke humming with energy. He dressed quickly and rolled out his prayer rug for morning prayers. His prayer rug was an oddity, an ancient Persian weave that showed the mosques and towers of a city on one half of the design. Most Arab designs were abstract; the idea of representational art was considered sinful and an attempt to emulate Allah. This rug, which Muallah had found in Baghdad over twenty years before, was very rare. He knew at once that it was meant for the One of the Prophecies. The city over which he knelt every morning was the rebirth of the Arab Empire. Allah had promised this to him in return for his service and devotion. Muallah prostrated himself on the rug, facing Mecca, and prayed.

When he left his room the smell of good coffee filled the air. His team was awaiting him in the large central room. The coffee was untouched, of course, for he would have the first cup. They knelt, twelve men with faces all alike in their devotion, waiting.

"Allah be with you!" Muallah said with a broad smile. The men smiled back at him, except of course for Ali, who never smiled. "Come, let us share coffee and break our fast, and we shall begin."

"Do we leave today?" the helicopter pilot, Assad, asked.

"This afternoon," Muallah promised. The pilot nodded and chewed his lip. His craft was an old Soviet Hind, lovingly maintained. Assad was a worrier, however. He wanted his Hind to be perfect, and there was always something leaking or separating or wearing out.

"The helicopter is ready," Assad said stoutly at a raised eyebrow from Muallah. As soon as the coffee was over, however, Muallah knew that he would rush to his machine for last-minute preparations.

"The weapons are ready," Haadin said.

"We just need to know where," Rashad said eagerly, sipping his coffee.

"There is a silo outside a town named Turtkul, in Uzbekistan," Mullah said. He nodded at Ali, who unrolled the maps they'd carried from Paris. Ali held one half of the map and Rashad held the other. The small town of Turtkul was marked with red pen. "We should be able to fly there within a few hours." The men leaned over the map, their coffee forgotten in their hands. Muallah sipped his with appreciation, leaning back against the comfort of the richly embroidered pillows.

"Is it well guarded?" Haadin asked.

"These silos are nearly forgotten," Muallah said scornfully. "The rotting hulk of the Soviet Empire fills the air with its stench. There may be four, five soldiers at most. They won't be prepared for us."

"Mahdi," Assad said softly. Assad, the worrier. Muallah knew he was a weak team member—perhaps because he loved his helicopter so much. The worship in Assad's eyes was dimmer than that in the others. He loved his Hind, perhaps more than he loved Muallah. That was annoying to Muallah. But Assad and his Hind were vital.

"Yes, my son?" Muallah said gently, though Assad was at least a decade older than he.

"What do we do here, Mahdi? How does this fulfill the Prophecy?"

Muallah couldn't help himself. He was so filled with excitement and delight, so ready for action after years of planning and waiting, that he threw back his head and laughed. His coffee cup rattled on the tiny saucer. His

202 • BONNIE RAMTHUN

Chosen Ones smiled at his laughter, not knowing why he laughed but glad that he was laughing. Assad, too, smiled. But his eyes were dark and worried above the smile.

"My son, it is time," Muallah said. "All of you, it is time to know the whole plan."

Ali, who knew the plan, watched the other team members instead of Muallah. As Muallah explained his plan, Ali gazed from one man to another. His eyes were as expressionless as his face. If any faltered, they would not leave the room alive. Ali reached inside his pocket and caressed the coil of wire that always lay within.

There would be no turning back now, for any of them.

•24

Colorado Springs

Joni's was uncrowded, quiet, and cool. The house was left largely intact, with separate parlor, dining room, and living rooms. The walls were decorated in the fussy, crowded Victorian way. The tables were generous and the chairs comfortable. There were no more than two or three tables in each room. The air smelled of fresh bread and herbs.

As they stood in the front hall a tiny woman appeared from the back and smiled broadly at Eileen.

"Eileen!" she said, and held out her arms. Eileen grinned and hugged her.

"Joni, this is Joe Tanner," she said, and the woman looked sharply at Joe. Joe smiled politely. Joni was an old woman, with a network of wrinkles across a miniature face. Her eyes were bright and sharp. Her lined cheeks were rosy from cooking. She had small white teeth and a halo of white hair, held back by a girl's flowered headband. She was wearing a flowered dress and a calico apron, a childish costume that suited her.

"Joe," Joni said. "Eileen finally brings a man to my place! I celebrate. Sit in your usual spot, my dear, I'll bring your coffee. Would you care for coffee, Joe?"

"A big glass of water first?"

"Of course."

Joni whisked back down the hall.

"She's a good friend," Eileen said with a half-embarrassed smile. "She got robbed two years ago, and I handled the case. We ended up friends." She indicated the passageway with her hand, and Joe followed her into the dining room. There were four small tables, one in a bay window nearly covered with vines. Eileen sat down at the bay window table.

"This is really nice," Joe said. "It's like being underwater." The westering sun poured through the leaves, lighting the alcove with shafts of gold and green. The afternoon breeze made the shafts dance and flicker, moving through the open windows and stirring the napkins on the table.

"My spot," Eileen said. "Joni doesn't save it for me, particularly, but if I call ahead she will, and if it's empty it's mine. I come here for breakfast almost every Sunday."

Joni appeared and set down water and coffee, giving Joe another of the quick, birdlike glances.

"I'm fixing roughy with Jamaican sauce today, sound good? You like fish?" She addressed her question to Joe, ignoring Eileen.

"Fish would be fine," Joe said.

"Good," Joni said abruptly, and vanished.

Eileen poured cream from a tiny porcelain pitcher, stirred her coffee, sipped it, and sighed in pleasure.

The Pentagon

The film Lucy Giometti was watching was produced in the same television studio where Eileen Reed was spending so much of her time. The film was professional and crisp, with the flavor of a documentary. The narrator had a deep bass voice, soothing and beautiful.

"The so-called Star Wars program was canceled in the mid-eighties," the narrator said. "But the new Ballistic Missile Defense program was born out of the ashes, born in secret and built under the blackest program since the Manhattan Project."

Somehow the dramatic words sounded just right in that buttery-rich voice.

"The President had made his decision," the narrator said. "The Missile Defense program would not be canceled. The following film is from a test made a little over a year after the public cancellation."

The view switched to an object in space, shiny as a tin can and shaped vaguely like one. Lucy wondered how large the object was, since there was nothing to compare it against. Then an arm came into view, the arm of the astronaut who was operating the camera. The object was tiny, Lucy realized. It was smaller than the astronaut.

"This is a Brilliant Pebble," the narrator said proudly, sounding like a father introducing his son, the doctor. Lucy grinned around her chicken.

The Pebble floated above the huge blue curve of the planet.

"Man, look at that little sucker," the astronaut-cameraman said in a Dallas accent. "She's so tiny. You gonna do this test, or am I gonna float on my ass out here all day?"

The Pebble responded by unfolding her delicate eyes. The goggles turned toward the astronaut, and he burst into delighted laughter as the Pebble appeared to wink at him.

"Wiggle that fanny, honey," the astronaut said, then laughed again as peroxide jets squirted out and made the little Pebble appear to dance back and forth.

"Could you can that, Major?" an irritated voice said over the communications link. The astronaut's body floated upward a few inches; he had shrugged inside his suit. The Pebble turned slowly until it faced the blue earth beneath it. The goggle eyes continued to scan back and forth, steadied by tiny bursts of peroxide jets.

"Beautiful," the astronaut murmured.

"We have Brilliant Pebbles," the narrator said. "The BPs are loaded with command software. They can destroy ballistic missiles in flight much like the Patriot missiles destroyed incoming Scuds during the Persian Gulf War."

"I heard the Patriots actually weren't very effective," Mills said.

"Disinformation," Lucy and Jefferson said at the same time. Lucy smiled at the aide, and he grinned back. She knew there was something fishy about those pooh-pooh reports after the war was over. She watched CNN every night and saw the missiles getting hit by Patriots. Somehow she couldn't make herself believe all the reports about how they "didn't really work very well."

"The Patriots had to be discredited or foreign governments might become suspicious about our 'canceled' Missile Defense program," Jefferson explained to Mills.

206 • BONNIE RAMTHUN

"We also have ground-based missiles much like the Patriots, even more powerful than the original missiles, capable of destroying a delicate reentry vehicle in flight and rendering the incoming missile harmless," the narrator continued.

There was another shot, this time one familiar to Lucy from her memories of the Persian Gulf war; a hissing, screeching missile launching itself skyward from a rack mounted on some sort of truck, and then the spectacular fireworks as the missile hit something in the sky. Lucy began to nod as the narrator continued, discussing the plans for the future installation of Patriot-type missiles around American cities.

The end of the documentary showed another shot from the Shuttle. The earth floated before them, blue and white and pure. For a moment the image held, and then it faded. Lucy couldn't take her eyes from the earth. It was heartbreakingly pure and beautiful. The image faded and the President's image appeared.

"I may not be the President now," he said. He was correct; he'd left office at the last election. "But what we Americans have is a great thing. We can stop a nuclear missile from destroying a million innocent people. No country knows that we can do this. Most Americans don't know that we can do this. But now you know."

The President leaned forward, and seemed to be looking directly at them.

"Your heart should be full of pride at your people, your countrymen and -women who made this possible. We have to keep funding for the shield. For all our sakes. For all our children's sakes."

The screen held on him for a moment, then went dark. Lieutenant Jefferson went to the back of the room and the lights came up.

"This is shown to senators and representatives, isn't it?" Lucy asked Admiral Kane. He was looking at her with sad eyes.

"Yes, it is. Any congressman who wants to get feisty about 'black project' defense spending gets a little trip to this theater. The members of the Armed Services Committee have seen this film. We get our funding."

"Why isn't it made public?" Mills asked in bewilderment. "I don't understand. We could be heroes to the whole world."

"The world is much less peaceful now that the Cold War is over. Nuclear weapons are in a lot of hands that I don't even care to think about."

"The shield works partly because few hostile countries know we have it," Jefferson explained. "Once they knew, they'd start figuring out ways to defeat it. Since they don't know . . ." He shrugged.

"I see," Lucy said. She was beginning to see, and she didn't like the direction her thoughts were heading.

"What about hand-carried nuclear devices—you know, like truck bombs?" Mills asked. "What good is the system against those?"

"Carry a nuclear device in a truck for a week and see how much hair you have left," Jefferson commented with a small, cynical smile.

"If a truck bomb could be nuclear, there probably would have been one by now," Kane agreed. "We're still worried that someone will figure a way to shield a bomb and transport it and set it off, but the logistical problems are intense. Governments are more likely to use a nuclear device and they are most likely to use airborne methods of delivery."

"Airborne," Lucy murmured.

"Can't other countries see the Brilliant Pebbles?" Mills asked.

"Oh, you mean with telescopes?" Jefferson smiled. "A Brilliant Pebble is tiny. Each one is about as big as a medium-size dog. Space is big. We can't even track them on our radar systems; we see them through radio signals that they send to us."

"Dogs," Lucy murmured.

"Doberman pinschers, more likely," Admiral Kane smiled at her. "Watchdogs."

"If the Missile Defense homicides case goes public," Lucy said slowly, feeling a taste like something terrible in her mouth, "then the whole project could be hauled into the light of day."

"Exactly, my dear. Which is why you are here today. Which is why we have to haul this project back into the black. We are dangerously close to breaking on this Schriever incident. If this police detective isn't taken off the case, she might discover our other problems."

"Our other problems," Lucy said. "Our twelve other problems. Our twelve dead problems. And the spy."

"They are twelve. We've got the life of the whole human race at stake here," Admiral Kane said, but he didn't sound pleased. "I don't like it either, but we have to continue down this course. We're not just Americans here, we're human beings. We could save New Delhi from a conflict with Pakistan. Or Seoul, South Korea, from an attack by North Korea. Our path was set by others, but we still have to follow it. We invented nuclear weapons, and now we are going to stop them from being used. We have to keep the secret."

There was silence in the little room. Lucy nodded finally, her shoulders bowed.

"I understand," she said in a low voice. "I agree, Admiral Kane. I'll let the Schriever case be buried as completely as all the other cases." She looked up at him. "But Fouad Muallah may be a bigger threat than we know. I would like permission to continue working on that case."

Admiral Kane considered, and Lucy's fingers clenched the armrests of her chair.

Then he nodded, and she heaved a sigh of relief.

"I trust your discretion, Lucy," he said.

"Thank you," she said. Even with that small victory, the taste was terrible. Those poor people out at Schriever. She was going to have to find a bathroom after all, it seemed.

"May I go now, please?"

"Of course," the Admiral said. Jefferson leaned toward her and spoke quietly in her ear. He was telling her the directions to the ladies' room, she realized.

"Thank you," she murmured to him, and gathered her bag.

She made it to the ladies' room with seconds to spare, but at least she hadn't lost her dignity by running.

Colorado Springs

For a space of time, in the green underwater light, nothing of blood or murder existed. Eileen asked Joe about his childhood, where he had grown up, what he had done as a little boy. Eileen loved to listen to people talk about themselves. Joe Tanner, not surprisingly, talked a great deal. Eileen had learned years before that her delight in listening to people's stories was extraordinarily useful. *Everyone* liked to talk about themselves.

Joe talked about his summer car trips, the swimming lessons, bright sunny days. His family was very poor, but all the children worked their way through college. His sisters and brother were all very close. He loved computers, loved the relentless logic of them and the satisfaction of making them work. He was a computer nerd with an athletic bent. He refused to turn pale and doughy like his other computer friends.

Somehow Eileen found herself, during the main course, explaining about growing up on her parents' ranch, near Devil's Tower in Wyoming. Her school years were spent farmed out in the Smithsons' family home in Belle Fourche, South Dakota. She told Joe how it was to wait through that last week of school, both dreading and longing for the day when she could be home with her mom and dad.

"No brothers or sisters?" he asked.

"No," she said. "A brother I never knew. He was only a few months old when he died. A heart problem, my parents said. That was before I was born."

"I'm sorry," Joe said. "Your parents must have been very happy to have you."

"They were, really," she said. "They never clutched, as you might've supposed after that. Just let me be. I was lonely for a brother or sister, I think, but it didn't really matter."

"Where are they now?"

"My parents? On the ranch, of course. They're only in their sixties; they still run over a thousand head of cattle on the land."

"Wow," Joe said, sitting back in his chair. "I didn't really think— Hearing your stories, I guess I had an image of *Little House on the Prairie,* you know, your mom in a bonnet or something . . ."

"Not exactly," Eileen said wryly. "They come to Denver once a year at least, for the Western Stock Show, and every few years they take a trip— Canada, Bahamas, England—for a whole summer. They like to travel."

"You didn't stay and be a rancher?"

"I joined the Air Force. I wanted to fly, I thought, when I would see those contrails and hear the jets in the sky."

"Why didn't you stay in?" Joe asked.

"I quit," Eileen said. "I flew A-10s—warthogs, they're called, ugly and fast. A friend of mine—"

"Well, hello," Joni said behind them, and poured more coffee. A silent busboy whisked away their plates. "Dessert, you must have dessert. Let me show this charming young man my very best."

"Dessert, of course," Eileen said, smiling at Joni and mentally shaking herself. The idea was to get Joe Tanner to talk about himself, not to listen to herself babble.

"What about your friend?" Joe asked.

"Oh, nothing," Eileen said, too brightly. "That's way in the past now. So how did you get this job at Schriever?"

Joe looked at her and grinned insultingly. "A poor segue," he said. "You're not supposed to be that obvious, Columbo."

Eileen had to smile back. "Caught red-handed," she said.

Joni came by after they'd eaten their flaky pastries. She brushed a kiss against Eileen's cheek. "On the house, my girl, today," she said. "Come back anytime, and bring this handsome devil too," and she smiled at Joe.

"You get your meals free there?" Joe asked as he held the door for Eileen. The summer night was upon them, rich and warm. A few bugs beat their wings against the porch lights.

"Not always. Not so often that I expect it, just enough so it's a treat."

"What favor did you do? You said she was robbed?"

"She was robbed and beaten and raped, Joe," Eileen said. "And I caught them, and talked her into testifying, and they are in prison for a long, long time because I did everything right. I got the paperwork all filed and I got Joni to have pictures taken of her in the hospital and I didn't violate any procedures. I won one, that time."

Joe put his arm through hers and hugged it against him. He didn't look at her. "I'm glad," he said. "I'm glad you won that one."

When his headlights lit the small dark shape of her car, she felt regret that the drive hadn't been longer. The Garden of the Gods was very dark, and the monoliths loomed over the narrow asphalt of the road. Joe got her door and took her hand to help her out, and for a moment they stood, listening to the crickets.

"Look at the stars," Eileen murmured. They were brilliant, made more visible by the stone spires blocking the light of the city around them.

"Let me follow you home," he said at last, dropping her hand with a regretful little squeeze.

"You don't have to do that," she said sharply.

The fizz abruptly went out of the night. Joe blinked and dropped his head to look at the ground. He rubbed his hand across his forehead.

"Well, that was a dumb thing to say," he said sadly. "I forgot everything. I just wanted to make sure you got home safely, that's all. I'm sorry."

"That's all right," Eileen said. She felt as sad as Joe looked. Under other circumstances . . . She held out her hand. Joe shook it warmly and tried on a version of the sunny grin he'd had earlier.

"Maybe when this is all over we could try another dinner," he said.

"That's a promise," Eileen said. She knew Joe Tanner wasn't the murderer. She knew it with all her heart. But she still waited until he had driven out of sight before starting up her own car.

•25

Ted Giometti held his wife and thought passionately about murdering that skinny WASP pipsqueak, that washed-out pale-eyed rat-faced creature, that Steven Mills whose headstone he would deface after he was buried, whose entire family he would . . .

"I can't tell you why," Lucy sobbed, grinding her flushed face against Ted's shoulder. His shirt was already damp from the flood of her angry tears. "I can't tell you why. I—" Here she broke down again, crying out her rage and striking at her husband's solid chest with her fists. Ted was not a huge man, but he was strong enough. He scooped up his pregnant wife and carried her to bed, managing not to stagger. He knew he wouldn't be able to do that soon. She'd weigh more than he did if she kept up her weight gain. He laid her on the bed and gathered her up in his arms.

She cried for a long time, long enough that he became worried. They were Italian Americans, he and Lucy, and their culture knew about grieving. Italian men didn't hold back their emotions, didn't absorb the poisons of grief into their system. Leave that to the pale WASPs like Steven Mills. Ted comforted himself with imagining Mills stumbling around his house, clutching his chest or his head as the heart attack struck or the aneurysm burst in his brain, blood flooding from his mouth and ears. Lucy's crying tapered off and finally stopped. Her breathing slowed and her body relaxed. She'd wept it out. She slept.

Ted held her, glad that she was all cried out. He kissed her damp forehead and slowly extricated himself from her sleeping grasp. He'd wake her in an hour, after he'd fixed some good pasta for her. After her cry, she'd be famished.

He paused at the door and looked at the rounded sleeping curves of his wife. Then he turned away to make his way to the kitchen and start supper.

Mashhad, Iran

A decade ago, Ala-ad's report would have been painstakingly typed, photographed, and mailed through various tortuous channels until it reached Langley, Virginia, weeks after it was written. Even after it reached the CIA, an analyst might never look at it; there was always too much data and too few analysts.

That was before the Internet. Ala-ad's boxy IBM computer had a pitifully small processor and a painfully slow modem, but for Mashhad he was far ahead of the times. Ala-ad used his computer to run his business accounts, print out his employee paychecks, and keep track of his aircraft fuel. He sold all types of aircraft fuel at the Mashhad airport.

Ala-ad typed his reports with two fingers. He had only two fingers on one hand, three on the other. His fingers were the least of his losses during the Iran-Iraq war. His wife and son were dead, used by the Ayatollah as human shields during the most desperate years of the fighting. Ala-ad should have been grateful to dedicate his wife and son to the glorious Ayatollah. He was not.

Ala-ad had some funny ideas for an Iranian, ideas that his wife, an Oxford graduate, had filled his head with during the short, sunlight-filled years of their marriage. The idea that all men are created equal, that Ala-ad should be able to have life, liberty, and the pursuit of happiness. These goals were reconcilable with the religion of Islam, Ala-ad knew. In fact, the Prophet Mohammed himself was the originator of the concept that each man is his own religious leader, not a sheep in some leader's flock. Somehow through the centuries Mohammed's ideas had been corrupted. Ala-ad had lost his wife and his child because of that corruption.

He sent reports that might be interesting to the CIA not because he had any real hope that Iran might someday be an Islamic democracy, but because it was something to do to pass the time until he could join his Liah and his beautiful little boy, Adda. There wasn't much in Ala-ad's idea of the future. That had ended with Liah.

Today he wrote about Assad and his precious Hind. Assad was worried that they would get shot down over Uzbekistan as they tried to take over some old Soviet silo. They were going to stage some sort of terrorist event, Ala-ad figured, but Assad didn't come right out with the plan. Assad loved his Hind and was worried he would have to leave it behind if there were no fuel reserves at the missile silo.

Before Ala-ad finished his report, he wrote down all the names Assad had mentioned, as he'd been trained to do by his dead wife's Oxford professor who had, in turn, been trained by the CIA. Ala-ad wrote down the names he remembered: Rashad, Ali, and the leader, Fouad Muallah.

Ala-ad sent his report via modem to a number in Tehran that was actually a rerouted number to Berlin. The Berlin office forwarded the electronic report automatically to Langley, Virginia, where it joined hundreds of thousands of documents from around the world in the huge databases of the CIA computers.

Within the computer Lucy's search engine was still running, looking for information about George Tabor, missing dogs in Paris, and the name Fouad Muallah.

Colorado Springs Investigations Bureau

For an entire morning, like a child stuck with homework during a beautiful day, Eileen sat at her computer. She was in Harben's office at seven-thirty, and from eight o'clock until noon she was embroiled in paperwork. Rosen briefed her on his investigations the night Arthur Bailey was murdered. Could it have been only a day ago? Eileen felt the sense of time slipping away. She was nearly frantic by the lunch hour.

"Everything we need is here," Rosen said sensibly. "You wouldn't learn anything more by driving out there."

"I haven't spoken to Sharon Johnson again," Eileen said, rubbing at her temples and glaring at Rosen. He was easier to glare at than Harben, although he seemed to be as unaffected by her impatience.

"Why would you need to speak to her?"

"Well, look at my notes. Every single damn one of them hated Terry Guzman. Every one of them had a good reason to wish her dead."

"How about Lowell?"

"Lowell particularly. Maybe he knew about 'Berto. Jealousy?"

"Could be," Rosen admitted. He was sitting across from Eileen and his long legs were propped up next to the keyboard. He wore sensible dress shoes that, like Eileen's, were actually running shoes. "But we have no indication he found out. You want to go talk to him? He's not out at Schriever today."

"No shards of metal found anywhere," Eileen muttered, changing the subject.

"No shards. No blood on any clothing in any of the Gamers' houses or apartments."

"Did you read the autopsy report from Rowland? I skimmed it, but I didn't see anything in particular."

"I didn't see anything either," Rosen admitted. "Nothing that would point a finger toward the suspects. I skimmed your Procell file, too."

"And?" Eileen prompted. Rosen had fallen silent. His face was turned to the windows. The massive flank of Pikes Peak showed the shadows of the first of the afternoon thundershowers.

"In my opinion they are murders," Rosen said flatly. Eileen was surprised.

"Really?"

"Yes, really," he said, and shrugged. "Nothing we can do about them. I don't think they're related to Guzman or Bailey. This case doesn't fit Procell's pattern."

"But you think they're related to each other."

"Yes," Rosen said. He glanced over at Eileen. "Nothing we can do. Scientists are being murdered in the Defense Department, and if the Defense Department chooses to do nothing, that's their business."

Eileen felt chilled. She'd removed all references to the Ballistic Missile Defense program before she'd placed the file on disk. The file was unclassified now, but what would Rosen have said had he seen the complete set of information?

"What we need to do is solve these murders, is what you're saying," Eileen said. "Do you know the OSI is going to be here in two days? I'd bet you my pension there will no longer be an investigation in two days." She ran her fingers through her hair. "We can't let that happen. We just can't."

"Well, that may be," Rosen said. "And may not be. Right now I think we need to blow off some steam and think things over. How about blowing away some targets at the range?"

Eileen glared at him for a moment more, then sighed and grinned.

"Lead the way, Ros," she said. "That sounds like heaven to me."

Central Intelligence Agency, Langley, Virginia

To Lucy, Fouad Muallah was like an itch between her shoulder blades, an itch she couldn't reach. The thrust of Muallah's master's thesis was an attempt to prove that the prophecy of al-Hallaj had not been fulfilled by the collapse of the Ottoman Empire. His thesis wanted to leave the reader believing that the prophecy was yet to be fulfilled.

Lucy picked up a sheet of paper. She'd printed out the poem just so she could look at the words on paper.

Prophecy is the Lamp of the world's light;
But ecstasy in the same Niche has room.
The Spirit's is the breath which sighs through me;
And mine the thought which blows the Trumpet of Doom.

Why was this poem important? What connection did it have to the Ballistic Missile Program? If only she knew what George Tabor had carried to Muallah. The information was somehow vitally important; Muallah had not only killed Tabor, but also his Parisian girl Sufi. He no longer had a base in Paris, and that obviously didn't matter anymore. Charles D'Arnot had no further information for her. Wherever Muallah had gone, it was beyond the bounds of the Paris police.

Lucy opened her food drawer and rummaged. Today her baby demanded beef jerky. She had six different kinds, every flavor the local 7-Eleven had provided.

"Teriyaki, is it?" she murmured to her baby, ripping a package open with her teeth. She'd never had beef jerky before today, until the person ahead of her in line at the gas station bit off a mouthful from a hunk of jerky he was holding. The pungent smell should have sent her to the bathroom. Instead, she'd bought every flavor she could find.

"Mine the thought which blows the Trumpet of Doom," Lucy said around a mouthful of jerky. There was something there, something that felt like cold fingers pressing along the bottom of her spine.

A cartoon police cruiser suddenly howled across her screen, tiny lights flashing, and skidded to a stop at the bottom of her screen.

Denver Animal Shelter

Fancy lay in her kennel with the sound of dogs howling all around her. She whined every once in a while, but she wasn't a howler. The kennel keeper, Debbie, was a stout young woman with short black hair. She fed Fancy and patted her on the head.

"I'm sorry your owner had to move away, Fancy," Debbie said as she hosed the kennel. "He was cute, wasn't he? What a pretty set of eyes, all that blue with those thick brown lashes." She sighed, rubbed Fancy's ears, then moved to the next kennel.

Later that day a puppy was adopted by a young boy. His parents stood and talked to Debbie.

"Good choice. Those pups are a good mix," she said approvingly.

"How big will he be as an adult?" the mother asked.

"He's a blue heeler mix. No more than forty pounds or so."

At closing time, Debbie walked down the kennel corridor and took away a German shepherd. Her face was set and sad as she walked the dog toward the back of the kennel. When she returned, alone, she hosed out the empty kennel and hung the leash on a hook by the door. She moved two dogs from an overcrowded kennel into the empty space. She turned out the lights.

Fancy stopped pacing. She lay down on the bare concrete and put her head on her paws. The silk of her fur was already getting matted and dull. Fancy, like Eileen, like Lucy, had only two more days to go.

Oklahoma

The Chinook developed engine trouble over Oklahoma. The pilots weren't happy about the performance of the new helicopter before they'd gone a hundred miles, but they weren't paid to be finicky. They had to have a reason to ground a helicopter that cost over a million dollars. To say "It just doesn't feel right" wouldn't do.

But the engines didn't feel right. They responded sluggishly in the thick Alabama air, and the pilots knew how helicopters did in the thin air of Colorado. In a word, terrible. Stillwell, in the back, had a sickening headache from the ill-fitting flight helmet. It felt as if a blunt drill were being ground slowly into his head. But taking off the helmet would be suicide to his eardrums. The noise of the twin-rotor helicopter was unbearable. Stillwell hung miserably on, unaware of the pilot's increasing nervousness.

Right around noon the oil pressure in the main engine sank. The pilot was paying very close attention to each gauge and dial in his complex aircraft. Things weren't right, and he was expecting trouble.

"Oil pressure!" he shouted over the comm link. "Autorotate!" He started the autorotation process. The autorotation of a helicopter consists of disengaging the rotor system from the rotor blades. The rotor blades can then spin free like the propellers of an aircraft. The free-spinning blades should provide enough lift to set the helicopter down, although roughly, in one piece. Stillwell, hearing the shout over his flight helmet's headset, clutched his flight bag to his chest and closed his eyes. Brightly printed on his mind's eye was the sight of two dead pilots whose autorotation system had failed. In that incident the controls of the aircraft were seized out of the pilot's hands as the rotor system locked up, ripped out of the bottom of the aircraft as the system disintegrated. There were blank looks of astonishment on the pilot's dead faces.

This time the autorotation didn't fail. The system disengaged and the ungainly Chinook dropped out of the sky and came to an abrupt, jarring landing in an Oklahoma field. Corn stocks rustled and crunched under the helicopter's landing skids. There was silence, and a series of rapid clicks as the pilots shut down their system.

"She'll be good to go in a week, I'd say," the pilot said cheerfully. "No systems are damaged." The copilot nodded and clapped the pilot on the shoulder.

"Damn nice landing, Richard," she said. "You okay back there, Major?"

Stillwell nodded, unable to speak. He still couldn't believe he was down safely.

"You wouldn't happen to have any shorts in that bag, would you?" the pilot said, unhooking his helmet and placing it on the floor of the aircraft. He turned toward Stillwell and climbed into the seat next to his.

"Let me take this off for you," he said, and as he removed the helmet Stillwell could hear him again.

"You have any shorts in that bag?" the pilot asked again, patiently.

"Yes," Stillwell whispered. His lips felt icy and numb. "Why?"

"Because I pissed myself," the pilot said.

"I'll borrow some if you've got three pair," the copilot said, removing her helmet and revealing a puglike, cheerful face. "I knew I should have worn my diaper today."

Stillwell looked out the windshield of the helicopter, and all he could see was corn. He looked to the sides, and when the three of them got out of the helicopter he looked to the rear of their landing, and in all directions the only thing he could see was unending rows of fresh growing corn.

•26

Turtkul, Uzbekistan

Muallah felt a lift of his heart as well as his stomach as the Hind swooped over a low, scrub-covered hill. Beyond was a stretch of barbed wire dotted with weeds. Within the fencing the huge concrete covers to the missiles looked like unfinished building foundations. There was one small building at the center of the six concrete pads, a building with clean white curtains and flower boxes outside the windows. The windows were clean and the building was freshly whitewashed. It looked like a farmer's cottage instead of a missile base command center.

But, of course, the command center would be underground. Muallah resisted an impulse to rub his aching forehead under the heavy Russian helmet. Flying in the Hind was exhausting. The noise was overwhelming, the seats were wretchedly uncomfortable, and the helmet was insufficient protection from the noise. He did not rub his forehead because he was Fouad Muallah, the Chosen One. His people needed to see his absolute confidence. And he was confident.

Muallah leaned forward and gave a thumbs-up to Assad. Ali, who was at the door of the Hind with his Uzi at the ready, nodded tensely as Muallah turned to him. He was ready. Rashad, at his left, was beaded with sweat and miserably pale. He'd been sick twice on the trip. Muallah nodded at him, and he squared his shoulders.

Below, Muallah could see two men leaving the house and running to the helicopter pad. They were pointing and shouting. Unbelievably, they appeared to be unarmed. Their uniforms were patched and well-worn, and one of the men had no hat.

The situation was better than Muallah had thought. These soldiers had made a home out of their missile silo. They were stranded by the decay of the Soviet machine, left behind as the old country was going through its difficult transformation. They probably had wives and children in the whitewashed cottage, vegetables planted around the missile silo caps. Muallah started to grin.

This was going to be easy.

Colorado Springs Investigations Bureau

"I need to talk to Sharon Johnson again," Eileen insisted to Rosen. The shooting range had been a fine distraction, but the day was getting along. The usual afternoon thundershowers were moving down Pikes Peak. "Maybe she'll give me some ideas. Then I need to talk to Lowell. After that, I'm out of ideas."

"I've got a request in to Major Blaine for the contents of Terry's desk," Rosen said. "I'd like to look through what she had there."

"That's something," Eileen said. "I'm going to make some phone calls."

She called Sharon Johnson and caught her just as she was leaving her house. Sharon was going to her Network class at the university. She agreed to meet Eileen after her class let out, at the Student Union. Eileen hung up the phone, glanced at her watch, and called Joe Tanner.

"Think of anything?" Eileen asked.

"Nothing so far," Tanner said. "How about dinner again? Nelson won't let any of us go back to work, and I'm driving myself crazy at home."

Eileen was astonished at the feeling of pleasure this gave her. It worried her.

"Come on," Tanner said soberly. "You can keep an eye on your suspect this way, can't you?"

"Six o'clock. I'll pick you up," Eileen said.

"Done," he said cheerfully, and hung up the phone with a crash. Eileen sat for a moment staring at her phone, then turned to see Rosen looking at her with his blank, impassive face. His Navaho face, she was beginning to think of it.

"A personal call," she said defensively. Rosen nodded without saying anything and turned back to his computer screen.

Oklahoma

"My goodness, look at you," the woman cried, and started laughing. "You're all sunburn and mosquito bites. You from that crash? What was that thing, anyway?"

"A Chinook helicopter, ma'am," Richard, the pilot, said politely. "May we use your phone?"

"Well, we don't have a phone this week since that tornado took out the lines. My husband should be back tonight around six o'clock. I would have come out to get you, but as you can see . . ." She gestured at her leg, encased in a bright blue cast. She was plain and brown-haired and young, with a handsome smile.

"But come in, come in," she said, and gestured them into the house. "I'm forgetting my manners. I saw you out there coming, so I've been cooking. I've got iced tea for you, and there's some fresh chicken I've done up myself. Tornado broke my leg and killed some of those blasted chickens. Proves some good comes out of every bad."

"How about some Calamine lotion?" Stillwell said ruefully, scratching, and she laughed her pretty laugh again.

"Plenty of that, too," she said. "Come on in."

Turtkul, Uzbekistan

Anna Kalinsk figured she might be a genius, although she could not be sure. She had finished only secondary school. College was a luxury beyond her family's reach or influence. She regretted that. Anna felt she would have done very well in college. Concepts and ideas that others seemed to have trouble grasping came leaping to her, complete and whole. Math was a joy to her in school. Literature wasn't much fun, since books were heavily censored. Now that the Soviet Union was Russia again, Anna had hopes that she might get her hands on some real books. Eventually.

She read her husband's Missile Command Center handbook more or less out of boredom. Soon he was coming to her for advice, though he never saw it that way. She made sure he never saw it that way. A merely smart woman would have made Dmitri feel uncomfortable at her intelligence. Anna was not merely smart.

Therefore, it was Dmitri's idea that the four wives move onto the base with their children. Dmitri divided up the underground into sleeping and living quarters, and put his wife in charge of turning the cottage into their communal living room and kitchen. Dmitri had a brilliant idea that they should grow a vegetable garden. Next year, Dmitri was going to have another great idea and build a barn. Then they were going to get some dairy cattle.

As long as the Russian Republic remembered them with monthly paychecks, Anna was happy to baby-sit the old missile silo. She knew there was no radiation danger to the children—not only had she read the Missile Command Center book, but she had a Russian's adeptness at reading between the lines. Only the open silos were dangerous. The little missile base was a fine place to raise her boys and grow her vegetables while the old Soviet Union slowly decayed. And, like her compost heap by her vegetable garden, she was sure the new Russian plant was going to be strong and fruitful.

Right now, though, the Russian Army was in horrible disarray. Many soldiers found themselves with no skills and no jobs, in a country that had only the most rudimentary idea of capitalism. Anna did not want that fate for her Dmitri or her boys. The new Republic realized the importance of keeping control of the old missile silos until they could be safely dismantled. Thus, Dmitri and his fellow officers received paychecks where thousands of soldiers did not. Anna was happy to live here in the middle of Uzbekistan, far from her Ukrainian home, as long as the money kept coming and they were left alone. Eventually the silo would be dismantled, but by then Anna was sure Mother Russia would be on her feet. Mother Russia, like Anna, was a survivor.

Everything changed for her in a single instant. She'd been doing dishes when the helicopter arrived. She was standing at the door of the cottage, wiping suds from her arms with her apron, when the chatter of the Uzi blew Dmitri backward. He had an expression of surprise and dismay on his dying face as he stumbled back from the open door of the helicopter.

Anna felt her mouth open in a soundless cry of denial and grief. Dmitri was dead. Her husband, full of sternness and unexpected laughter, putting on weight as he aged and developing a touch of gray in his hair, was dead. Dmitri was dead. Anna looked at the Hind and saw the patches, the faded Red Star on the side. All this while Dmitri was still stumbling backward and the Uzi was aimed at Serenko. Anna saw the black hair and the dark complexions, and all computations came together in a flashing instant.

"Downstairs!" she cried. Boris Berezovo ran to the doorway instead. Luckily the other women and the children were downstairs with their afterlunch stories. The little ones would be put down for naps and the older ones settled with books or quiet chores. Anna ran for the stairs and ignored the chatter of weapons fire that meant Boris had not listened to her and was now dead. She threw the bolt on the inside of the door and ran eight flights of stairs as though she were still a fleet-footed girl. The door would hold them for a little while. It was steel, and the bolt was good. But it wouldn't hold against a grenade. She heard the first bullet thumps booming down the stairs after her as she reached the bottom.

The door at the bottom of the stairs was also merely steel. Anna threw this door too, and bolted it. Dmitri, Serenko, and Boris, all dead. She had to tell their wives. She had to make the younger Boris, whom they all called Boriska, understand. Somehow she had to get everyone to a place the terrorists could not come. She knew where that place was.

"Anna!" The frightened face of Ilina peered around the corner of the Children's School, a long tube in the ground that had once held ordnance.

Boriska came running from the command center. Today had been Boriska's watch in the center. Anna felt a brief burst of hate for Boriska. Why couldn't today have been Dmitri's turn?

"What is going on?" he shouted.

"Listen to me," Anna panted. "We don't have much time. There are terrorists outside. They killed Dmitri and Boris and Serenko." Ilina made a grotesque face, her mouth pulling down and her eyes squinting shut. Her hands went to her hair and tugged as though she were going to pull her hair out by the roots. But she made no sound. Anna looked away. She had no time for grief, either.

Boriska went pale.

"They want the missiles?" he choked.

"I don't care what they want," Anna said. "We can get into silo number six, the empty one. We can bar it from the inside with a metal bar and they'll never be able to spin the door lock. All the grenades in the world won't break that door, either."

"I'll get the children," Ilina whispered.

"We have maybe ten minutes," Anna said, closing her eyes for an instant and visualizing bullets, grenade, careful negotiation of the eight flights of stairs, and another grenade or two. "Ten minutes."

"I will send out the warning," Boriska said stiffly. "It is my duty."

"Come to your wife, Boriska," Anna said. "Don't be a hero."

"I will come if I can, Anna," Boriska said. His face was ashen white, but he was not trembling. "Take care of my babies."

"I will, Boris," Anna said, and turned away. She did not look back.

•27

Central Intelligence Agency, Langley, Virginia

"I'd like to speak to Lieutenant Jefferson, please," Lucy said. Her fingers clenched the phone. Sweat beaded her hairline yet again.

"He's not at his desk right now. Would you like to leave a voice mail?" the voice said cheerfully.

"No, this is very important. Can you page the Lieutenant and tell him Lucy Giometti from the CIA would like to speak to him?"

"Well, all right," the voice said, not as cheerfully. "But you'll have to wait."

"I'll wait," Lucy said. She massaged her temple with her finger, switched the phone, and massaged the other one. She'd never felt so angry in all her life. She was sure Mills was feeling just grand.

Mills had refused to take her report to higher levels. It was too much of a leap, he said. The potential attack on a missile silo was not confirmed by any other source except an Iranian fuel clerk's gossip, he said. The idea that Muallah was going to attack an American city using nuclear weapons because of a poem written in 922 was ridiculous, he said.

Lucy had watched the smile bloom into a grin on Mills's face as her frustration became apparent. Her logic was infallible. The report from Mashhad fit in perfectly with everything she'd learned. But Mills was not going to take her analysis and use it.

Finally she realized why Steven Mills was grinning. He had her, finally, and he knew it. She could quit, she certainly could, at any time. Steven Mills had never been able to have power over her, the way he longed for power over his subordinates. Now Lucy had handed him a collar and leash. She desperately wanted to complete her case, and only Mills could do that for her. He finally had power over her, and he loved it.

"The report is interesting," he said, and pushed her report to one side of his desk. "We'll see if it's confirmed by additional sources."

"But—" Lucy bit off the words she was about to say. She stood for a moment, looking at Mills, and nodded slightly. "I see. Well, then, you have my report, Mr. Mills. I'll be getting back to my other work, then."

Mills looked at her suspiciously for a moment, then nodded. His grin was still there, though. Mills was having a great day. Lucy left to find the bathroom and throw up.

"Lieutenant Jefferson here," a voice spoke suddenly in her ear. Lucy started, lost for a moment in her musings over the horrible scene in Mills's office.

"This is Lucy Giometti, Lieutenant Jefferson," she said.

"Ah yes, Lucy," Jefferson said warmly. "What can I do for you?"

"I'd like to send you a small analysis I've done," Lucy said calmly. This might be the end of her career at the CIA. Lucy understood the risk of going around the chain of command. "Do you have a computer at your desk with on-line capability?"

"Of course," Jefferson said warily. "This will be encrypted, of course?"

"Of course. The key is—" Here Lucy thought for a moment. "The key is the word you said your wife was when she was pregnant. Remember?"

"I remember," Jefferson said.

"Are you at your desk?"

"I'm at my desk, Miss Lucy. This sounds important."

"It is important," Lucy said. "Desperately important."

"Then why isn't this going through channels?" Jefferson said sharply.

"Because channels are closed to me right now," Lucy said grimly. "My companion at our little dinner party is not interested in furthering my reputation, shall we say?"

"In the military world, this is a very dangerous thing to do, my dear," Jefferson said.

"This is my world," Lucy said, then winced at the arrogance of her remark. "Well, I mean—" Jefferson laughed in her ear, but it was a kindly laugh.

"You are very young," he said. "But I do like your style. So does my friend."

"Give me your e-mail address," Lucy said, typing in "Peckish" as the encryption code to her report. She typed in Jefferson's address rapidly and punched the Send button before she could change her mind.

"What am I supposed to do with this?" Jefferson said in her ear.

"Whatever you think you should, Lieutenant," Lucy said grimly. "Whatever you think you can."

University of Colorado, Colorado Springs

Sharon was waiting when Eileen found her way into the Student Union. The University of Colorado at Colorado Springs sat along the slope of a bluff. The buildings were the usual college mixture of old and new. The union was new, all glass and concrete, and was empty except for a few solitary students studying at the tables. Sharon was studying as well, but she put her papers neatly together and put her books and papers in her knapsack as she saw Eileen approaching.

"Would you like some coffee?" Eileen asked. "I was going to get a cup."

"Nothing, thank you," Sharon said. She was dressed in old black jeans and a long sweater, and she wore old squashy loafers on her plump feet. Sharon Johnson looked puffy and tired. A woman who was mourning. Eileen got a cup of deep black student coffee and poured half a cup of milk into the Styrofoam cup before the liquid turned a muddy brown. She sat down across from Sharon and took a cautious sip.

"I'm sorry about Art," Eileen said finally. Sharon blinked and nodded and looked down at her folded hands.

"Art's in God's hands now," she said. "I'm sorry you didn't find the murderer before, but I hope you still will. Arthur was a good man."

"I talked to Joe Tanner about Sully," Eileen said. "I found out about your mysterious coder, as well."

Sharon looked up in surprise and with the faint beginnings of a question on her lips. Eileen shook her head, and Sharon nodded immediately.

"I understand," she said. "I don't want to know. I hoped that would help you find—whoever it was. But it didn't, did it?"

"No, I'm afraid not," Eileen said. "I'm fresh out of ideas."

"You're not supposed to tell me that, Detective," Sharon said wryly. "I'm one of your suspects still, I suppose."

"Yeah, you are," Eileen said, and sipped her coffee. "I want to know something from you, and it's probably not going to be easy for you. So I'll start off by saying I don't think you killed Art."

Sharon nodded gravely and moved the loafered feet in a slight whispery sound on the tile of the floor. That was the only sound she made, although Eileen thought she saw a slight relaxation around the tired brown eyes.

"So you're off the hook, maybe."

"Thank you, Miss Reed," she whispered.

"Now I want to know what Terry had on you."

"Pardon?"

"I think I knew Terry. Perhaps better than any of you did. Better than Lowell did, even. She had to have something on everybody. I'll be talking to Lowell tomorrow; perhaps the only thing she had over him was his love for her. I'll find that out tomorrow. But every other Gamer had a reason to hate her. Tell me what she tried to do to you."

There was a period of silence. Eileen tried to keep her expression open and friendly and slightly pleading. She wouldn't threaten this woman.

Sharon Johnson sighed.

"Well, I'll tell you," she said. "I don't know what Terry did to the other Gamers. But she hated me. She hated me and she knew just where I was the most vulnerable, the little bitch." Sharon spoke the word with a total lack of passion that came off as somehow deadly.

"Where was that?"

"My children, of course," Sharon said. She looked at Eileen with black eyes that suddenly seemed even blacker. "She was trying to get me fired. Because of my work. I told you that the first day."

"I remember," Eileen said. "What did she do?"

"She knew I couldn't afford the Colorado Springs school. Not without this job. She knew I couldn't afford this school unless the government was paying for my classes. I have three children. I have to pay for my neighbor to look after them while I'm in class, so there's that money too."

"Why did she think she could get you fired?"

"Because I'm not that good, or I wasn't. I struggled a lot that first year. Sully, I thought she hated me. I didn't know how to think my way through the whole problem. I kept missing things."

Sharon looked down at her fingers, twined together, then spread her hand out and looked at it.

"I didn't know what a parameter was. It was a complete mystery. I didn't dare ask. I worked so hard, but I didn't know how to write a good program. Even Terry was better than me at first. They hired me because I talked Paul Wiessman into it. And my race helped, too," she said, and her mouth twisted bitterly. "I wanted to prove to everyone that I could pull my own weight."

"What is a parameter?" Eileen asked, smiling.

"A list of things you pass to a program," Sharon said promptly, and her grave look lifted for a moment. She smiled back at Eileen. "Like your program is going to sort fruit, so you run the program and you pass along an apple, an orange, and a banana. Those are the parameters to the program."

"I see," Eileen said. "You make it sound simple."

"Those are Art's words," Sharon said, and she blinked rapidly. "I finally asked, late at night. He came by and I was in tears. I don't cry easily. I knew I was beat. He sat down and flat out told me he was going to help me, and for me not to get my damn southern back up about it."

Eileen could see the vision Sharon presented to her. She could see the half-darkness of the empty office space and the weeping woman in the front of the blank face of the computer terminal. She could see Art's friendly expression and the simple explanation of apple, banana, orange.

"He tutored me for months," she said, and reached down to her purse. She blew her nose briskly on a tissue. "I started to get it. Before then, Terry didn't hate me. I wasn't worthy. People have to be beneath her, that's her kink. When I was the worst programmer on Gaming, she didn't notice me. Then I started understanding. Then the computer started to become a machine to me, not this living creature that hated me.

"Then Terry started making remarks about my work. My code. We'd run a test and she'd find some flaw with my work—that was easy at first—and she'd throw up her hands and declare she couldn't do her tests unless the product was stable, unless she had good code to work with. She'd be just loud enough. Lowell had a talk with me."

"Lowell talked to you?"

"He'd do anything she wanted, poor man. He loved her so. I can't imagine sleeping next to that woman. It would be like sleeping next to a nest of cottonmouth snakes. She'd talked to him about me, I imagine at home, and so he wanted to ask me about my work."

"What about Nelson?" Eileen asked, although she already had a pretty good idea about that.

"I didn't talk to Nelson," Sharon said after a moment. "He didn't concern himself much with this sort of thing."

Eileen nodded solemnly. Sharon had a tender heart. Nelson Atkins was a worthless manager, but he was a sweet and caring man. She wouldn't reveal Nelson's inadequacies to Detective Reed.

"What did Lowell say?"

"He wanted to know how I felt I was doing. Perhaps Terry thought I would be an easy pushover, that I would cry and beg to be kept on. It was so odd to see his face and hear his voice saying words that I knew had been spoken by her.

" 'Do you think this job is going to be too much for you?' he asked, and I took my courage and I fixed him with my eye and I said 'I don't think it is. I'm doing well and I'm getting better every day. I've done code counts and problem counts, and I could print you out a chart if you'd like. Sully helped me with a program that shows my improvement over time.'

"Terry didn't know I was making friends, you see. She thought of everyone as a separate island, vulnerable. Sully put a sword in my hand. Sully knew I was supposed to go talk to Lowell. I don't know how she knew. But there she was, with her hair all sticking up every which way, and she showed me this program that she'd put together. She showed me how my code and the quality of my code was shooting up every week. She showed me her code, all flat line and basically perfect, and she winked at me and showed me Terry's code, flat line and at the bottom. Then she put my code up against Terry's and she turned and just walked away."

"She helped you," Eileen said. She was choked with admiration and jealousy over a woman two years dead.

"She knew what I was going up against. If I had shown any weakness, maybe Lowell would have tried to get Nelson to set my rating back to technician instead of engineer. That would have been a big cut in pay. She wanted to punish me through my children. I would have had to pull them out of the private school. She wanted me beaten."

She almost did it, Eileen thought, and remembered the deadness of Joe's eyes when he spoke of Sully, the tortured penance of 'Berto, and the exhaustion and guilt of Doug Procell.

"She didn't know I'd have my friends. She took Sully away, but there was Joe, and 'Berto, and Doug. She didn't beat me. But she never gave up, either." Sharon looked at Eileen, and her eyes were implacable.

"Whoever killed that woman did us all a favor," Sharon said. "I'm ashamed of myself for thinking that. Then God took Art away from us. He was the best of us, Art was. Now he's gone. Perhaps that's our punishment."

Turtkul, Uzbekistan

Muallah toed the body of the Russian soldier. He was a young one, perhaps no more than twenty or so. He'd gotten some sort of message out over the communications set before Rashad shot him carefully in the back. There was no sign of anyone else, although Muallah was sure that there were more people here. Women, probably, and perhaps children. The curtains at the window. The vegetable garden.

"Ali," he said softly. "There are more here. Find them."

Ali touched his lips with his right hand and ghosted out of the room alone. Ali needed no help.

"Ruadh," Muallah said, and gestured at the console. Ruadh, a tall beefy man with a shadow of black beard across his sweating face, looked more like a camel driver than a Scud missile controller. Ruadh had fought well in the Iraqi acquisition of Kuwait. It was not his fault the damned American Patriot missiles kept shooting down his Scuds. Rashad had found Ruadh morosely smoking hashish in a filthy hovel in Baghdad, victim of Hussein's rabid attempt to lay blame down the line of command. Ruadh barely escaped a prison sentence, simply because his equipment was outgunned by the Americans and he was of a small and unprotected rank. The purge left Ruadh without a livelihood and with a deep hatred toward America, which he considered the source of his troubles.

"I will need time," Ruadh said shortly, and started pulling books from the shelves of the command center. Muallah gestured toward Rashad to remove the dead soldier. There were comfortable furnishings in the helicopter, even a silver coffee service. Muallah required his small luxuries. Unfortunately, there was no woman to serve the coffee. Unless . . .

"Rashad," he said softly. "Tell Ali to let one woman live. To serve us."

Rashad grinned and nodded. He dropped the dead feet of the soldier and darted from the room. Ali was very efficient in his work. If there was to be anyone left alive, Rashad had to hurry.

Moscow, Russian Republic

The call from the Uzbekistani missile silo, what would be called a Mayday call in America, was picked up immediately in Moscow by the GRU, the intelligence branch of the military. This was not a matter of luck. There were huge amounts of money pouring into the former Soviet Union, much of it American and all of it welcome. One of the more interesting strings attached to the U.S. government money was the establishment of a firm control structure over former Soviet missile silos. U.S. West, unrolling phone wire in Russia as fast as they could pitchfork the bales out of trucks, donated a staggering amount of communications equipment to the Moscow GRU. IBM delivered some gorgeously appointed computers. All of it free. The Center was almost American, it was so modern.

Colonel Sergei Kalashnikov, a second cousin three times removed from the man who invented the rifle, was grouchy for many months about the massive and typically heavy-handed American influence in what should be a Russian problem. His superior, Major General Cherepovitch, was equally grouchy but had received The Word from on high, from the President himself. Let them help. Don't lose control.

For four years Kalashnikov had complied with this strategy, finally admitting that the system was indeed very helpful. The American advisers were almost tolerable. They were even learning how to drink vodka.

His own home village of Salekhard in the western Siberian lowland was now under the enormous wing of Exxon. Exxon was building roads, schools, housing, a landing field, and installing a model waste-treatment plant. Exxon seemed to be intent on turning every Russian oil field site into a showplace. Of course, it was making money in bundles from the new and previously untapped oil fields. This was not causing the Russian people, who discovered that Exxon considered them to be "private property owners" of the land and the oil fields, any pain. Kalashnikov's uncle just sent a letter asking Sergei to resign his commission and come home to help run the family business, a grocery store. Business was booming. The lease rights from the oil fields were stunning. And every house in Salekhard had running water!

Kalashnikov didn't seriously consider resigning his commission. Moscow was also benefiting from the Western invasion. Kalashnikov's wife liked the ballet, the new restaurants, the beginnings of a shopping district. Moscow suited them very well.

When the cold and emotionless voice of Boris Pavlovsk broke through static on the emergency line, Kalashnikov's musings over Salekhard and the grocery store ended abruptly. The systems were set up to record all incoming radio traffic, so all Kalashnikov had to do was listen. Hearing what he heard was like seeing a gun unexpectedly aimed at his head.

"Oh my God," Major Thomas Paxton said when the transmission ended with a very brief, very final gunshot. The American major was standing shoulder to shoulder with Kalashnikov, staring at the blinking light on the Russian map that pinpointed Turtkul, Uzbekistan. The Center was in a large room in the basement of the building that used to house the KGB. Four other soldiers sat at their consoles, looking with wide eyes at the two ranking officers. They knew, too.

"Boris Pavlovsk will get the highest medal for this," Kalashnikov said through numb lips. "He warned us instead of hiding with the other families."

"We have to believe they're safe in the empty silo," the Major said, clearly not believing it. "The terrorists must want the missiles."

"Before we contact them, we have to get a higher authority involved," Kalashnikov said coldly.

"I must contact my chain of command too," Major Paxton said formally. He said it like the Americans said everything they knew you didn't want to hear—like a man who takes a forbidden bone from a dog's mouth. Gently, reluctantly, but with a clear sense of mastery. Kalashnikov hated that.

"Of course," he said, and his tone was pure frost. "We have no idea who they intend to threaten, or what they intend to do. You must use your best judgment."

The Major nodded quickly and went to his phone. Kalashnikov found himself looking over at the Major after he dialed the number marked in red on the sheet taped to the phone. The Major was looking back at him, and his face was as grim as Kalashnikov felt.

"God help those poor women and children," he said softly to the Major, for Kalashnikov was Russian Orthodox and believed very deeply in God. "God help us all."

•28

"They are in a missile silo marked number six," Ali said. His face showed the slightest hint of dissatisfaction, which meant Ali was in a thundering rage. "We cannot enter, Mahdi."

"You cannot enter?" Muallah asked, incredulous. Ali, fail? This was impossible.

"The doors are very thick. We checked number five after three grenades failed to open number six. I cannot enter."

Muallah looked silently at Ali, who paled and lost his look of dissatisfaction. Ali smelled sharply of gun smoke and sweat. The breast of his jacket was splattered with a few drops of the Russian soldier's blood. His hair was disheveled and flopped over his forehead. Muallah frowned.

"Can you lock them in so they cannot escape?"

"I have already done so, Mahdi," Ali said.

"Then they are rubbish. Assad, you must make the coffee." Muallah smiled at Assad to take the sting from the demeaning task, one fit only for a woman. Assad nodded and left immediately. Ali waited in silence as Muallah glanced at Ruadh. Ruadh was buried deep in the missile manuals.

"How long, Ali?" Muallah said softly. "Until they get a team together that can attempt an assault?"

"Perhaps a few days. No less than twenty-four hours."

"Ah, good. And bombers?"

"They could attempt a bombing, but we are well protected from anything but a nuclear strike, which of course they will not risk."

Muallah knew all this, but he was jittery from nerves and excitement. He needed Ali to confirm his flawless plan.

"Excellent," Muallah said. He stretched back on the pillows and Persian carpeting they had brought on the Hind. "Now all we need is coffee."

Colorado Springs

Joe Tanner opened the door.

"Well, hello," he said, and smiled at Eileen.

"Hello back," she said, absolutely convinced she was looking at a murderer and absolutely convinced he was innocent, all at the same time. Joe was wearing a plain white shirt and jeans. His hair was just washed, thick and brown and bristly, like a mink. His eyebrows were thick and arched over his green eyes. He'd cut himself underneath the chin while shaving.

"Shall we take my car again?" Joe asked, turning away to lock his door.

"Sure," Eileen said. "Where are we going? You said it was your choice?"

"The Broadmoor," Joe said with a wicked grin. "My choice."

"Oh, no, we can't go there," Eileen protested. "It's too—"

"Expensive? Of course," Joe said. "I'm loaded, Detective."

"Not expensive," Eileen replied, trying not to laugh. The income from her portion of the cattle on her parents' ranch was more than her yearly salary as a detective, and that wasn't half bad. Money was not the reason she'd never been to the Broadmoor. "Snooty, Joe. That place is a five-star resort hotel. They're snooty. Look at me."

"You look ravishing," Joe said. "Don't you know that?"

"I'm wearing pants," Eileen explained, feeling her face start to flush.

"I noticed," Joe said dryly. "Why would you wear anything but pants? You look like a young Katharine Hepburn, only in color. You should always wear khakis."

"Thank you," Eileen murmured, inwardly amused at her own reaction to Joe's flattery. She wasn't that young or foolish, to feel warm over a compliment.

"I like the Broadmoor," Joe continued, taking her elbow in a warm grip and leading her down to his car. "It's the Gamers' place to go after a successful war game. A *four*-star place is snooty. A *five*-star place is just like home, only better. They've got this huge patio overlooking the lake, with the mountains just above it. It's the best place in Colorado Springs. I can't believe you've never been there."

"Well, I've been there, professionally," Eileen said, settling into the car and pulling the seat belt across her lap. She got a sudden, vivid image of the gorgeously appointed room 104, with the view of Cheyenne Mountain through the windows and the sprawled sad legs of Suzanne DeBeau, lady golfer and cocaine addict, making a sloppy X on the plush green carpet.

"Yikes," Joe said, getting into the driver's seat. "A murder?"

"Accidental death," Eileen said, "but let's not talk about work."

"Let's not," Joe said, and smiled over at her again. "There's lots to talk about besides war games and murders. I want to know what herding cattle is like."

Eileen laughed. "It's hot and stinky," she said. "But if you really want to know, I'll tell you all."

When Joe turned onto Lake Drive a few minutes later, Eileen looked doubtfully at the enormous hotel at the end of the street.

"There used to be a railroad that went right up Lake Drive, did you know that?" Joe said. "This whole city was founded as a resort community. The Broadmoor was the first hotel, and it's the grandest. I always feel like I'm going back in time when I come here."

He looked up with a kind of familiar pride at the facade as they pulled into the parking lot. The stone was painted a dull putty color and the roofs were red slate. The flower beds were impeccable and their scent filled the air. A little fountain played by the entrance. It should have looked European and out of place, but it didn't. The building had been designed by someone who knew how it should look against the setting of Pikes Peak and Cheyenne Mountain.

"It is beautiful," Eileen said grudgingly.

"This'll really be a treat," Joe said greedily, and rubbed his hands together.

Just as at Joni's, a kind of bubble surrounded Eileen. Nothing existed beyond the present moment. The sun was setting slowly behind the Front Range as they were seated in the enormous dining room. Eileen ordered seafood fettuccine. Joe ate a filet that was smothered in asparagus and crab, and he insisted that Eileen have a bite. She took the beef from his fork, and the meat was so tender it was like butter in her mouth.

Nothing was said of the murders during the dinner. They spoke of college days, of Joe's family, the latest movies. They rambled easily from one subject to another.

"You can't brand cattle when they're wet," Eileen explained at one point, waving a chunk of crab at the end of her fork. "If you do, then the whole area just kind of scabs up and falls off, so you get this big round scar instead of a nice clean brand." She stopped, and Joe started laughing.

"That's disgusting," he said.

"Sorry," she said, and ate the piece of crab. She grinned over at him. "But who was telling me about the road rash from that bike crash, huh? A whole leg of scabs for a month?"

"I've got an iron stomach," Joe explained. "Nothing bothers me. My aunt was a nurse, and she lived with us for a summer when she first got divorced. Her and her kids. What a great summer. She'd come home and shower up and talk to my mom about her day in the emergency room. We'd be eating supper and she'd be telling Mom about the gunshot wounds and the car wrecks. We'd listen with our mouths hanging open as they'd laugh and talk."

"How many cousins do you have?"

"She had three kids, all boys, all right around our ages, me and my brother and sisters. We had such fun! There were a couple of ponds, and we would go fishing for sunfish and crappie. The moms signed us all up for swimming lessons, too, so we'd all troop off in the morning for those." Joe shook his head. "I miss the guys to this day, I do. Aunt Rachel moved out, but she was still close by. We still visited together all the time. We used to take our summer vacations together."

"We didn't take many vacations," Eileen said. "One to Disneyland. Of course."

"Of course," Joe laughed. "Everybody goes to Disneyland, don't they?"

"I almost got kicked out. I sneaked away and went over the fence at Jungle Safari, because I swore those were real crocodiles in the river. So I get three steps and I've got one of the Disney Secret Police holding me by the scruff of the neck."

"You went over the fence at Jungle Safari? In *Disneyland*?"

"I was interested," she said, trying to put on her best wide-eyed innocent look. She was rewarded by a burst of laughter.

"You talked your way out of it? I don't believe it."

"My mom did," Eileen said. "She could sweet-talk the birds out of the trees. They let us stay. As long as she was holding me by the hand."

"We went, too," Joe said. "When I was seven. Pretty exciting, even for a big-city kid."

"Rapid City was the big city to me," Eileen said dryly. "And Laramie, Wyoming. Wow, that was such an adjustment."

"Belle Fourche," Joe said in a marveling voice. "I can't imagine what it would be like to go to boarding school."

"It wasn't a boarding school, just a regular high school. But the ranch kids boarded with local families. You know, parents whose kids were gone or families with an extra room. I had a good time in high school," Eileen said. "It's lonely at first because you still want to be with Mom and Dad. But in high school we had a whole crowd of boarders that hung out together. The family I lived with, the Smithsons, they couldn't have any children. They're probably still boarding ranch kids. They had another boarder when I went to school, Owen Sutter. My buddy Owen. He couldn't figure out why I wanted to go into the Air Force. He wanted to work the ranch and be a cowboy forever."

"Does he do that now?"

"He sure does, and he's got three kids. He married Molly, we were friends with her in high school. Molly Williams, there's a girl for you. She could ride a horse. Still does, I imagine." Eileen winked at Joe. "I'm glad Owen married her, actually, don't be thinking there's some tragic romantic story here. Owen was the brother I never had."

"What was it like when school ended for the summer?"

Eileen looked at him doubtfully.

"I really am interested. You are so different than I expected, so—"

"Not coplike?" she said.

"Exactly. Though I don't know any cops, personally. Until now." Joe regarded her across the remains of their supper, now being whisked away by the silent, impeccable Broadmoor waiters.

242 • BONNIE RAMTHUN

"I like listening to people's stories," Eileen said. "I like brainteasers and puzzles, but best of all I like figuring out what makes people the way they are. Being a cop suits me."

"How about the gun? Doesn't it feel strange, carrying a gun?"

"Oh, yes, the gun too," Eileen said, and patted her side affectionately. "I've carried a gun since I was ten. Mountain lions like to snack on calves, and they'd be happy to snack on me too. Mom and Dad taught me to shoot. I don't feel right without a gun."

"I don't think I'd feel right with a gun," Joe said. Eileen's bubble fled as, for just a moment, she contemplated Joe Tanner sharpening a deadly screwdriver stiletto, humming as he shaved metal particles from the blade. Then she blinked, hard, and the image disappeared. Joe was not the murderer. He was *not*. Not tonight, anyhow.

"Sometime I'll take you shooting," she said lightly. "You'll be hooked, I bet. When I first took Joni shooting she'd pucker her face up and barely get a shot off, her hands would shake so bad. Now she can hit the X ring half the time."

"Joni has a gun?" Joe asked in surprise.

"She was carrying a gun when you met her, Joe," Eileen said. "Concealed carry permit. Nobody is going to mess with Joni again."

"I like that," Joe said slowly. "I don't want anybody messing with Joni either."

"Time for coffee and dessert," the waiter said with a grin, rolling a cart to the table that was packed with confections. "Don't try to get away without dessert."

"We have to have coffee," Eileen said, eyeing the cart.

"But of course," Joe said gloomily. "I'll just run about twelve miles tomorrow to work this off, that's all."

The night fizzed around her like champagne as she laughed, and Eileen understood in the cold and rational part of her that the danger was a part of the fizz. The danger that she might be falling in love with a madman and a murderer. Eileen knew with all her heart that Joe Tanner was innocent, that he was intelligent and good. But the tiny rational voice in her head stayed awake and aware, looking with cold lizard eyes out of her head and assessing every movement and nuance of Joe Tanner. The rational part of her,

her lizard part, would not trust Joe Tanner until she had the real murderer in custody. No matter what her heart was telling her.

THE NIGHT BREEZE blew through the car windows and stirred Eileen's hair as they drove to Joe's home.

"That was the best dinner I ever had," Joe said after he pulled to a stop. "Do you want to come in for coffee or something?"

"I don't—"

"Please? Just for a bit. I don't want the night to end."

He leaned forward and kissed her, and his mouth was as soft as she imagined it to be. His kiss was maddeningly gentle.

"All right," she said.

His apartment was small and indifferently decorated, as she knew it would be. There was no particular style, just nice furniture and lamps and a couple of prints.

"Let me fix decaf," he said, "or I'll be up all night. I'll probably be up all night anyway."

Eileen didn't answer. She was looking at a framed picture of Harriet Sullivan. Eileen felt a withering rage and jealousy of this dead woman, for the second time. She couldn't help it, even though she knew it was useless.

"It was two years ago," she said.

"It feels like yesterday," he said, his face abruptly as expressionless as stone.

"I've heard a lot of stories about Sully," Eileen said. "Sharon told me what she did when she thought she was going to lose her job. I think—"

"You think I killed Terry because of Sully," Joe said sharply. He was clenching the coffee grinder in his hands. He looked furious.

"I don't know," Eileen said, from the lizard part of her. Then she folded her arms and bowed her head. "No," she whispered from her heart. "Not you."

The coffee grinder thumped to the counter with a clatter.

"Not me, Eileen," Joe said. He walked to her and took her in his arms, as naturally as though he'd done it a thousand times. "It wasn't me." Eileen could feel his heart beating under her ear, and she put her arms around him and held him tightly. Lost, she was lost, and she didn't care.

"I know it wasn't you."

Great Falls, Virginia

"Lucy, Lucy," Ted called to her.

Lucy could hear her husband's voice, but the smoke swirled around her and she couldn't see. There was a frantic crackling sound that had to be fire. There were sharp rubble and rocks under her feet. She looked down, in the queer fishbowl vision of a dream, and saw that her feet were encased in stout boots. Underneath her feet were brick shards and shell casings and white tiny sticks that she understood were children's bones.

"Ted!" she screamed, but the scream came out of her throat as the tiniest of whispers. She tried to look around, but the smoke was choking and thick and studded with particles that glistened like crystals. The smoke was shimmering, but the taste was foul, like death.

The smoke haze lifted and she saw the Tower of London, broken, one part of the spire sticking up like a brutally sharpened pencil, and then the shimmering clouds swirled it away again. She'd visited London as a college student on spring break and never forgotten her first breathtaking glimpse of the Tower. Now it was destroyed.

Lucy felt the scream sticking in her throat, and knew she was walking through radioactive clouds. Then she realized she was carrying a child, and knew that the worst part wasn't that she was dead, but that her child was, too.

That broke the scream free and sent her up and out of the nightmare, and she opened her eyes in the darkness and Ted was there, holding her. There was no smoke.

"Lucy," Ted said. He was near tears. "Don't scream, Lucy, don't."

Lucy put her arms around his neck and sobbed, feeling her sweat running down her body and soaking her nightshirt.

"Oh, Ted," she said. "I had the most horrible nightmare."

"It's okay now, baby, it's okay, it was just a dream," he soothed, and held her.

But it was a long time before Lucy fell asleep again.

•29

Oklahoma

"Have you finished Chapter Twelve yet?" Major Stillwell asked Richard, the pilot. They were sitting in a Greyhound bus stop in Oklahoma. The bus stop also served as a gas station and liquor store. The bugs swarmed around the light at the front of the station.

"Almost done," Richard said absently. Richard was bringing home a romance novel for his wife, a gift. She loved romance novels. This was the only reading material anybody had. They'd split Richard's book into chapters and were sharing the chapters around as they read. They'd tried reading it together, but Gwen was too fast and Stillwell was too slow. The gas station's one video game had an Out of Order sign on it that was so sun-faded as to be illegible.

The friendly broken-legged farmer's wife had fed them some terrific fried chicken for lunch and some cherry pie for dessert that Stillwell thought he might remember forever, it was so good.

After the lunch—the farmer's wife called it dinner—there was a long, boring wait for the farmer to return from the fields, and a long, boring drive to the nearest town, and then a long, boring wait for the bus.

The bus tickets weren't that expensive, but all three groaned when they found out the next bus wouldn't pull into town until two that morning.

"I was supposed to be in Colorado Springs tonight," Stillwell said.

"We all were," Richard said gloomily.

RICHARD FINISHED his chapter and handed it over to Stillwell. Stillwell set his chapter carefully on the growing stack by his chair. Gwen, the quickest reader, was the first in line.

"Chapter Twelve," Stillwell said to himself, " 'The Wolf and the Dove.' "

This was his first experience with historical romance. Gwen told them she liked this one because the beautiful heroine was full-bodied and chunky, like Gwen.

"Those were the days," Gwen said.

Stillwell sighed and tried to find a comfortable position in the hard plastic chair.

Colorado Springs

Joe's mouth was soft and salty and hot, just the way Eileen imagined it to be.

"I want you," he said against her mouth. "Everything is right when you're around me."

How long had it been? Forever. The rational part of her brain was calling to her, crying out in a sharp commanding voice, but it was far away and she didn't want to listen to it. She wasn't going to listen to it.

"I want you too," she said through the thudding of her heart.

He pulled her against him and kissed her. She could taste the salt and the softness of his mouth. His shirt was untucked at the back and she slid her hands underneath, hungry to feel his bare skin.

"Yes," he said, and pulled her to the couch so they could sprawl down upon it. The landing was awkward, which made them both laugh.

She opened her eyes as he stopped kissing her, because she wanted to look at him. Eileen wanted to look at his face. Joe showed everything. If he was doing this as a way to finish his mourning over Sully, or to forget his friend Art, Eileen wanted to know. She wanted to see more than desire in his face, because what she felt was more than just desire.

He let his head fall back against the couch cushion, as though he understood what she wanted. He smiled at her, his wicked and unabashed grin.

"I want you," he said. "Not somebody to take her place. Is that what you want me to say?"

"Yes," she said, laughing.

"I want you, Eileen," he said strongly.

Eileen kissed him again, fiercely, her hands moving to his shirt buttons. She had to feel his skin against hers. She had to feel all of him.

Eileen fumbled with his buttons as he fumbled with hers, which set them to laughing again while they were kissing.

"Oh, wait, darn it," she said as he tried to strip her shirt off. She unbuckled her shoulder holster and casually set it on the floor. She tossed his shirt on top of it. He finished stripping her shirt off, her thin cotton bra showing the hard points of her nipples. He murmured in admiration as he took the bra from her, his hands meeting across her back as he brought her breasts to his mouth. Eileen pushed against his shoulders as his mouth pulled and licked at her nipples. His teeth closed softly around the hard point and she groaned, trying to pull away. He growled against her and smiled up at her, his lips against her breast. She laughed, cradling his head against her, twining her fingers through the thickness of his hair.

"Oh, it's so good," she whispered.

"Yes," Joe murmured, and unbuttoned her pants, unzipping the zipper and letting the fabric fall down her hips, pulling them free and kissing her ankles as he stripped the khakis from her. She reached for his pants, the waistband. She was now clad only in the silkiest of panties. His hand smoothed downward and cupped her bottom.

"I'm very excited," she whispered, and he pulled her against him and kissed her hard, his breath nearly a pant.

"Oh, God, yes you are," he said. She struggled with his waistband, her hands clumsy, and finally the tongue of the zipper went down and she reached in to touch him. His head fell back as she struggled to release him. He stood up, impatient, and stripped his pants off. Eileen sat on her heels, knees apart, and as he tossed the pants aside she reached out with her own hands and caught his hips. Then she was nuzzling and kissing the smooth length of him, tasting him with her tongue and her lips. He stood, head forward, looking at her mouth against him, his hands reaching out to her shoulders to steady himself. Then he pulled away, shaking his head, needing to slow down, and it was her turn to smile. He pushed her back against the sofa and she lay back for him as he peeled her panties from her and covered her body with his.

"I can't wait," he gasped against her ear, kissing the curve of her neck.

"Here," she said. "Ahh, here." She tilted her hips to him.

"More," she said. "Oh please."

Soon she cried out and caught at him as he, too, groaned and sighed and then his weight came down on her, sweat slicked, and their hearts thudded together.

"Oh, yes, yes," she whispered. "Oh yes. Oh Joe."

"I think I love you," he said in a sleepy, blurred voice.

"I think I love you, too," she said, and sleep took her under like a black wave.

Central Intelligence Agency, Langley, Virginia

"I couldn't sleep," Lucy said shortly to Mills. She had her desk light on because the sun wasn't up yet. It was very early for Lucy.

"That's unusual," Mills said to her in a smugly friendly way. Lucy looked at him for a moment, puzzled, then realized Mills thought she was in there to impress *him*. He had her under his control now, or so he thought.

"Just couldn't sleep, that's all," she said shortly, and turned her head back to her computer screen, clearly dismissing him. He closed the door softly with a small chuckle, which she ignored.

After he left, Lucy took another donut out of her desk drawer. They were incredibly fresh at four-thirty in the morning, she had just discovered. The bakers were still putting them out on the racks when she stepped into the bakery. The smell of fresh-baked donuts was mouthwatering.

"I hate that man," she said, her mouth muffled by donut. There didn't seem to be anything more on Muallah, any piece of information that could get her report off Mills's desk and into the DDCIA's office.

The phone rang. Lucy swallowed hard.

"Yeth," she said, because her voice was still mostly choked with donut.

"Is this Lucy Giometti?"

"Yes, Lieutenant, this is Lucy," Lucy said. She sat straight up in her chair. "Did you read it? What did you—"

"We've got all the confirmation we need now," Jefferson said grimly. "Kane wants you over at the Pentagon right away. You are now our Muallah expert."

"I have to talk to Mills—" Lucy started, grimacing. Mills was not going to be happy about this.

"I've already called him," Jefferson said. "We're going to let him have the opportunity to take the credit for your brilliant analysis. If he chooses to try and nail you for going around the chain of command, he's going to bounce so far on his ass you'll see skid marks on the pavement. Now, get over here, Miss Lucy. We've got a Situation."

"I'm on my way," she said, and hung up the phone just as Mills stormed into the office.

"What's the meaning of all this?" he squealed, his face mottled with red and white.

"The meaning is that you were wrong and I was right," Lucy said. "But you can still get the credit if you want."

Mills stood there like a fish on a dock, his mouth opening and closing, as Lucy gathered her purse and closed down her computer and contemplated the donuts. Finally she shrugged, closed the donut box, and tucked it under her arm.

"We need to go," she said to Mills. "Plan your revenge later. We need to get to the Pentagon."

Lucy found she regretted that remark very much, later on.

Oklahoma

"The bus is here," said Gwen. Major Stillwell came awake with a start. His left foot was asleep and started tingling when he moved in the hard plastic chair. He groaned.

"Oh, thank God," said Richard. He was sitting rigidly in the bus station's hard, brightly colored chair, his eyes locked on the big blue and white form of the bus. Three other sleepy passengers stirred in the tiny waiting room of the gas station that served as a bus stop.

"What time is it?" Stillwell asked.

"Two o'clock," Richard said.

"I was almost willing to fly that Chinook out of that cornfield," Gwen said grimly.

"I thought about it," Richard said to her.

"You're a fruitcake," she said, which puzzled Stillwell.

The bus was mostly empty. Everyone on board seemed to be asleep. Stillwell felt sweaty and rank in the close confines of the bus, but he realized everyone else smelled that way too. He took a seat, and Gwen and Richard sat together on the seat across from him.

"See, we're safe now, you big baby," Gwen said as they pulled away from the station. "We'll be in Oklahoma City in a couple of hours and home by tomorrow night, I bet."

"I want a shower," Stillwell said. "And some sleep in a real bed."

"I'm just glad we made it out," Richard said. He did look better. The color was beginning to return to his face.

"What's the deal?" Stillwell said.

"Too many scary stories when he was a kid," Gwen said. Richard looked out the window as though he were annoyed, but Stillwell could see the beginnings of a grin.

"There was a movie called *Children of the Corn,* from a Stephen King story," Gwen said.

"Oh, yeah, I caught that on the late night a long time ago. It was pretty good," Stillwell said.

"I hate cornfields. Always have. I've always thought there was something in there, when I was growing up in Kansas. Then I saw this movie. So here we go, crashing in a cornfield. Then we have to sit in a little redneck town all day," Richard said.

"Richard was waiting for the natives to come swarming out and sacrifice us to the corn," Gwen said.

"Well, I would have made it," Richard said. "I would have given them you to sacrifice, and saved my own ass."

They laughed together, and Stillwell found himself laughing too. He was finally moving again. It was too bad that he was going to be late to investigate the case at Schriever, but at least he was alive. Tomorrow would be soon enough. Stillwell laid his head back in the bus seat and tried to find a comfortable position so he could get some sleep.

Colorado Springs

Halfway through the night Eileen woke Joe by tugging at his arm, trying to get him to stand up.

"We're going to the bedroom," she said, getting her shoulder under his arm.

"What?" Tanner said sleepily.

"Bedroom," she said. His body, naked, shone in the darkness. "We're going to sleep in a bed. You're crushing me on this couch. Come on now, it's just down the hall."

Joe didn't resist. He was still mostly asleep. He let her lead him to the bedroom. The sheets were wonderfully cool and smooth, and the comforter she pulled over him was soft and warm.

Eileen hurried quickly to the living room. She fetched her gun and their clothing and set her holster by the bed, dumping their clothes by the door. She crawled in and curled her body up against him. He sleepily put his arm around her. She felt a vast sense of peace. She slept.

Turtkul, Uzbekistan

"They will rescue us," Anna whispered confidently. She held her youngest, who was seven and usually unwilling to submit to baby treatment, firmly against her bosom. He was sleeping, mouth open, eyelashes fanned against his perfect rounded cheek. Salt tears had dried in tiny streaks from his eyes. He snored.

"We can survive only three or four days," Ilina whispered.

"That will be more than enough," Anna soothed. "You brought plenty of food. We are safe, Ilina. Do not worry."

Anna, though, was worried, and deeply. What she knew, and hoped the murderous terrorists would not figure out, was that missile silo number six was capped by a concrete cover that could be blown off, just like every other silo with a nuclear warhead within. Blow the cover off and the women and children would be like mice at the bottom of a barrel. If the terrorists figured this out . . . Anna shook her head and stroked her sleeping son, and made a small offering to the God she'd been taught all her life did not exist.

"Please, God," she said to herself. "Please, God. Don't let them be as smart as me." She looked upward into the darkness at the top of the silo, and she prayed.

•30

Colorado Springs

"I shall fix you French toast," Joe whispered to Eileen. She woke abruptly and for a moment didn't know where she was. Joe was on his side next to her, his chin in his hand, looking into her eyes exactly like her cat Betty liked to do.

"Good morning?" he said, and there was an awkward silence for a moment.

"Good morning? Good morning!" Eileen said, recovering herself. She put her arms around Joe and hugged him hard. He rolled over in the bed until she was underneath him.

"When I woke I thought it was another of those dreams I've been having since I met you," he said solemnly as she started to laugh.

"I thought Betty had figured out how to open the cat-food cans and had gotten huge."

"I guess I am huge," Joe said with a smirk.

"You're gigantic . . . for a cat," Eileen said. He started kissing her.

"My mouth tastes terrible. But I can't stop."

"I'm going to fix you breakfast," he said again, laughing, but his arms were around her neck and he was kissing her.

"Later," she said.

Denver Animal Shelter

The dark-haired girl, Debbie, hung up a tag on Fancy's door when she fed the little spaniel that morning. She hosed out Fancy's kennel and patted the dog, and moved down the line to the next kennel. Fancy's time was going to run out the next day.

Colorado Springs

"I might have something," Dave Rosen said to Eileen. She wasn't late, but he was there before she walked into the office. Was he always early? She'd never noticed before.

"On the Schriever case? What is it?" Eileen was heading for her desk but changed direction. There was a purse on Rosen's desk.

"This is Terry Guzman's purse," Rosen said. "I realized when I was going over the autopsy report that she didn't have a purse."

"I missed that," Eileen said, and touched the edge of the leather bag with her finger. She wanted to snatch it off the surface of the desk, but this was Rosen's find. "Have you opened it?"

"It just got here," Rosen said. "She left it at her desk. Nobody touched her desk and nobody asked about a purse, so it wasn't turned in until the Game Director found it yesterday. He found it in her desk; they were boxing up her stuff. He sent it in."

"At your request, you mean. Stop teasing me, dammit, open it," Eileen said. Rosen smiled. He opened up the top and carefully shook out the contents onto the desk.

On the desk was lipstick, a checkbook, a comb, a small bottle of hair spray, a nail file, a bankbook, a coin purse, a pink oval case ("birth control pills,"

Eileen said to Rosen), a folding toothbrush in a clear case, a traveler's tube of toothpaste, a vial of perfume, an ancient granola bar, and a set of car keys.

Eileen felt a deep sadness when she saw the pitiful contents of Terry's bag. These were the private items of a woman's life, spread out for inspection.

There was so much happiness in her life this morning, she couldn't feel bad toward anyone. Everyone should have a fresh chance at life. Everyone should have the chance to feel like she did today. She thought guiltily that her mood must show. After the glorious morning lovemaking, Joe fixed Eileen French toast that was crisp and tasty. And coffee. Joe was a coffee drinker. His coffee was strong and good, just like him, she thought in amusement. Her brain was temporarily on vacation, obviously. She looked down at the desk.

"Let me see the checkbook," she said. Rosen handed her the book and then took up the bag and hefted it, trying to see if the weight was wrong. If there was an unexplained heaviness, there might be a hidden pocket or two. Purses often had little compartments that were easy to miss.

Eileen started looking through the check register. There were the usual utilities, car payment, ATM withdrawals. There was the monthly deposit of her paycheck, an amount that made Eileen draw in a deep breath. Did they really pay engineers that much? She remembered the huge and costly machines in the Gaming Center. Evidently the engineers were worth that kind of money. Eileen flipped through the checks and felt an unexpected hardness at the back of the checkbook.

"What's this?"

Rosen peered over Eileen's arm as she looked through the checkbook. She finally found the hidden compartment and pulled out a slim blue bankbook.

"She had two savings accounts?" Rosen asked. "Hey, now."

Eileen opened the savings account book and saw the name.

"Teresa James."

"That was the last name of her first husband, right?" Rosen said.

Eileen nodded. She pointed silently to the listing of deposits.

"My God," Rosen said. "Fourteen thousand dollars. Twelve thousand dollars. Fifteen thousand dollars. Where was she getting the money?"

"What did she have worth selling?" Eileen asked wearily. The sunshine had abruptly gone out of her day. The moment she'd seen the first amount she realized what Terry Guzman was doing to earn it.

"Secret documents," Rosen said. His face was shuttered, but his hands were clenched on the tabletop in excitement.

"Surely," Eileen said. Her fingers felt numb. This was it. This had to be it. All the trails led here. "She screwed everyone she could. Figuratively as well as literally. She tried to find everyone's proudest point and make it dirty. Look," she said, ticking the names with her fingers. "There's 'Berto. He was proud of his beliefs, his religion. There's Doug. He loved his wife, his new little girl."

"Procell had to work nights and couldn't see them," Rosen said. "And 'Berto, she made him guilty by sleeping with him. What about Joe? And Sharon?"

"Joe lost Sully. Terry destroyed him without even setting him up," Eileen said grimly. "And she got rid of Sully permanently, even if it was an accident. Sharon loves her kids. Terry was trying to get Sharon switched to a lower-paying position so Sharon would have to take her kids out of private school."

"Nelson?"

"I don't know. And Lowell? Did he know about this?"

"What about Art? Did she try anything on Art?"

"I don't know. We'll probably never know now," Eileen said, and started turning the pages of the bankbook. There was something written on the back page.

"Phone numbers," Rosen said in a strangled yelp. "Look."

Eileen looked at the first phone number. She knew the number. She felt a burst of savage excitement, and Rosen saw the look in her face. His face flushed a dusky red color.

"Whose is it? You know?"

"I know," Eileen said in satisfaction, and punched Dave Rosen on the thick part of the arm. "Feels good, doesn't it? We've got the bastard now."

"Who?"

"It's Major Blaine."

Central Intelligence Agency, Langley, Virginia

Lucy's screen was full of windows, but her mind refused to process any of the information. She was exhausted. Lieutenant Jefferson and four other officers had grilled her all morning in the stuffy room at the Pentagon. Mills, wisely, said little. He sat next to her on the hard folding chair and nodded sagely at all the right places. Lucy talked until she was hoarse, then talked some more. She shared her donuts, which had suddenly lost their taste. She longed for some more beef jerky, the greasy teriyaki kind.

Jefferson gave a little information away. Yes, there had been a takeover of a Russian missile silo. And yes, since Lucy seemed to know about it before it happened, it was in Uzbekistan. Even though Uzbekistan was now technically a separate country, the silos were still considered Russian territory, with the cooperation of the Uzbekistani government. Jefferson refused to discuss anything else.

Lucy did her best. She believed Jefferson was a listener. He was a smart man. The other officers might be of the same mettle, but it was Jefferson she spoke to. And, through Jefferson, Admiral Kane.

"Look, I know how this sounds," she had said. "You don't want to wade through Muallah's master's thesis. But if you did, you'd understand this guy really believes he is the One of the Prophecies. He believes he will blow this 'Trumpet of Doom' and unite the Arab countries into a new empire. What else could his trumpet of doom be but a nuclear bomb?"

"Saddam Hussein will eat him for breakfast if he tries a stunt like that," one of the unnamed officers said. He was a Marine, with cold eyes. Lucy didn't have to stretch to figure this guy was a veteran of the Gulf War. Mills made a little wiggling gesture in his chair, as though to apologize for her. She could have killed him then.

"I didn't say it was a *good* plan," Lucy said patiently. "The man is a freak. He killed a girl in Paris right after he killed Tabor. He—" Here Lucy stopped. She realized she was about to make a horrible blunder. Charles D'Arnot understood about Sufi. But he was French. These men, American military men, were not going to understand the monstrous ego behind the murder of Sufi. She was not going to score points by trying to explain.

"He's a murderer, a casual one," she finished lamely. "He kills for fun. He's going to launch that missile."

"There is no way a terrorist is going to launch a nuclear missile to unite the Arab countries," the Marine said dismissively. "The Arab countries wouldn't unite even if he single-handedly destroyed Israel on live television. No, he probably wants money. Or the release of a few of his buddies from Israeli prison."

"I didn't say it was a *good* plan," Lucy said again, feeling hopeless. Jefferson nodded sympathetically at her. There were a few more questions, but the session was over. She felt she had failed.

The phone rang. Lucy started, and realized she had a half-chewed piece of teriyaki jerky in one hand. Pregnancy really sucked. This whole day sucked, and it was only noon.

"Hello, Giometti here," she said.

"Lucy! What's up? Got something for me on the Tabor case?" The voice was cheerful Californian surfer boy. Fred Nguyen.

"Fred!" she said happily. She couldn't be depressed with Fred on the line. He positively crackled with energy. "I do, actually. But I'm muzzled right now until things settle out."

"Bummer," Fred said. "You're gonna let me know when everything's over, right?"

"I will," Lucy said firmly. She was of the younger generation at the CIA, and didn't buy into the old rivalry between the services. Nguyen was of her generation as well, and he laughed.

"Good," he said. "That Tabor case was a real wreck for my boss. I guess they'd been closing in on this dude for a while. Me, I just keep thinking about that poor damn dog he left behind. I wish he'd given her the cyanide pills, for sure."

"Why?" Lucy asked.

"Oh, come on. You think anyone's going to adopt her? She's a full-grown dog. She'll live for another day or so and then they'll put her to sleep. Damn spy couldn't even kill his own dog. I guess I can understand, but it pisses me off."

"Poor thing," Lucy said.

"Yeah. I'd adopt her myself, but my youngest has asthma. Can't have a dog. So, hey, keep in touch."

"You betcha," Lucy said, and rang off. She felt better after talking to Fred, even if no one else believed her. She bit off another hunk of jerky.

Steven Mills walked in. His thinning blond hair was askew and his pale eyes were bloodshot. He had the beginnings of sweat dampening his forehead, but a small smile sat on his lips, an odd, satisfied kind of smile. Lucy didn't like his smile at all.

"Giometti, we have a problem," he said without preamble. "Stillwell is stuck in some backwoods Oklahoma airport and won't make it in before midnight at the earliest. You need to get out there today and do some damage control."

Lucy nearly choked on her jerky. She chewed hard, and swallowed.

"Are you kidding? With Muallah in the missile silo? You're sending me to Colorado?"

Mills looked at her without expression. "Why, yes," he said. "We need you out there to help with the cover-up."

Lucy felt a sinking sensation in the pit of her stomach. She was being put Outside. Put out of the way.

"What about Jefferson?" she choked. "He probably wants to talk to me—"

"Nope, the Pentagon is done with your analysis," Mills said smugly. "You aren't needed on that effort any longer. I called Lieutenant Jefferson on that issue and he agreed that you could be sent to Colorado."

Lucy sat for a moment, then swallowed hard.

"Well, sure, Steve," she said mildly. This took enough effort that she could feel tiny sweat beads in her hairline. "You get Travel to set up the airline tickets, and I'll call Ted."

"I really appreciate it," he said. "What shall you go as? Air Force?"

"How about DIA?"

"Great idea," he said, and left the office.

Lucy leaned over her desk, eyes closed, feeling betrayed. How could Jefferson do that to her? Then she raised her head and blinked hard.

"Oh my God," she said suddenly, alone in her office. What would be the most likely target of a missile aimed at the United States? Why, Washington, D.C., of course. Washington, D.C., was always the first ground zero, the first target. Jefferson *believed* her. He was trying to get her out of harm's way. Lucy grinned. Damn chauvinist. What a wonderful man. Lucy picked up the phone and dialed quickly.

"Ted," she said. "I'm being sent out of town. Colorado. Do you think you could take a plane to your sister's place in Florida for a few days?"

•31

Colorado Springs

"So you want to bring him in?" Harben sat behind his perfect desk, his fingers folded neatly in front of him. His tie was narrow and black and his dark brown hair was combed. He looked back and forth from Eileen to Dave Rosen.

"Look, he's got to be the one," Eileen said. "He's her contact to get information out. He's the one who delivers the money to her. We found three numbers in that bankbook. Two of them are disconnected."

"They've been disconnected for two days," Rosen said. "I checked with the phone company. The services were canceled the day Guzman was murdered."

"The foreign spies," Harben said.

"Yes," Eileen said. "There isn't a single thing she could do that would be worth fourteen thousand a pop except for drugs or espionage."

"How about drugs, then?"

"The only indication we have as far as drugs go is Blaine's apparent marijuana use the night Art Bailey was killed," Rosen said crisply.

"I missed that," Harben said. "Eileen?"

"Maybe he was a little stoned the night Art was killed," Eileen said reluctantly. "I put it in my report. Maybe it was dope. Maybe it was because he'd just murdered Art and it wasn't as well planned out as Terry."

"Maybe he has a drug habit," Harben said. "But that doesn't matter, because espionage takes this case right out of our hands. You know that, don't you?" He addressed his remarks to both of the detectives. Rosen's lanky frame was slumped in the chair in front of him. Eileen sat forward in hers, forearms on her knees, her head propped in her hands.

"I know," Eileen said glumly.

"We could haul him in and have a few hours to interrogate him," Rosen said. "Just by arresting him we could make him talk, maybe."

"Maybe so," Harben said. "But we won't. The Air Force OSI officer called me this morning. He'll be arriving this evening and he'll take the whole case out of our hands. We turn our documents over to him and it's his ball game."

Eileen stared at the floor.

"It all fits," Rosen pleaded. "Blaine was there. He's got a motive. He's our man."

"He'll be the FBI's man, if he's anybody's," Harben said. "This is a federal case." Eileen looked up at Harben. Her captain was staring at her, and as always there was no emotion in his face.

"Eileen, you've done a fine job here," Harben said. "And so have you, Dave. I'm sorry you can't close this case. I want you to wrap up the documents and get them printed for the OSI officer."

"I'd like to talk to Lowell Guzman one more time," Eileen said in desperation. "Maybe he knows something about Terry's dealings with Major Blaine. I won't blow the case, I swear. I just have to wrap up the last loose ends."

Harben opened his mouth, then hesitated.

"Lowell might be in danger from Blaine, actually," Rosen said, and Eileen and Harben turned to look at him. "Wouldn't Blaine want to make sure Terry didn't have anything that pointed a finger at him? I wonder why he didn't search Lowell's house already."

"Maybe he hasn't gotten around to it," Eileen said.

Harben leaned back in his chair. It didn't squeak. Nothing was ever out of place around Harben.

"Please," Eileen said. "Don't let it just end like this. We can wrap it all the way up and they can just—tie the bow on the thing. I don't want to let them stuff this case in a drawer somewhere, or screw it up. Please let me— I mean, us—finish this."

There was silence.

"Go check on Lowell, Eileen," Harben said. "You could suggest he spend the night at a hotel until the OSI has Blaine in custody."

"I can't believe we can't arrest him right now—" Rosen started, and Harben waved him down.

"I won't allow that. They might want to let him run, to see if he reveals anyone else. We don't deal with espionage. But I have," Harben added dryly, "read up on it. Check on Lowell Guzman."

"I'm on my way," Eileen said.

Turtkul, Uzbekistan

"I am Fouad Muallah," Muallah said proudly. Behind him, Ruadh had finished his research and was now examining the launch control panels. The microphone in front of Muallah smelled faintly of garlic.

"What are your intentions, Mr. Muallah?" the voice asked respectfully. The speaker was Russian but spoke a passable Arabic. They knew who he was, then.

"Let my intentions be known to the world," Muallah said grandly. "Let the name of Fouad Muallah be repeated around the world, as the One of the Prophecies. Allah has sent us here today to complete a holy mission a *jitan*. This you shall know. Let all know my name."

With that, Muallah gestured to Ruadh, who obediently left off his examination of the launch panel. Ruadh turned off the radio and returned without a word to the panel.

"When?" Muallah asked tensely. This was taking longer than he expected.

"Very soon, Mahdi," Ruadh said serenely. "Very soon."

Moscow, Russian Republic

"What the hell does that mean?" Major Paxton said in bewilderment. Lucy Giometti could have told him, but Lucy was boarding a United Airlines flight for Colorado Springs.

Major Sergei Kalashnikov didn't like the sound of Muallah. He didn't like his tone, and he didn't like what the man said, once it was translated from Arabic by the sergeant who spoke the language.

"I don't like the sound of this," Major General Cherepovitch said.

"I have been instructed to offer you American Stealth bombers," Major Paxton said unexpectedly. Cherepovitch and Kalashnikov turned to the Major, who was not looking much like the master of anything at the moment. His hair looked sweaty and rumpled.

"We can blow the covers off the silos and drop bombs down the tubes in two bomber waves, guaranteed," the Major said reluctantly. His face was definitely flushed. He was not a happy-looking man.

"That will kill the Russian women and children in silo number six, won't it?" Kalashnikov said softly. The Major's flush deepened. He knew that.

"Yes," he said shortly. There was a long moment of silence.

"Let's see," Cherepovitch said slowly. "You want to send American bombers over Russian soil and bomb Russian women and children in order to kill a terrorist. Is this correct?"

"We have some background on Muallah that suggests he might launch," the Major said stubbornly. He refused to look Kalashnikov in the eye. "Wherever that bomb might hit would kill far more women and children than are in silo number six."

"Thank you, no," Cherepovitch said coldly. Kalashnikov wanted to cheer. "My country declines. We have a ground assault team that can be there in twelve hours. We will take our missile base back and rescue our comrades, Major Paxton. Please express our regrets to your government, and our thanks at your offer."

Cherepovitch turned to Kalashnikov and gave him a solemn wink. Kalashnikov barely suppressed a grin. God, that felt good.

Now their assault team had to succeed, that was all. Kalashnikov said another silent prayer as Major Paxton, shoulders slumped, went to his secure phone.

The Pentagon

"They said no?"

"They said no," General Knox said to the Secretary of Defense.

"What is your assessment?"

"Mr. Secretary, the Russians are the Three Stooges of the military world," Knox said rudely. "They'll probably kill each other and launch the missile themselves."

The Secretary licked his lips nervously. Was this man serious?

"And?"

"I suggest we get the President in the air and as many members of Congress out of town as quickly as possible." Knox knew he'd convinced the Secretary when the man paled to a nice tone of paper white.

"Oh my God," he said.

"We have one card up our sleeve," Knox said. "If this madman does happen to launch."

"The Missile Defense program?" the Secretary whispered.

"That's correct, sir," Knox said. He'd argued for years against spending on those damn foolish space toys. Now here he was offering the program like a life preserver to a drowning man. He hated the words coming out of his mouth. "After we get the President out of danger, I suggest we get Admiral Kane to fire up this system and see if all the billions we spent pays off."

"First things first," the Secretary said, still pale. Knox kept a contemptuous smile from curling his lip. The Secretary would be on Air Force One with the President. The coward. The Secretary picked up the phone.

"Operation Scramble," he said.

Colorado Springs

Lucy Giometti, who left Washington, D.C., a day after Major Alan Stillwell finally left Alabama, beat him into Colorado Springs by a margin of
better than four hours. Her commercial flight landed at the Colorado
Springs airport and taxied to the entrance in the late afternoon.

Colorado Springs still managed to retain the flavor of a small-town airport. The business out of the huge Denver International Airport, sixty
miles north, consumed most of the air traffic in the area. So Lucy found
herself in a small, nearly empty terminal building framing a breathtaking
view of a single towering mountain.

"What's that mountain called?" she asked the rental-car attendant.

"Pikes Peak," the girl said with a bored expression. Lucy nodded and set
down her bag. Her legs ached from the flight and her stomach felt awful.
She hadn't thrown up, but it had been a near thing as they'd bumped their
way down the Front Range. She turned again to regard the amazing bulk of
Pikes Peak. There were thunderstorms rising lazily in the afternoon heat,
building up along the shoulders of the Peak. Lucy thought she could look
at the view forever and never grow tired of it.

The FBI office was fairly close to the airport. The directions Fred
Nguyen had given Lucy were simple, and she found his office without any
trouble. The air was hot but fresh and dry, and she stretched luxuriously
outside her car before entering the office building.

"Fred?" she asked. There couldn't be a doubt. The Asian man who was
sitting at the front desk in the empty office could only be Fred Nguyen. He
had a phone to his ear and his feet were up on the desk. He was wearing the
FBI suit, but the thick black hair was cut so that it stood up wildly all over
his head. A grin split his face when he saw Lucy in the doorway.

"Gotta go, hon," he said, and hung up the phone. "You must be Lucy."

"I'm Lucy, and I'm hungry," she said, and grinned back at him.

"Hey, you're pregnant," he said, standing up from the desk and walking
around to shake her hand.

"Not really," she said soberly. "It's all part of the disguise." He looked at her closely for a second, then threw his head back and laughed.

"You kill me," he said. "Hey, how about genuine Vietnamese food? I asked Kim if she'd do us up a real meal and she said sure. That okay with you?"

"That sounds great," Lucy said.

"Let's head right to my house, okay?" Nguyen said. He escorted her out and locked the office behind him.

"Everyone's gone?"

"Hot line's in Denver," Nguyen said with a grin. "This here is the backwater. Gone fishin', gone skiin', we take any excuse to take off. That's why I like this place." His smile was warm and without cynicism, but Lucy knew the real story. Nguyen just didn't have the look of an FBI agent. He wasn't white and he wasn't tall, and so he was assigned to Colorado Springs, not Washington, D.C. Nguyen caught her look and offered a small, cynical shrug.

"Heck, it could have been the Navajo Reservation," he said. "Or up in Rapid City. Colorado Springs has a knock-your-socks-off symphony."

"A symphony," Lucy murmured. Here she was, safely out of Washington. At least Ted was safe in Florida. If anything happened, that is. Lucy looked toward the west again and realized uneasily that NORAD was in those mountains. Wouldn't that be a good joke, if Jefferson sent her to ground zero?

"Almost heaven," Nguyen said. "You'll be in heaven when you taste my wife's cooking. Now, that's paradise."

As they went to their cars, an afternoon thundershower started booming off Pikes Peak, sending gray sheets of rain drifting through the dry afternoon air.

Garden of the Gods, Colorado Springs

Joe Tanner had an idea. An Idea. Perhaps the thunderstorms inspired him. He'd read once that thunderstorms created an electromagnetic field that caused people to do better on tests. The thundershower hadn't caught him on his run through the Garden of the Gods, but only because he'd sprinted the last half mile to his car. He was a native and knew the weather patterns, so he'd timed his run to end before five o'clock, when the first of the showers should be striking down from the Peak. They hit just as planned, and now he sat in his car, panting, as the first big drops splattered against his windshield. Thunder boomed, and he smelled the glorious wet sage smell of Colorado rain.

"Ahh, beautiful," he said to himself, and leaned back in the seat. He was happy. To wake up with Eileen Reed was something he was going to like getting used to, he decided. Fixing coffee was a whole new experience. And that shower they'd had together! He shivered with sudden goose bumps. The rain fell harder and a few hailstones bounced off the windshield. Joe kept the window open so he could smell the rain and the sage, even though a hailstone or two bounced into the car. He remembered Sully, and the memory didn't hurt. Remembering Sully made him think that Art would be so happy for him that he'd found someone—and his thoughts dissolved in confusion and grief. Art was dead and he'd never know now. He watched the hard rain bouncing off the hood of the car. Art had been trying to prove to Eileen that he hadn't killed Terry. Art hated the thought that he was a suspect. He'd told Joe on that last afternoon that he was going to try and figure out a way to prove who'd done it. Or at least, prove that *he* hadn't. There really wasn't any way for him to do that, unless . . .

That was when he realized what Arthur Bailey had been doing.

Joe sat straight up in the car seat. His eyes stared at nothing. The sweat that beaded his face from his run dripped, unnoticed, from his nose and chin.

"That's what he was doing!" he said aloud, to himself. "Why didn't I think of that? I'm so stupid. I'm so stupid!"

He pulled his seat upright, fumbled for the keys, and started his car. He pulled into the roadway with a scattering of wet gravel, and headed down the road.

Washington, D.C.

"Ouch, goddammit, you're hurting me!" Richard yelped as the Secret Service agent carried him over his shoulder like so much baggage. Richard was not small, but the agent ran down the hallway at a near sprint. When Richard was dumped into the helicopter he rubbed his arms and glared at the agent, who was panting and red-faced.

"Sorry, sir," the agent said, obviously not meaning it.

Richard was preparing to go into what he fondly considered a high fury, but then he saw the wildly waving legs of his younger brother being carried upside down by a very determined-looking Secret Service agent. Richard was instantly diverted.

"That's funny." He laughed. "I can't wait to see Dad . . ." His voice trailed off as the enormous bulk of his father came shooting out the White House door right after his brother. The President was upright, but his feet weren't touching the ground. His agents were carrying him, actually *carrying* him. Richard wondered if he was imagining this. No, his father's feet really were off the ground. The President of the United States had been enormous before he was elected. Now he was of legendary proportions. The two agents who were carrying him looked very distressed and were trying to hide it. Their grip made the President, at a distance, keep his dignity. But his tiny feet paddled inches above the ground as he traveled faster than a normal man could run. Richard covered his mouth to stifle a giggle.

"Ha, Steve," he said as his brother was shoved in next to him. "You sure looked stupid, upside down like that."

"Shut up," Steve panted. "What about Mom?" he asked his agent.

"She's already in the air," the agent said. The First Lady was on a fund-raising trip and wasn't due back from Florida until the end of the week.

The President was hustled in the door, and Richard made as though to sneak over and sit with him. The agent who'd carried him out briskly reached over and fastened his seat belt.

"This is going to be a very rough ride," he said softly and not unkindly. "You'll be able to sit with him on the plane."

The helicopter leaped into the sky with a very nasty jerk, and the engines revved up into a scream. This was not the usual helicopter ride from the White House.

Suddenly the whole picture fell into place for Richard.

"Oh my God," he said, horrified. "Is it aliens?"

His father was panting too much to talk. Steve, who was a worm, sneered at him. Steve was brilliant. Richard had lived his whole life with a little brother who could think rings around him. And Steve wasn't a wormy-looking geek, either. He was tall and straight and had wavy brown hair and snapping blue eyes. He looked like a little superhero. Richard, who shared Steve's height and hair and eyes but who was built like Dad, held out hope he would keep from getting quite as fat as his father. In the meantime, algebra and his brother were the banes of his life.

"Look in the sky, bat-brain," Steve said nastily. "Do you see alien space-ships?"

"No, I don't, Wormy," he snapped back. "But if I were President, I'd get out before they hovered over the White House."

His agent, Carlton, grinned at him affectionately.

"So let me in on the joke," Dad said, having finally regained his breath.

"Yes, Mr. President," the head of Secret Service said. He was very tall and very grave and, to Richard, looked like he was about a million years old. "There is a potential nuclear threat against the United States . . ."

Richard stopped listening. He reached out blindly, and Steve took his hand. They sat huddled together as the Secret Service agent spoke of monstrous terrors in his low and soothing voice. The helicopter screamed through the skies over Washington, D.C., headed for the airport and Air Force One.

• 32

Colorado Springs Investigations Bureau

Eileen cursed and hung up the phone.

"What's up?" Rosen said. He was tilted back in his chair and had a wet washcloth pressed to his forehead. Rosen didn't believe in drugs of any kind and so used the washcloth method to get rid of a headache. He informed Eileen it worked much better than the aspirin she was going to swallow.

"Uh-huh," Eileen said, and swallowed the aspirin.

Now she let her head rest against her arm and cursed again.

"Let me guess," Rosen said from behind the washcloth. "Guzman still isn't home."

"No, he's not. It's six o'clock," Eileen said in frustration. "Where is he?"

"Could be anywhere," Rosen said.

"I've got a date tonight," Eileen said reluctantly. "I've got possibilities of developing a life here."

"With Joe Tanner?" Rosen said. His face was hidden behind the cloth, but his voice was reassuringly bland.

"Yeah," Eileen said, unsurprised. Dave Rosen was no dummy. She rested a hip against the desk. "We're going to be working together from now on, it looks like. I don't think I should start out by lying to you." She felt the heat rise in her face. This was difficult for her. She didn't have any brothers, although she had had Owen Sutter, her fellow high-school boarder, when she was a child. A new partner always presented some challenges.

"That's a good idea," Rosen said. "Not lying, I mean." He took the washcloth from his forehead and looked over at her. "I don't think dating Joe Tanner is a real swell idea right now. I know all the signs point to Major Blaine, but he's still contaminated by all of this. I hope you don't lose your perspective on that."

Eileen took a deep, angry breath, then blew it out again. She shrugged at Rosen, then grinned at him.

"I guess that's what you're around for," she said. "Right?"

Rosen looked at her for a moment, then leaned back in his chair and put the washcloth back over his face.

"Right," he said. "I wouldn't want to work with anyone else. You know Guzman might be at his house. He might have turned the phone off."

"Hey, good idea," Eileen said. She was a little disconcerted by the compliment. "Good idea. I think I'll drive out there. Let me call Joe first, though."

She dialed, but there was no answer there either. Eileen frowned and left a message on the machine.

"Now, where could Joe be?" she wondered aloud, then realized he was probably working out at the health club near the Garden of the Gods. Nelson had said he swam or ran there nearly every day. She got her keys from her desk.

"You got the rest of this?" she asked Rosen. He was still relaxing, feet up on the desk.

"I got the paperwork going," he said, and flapped a hand at her. "Go on."

As Eileen took her jacket from the hook by her desk, Rosen spoke behind the wet rag.

"Eileen?"

"Yes?" she said, shrugging into her jacket and checking her holster.

"You sure you don't want me to go? I got a funny feeling about this one."

Eileen felt a run of goose bumps.

"No," she said, after thinking for a moment. "We have to get that paperwork out the door. I'll only be an hour at the most."

"Okay," Rosen said. "Just watch your back."

"I will." She smiled at the washrag. "Don't worry."

Colorado Springs

Lucy leaned back in her chair, sighing. She'd had to pass on the plum wine because of her pregnancy, but she'd eaten the other dishes until she was stuffed.

"This plum wine isn't authentic anyway," Fred Nguyen said. Fred's wife Kim was another California Vietnamese with the same mixture of Asian features and beach girl mannerisms. They had two children, a boy and a girl.

"I'm afraid of labor," Lucy admitted. "But it's worth it to have a baby."

"You're going to love being a mom," Kim said, stacking dishes. "Labor isn't all that bad."

Behind her, Fred rolled his eyes.

"I need to get to my hotel room," Lucy said, smiling. "I've got to get ahold of Colonel Ellison. And maybe Detective Reed, if she's around."

"Sure you can't stay?" Nguyen asked. He'd already given Lucy his sheaf of documents, which she'd locked in her little travel suitcase. The suitcase was the only CIA-made object in her wardrobe. No poison pens or little laser-beam penlights, she'd thought with a sigh. The suitcase was aluminum reinforced and had a tiny acid container in the locking mechanism. If the case was forced the acid would dump and destroy the contents of the case.

"Cool," Lucy muttered when Mills gave her the suitcase on her first business trip.

"Don't forget the combo," Mills had said.

"Or the acid will eat my shorts." Lucy grinned. Mills didn't laugh.

"I do have to work," Lucy said. "Thank you so much for the meal and the company."

Looking at the two of them made Lucy miss Ted terribly. She wished she'd talked him into coming with her instead of going to Florida. For whole blocks of time she could make herself forget Fouad Muallah and the Turtkul missile silo, then she would remember. Remembering felt awful. There was nothing she could do, she reminded herself as she shook hands with Fred. Her analysis was complete and that's all she was, an analyst. She wasn't some kind of movie hero, to go with guns blazing into Uzbekistan and somehow ruin Muallah's plans. She just had to wait it out.

"Good luck with your little one," Kim said, woman to woman, and they smiled at each other.

"Take care, now," Fred called as she walked to her car, and a shiver ran up her spine like the cold touch of a hand. Muallah. Nuclear threat. Lucy held one hand over the rounded swell of her belly as she got into the car.

Air Force One

Richard, attached like a round little barnacle to the side of his father, heard the whole conversation. Air Force One was in the air and there were no aliens, just a crazy Arab terrorist who might launch a nuclear missile. Some CIA analyst had decided he was going to launch at the United States instead of the obvious target, Israel, and the Russians refused to let the Americans take the missile silo out. Evidently there were some Russian hostages.

Richard had great problems with algebra, but he had a keen grasp for detail. What was most important was that the chances of America getting nuked seemed pretty small. The atmosphere inside Air Force One was definitely more relaxed.

"Admiral Kane," Dad said in his Mr. President voice.

"Sir," said the voice over the radio. Kane sounded old, Richard thought. Or perhaps he'd been up for many hours.

"You're requesting authorization to enable the Missile Defense System?"

"That is correct, sir. The sooner the better. If there is a launch and the system is already set up for tracking, we should have a better chance of shooting it down."

"More than a chance, I hope, Admiral," the President said harshly. "For the money we've spent."

"Mr. President, the system is still in the start-up stages. It's not fully operational. But we feel confident the system will work."

"Any chances of the system being compromised?"

"None as far as we can tell, sir."

"Approved," the President said, and waved his hand to cut the communications link. "Now let's get to work on the Russian situation."

One of the Generals in the cabin looked quickly at Richard and Steve, then looked at the President. The President glared at him.

"They stay," he said, and Richard gave a smug grimace at the General. "As long as they don't say a word." Richard pressed his lips together firmly and looked over at Steve, who nodded back. They weren't going to get kicked out. This was much too interesting.

Colorado Springs

Eileen finally found the Guzman residence. Rosen had been here, but she hadn't. It was merely another handsome tract home on a quiet cul-de-sac, a location innocent of any atmosphere. She turned off her lights and coasted to a stop against the curb. Her tires made a mild crunching sound over the few pieces of gravel on the road, and a dog barked a long way away. The thundershowers had stopped and it was almost dark. Water ran in the curbs, drying quickly in the warm evening air.

The porch light was on. There were lights on in the house, and there was the faint sound and flickering of a television. Eileen rang the doorbell.

Silence. The dog barked again, down the street. The slight breeze brought a heavy scent of summer roses. The Guzmans must have a rose bed somewhere. Eileen rang the doorbell again. She couldn't figure out why she was so nervous. Perhaps because she knew about Terry Guzman. She knew the spider this house was home to. Eileen wondered about Lowell Guzman. Could he not know what he was married to? Was there some deep feeling of relief under all that grief over her death?

Still no reply. Eileen drew a deep breath. Perhaps Guzman couldn't hear her because he was already dead. Maybe Lowell was the next victim. Eileen walked quietly around the side of the house. Her breath was light and quick. She came to the living-room windows and saw the television and the back of Lowell Guzman's head. The head was slack, resting in a big arm-chair. One limp hand hung around a glass of what looked like Scotch. The arm seemed too still. It looked more than passed out. It looked dead. Eileen felt her whole body prickle with goose bumps. She drew her gun carefully from her holster.

The back-porch door was locked, but the window next to it was open. It took only a moment for Eileen to unlatch the screen and reach through to the door. She stepped into the house.

Gaming Center, Schriever Air Force Base

Joe Tanner took a deep breath and sat down in Art's chair. His terminal keys were dirty, he saw; the F and the J were particularly grubby. For a moment unexpected tears stung his eyes, and then he blinked them away. Art was shorter than he was. Joe had to adjust the chair. The workstation screen was dark. Joe posed his hands over the keyboard, fingers lightly touching Art's keys, and pressed the return key with one finger.

"Login." The words printed in cold white on the dark screen. Joe had three chances to log in to the computer network that controlled the simulations. If he failed three times and tried again, the computer system would appear to let him in, while screaming for help at the main operator console. There was a computer security program that would spill false data to an unsuspecting pirate. By the time the invader figured out that the system wasn't responding quite as it should, the FBI would be knocking at the door. Or, in Joe's case, he would call the operator and receive a tongue-lashing for his thick-fingered clumsiness, while the operator shut down the emergency alarms. It had happened to some Gamers, but not Joe.

Joe looked around, even though he knew no one could possibly be there this late at night. Besides, the door to the computer Center was a huge, noisy thing that beeped loudly when opened. Still, he was about to commit a computer crime.

He took another breath and typed Art's name and password on the screen. Art and Joe always shared their passwords, a secret they told no one else. Sharing a password was a crime, but it made their work easier during the long preparation hours for a War Game. Neither the name nor the password appeared, another security feature that Joe found irritating. The workstation seemed to muse for a moment, chewing over his request for access. The screen flashed white, then cleared. He was in.

Colorado Springs

Eileen walked down the dim hallway toward the family room, where the TV chattered meaninglessly. A burst of canned laughter tensed her briefly. The sound of the TV, the darkness of the hallway, the absurdity she was involved with, made her feel unreal, as though she were part of some television drama. It was a soothing and dangerous thought, as though if Major Blaine were to leap from some unknown corner and stab her, Eileen could just wipe the blood away and shoot the next scene. She caught sight of the back of the armchair, the shock of brown hair, and the checkered bathrobe arm as limp as a store dummy draped over a fragile side table.

The armed moved stiffly, and the glass was brought to the front of the chair. Eileen felt her whole body relax in relief. She wet her lips and entered the room.

"Mr. Guzman," she said softly. "It's Detective Reed. Can we talk?"

There was no reply. Eileen moved in front of the chair and froze in surprise. She faced a nubbled yellow face without eyes or mouth or nose, topped by a snarl of brown hair. It took her a moment to identify the face as a foam football, turned on end and impaled on a thin pine board. Beneath the head, settled into the armchair like some malevolent broken toy, a nest of wires and circuit boards moved a bathrobe-clad robot arm toward the football. The glass turned, the Scotch rose smoothly up the side of the glass, the arm moved back toward the table. There was a gentle humming.

Behind Eileen the television flickered and launched into a loud musical commercial. The seamless face of the robot seemed to mock her. She caught a movement from the corner of her eye and turned to look, tensed in an instant, the sweat turning icy on her face.

The motion was from a house next door. A woman was in her kitchen. The woman's blinds were up, and the French doors in Lowell's house had the curtains pulled back. The woman was too far away to see an expression, but she could obviously see Eileen in Lowell's living room, and her posture spelled confusion.

Eileen moved carefully to one of the other chairs and sat down calmly, as though invited to do so by the faceless thing in the armchair. She saw the woman lose her suspicious posture and go on with some sort of homey evening cooking, probably cookies or some kind of treat. Eileen could almost smell the chocolate.

It was then that she realized, all in a rush, what the robot and the woman meant. The neighbor would swear Lowell had been there; she'd seen him in his armchair all evening. And that could mean only one thing: Lowell needed an alibi because he was going to commit a murder. Another murder.

Lowell Guzman was the murderer, not Major Blaine. Eileen couldn't move in the armchair. Everything came rushing together. It all fit. Lowell must have found out that Terry was selling secret documents. If she were discovered and convicted, he would go to jail, or at the least lose his clearance. Lowell was in the Gaming Center the day Terry was murdered. Lowell was the damn fine actor that Eileen watched on the videos of the Game, crumpled and weeping in the arms of 'Berto and Sharon Johnson. It wasn't Major Blaine at all. It was Lowell.

•33

Gaming Center, Schriever Air Force Base

Joe walked from room to room, flipping on lights and punching the buttons that turned on the graphics terminals. He had done this a thousand times, but always with Art chattering on the keyboard in the main room, or racing him to see who could turn on more terminals. His death surrounded Joe like a rough sea: sometimes it surged around him quietly and sometimes it took him and dragged him under and scraped him raw. It hurt. Then he thought of Eileen, and he knew how much better it was to feel, even if it hurt. For the two years since Sully died he hadn't felt much of anything. Now he was living again.

Then the seas quieted down around him and he forgot everything but the minutiae of the simulation, the terminal stations up and going, the computer network functioning without error, the ports between computers connected and transmitting perfectly. If anything was slightly less than perfect, his attempt would not work.

Joe returned to the main console, his fingers moving rapidly over Art's grubby keyboard. His eyes, lit by the screen, showed a dazed, slightly puzzled look of concentration.

Eventually he paused, sitting back in his chair and putting one foot up on the table where the terminal sat. The computer screen was full of square windows, each one filled with words. Joe flicked his gaze over each window, then nodded in satisfaction and punched the return key.

The screens in the Gaming Center went dark, one by one, then lit up again with the blue globe of the Earth. Joe went to 'Berto's console and stood plucking at his lower lip. He wasn't aware he was copying Art's favorite expression. On the console, the arrow that represented the mouse control suddenly jerked and moved across the screen, although there was no hand at the mouse. Joe nodded to himself, unsmiling.

The arrow moved again, and the globe shifted to a view of the United States. Joe watched, fascinated, as the slightest move of Roberto Espinoza was played back in front of his eyes. Every move that he had made on the keyboard, every tremor of muscle or finger key-click, had been recorded faithfully by the computer system. Joe, as he suspected Art had done before him, had set the system up so that the recording was being played back, exactly as the Game had happened on the day of the murder.

Somewhere, on one of the eight terminals in the Gaming room, one arrow would grow still. During a War Game the participants were required to have their hand on the mouse at all times, to monitor the battle and send the right commands.

On one screen, the mouse would stop moving. The screen would stay unchanged. The person whose fingers should have been on the mouse, making it move and shift around the screen, would be gone. The mouse would stay absolutely still while the murderer crawled under the Gaming Center floor and rose up behind Terry Guzman like a cobra from a basket. The mouse wouldn't move again until the murderer was back in his seat, pretending all was well.

The missiles burst from the ocean and 'Berto's terminal flickered toward the launch. Joe stood and watched as the missiles lifted and flared and eventually detonated in Washington, D.C.

He sighed, and walked back to Art's console. He pressed a series of keys and the screens went black, then lit up again with the blue globe of the Earth.

Joe knew that the screens hadn't been live when they'd found Art. Art must have created a program to check on each of the terminals and make a decision when one was silent for too long. That was the "Found" phrase on Art's computer that Nelson told her about when Major Blaine discovered Art's body. Joe knew he could duplicate Art's code, but it would take him days where it had taken Art hours. He figured it would be easier to just replay the Gamers' screens and watch them one by one, in each person's room. Art was so good. He felt a surge of panic as he realized if there were more games to be played, it would be Joe Tanner at the helm now. He wouldn't ever be able to fill Art's shoes, but he'd have to try. He rubbed his hands together furiously and blinked hard. Finding out Art's murderer would be a good start.

Joe walked to Doug Procell's terminal, and the light from the screen lit his face as he stood motionless, watching.

NORAD, Cheyenne Mountain, Colorado

General Kelton was on duty that night. There were three American generals and one Canadian general who shared the on-call duty at NORAD.

Now that the Missile Defense program was more or less on-line, crucial decisions had to be made. Most important, the whole system wasn't operational yet. Control of the system alternated between NORAD and Space Command, out at Schriever. Eventually control would rest at NORAD, as it must, and Schriever would continue as a research-and-development station. For now there was always a bit of a battle whenever there were War Games going on.

Kelton, who considered himself a tough son of a bitch and a damned fine soldier, contemplated the Real Thing. He'd been at NORAD for almost three years and he dreamed about incoming missile tracks. Sometimes he wondered if they weren't printed on the inner side of his eyelids. He'd played enough War Games to understand decisions had to be made at lightning speed. Missiles were rockets, godddammit, *rockets,* and they came fast.

So Kelton drank Coke all night long and slept in a darkened room with special window shades during the day. His children were grown and gone, so his wife good-naturedly moved her schedule around to match his.

The alert phone rang. Kelton picked up the red phone and heard a dial tone. The phone rang again. He looked down and realized the gold phone was ringing. *The gold phone.*

"Alert!" he roared, and picked up the phone.

"General Kelton, this is Admiral Kane," the Admiral's voice crackled.

"Admiral Kane," Kelton said. Around him, the Command Center at NORAD was exploding with running feet and flashing lights. But silently, silently. Kelton established silent alerts when he took command, and now his people were as quiet as ghosts. His punishment for noise was a suspension of cafeteria privileges. No one messed up twice after having to eat sandwiches from a cooler when the rest of the crew were devouring the gourmet meals dished up at NORAD.

"We have a Russian missile silo taken over by an Arab terrorist group," Kane said briefly. "There is a potential for a launch at an American city."

"Yes, sir," Kelton said, and pumped his forearm at the Colonel standing four feet away. Kelton poked his index finger out of his fist, and the Colonel went white. Kelton glared at him so fiercely, the Colonel should have burst into flames like a newspaper in the path of a flamethrower.

"Button up!" the General whispered, covering the phone with one hand. "Button up!"

"You need to enable the Missile Defense system," Kane said. "If this missile flies anywhere, we want to shoot it down. Europe, Israel, South America, anywhere."

"If it flies, it dies, sir," Kelton said grimly.

"Keep me informed."

"Yes, sir."

Kelton heard, through the earth that surrounded him on all sides, the shuddering sound of the blast door slamming shut. NORAD was sealed.

Colorado Springs

Eileen sat in Lowell's chair, frozen with indecision. Who was going to be murdered? For precious minutes her mind raced without purpose or coherence. The sweat beaded and dropped down her back. The bland empty face of the robot stared straight ahead, the glass rising and falling in the metal hand, rising and falling. The robot would have been in this position the night before, when Art was being murdered. Eileen felt the rage rise and blossom in her body. She nearly reached out and swept the mechanical man from the chair. The urge was so overwhelming, she found herself on her feet, fists clenched, wanting to kick and hammer and destroy. But Eileen wanted Guzman, wanted him behind bars or perhaps dead and rotting in a coffin.

And if Eileen didn't do some fast thinking, there would be three Guzman victims instead of two.

Eileen straightened with a jerk. She leaped to the phone and pawed at it for a moment with clumsy and sweat-slicked hands. She dialed Joe's number from memory, waiting an agony of seconds before the connection was made and the phone began to ring.

She knew he was gone—or dead, a tiny cheerful voice in her head informed her—before the answering machine picked up and Joe's precise, velvety voice asked her to leave her name and number. Eileen almost put the phone down, then stopped.

"Joe, this is Eileen. Please get out of your house, right now. Go to a phone and call the police. Don't talk to anyone or get close to anyone, do you understand? If you are hearing this, please get out and get to a phone now!" Eileen bit back a strangled sound as she slammed the phone on the cradle and headed for the door.

NORAD, Cheyenne Mountain, Colorado

"What do you mean, you can't enable the system?" Kelton said in a voice as cold as frozen iron.

"I can't enable," the Captain said miserably. Her hair was in disarray and her uniform skirt was rumpled. "We suspended the system when that girl got murdered at Schriever. The system hasn't been reset, sir."

"That means we have to enable at Schriever," Kelton said. His lips were numb. "Get the emergency helicopter ready to fly. Shelly, we'll send you to Schriever to—"

"Sir," Shelly squeaked. "Sir—"

"Yes?"

"The Gaming Center has to be kicked on—started up, sir. I don't know how to do that."

Kelton stood contemplating Captain Shelly for a moment. He was in a cold rage, but he was thinking fast. Rockets were so goddamned *fast*.

"Who knows?"

"The Truth Team leader got killed too, sir," Captain Shelly said. "But the Game Leader, Nelson Atkins, he should know how to do it."

"Find out where he lives," Kelton snapped at Colonel Maclean. "Get the helicopter ready for Maclean and Shelly," he snapped to Major Dunn. "And open that goddamned blast door!"

Turtkul, Uzbekistan

Anna Kalinsk was allowing herself to feel a little kernel of hope. The terrorists hadn't figured out how to blast the silo top off, or they had decided the little group of women and children weren't worth the effort. She didn't care about the reason, only the result. Her sons might live, after all.

"Will our comrades send troops, Anna?" Ilina whispered fiercely. "Will they come?"

Anna closed her eyes and thought for a moment. Yes, troops could be brought in using Hinds. Would the little missile silo be worth it? Of course. Anna counted the hours in the silo, the last radio transmission by Boriska, the probable response time. . . .

She opened her eyes and smiled at Ilina.

"Why, they should be here anytime!" she said brightly, and as though her words were a cue, they heard the booming sounds of heavy guns.

Ilina looked at Anna with her mouth hanging open. Anna offered a small shrug, and blushed.

"Just luck," she said.

Gaming Center, Schriever Air Force Base

Joe watched Sharon's console next, although he felt sure Sharon Johnson couldn't kill anyone. Sharon's was the next in line, and Joe was a logical person. He wondered where Eileen could be. He'd called her at the office and they'd said she was out. He was nervous about telling some dispatcher that this was an emergency—what if he were wrong? So he said it was a personal call, and he left a message for Eileen at her home machine.

The globe of the Earth showed blue and white and spectacular. Sharon, manning some of the communications satellite views, was positioned casually north, near England. That way the launch could be seen at Bermuda but she wouldn't commit the mistake of hovering directly over a launch that she shouldn't know was going to happen. The view shifted constantly. Joe gazed at the terminal and wondered if Nelson was going to call him at the Center. He'd left a message for Nelson on voice mail since he hadn't been able to contact Eileen. Maybe Lowell would call. Sometimes he picked up Nelson's voice mail when Nelson was out. Joe sighed, watching Sharon's mouse key move through the course of the game. Not Sharon, then, but he could have guessed that.

Colorado Springs

Eileen made the call as her Jeep squealed out of the subdivision. Rosen was still in the office.

"Thank God," she said to him. "Listen. I've been to Lowell's house. He's got a robot there, something that looks like him from the windows."

"It's Lowell," Rosen said immediately. "Oh, shit, it's Lowell."

"Could be Lowell and Blaine both, for all I know. I think he's after someone. He used that alibi the night Art was killed."

"I'll send out cars to all the Gamers' houses," Rosen said. "I'll take Lowell's house myself. We'll get the crew there to photograph for evidence. You're on your way to Joe Tanner's house?"

Eileen felt warmth in the cold yawning pit of her insides. Rosen was going to be a great partner.

"On my way there," she said. "Yes."

"I'll get a warrant for Guzman and Blaine both," Rosen said. "We haven't had word one from Stillwell."

"Clear. I'll contact you when I'm there. Out."

Eileen's stomach felt like a slick stone in her middle, and her mouth was so dry she made a little clicking sound when she swallowed. Joe, Joe, she mouthed.

She saw Constitution Avenue. The road upon which she would turn to go to Schriever Air Force Base. Eileen stared at the crossing, and the answer came to her. It was so simple. She swerved across two lanes and made the turn to Schriever, and the sudden hope in her chest was more terrible than the fear. She picked up the phone to call Rosen.

Peterson Air Force Base, Colorado

"Captain Stillwell?"

Stillwell, in the hangar at Peterson Air Field, was just hanging up the pay phone. He felt dirty and tired and confused. That seemed to be his fate lately. He looked up and saw the on-duty officer holding a phone and gesturing to him. Behind the on-duty officer Stillwell could see Gwen and Richard and the flight commander of the base. The flight commander looked crisp and fresh. Gwen and Richard looked dirty and exhausted, but their faces were animated. They were standing at a map and discussing the salvage operation.

"For me?" he said. The on-duty officer nodded and held out the phone.

Stillwell felt sick to his stomach. He hadn't lost his lunch when the Chinook dropped out of the sky into a cornfield, but now his stomach was rolling like a ship at sea. Colonel Ellison had just told him to shut the investigation down, and the order wasn't even disguised as a polite request. Stillwell intended to follow orders, but he didn't have to like them.

"Hello?"

"Captain Stillwell?"

"Yes," he said. "Who is this?"

"My name is Lucy Giometti. I'm from DIA. I just spoke to your Colonel Ellison, and he told me you'd just gotten into town. Did he talk to you?"

"I'm in town," he said. "And I just finished talking to him. Why—what are you to do with all this?"

"I'm here to help out," the voice said. "Let's just say, I'll hold up the edge of the carpet while you sweep."

Stillwell closed his eyes. "I see."

"Not too pleasant, I know," Lucy Giometti said.

"Alan," Stillwell said. "Call me Alan. I was planning to shower and change. I've been—"

There was a tap on his shoulder. The harassed-looking on-duty officer was holding out another line.

"Hang on," he said, and took the phone to his other ear.

"I called the Colorado Springs Police to tell them you were in town and to arrange a transfer from Captain Harben," Colonel Ellison said in his deep, clipped voice. "And they tell me the detective is at Schriever right now. She called in an assault."

"I'm on my way," Stillwell said immediately.

"Good," his commander said. "This is turning into a royal mess, Alan. I want you to get this under control."

"Yes, sir," Stillwell said, through the click of the disconnecting line.

"What was that?" Lucy Giometti said in his other ear.

"That means I don't get a shower," he said. "Where are you?"

"Day's Inn, next to the Colorado Springs airport," she responded instantly.

"Be out front. I'll be there in ten minutes. We have to get to Schriever," he said.

"I'll be there," she said.

Stillwell handed both phones back to the on-duty officer.

"I need a car," he said. "Mine is at the Denver airport."

"My car is here," Gwen said from across the room. "You can borrow mine."

•34

Joe configured for Lowell Guzman's terminal.

Colorado Springs

Lucy Giometti pulled thick white socks over her feet. Her pregnancy pants were really horrible looking, but they were comfortable and they fit. She pulled on a white button-up shirt—also a pregnancy shirt—and laced her running shoes tightly. Her heart was pounding and there was a slick feeling at the back of her throat. Part of her brain was telling her to stay in her safe little rabbit hutch of a room. That part of her brain was telling her that she was pregnant. Going into danger while pregnant was not right. She should be protecting herself. She should stay put.

The other part of her remembered the Tower of London, shattered and smoking. That part of her checked her gun. The shoulder holster fit under the baggy white shirt. Lucy slipped an extra clip into her hideous pregnancy pants, where it rested coldly against the swelling of her stomach.

"Here I go," she said to her reflection in the mirror, and blew out a trembling deep breath.

Lucy remembered her room key and headed for the door.

Highway 94, Colorado

The highway was dark and empty. The cattle stood sleepily by the fences, washed momentarily by Eileen's headlights as she held the Jeep on the bare edge of control. One large stone, one clod of debris, could tear the steering wheel from her hands and send her hurtling into the ditch. The Jeep was not meant to be treated like a sports car. Eileen took the chance that there would be no stone, and kept her foot on the accelerator.

Turtkul, Uzbekistan

Muallah was extremely unhappy with Ruadh. He was supposed to have targeted the missile and blasted it off within twelve hours, and look at him. He was still humming, still running his fingers on the console, still consulting manuals.

"Ruadh," Muallah said finally. "You must start the countdown to launch. We cannot wait any longer. Or you must admit that you cannot do it."

Ruadh looked over, and Muallah made sure he saw the look in his eyes. Admitting failure meant a very quick death at the hands of Ali.

"I—" Ruadh looked stubborn for a moment, then sighed. "I can begin for you. I would like more time, but—"

"Then begin!" Muallah shouted.

At that moment, there was a booming sound from far above. A shot.

"Attackers!" Rashad shouted, and left the Command Center at a dead run.

"Stay with me, Ali," Muallah commanded. "Ruadh, be quick. For your life, be quick."

Gaming Center, Schriever Air Force Base

Joe watched Lowell's terminal, bored now and impatient. He wanted to go home and take a shower and think about Eileen, not stand here in the gloom and watch another Game. He was hungry. He wondered where they would go tonight. Joni's, perhaps? Would Joni see that they were lovers? Perhaps she would. This replay idea seemed so good a few hours before. Now it was boring. Maybe Joe would fix dinner for Eileen himself. Maybe they'd order out for pizza, because he wanted to take her clothes off as soon as she got there and crawl into bed with her and find out if every touch was as incredible as he remembered.

The screen stopped. The mouse arrow stopped. The globe froze in place. Joe froze, one hand to his mouth, eyes widening. He looked at the Game clock, a display in the corner of each screen. It stood at 9:12 A.M. The mouse was still and unmoving and the globe turned, unattended, as Lowell Guzman crawled under the floors and rose up behind his wife with a screw-driver and drove it into her back.

It was Lowell.

"Oh dear God, it was Lowell," Joe whispered. The strength ran from his bones and he sat back in the chair. Then he leaped out of it as though stung. This was Lowell's chair.

His heart started pounding. He'd called Eileen, but she wasn't home. He'd called Nelson, but he wasn't home either. Probably out feeding the horses.

Then the enormity of what he'd done hit him. He'd called Nelson. Just like Art. Just like Art. Lowell had Nelson's voice-mail password. He'd done exactly what Art had done.

Far away, down the long sloping corridor to the front of the Gaming Center, Joe heard the key clicks as someone on the other side keyed in the combination to open the door.

Black Forest, Colorado

Caleb Atkins loved his Appaloosa horse business. He was a genuine horse nut. His father insisted he attend college classes at the University of Colorado, and Caleb grudgingly admitted his business degree was going to help the business quite a bit. But he still felt like a six-year-old when the last class ended and he could come home to the barns and the stalls and the creatures that he adored.

When the thudding sound of the helicopter rose out of the forest, Caleb was looking at the slightly swollen foreleg of Annamarie in the Big Barn, where the pregnant mares were kept. Annamarie whickered softly. The barn smelled of warm horses and hay and disinfectant. Caleb stood up from Annamarie's leg, eyes wide.

The stories of the Black Helicopter of the Black Forest were many and varied. Some claimed the helicopter was merely some Army training mission from down at Fort Carson. Some claimed whoever saw the Black Helicopter always had missing time afterward, and bloody noses at night. Always. Caleb didn't believe in UFOs. He had no time for them. But everyone who lived in the Black Forest heard about the Black Helicopter.

Caleb looked out the open barn door, stunned, as a huge black helicopter with absolutely no markings swooped over the trees and settled in for a landing in front of the main house. Annamarie whinnied sharply at the sound and shifted, pressing her warm shoulder into Caleb. Caleb clenched his jaw. They were coming for his dad, who worked out at Schriever on something that was so top secret he never spoke about it. That helicopter was going to abduct his dad.

"No, it's not," Caleb said. Cassie Atkins's shotgun was behind the barn door, fully loaded. It was a Defender combat shotgun intended to kill rabid dogs, crazy mountain lions, and any Bad Men who had intentions about Cassie. Caleb's mother had taught him how to shoot her Defender years earlier and insisted Caleb keep up regular practice. Caleb kept the shotgun and kept in practice, just as she would have wanted him to do. The length of her final illness had left them plenty of time to say all their good-byes, but it didn't mean that he still didn't miss her.

Caleb hefted his mother's shotgun and ran into the darkness as the helicopter settled on the grass and two figures ran for the door.

He moved behind the helicopter, keeping to the trees, and scuttled toward his front door. The smell of jet fuel was choking. The two figures were knocking—knocking? he thought blankly—and when his father opened the door in bathrobe and reading glasses, one of them grabbed his arm as though to hustle him to the helicopter.

"Oh no you don't!" Caleb roared, and stood up. He leveled his shotgun at the closest figure. "You take your hands off my father!"

Highway 94, Colorado

Eileen slowed to take the turn onto Enoch Road, her eyes leaping ahead to the lights of the base. She was looking for flashing colors, the police lights that would mean she was too late. She kept mouthing Joe's name. He had figured out what Art had done. Eileen had realized why her mind had supplied Joe's image, and where he must be, when she saw the turn to Schriever. Who else but Joe, Art's partner, would be able to figure out what Art had done? Lowell must have found out what Art had discovered. What had Art known? Eileen would have pounded the steering wheel in frustration if she dared to take her hands from the wheel.

She hoped that Lowell was even now in Joe's house, waiting for him to return home, ready to kill him on the off chance that Joe might find out what Art had discovered. Lowell would be caught if he were, and Joe would be safe. But she knew she was foolish to think that. Lowell left the robot alibi in his house because Joe was out at the Gaming Center. Joe knew what Art had done, and Lowell had found out.

Eileen bit her lip hard enough to draw blood, her hands cold and slick on the trembling wheel of the Jeep. Her portable siren was flashing on the top of her car, and she flipped the audible on as she blew by the guard station at the entrance to Schriever. She saw the guard in the rearview mirror as he ran out into the road and stood staring. Then he ran back into his shack, and Eileen knew he'd be calling the other guards. Good, she thought.

She pulled the Jeep up to the vehicle gate at the retinal-scanner building. The Entrance Portals, Major Blaine had called them. Eileen left the siren blaring, and in a few seconds there were soldiers at her car, looking dazed and frightened. Eileen flipped the siren off.

"Colorado Springs Police," she shouted. "We have an emergency at the War Game Center. I need to get on this base now!"

"Ma'am, we can't let you drive on this base," one of the guards said. He carried an M-16 on his back, but Eileen doubted it was loaded. He looked obstinate and afraid, the way Eileen remembered all enlisted people looking when she was in the Air Force.

"Look, we've got a possible assault in the Gaming Center," she said. "You want to drive me? You can drive my car. You can get me there any way you want. But I need to get to that Center now!"

"Do you have authorization to be on this base, ma'am?" the soldier asked.

Eileen pulled out her police badge. Her Schriever badges were tucked in behind.

"Will this do?" she said, trying to keep her voice even. The best way to deal with the military was to follow all the right forms. Otherwise you ended up splattered on a mountain, the words "pilot error" engraved on your headstone. Eileen never wanted to pull her gun and try to force her way as much as she did at that moment. But there were six of the guards now, and they all looked concerned. The gates were solid. In the movies she would be able to drive through eight-foot-tall chain link, but not in reality. Her Jeep would give a great bounce and a lurch and never run right again.

"Yes, sir," the guard said. "Let me call my commander and see if we can give you a ride over there."

Eileen got out of her Jeep and ran into the retinal-scan building, and for one horrified moment as she felt the glass doors lock behind her she thought she'd forgotten the number. Then it sprang into her brain and she keyed the access code. The green light flashed in her eye, the door clicked open, and Eileen burst through the other side, officially on base. The guards stared after her. The head guard shrugged his shoulders to the other guards, as if to say, "What can we do?" Then he went in to call his commanding officer. They wouldn't get in trouble, at least. They'd followed all the right procedures. The woman had entered the base the proper way.

Eileen ran into the darkness, her clever running shoes making no sound.

Black Forest, Colorado

"Oh my God," Nelson Atkins said. "You need me to start up the *system*?"

Captain Shelly, her hands locked firmly behind her neck, glared at the tall boy with the shotgun.

"Can you tell your son to let us go now?" Colonel Maclean said gently. His hands were behind his neck too, and he didn't like it any more than Captain Shelly did. Why hadn't they brought side arms? The boy held the shotgun firmly, and Maclean felt the sweat start to drip down his sides. The opening of the shotgun seemed about as large as the Eisenhower tunnel. "We need to get you to Schriever to enable the—uh—system. There is a potential that the system might be *used*. Do you get my meaning, sir?"

Nelson paled further.

"Stop scaring my dad," Caleb snapped. "And what are you talking about? What system?"

"Son, this is about my job," Nelson said gently. "They're from where I work. I didn't know they were coming or I would have said something. Can you put the shotgun up? They need me to do something very important. Okay?"

Caleb put up the shotgun at once. Maclean could see the blush climbing up the boy's cheeks. Caleb thumbed the safety switch and shrugged again.

"No hard feelings," Captain Shelly said with a wobbly grin, taking her hands down from her neck.

"None at all," Maclean said, working his shoulders and sighing. "You did a fine job of protecting your dad, son."

"Thank you," Caleb murmured, flushing an even brighter red.

"We need to go, sir," Captain Shelly said.

"I'll be back," Nelson said to Caleb. He didn't go into the house to change out of his bathrobe, or put his reading glasses away. He hurried with the two Air Force people toward the helicopter, a section of the newspaper still clutched in his hand.

Turtkul, Uzbekistan

"Our men can hold the stairway for hours, Mahdi," Ali said confidently. "The foolish Russian could have held us off until his ammunition gave out. We have plenty of ammunition."

"Grenades?" Muallah asked tersely, not taking his eyes off Ruadh. Ruadh was sweating heavily, but at long last he appeared to be doing something. He'd fetched keys from all the dead Russian soldiers hours before and had three of the keys in slots on the control panels.

"The stairs are reinforced and block the bottom doorway. The only way they can blow the door again is by reaching the bottom of the stairs as we did. Rashad, Haadin, and Assad will not allow that."

"Our escape?" Muallah murmured. Ali said nothing.

"Many of the Russians will be dead shortly," Ruadh spoke up, startling Muallah. "The silo tops blow sideways with explosive charges. I'll blow them all, Mahdi."

"Excellent." Muallah grinned. "Soon?"

"Now, if you are ready," Ruadh said, his sweaty face glowing with pride. "We need to turn the two keys at once." Muallah knew this drill from a dozen Western movies. He went to the panel and watched as Ruadh took hold of the little silver key.

"Two turns. On my count of three make the first turn," Ruadh said. "One. Two. Three!"

As Muallah turned his key, he heard a glorious roaring sound from eight stories above his head. Then the ground shuddered as the giant concrete covers, blasted sideways by explosive charges, thudded to the ground and shattered. The covers were the size of basketball courts. Any living thing in their way was now so much ground meat.

"Now we launch," Ruadh said. "I've set silo number two for the launch sequence."

Muallah nodded at Ali and watched as Ali slipped silently from the command center. Ali would see how many of the Russians were left. Muallah's plans did not include a Russian prison.

"On my count of three, again," Ruadh said, and took hold of the second of the two sets of keys.

Gaming Center, Schriever Air Force Base

For a moment Joe couldn't move. The fear poured into his body, and he saw white specks in front of his eyes. There was a roaring sound in his ears, and he wondered if he was going to pass out. Then he heard the door open down the long hallway, and the trance broke.

He looked around Lowell's room. Everything seemed very bright and very clear. He noticed with one part of his brain that the clock on the computer had slowed down. Each second ticked by an eternity after the last. The gadget to pick up the metal floor tiles was in the television studio, a few feet from Lowell's room.

Joe leaped to the television studio and, device in hand, was levering up a metal square while one part of his mind was still contemplating the curious slowness of the simulation. He left the carpet square folded up, hoping it would drop back down as soon as he put the tile down. If Lowell found him, he wouldn't have much of a chance. A tile opener against a sharpened knife wasn't much. But unlike Art Bailey, Joe Tanner knew who the murderer was. Joe wasn't going to stand there and let Lowell rip out his throat. He was going to fight.

He had no flashlight, but that didn't matter. He kept the suction device, the weight reassuring to his hand, and squeezed into the blackness beneath the floor. As he lowered the tile back down, he heard Lowell calling his name.

Highway 94, Colorado

"Colonel Ellison didn't tell me why!" Stillwell shouted over the screaming of the little Datsun's engine. Gwen's car was a pickle-green B-210 with rusted-out side panels and an engine that probably shouldn't be driven over forty.

Stillwell held the engine at sixty, and the sound of the wind shrieking in through every faded seal was matched by the howl of the tiny engine. Lucy held on to the frayed dashboard.

"Have they found another body? Did he say that?"

"No!" Stillwell shouted. He banged the steering with his fist, and Lucy jumped and shouted.

"What?" he yelled. "What is it?"

"Don't hit this car!" she shouted back. "Are you crazy?"

Stillwell started roaring with laughter and Lucy, after a moment, joined him.

•35

The weight of her gun kept bumping against Eileen's ribs, but she was used to that. The night air was soft and warm against her hot face. The long dark bulk of the CSOC loomed over her. A brief flicker caught her by surprise and she lost her pace for a moment, seeing something moving in the grass. Then she saw the white flip of a tail and realized she was seeing a jackrabbit. They must live on the base and come out at night to feed on the alien Kentucky bluegrass. What a treat for the rabbits.

She crossed the road and headed up the slope toward the Gaming Center, and she felt as if she could run straight up the side of the building. The fear was over now. This was the time for action. She no longer had to sit and wait. She would finish this. She would save Joe or she would avenge him. There were no other options open to her. She ran.

Peterson Air Force Base, Colorado

"I'm the commander of Schriever Air Force Base," Colonel Willmeth said into the phone. "And you are going to listen to me very closely. We have an inbound helicopter on the way to the Space Command building. This helicopter is authorized to fly over Schriever and land undisturbed. Do I make myself clear?"

"We're not supposed to—"

"Tonight, you will," Willmeth said. He was struggling into his clothing and was hopping on one foot as he spoke. What the hell was going on out there? Not for the first time, he cursed an assignment where he could not live on the base he commanded. He knew General Kelton from NORAD only slightly. Kelton's usual clipped voice had been flat with stress when he'd woken Willmeth out of a sound sleep minutes before.

"I'll be there in twenty minutes," Willmeth said to the on-duty officer at Shreiver. "If that helicopter has any troubles with my base guards, I'll gut you like a fish. Now follow your goddamn orders, Captain!"

He set the phone down and struggled with the zipper of his uniform pants. His hair could wait, he decided. His teeth could not. He grabbed his toothbrush and squeezed an enormous minty-smelling gob of paste on the bristles. The toothbrush went into his mouth. Car keys in hand, Colonel Willmeth ran for his car.

Schriever Air Force Base

"Captain Alan Stillwell," Stillwell repeated. He could feel his temper threatening to float away like a balloon. His head felt like a balloon, full of the pound of his furious heart.

"We can't let you in here," the Air Force soldier said stubbornly.

"We had a call from Colonel Ellison that Detective Reed from the Colorado Springs Police Department had called in an assault," Lucy said. Her face was pale, and two red spots burned on her cheeks. Lucy looked furious.

"Yes, ma'am, she came out here and tried to drive in on base, but we can't allow vehicle traffic on base."

"How did she get in?"

"She had her badges, ma'am."

Lucy drew a deep breath and stepped up to the airman.

"You listen to me, soldier," she said. Her eyes were narrowed to slits. "You have two options. You can escort us onto this base, or you can keep us here. If you escort us on base, you might get in trouble. You might even lose a stripe." She looked at his two stripes. "If you keep us here, and you are wrong, which you are, I will guarantee that you will be charged with criminal negligence, conspiracy to commit a crime, and obstruction of an officer in the commission of his duty. That means Leavenworth. Is that clear?"

The airman was no longer looking stubborn and scared. He was now just looking scared. Stillwell looked at Lucy in admiration.

Lucy was just getting started.

"Your commission, your oath, is to your duty. You are not a robot. You are supposed to think. You do not shoot babies. You do not let innocent people die. If you do, you hang for it. You go to Leavenworth for it. Is that clear?"

"Ma'am," the airman said weakly, "I—"

Lights suddenly washed across the group as a Chevy Blazer roared up the road. The truck came to a skidding stop.

"Major Blaine here," said a trim-looking man from behind the wheel. "I'm chief of security. I need to get through—" He stopped and looked with an unsettling blankness at Lucy and Stillwell. "Who are you?"

"Captain Stillwell, OSI," Stillwell shouted. "And Lucy—ahh—Lucy from DIA. We need to get on this base!"

"OSI?" Blaine said. For a moment Stillwell saw a look of fright on his face, but it was gone so quickly he couldn't be sure. "Why are you here?"

"Detective Reed called in an assault," Stillwell said with the last rags of his composure. "We need to get on this base to contain this situation, Major Blaine."

Major Blaine was silent for an endless second, his face smooth and blank.

Stillwell glared at Blaine. Didn't the stupid Security Chief understand the phrase? In all military services, containing the situation means one thing and one thing only. Cover-up, burial, *containment*, damn it.

Blaine at last seemed to understand, or to come to some kind of conclusion.

"Open the gate, Airman," Blaine said, and held up his badge. "Get in the car," he said to Stillwell and Lucy. "I'll take you in."

Gaming Center, Schriever Air Force Base

Joe lay prone in pitch blackness among the hum and pulse of the computers, trying to make his breathing slow down. This was the nightmare of childhood, hiding in the darkness while the monster stalked. He crawled away from the spot where he hoped the carpet lay undisturbed.

There was a thumping sound off to his right. Joe concentrated fiercely, but he couldn't hear anything over the hum of the machinery.

A tile lifted suddenly, off to his right. A bright shaft of light speared down and a hissing, squealing sound broke from his throat as he scrambled away from the light. He could see the support shafts now, too small to hide him. The whole area seemed to be lit up to his night eyes.

Another floor tile lifted suddenly, this one down by the doorway. Joe knew what Lowell was doing. When there were enough tiles lifted, he would be able to drop down and see him. Lowell knew where he was. He scrambled away from the lights, trying to think. A red mist tried to swamp his brain, a mist that told him he could kill Lowell, yes he could, he could kill Lowell with his bare hands, just stand up and fight, kill, *kill him.*

"No," he mouthed to himself, although he made no sound. Lowell outweighed him by fifty pounds. Joe didn't know how to fight. He'd never taken boxing or even wrestling. He did *track* in high school, for godsake. Lowell would take him apart. The only thing he had were his brains and his speed.

Joe started to work his way toward the far end of the Center. If he could just lead Lowell away from the door, he might have a chance to make a break for it.

He clutched the tile-lifting tool to his chest, and as he crawled under the floors he started to pry the rubber suction cups off, leaving the sharp metal edges exposed. Just in case, he told himself, dropping the suction cups to the floor. Just in case.

Schriever Air Force Base

"I got the information from the base commander," Blaine said as the Blazer roared across the grass. Lucy held on as they bounced over a gully. Surprised jackrabbits scattered everywhere across the damp grass.

"We heard from the Peterson base commander," Stillwell shouted. He was still half deaf from the cruise in the screaming Pickle.

"Colonel Willmeth said Reed had called in a possible assault, not a murder," Blaine said forcefully. "I hope to God we're not too late!"

Lucy, from the backseat, looked at Major Blaine. Blaine was a horrible actor. There were big beads of sweat in the crisp hairline. There was a tic at the corner of his mouth. Blaine's voice wasn't steady. His face showed concern, but his eyes were ringed in white and wild with anxiety.

Lucy knew someone had tipped off George Tabor. It couldn't be anyone in the Gaming Center; they were all locked in the Center until the Colorado Springs detective arrived. Colonel Willmeth was a brand-new base commander and so could hardly have been George's contact. Lucy had tentatively marked Major Blaine as a possible risk, and now she decided that he was a very probable risk. She was certain of it. Major Blaine was not playing for the Home Team.

Lucy braced herself against the bouncing of the Blazer and decided to ride this one out. She would see what Major Blaine was up to. She could be wrong about him. But she had no intention of letting Major Blaine out of her sight.

Gaming Center, Schriever Air Force Base

Eileen held up her Schriever badge and her police badge and ran by the guards in the Missile Defense Center. She was too out of breath to explain anything to them, and she assumed the base guards would be along shortly.

The long stairs were the cruelest part of her run, and she was nearly done when she reached the third floor. The air was thin with little oxygen, and Eileen could feel the sweat soaking through the back of her shirt. She gasped and wheezed and then picked up a run again, nearly staggering.

The submarine-style door bashed against the wall as she flung it open. She didn't bother to close it behind her. Later on, they would show her the long groove the door handle had punched into the wall and the spray of blood from the knuckle she'd skinned when she spun the wheel. Eileen ran down the hallway to the last door, unaware of her bleeding hand, and as she came to the Gaming Center she reached under her arm and brought out her gun.

The number didn't work. She keyed the clicker twice, fingers trembling, before she realized she was keying in the proper number in reverse order. Eileen cursed, keyed in the number in the proper order, pulled the door open, and raced up the hallway.

As she entered the Gaming Center she saw the patchwork of tiles. Carpet squares lay everywhere. The metal tiles were flipped on their backs, metal gleaming sharply from their undersides. Every console in the Gaming Center showed the vision of Washington, D.C., in the last seconds before impact. Eileen recognized the simulation. It was from the War Game that had played just a few days before.

Lowell Guzman, hair soaked with sweat, was flipping open another tile. His soft burly body was crouched over the opening, and the glitter of his screwdriver was murderously sharp in the gloom.

As Eileen appeared in the doorway Joe leaped up from an opening a few feet from Lowell. His eyes were grim and narrow and his cheeks were patchy with red and pale white. He clutched a bare levering device in one hand and he was heading for the doorway, directly toward Eileen.

For a moment he didn't see her. His eyes were at his feet as he sprinted from opening to opening, fleet-footed as a deer in the snow. Behind him, Lowell roared and sprang after him, dropping his own tile-opening tool and raising the sharpened screwdriver high.

Joe was quicker than Lowell. But he raised his eyes, saw Eileen, and stumbled, arms flung wide. Lowell, behind him, still shouting, raised the screwdriver above his shoulder to drive it forward into Joe's back.

"Drop!" Eileen shouted, and Joe tucked into a ball and fell into the next opening like a magician through a trap door. He was gone, and Lowell saw Eileen.

Eileen raised her gun in slow motion, seeing every bead of sweat and the surprise and the frustration on Lowell's face. Behind Lowell, the giant screens blossomed with nuclear detonation. A climbing mushroom cloud stood over Washington like an angry fist. Then Lowell was gone, too, tucking up exactly as Joe had done and dropping into the floor.

Eileen shouted in frustration and ran forward. She didn't have a chance to make a shot at Lowell, and now she couldn't. She might hit Joe. She stood on a tile where the two had been, and as she looked for Joe the tile underneath her erupted up and she stumbled, staggering. Lowell burst up through the floor, and in the patchwork of the room Eileen could not find a footing. She curled up and rolled over a tile. The gun spun from her hands as she instinctively tried to keep from dropping into one of the holes in the floor. Lowell scratched a long silvery streak in the metal floor as his home-made stiletto missed Eileen by a bare half-inch.

Eileen dropped into the hole in the floor. Lowell came after her. Lowell was mad, eyes completely senseless in his beefy face, sweat running in streams. He drew back for another strike as Eileen scrambled to her feet. Eileen reached under Lowell's arm and hit him smoothly in the throat. Most people hit in the jaw, thinking about the movies. Jaws are hard objects that in real life have a tendency to break what hits them, like hands. Throats, on the other hand, aren't very hard. People protect their throats with their jaws in a fight, but Lowell wasn't expecting Eileen to strike him there. The blow struck Lowell directly in the windpipe, immediately cutting off his breath.

Eileen danced backward, and that was her mistake. The edge of a floor tile caught her in the upper thighs, sending exquisite pain through her legs.

She doubled over and barely avoided Lowell as he tried to strike at her again. His eyes were bulging and he was trying unsuccessfully to breathe.

Lowell stood up for a third strike, and that was when Joe rose up behind him with the tile opener held in both hands. He swung the bulky thing like a baseball bat and connected solidly with the back of Lowell's head. There was an amazing spray of blood from Lowell's scalp as the metal edges tore through his hair, and the sense and madness fled from Lowell's eyes. He stood for a moment, a childlike, puzzled look on his face, then fell forward. He landed half on, half off a tile that was still in place. His feet dangled to the floor below.

Joe stood staring, then dropped the bloody tool from his hands.

Eileen secured her gun before she handcuffed Lowell Guzman, and she did both of those before she turned to Joe Tanner.

"I told you I didn't do it," Joe said shakily.

"I knew you didn't," she said. She looked at Guzman and realized he was breathing, which relieved her. She wanted to have a long talk with Lowell Guzman. Several of them. It was going to be a pleasure. "Gotcha, you bastard," she murmured.

"*I* got him," Joe said, smiling ferociously.

Eileen put her hands on the crossbars of the tiles and swung herself out of the floor. She dusted her hands and grinned.

"You got him, yes you did," she said. "Have I said thanks yet?"

"Not yet," Joe said, and scrambled out of his hole in the floor. There was an empty floor tile between them.

"Thank you." Eileen laughed, and leaped at him.

•36

Schriever Air Force Base

The Blazer scattered gravel into the grass as it slid to a stop in front of the building. Blaine got out of the Blazer and ran toward the doorway, not waiting for Lucy or Stillwell. Lucy cursed, struggling with the backseat release. She passed Stillwell as they ran for the entrance.

"What's going on?" Stillwell asked.

Lucy ran without answering. She sprinted by the desk without seeing the guards, following Blaine. Her stomach felt heavy and unfamiliar, but her legs were toughened by years of running. Stillwell was a distant third as Blaine headed up the stairwell.

She was silent in her running shoes. She hoped her intuition was wrong. She knew it was not. The building seemed enormous, and she could not quite catch up to Blaine. There didn't seem to be any oxygen in this Colorado air.

As she rounded a curve, she saw Blaine in an open doorway. He was looking at something, and as time slowed down for her she saw him pull a pistol from his shoulder holster. Her pistol matched his, flying into her grip with absurd and dreamlike ease.

He raised the pistol. Lucy didn't raise hers. She knew she couldn't hit him while she was running, and she hoped she could reach him before he fired.

He fired.

Turtkul, Uzbekistan

The sound was enormous. It was unbearable. Anna Kalinsk shrieked and huddled over her two youngest boys, trying to hold her body over theirs and protect her ears at the same time. She knew everyone must be screaming, but she could hear nothing.

Suddenly daylight poured over her. Anna hunched over her boys, trying to gather them under her like a duck hiding her ducklings, knowing that it would do no good. Her body would not stop the bullets. They would go through her and into her sons, and it would be over.

Not for the first time, Anna wished she had a rifle. At least she could try and take some of the husband-killing, father-killing murderers with her. She looked up, teeth bared, to meet her death face-on.

There was no one at the opening of the underground silo. Nothing but clouds of billowing dust.

Gaming Center, Schriever Air Force Base

There was a movement at the entrance to the Gaming Center. Eileen turned from Joe's arms, expecting to see a whole platoon of base guards, and instead saw Major Blaine standing at the end of the hallway. He had a pistol, and as he raised it to his shoulder Eileen twisted around and pulled Joe into an open space between the floor tiles.

They hit the subfloor together, with an impact that drove the air from her lungs. Joe had landed on top of her. Blaine's gun went off with an enormous coughing sound. It was not the thud of a bullet hitting meat. Eileen whooped, and Joe shouted. He scrambled off her and tried to stand up.

Eileen put her hand on his shoulders and pushed him roughly down. She couldn't seem to take a breath. She leaped out of the floor.

The office chair in front of the unconscious form of Lowell Guzman was shredded and smoking. It had been a near miss. The stink of gunfire was choking. Eileen ran toward the entrance, gun in hand.

Blaine was down. He was flat on his face, one arm twisted high between his shoulder blades. He was breathing heavily. A woman sat on him, holding his arm neatly. She was panting. Both of them had obviously arrived at a run, which explained Blaine's poor shot. He didn't have time to take a good stand and steady his aim. If he had, Lowell Guzman would probably be dead.

Eileen stopped in the doorway, bent over, put her hands on her thighs, and drew a deep harsh breath.

"Ahh," she said.

"Anyone shot?" the woman said.

"Just a chair," Eileen wheezed.

Another man came running up, wheezing as badly as Eileen.

"Was he trying to shoot a bad guy or a good guy?" the woman asked. She was dark-haired and very pretty, and dressed in civilian clothes. Eileen had never seen her before. "Tell me I did the right thing."

"You did the right thing," Eileen whispered hoarsely. She took a couple of breaths and choked out a laugh. "I'm out of handcuffs."

"He's not," the other man said, pointing at Blaine. Eileen looked at the new man. He was a short Air Force major in a rumpled uniform. The uniform was not merely rumpled. There were wrinkles on the wrinkles. Dust was creased into the wrinkles at his ankles. There was a big stain on the shirt. He was sunburned and mosquito-bitten. He looked as if he'd been hopping freight trains for a week.

"Lucy Giometti, DIA," the woman said. She was very pale. She unhooked Blaine's own handcuffs from his belt and used them on him. As she stood up Eileen realized the woman was pregnant.

"Eileen Reed, Springs Police," Eileen said. Her breath was coming back. "Are you okay?"

"I'm okay," Lucy Giometti said. She was feeling her stomach, patting it all over, as though she were checking to make sure it was all there. She grinned at Eileen and held out her hand. "I don't want to do that, say, for regular exercise, but I'm okay."

"Thank God," Stillwell said as Eileen and Lucy shook hands. "I couldn't get here as fast as she did. What a hit! Where did you learn to do that?"

"Girl Scouts," Lucy said primly.

"I'm Captain Stillwell, OSI," the raccoon-eyed major said, turning to Eileen.

"Nice to meet you," Eileen said. "You're supposed to take over the investigation, right?"

"That's right," Stillwell said, and started to grin. "Looks like the only thing you left me was some paperwork." He held out his hand, and Eileen shook it firmly.

"I'm glad," Lucy said.

"Me too," Joe said from behind Eileen's shoulder. He was looking at Major Blaine with a wondering expression on his face.

"Me three," Stillwell said.

"Let me up," Blaine said from the floor.

"Shut up," all four of them said at once.

Turtkul, Uzbekistan

Ali appeared at Muallah's right. Muallah was watching the countdown clock with satisfaction. Only four minutes and Fouad Mullah would fulfill his destiny. The Trumpet of Doom would sound, and the world would never be the same.

"Mahdi," Ali murmured. "I predict survivors. We can climb from silo one."

"We need Assad," Muallah murmured, understanding instantly what Ali meant. Rashad, Haadin, and Ruadh would hold off the soldiers while Muallah and Ali escaped. They needed Assad to fly the helicopter, but the others were disposable.

"We need Assad to set the explosives in this room," Muallah said aloud to Ruadh. "Take his place and send him here."

"I can—"

"I require Assad," Muallah ordered. Ruadh bent his head and left, with a last glance at the control panel.

"Only three minutes left," Ali said, gazing at the red numbers.

"I want to be outside when the Trumpet sounds," Muallah said. He felt rapturous, transported. His moment was at hand.

"We need to hurry," Ali said.

Gaming Center, Schriever Air Force Base

"Who's in the Center?" Lucy asked, holstering her gun.

"Lowell Guzman," Eileen and Joe said together, and grinned at each other.

"Lowell," Lucy said wonderingly. "He's the murderer? And Major Blaine was trying to shoot him?"

"He sure wasn't aiming at us," Eileen said. "I think—"

She was interrupted by the earsplitting shriek of a siren. The hall to the Gaming Center lit up with swirling red lights.

Lucy and Stillwell jumped. Joe Tanner gasped.

"Oh my God," he shouted.

"What is it?" Eileen said, shouting over the whooping of the siren.

"It's a launch," Joe shouted back. "It's impossible. It's—" Then he turned and was gone, bounding up the hallway into the Center.

Stillwell and Eileen looked at each other, then at Lucy. The color was draining out of Lucy's face.

"What is it?" Eileen asked.

"Muallah," Lucy whispered from ashen lips. "Muallah is going to launch."

Turtkul, Uzbekistan

Anna saw the distant silhouette of a figure at the top of the silo, the figure she'd been dreading, and she felt her whole body go rigid. As if that would help stop the bullets.

"Hello?" a voice echoed down the silo. Anna blinked in disbelief. The voice and the language were Russian. *Russian.*

"Hello!" she screamed. "Hello, help us, please!"

Ilina stood, dislodging children left and right, her face wild with hope.

"Help us, we are Russians, we are women and children, help us, please!" she shouted, then burst into hysterical laughter.

"They are Russian, Ilina, Russian!" Anna shouted, and then everyone was on their feet, shouting and laughing and crying, as the first ropes came down the silo.

A very tough-looking Russian soldier slid down the rope like a circus acrobat, facefirst, a wicked-looking rifle at the ready. He landed on his feet and bounced like a tiger. His eyes darted everywhere.

"You okay?" he asked Anna.

"We are okay," Anna said, wiping at her face with her apron. "The terrorists? You have killed them?"

"Some of them," the soldier admitted. "We need to get you out of here as quickly as possible. Do any of you need a doctor?"

"No," Anna said, and bit her lips to keep from laughing aloud. Was it wrong to feel this joyful when Dmitri lay dead so close by? But she could not help it. She had survived, and so had her children. "Tell us what to do."

Moscow, Russian Republic

"They have the women and children," Colonel Kalashnikov shouted. This turned the gloom of the Command Center into sudden excitement. Losing twenty men and three assault helicopters was a terrible blow. The silo covers had blown without warning. Now that twenty trained soldiers were dead, it was easy to see how stupid they had been not to plan for such an event. Now that the covers had blown, that is.

Cherepovitch was still a mottled shade of purple. Major Paxton was white with anxiety. He'd received more information from his superiors in Washington, and none of it was good. Muallah hated America, it seemed. The Russian Republic was not a likely target if Muallah got a missile off after all.

"We will succeed, Major," Kalashnikov said softly. "We have half our force left, after all. We will kill them."

"I hope so, sir," Paxton said woodenly.

Gaming Center, Schriever Air Force Base

Joe slapped the commander's console and the siren stopped in midwhoop. He bent over the console, fingers waving in the air uncertainly, then punched the access keys to NORAD.

"Get in here!" he roared in the direction of the doorway. Then he keyed the microphone to NORAD.

"This is Joe Tanner?" he said. "War Game Center? What—"

"Oh my God," a voice burst from the console. "General, we've got someone! We've got someone!"

"This is Major General Kelton," another voice said calmly. Joe barely noticed Eileen and Lucy and Stillwell joining him at the console. "We are unable to release the Missile Defense system from NORAD. We have a possible launch event. Is this clear?"

"That is clear," Joe said with lips as pale as Lucy's. "Uh, sir."

"The system has to be enabled from the War Game Center. We predict—" There was a brief pause. "Perhaps twenty minutes to launch. Can you get the system enabled and released?"

"Yes, I can," Joe said slowly. He looked around the Center uncertainly, looking bewildered, then focused on Lucy and Stillwell and Eileen. He nodded. "I have enough people to run the consoles."

"Who is this?" the General's voice asked. But Joe was already gone, leaping from floor tile to floor tile on his way to the Truth Team room.

"I've got to start it from here!" he shouted. "Follow me!"

Eileen immediately followed. Stillwell glanced at the console, and Lucy waved him on.

"Go," she said.

She pressed the same key Joe Tanner had used. "This is Lucy Giometti, CIA," she said crisply. "Joe Tanner is going to start up the system, but he needs our help. We'll contact you when we're ready. Over and out."

Cheyenne Mountain, Colorado

"CIA? What do you mean, CIA?" General Kelton was shouting, but the connection was dead. "How long until the helicopter gets to Schriever?" he snapped.

"ETA twenty-eight minutes," Major Parker said in a dead voice. "It's going to be way too late."

"I know Joe Tanner," a captain piped up. She was at another communications console. All faces turned to her. "He's a Truth Team guy. I talked to him last time we were out there for a demo. He knows how to start up the system. He does it all the time."

"Sweet Holy Mary," murmured Major Parker.

"What is Joe Tanner doing at the Center at ten o'clock at night?" the General asked. "And what is a CIA agent doing there? Get me Admiral Kane," he said to the Captain.

General Kelton scrubbed his hands over his balding head. He was furious because he was helpless. He stalked up and down the room, watching the screens, waiting for the telltale plume that he could do absolutely nothing about.

Gaming Center, Schriever Air Force Base

Eileen watched as Joe Tanner's fingers flew over the keyboard. Joe bit his lips into a bloodless line as his eyes flickered back and forth across the screen.

"Thank God I was already set up for play," he said. "All I have to do is—"

"All you have to do is what?" asked Stillwell after a long moment. Eileen glared at him and made a shushing sound. Joe ran his hands through his hair and looked at the screen. He kept on typing. Eileen and Stillwell and Lucy stood like statues behind him, looking at a screen full of windows that were full of words that meant nothing to them.

Joe stopped typing. He put his hands on his forehead and squeezed his fingers around his temples. He sat and stared at the screen for long endless seconds. Then he nodded.

"Eileen, go to the commander's console," he said crisply. "That's the one I was just standing at. Uh—you, pregnant lady, go sit at her left. That's Missile Launch Control. Major, go to the Space Command console."

"Where's that?" Stillwell asked humbly.

"Third door on the right," Joe snapped. "Go!"

As they hurried out of the room, Joe shouted after them. "Push the button on the bottom left of your communications box, that's the green button. That gives us hot-mike communication."

Eileen sat down at the commander's console. It showed the swirling cloud of nuclear detonation over Washington, D.C., the same one she'd seen days before. Joe had been replaying the game, she realized. Lucy was staring at her screen with horrified eyes.

"An old simulation," Eileen hissed. She punched the green button on her communications console. Suddenly the screen in front of her went dark. The whole room darkened as the large screens went dark as well. Then, one by one, the screens lit up with a perfect blue and white globe. The earth.

"This is a simulated earth," Joe Tanner said. His voice seemed to come from everywhere. "But everything on it is real. We can't do real clouds and we don't need to, not really."

"Why not?" Eileen whispered. Her voice came out of every speaker in the Center, and she winced.

"We can see through clouds," Lucy said matter-of-factly. Her voice echoed from every corner of the room. "Welcome to the world of Top Secret, Detective."

"Okay, I want to engage the whole Brilliant Pebble system," Joe said. "I don't know where the launch is and I don't care—"

"Uzbekistan," Lucy said.

"Okay, we'll focus our best satellite sensors there, after we get the system enabled," Joe said. Eileen looked over at Lucy, and Lucy offered a tiny shrug.

"CIA?" Eileen mouthed silently, and Lucy made a mouth. Eileen grinned like a child.

"We have to engage in sequence," Joe said. "Eileen, you're Command. I've hooked us to the hardware-in-the-loop. When we're fully integrated and on-line, your console will show the Enable key. When it does, you press it with your mouse key. Understood?"

"Understood," Eileen squeaked, then coughed in embarrassment.

"Next, pregnant lady. You're secondary command. Your key will light after Eileen presses her key. That's the second key. You have to press it within ten seconds of Eileen or we'll have to start over. Okay?"

"Okay," Lucy said.

"Major, you're Space Command. You have Brilliant Pebbles. You have a bunch of choices on your screen. Ignore them all. Punch the All Enable key, it will light up after the pregnant lady—Dammit, what's your name?"

"Lucy," Lucy said.

"After Lucy presses her key. Don't screw up. Okay?"

"All right," Stillwell said. Eileen could see him through the open door of his room. He was sitting at a console just like the one where Terry Guzman was found, his computer on a spindly table with a single stalk for a leg. He looked out at her and Lucy, and gave a little wave. Eileen looked over at Lucy and saw that she was smiling.

"We can do this," She said confidently. Her voice came out of all the speakers.

"Of course we can," Joe said absently. "Waiting to go on-line." Suddenly one of the big screens of the globe disappeared and was replaced with an odd-looking chart of satellites and lines. The lines connected the satellites together. All but three of them were green.

"Come on, come on, come on," Joe said tonelessly. "Come on, you bastards. Hook up."

Turtkul, Uzbekistan

Muallah was twenty feet from the lip of the silo when the world suddenly filled with sound. Ali was ahead of him and Assad behind him. He could see a crescent of sky beyond the nose cone of the missile in their silo.

"Allah akhbar!" he screamed, but he could not hear himself. He looked up, into the blue day, to see the Trumpet flaming upward into the sky. Muallah screamed in triumph as the roaring filled the world with sound.

•37

Cheyenne Mountain, Colorado

"We have a launch event," Major Parker said tonelessly. General Kelton stopped his pacing and sat down in the commander's seat.

"Well, people," he said calmly. "Here we go. Get me Air Force One."

Gaming Center, Schriever Air Force Base

"We've got a launch," Lucy said. She was staring at the big screen, her eyes huge and bruised looking in her pale face. Eileen looked away from the communications console, where one line remained red, and gulped. There was a big black dot in the map of Uzbekistan.

"Ignition plume," Stillwell said in a gulping voice.

"Be ready," Joe warned, his voice tight and angry. "Goddammit, you all just be ready."

Eileen held her finger over the mouse key, her mouse pointer hovering over the Enable key, which was dark and useless. Her finger trembled over the mouse. She looked away from the screen.

"Where is it headed?" Lucy whispered.

"Don't look," Joe snapped. "We're almost there, almost there, almost there . . ."

Eileen focused her whole body on the dark Enable button. "Light, light, light," she whispered.

The button flashed green as Joe shouted "Now!" from the Truth Team room. Eileen stabbed her mouse key, and her button started flashing. She looked over at Lucy. Lucy was clicking on another green button. They got up together and ran toward Major Stillwell's room, leaping awkwardly over the empty floor tiles. Joe appeared from the Truth Team room and beat them both to Major Stillwell.

"Here, here?" Stillwell panted. His console was a confusing mass of flashing buttons and weird-looking symbols. His unwashed hair flopped on the back of his neck. Beads of sweat stood out on his face.

"Right there," Joe said, and his voice was reassuringly calm. "Punch it."

Stillwell punched the button, and the console flashed yellow, then green around the edges.

"Done!" Joe shouted. Eileen and Lucy crowded in the doorway. "We did it!"

"How long 'til they shoot it down?" Lucy asked.

"Minutes," Joe said confidently. "We got it released in time, I'm sure of it. Now let's go see where it's headed."

"Should I stay here?" Stillwell asked.

"No, we can all go to the commander's console," Joe said. "We need to tell NORAD we got the Pebbles enabled."

Like children playing follow-the-leader, Eileen and Stillwell and Lucy leaped back to the commander's console, following Joe. On the way, Eileen spared a thought for Lowell Guzman, unconscious and bleeding less than ten feet away, and Major Blaine, facedown in the hallway. Then she put them out of her mind.

Joe punched the NORAD sequence again. "Pebbles are released," he said. "Uh, General. Sir."

They heard faint shouts and cheers from Cheyenne Mountain.

"What about a follow-on?" Joe asked. "Is there going to be more?"

"No follow-on," General Kelton said. "The Russian troops secured the base just as the missile took off. The terrorists are all dead."

"Good," Lucy said fiercely.

"Where's the impact location? The President needs to know."

"We all need to know," Eileen said dryly.

"General impact location is the northern United States," Joe said, looking at the globe of the Earth on the console. Eileen saw a large gray splotch over the northern part of America. It looked horrible, like a monstrous amoeba.

"Northern United States? Not Washington, D.C.?" Lucy asked in surprise.

Joe typed on the commander's console. The screen in front suddenly shifted to a view over the United States. The blotch was shrinking rapidly. It now covered the Great Lakes regions and was decreasing by the second. Eileen realized the computers must be predicting the impact from the missile's trajectory.

"It's the gut shot," Joe said numbly. The microphone to NORAD was still live.

"The *gut shot?*" General Kelton said.

"The gut shot," Joe repeated. "The body blow. The kidney punch. You know. Chicago, Illinois. We play that one all the time. You take out the industrial heartland. You take Chicago, you poison Detroit, Gary, Indiana, all the industrial centers. Then the fallout drifts over Ohio, Pennsylvania, New York. America loses her industrial capacity all in one strike. Not too good for crops in the Midwest, either."

"Oh my God," Eileen said faintly.

"Much more effective than the decapitation strike," Lucy murmured.

"Decapitation?" Eileen whispered.

"Of course," Joe said. "Decapitation is Washington, D.C., Eileen. Take out the federal government and supposedly you destroy our country. Cut off the head, you kill the body. But anyone who does their homework knows we don't really depend on Washington, D.C."

"Bomb Washington, D.C., and you just piss the hell out of America," Stillwell said, nodding. "And you don't have much of a chance of getting the President. They can get him out of Washington *fast*. You can't decapitate us, not really."

"Well, it would hurt pretty bad," Lucy murmured, and Eileen remembered the other woman was from Washington.

"We'll let the President know. God grant those Pebbles will work," the General said over the loudspeaker, startling them all. "God grant we were in time."

Turtkul, Uzbekistan

"You think this was the guy?" the soldier asked, rolling the body over with his toe. The arms flopped limply and the eyes gazed at the brilliant sky. The eyes blinked; the man was still alive, but he wouldn't be for long. The blood was pouring out of three bullet wounds in his chest.

"He doesn't look like a leader," the other soldier said doubtfully. "He's too young."

"Maybe this guy," one of them said to the other, going to the other body lying limply in the dirt.

Behind them, Muallah gazed at the sky. It was a brilliant and beautiful blue. The faint contrail of the missile crossed one side of his vision. He would have liked to move his eyes to see if he could see the missile still climbing into the heavens, but his eyes no longer obeyed him.

He would go to Allah, and that would be good. He would bring with him all the souls of the American infidels to be his slaves. Allah had decided that Muallah was not to be the leader of the new Arab empire, and that was the will of Allah. Muallah had fulfilled his *jitan,* his holy mission, and that, too, was the will of Allah.

Allah akhbar, he tried to whisper, but the sky was growing dark around him, swirling in black flakes like the fires that would consume the Western world. *Allah akhbar.*

Air Force One

"Hold on," the Secret Service agent said. The plane didn't just bank; for a moment Richard thought he was going to pass out as he was pressed deeply into his seat.

"Secondary sanctuary is Florida," the Secret Service agent said through compressed lips. Air Force One was doing a complete reversal in midair, turning on her tail and fleeing back in the direction from which she had come.

"Maine wasn't such a good idea after all, I guess," Steve said, his eyes sparkling with excitement. He loved roller-coaster rides. Not that he'd had a chance to ride on any in the past three years. The Secret Service would simply not hear of it.

"Oh my God, Chicago," the President said. Richard tried to pat Dad's arm, but his own arm wouldn't leave the seat. Dad was a terrible ashy color. Nobody else looked very good either, and it wasn't because of the g-forces.

"We have the Brilliant Pebbles, sir," the Secretary of Defense said with a grotesque attempt at confidence.

"I hope they work," the President said, and blinked rapidly. He bowed his head, and for a moment Richard couldn't figure out what he was doing. Then he realized his father was praying.

Moscow, Russian Republic

Kalashnikov could not bear to look at the American. But he could not live with himself if he did not. The Command Center was sick with tension. The radio communications link was open, but was silent except for a slight hiss of static. The roar of the missile launch had been clearly audible over the link. The projected impact had come in a scant two minutes later. The United States. After that, everyone had fallen into a helpless silence.

"General Cherepovitch," Major Paxton said abruptly. His words were slurred and drawn out, as though he were speaking an entirely different language than English. Oddly enough, Kalashnikov had recently seen *Gone With the Wind* in the theater and recognized the accent immediately. Kalashnikov looked at Paxton and saw that the Major's face was pale and his lips were bitten to a bloodless line. His precise and unaccented English was gone, but his eyes were still sane.

"Major Paxton," Cherepovitch responded formally.

"We must prevent war between our countries," Major Paxton said. For a moment Kalashnikov didn't understand what he meant; in Paxton's accent, thick with stress, "war" had come out as "wah."

Cherepovitch bowed his head. Kalashnikov realized his palms were damp and stinging. His fingernails had bitten through the skin. Was this to be the end? Not just the end of Salekhard, democracy, clean water and food and opportunity, but the end of everything?

Like the films his wife so loved to see, Kalashnikov could see the course of disaster. A Russian missile destroying an American city. A million dead, thousands more screaming in blind, burned agony. Thick radioactive ash falling over American soil, killing animals and plants, sickening children. All of it on television, all of it traceable to a Russian missile silo, a Russian bomb. Would the terrorist who launched the missile matter in the end? Or would the American people, mad for revenge, demand a response? Kalashnikov squeezed his fingers in his palms and felt the warm stinging of blood. He looked at Major Paxton and saw the man looking back at him with haunted, sickened eyes. They both knew there would have to be a response, and the result would lead to war.

"We will help you however we can," Cherepovitch said simply.

"I would have done the same as you," Paxton said heavily, reluctantly. "I would not choose to save my country over the bodies of your women and children. You did your best."

"We did our best," Cherepovitch said. "I'm sorry that it was not enough."

Gaming Center, Schriever Air Force Base

"Come on," Joe said. They looked at the main console, watching the missile track grow and grow. He typed rapidly on the commander's console,

a frown pinching his forehead. Eileen looked on helplessly. Lucy and Stillwell stood with their hands at their sides.

"Everything is enabled. They have to get an intercept solution. They
have to!" Joe said.

"It's almost to the Pole," said a voice from NORAD.

For an eternity they stood, staring at the growing black track. Eileen
thought of the babies being born in Chicago hospitals, the cops patrolling
neighborhoods and chasing drug dealers and prostitutes and doing their
best to keep the streets just a little bit safe, just a little bit sane, and this in-
sanity was flaming toward them and it *wasn't stopping*. There were late-night
restaurants and millions of people sleeping sweetly in their homes and they
were going to die, all of them, if that curve didn't stop growing. There had
to be something else they could do.

"Is there something else we can do?" Stillwell asked, his face in agony.
Joe put his hands to the sides of his face and shook his head back and forth,
eyes stricken. Lucy choked back a sob.

"Come on, baby, come on!" Eileen suddenly shouted. She couldn't
stand it anymore. "Come on, baby, find that bastard. Come *on!*"

Lucy glanced at Eileen and then shook her fists at the screen, grinning
wildly.

"Comeon! Comeon! Comeon!" she shouted.

"Find the ball, baby," Joe shouted, jumping up and down and laughing.
"Find the fucking ball, baby, you can do it!"

There was nothing from the speaker at NORAD; perhaps they thought
this weird set of Gamers had gone completely off the deep end.

Stillwell joined in, his face flushing red.

"Go for it, man," he shouted in a hoarse voice. "Go for it!"

Eileen started laughing. They were all shouting at the computer screens,
screaming at them, and it wasn't doing a damn thing, but it *felt* good, it felt
as if they were doing something.

She was looking at the center screen when there was a flash of brilliant
light. The light was nearly blinding. The whole room lit up fiercely, and
then the light was gone.

"Did you see that?" she gasped. They all stared at the screen, silent and
still in an instant.

"Yes," Joe said.

"Yes," Stillwell said.

"Yes!" Lucy shouted.

The gray splotch over Chicago, the projected impact point, disappeared without any fanfare. One moment it was there, the next it was gone.

"The missile has been shot down," Joe said quietly, voice trembling. He looked at his console and typed rapidly for a few moments.

"This is NORAD," General Kelton said from the speaker. His voice sounded shaky and young, like a boy's voice. "Can you confirm what we're showing?"

"I can confirm it, sir," Joe said. "No threats are in the air."

"The skies are clear?" Lucy asked, her face unbelieving. "Clear?"

"All clear," Joe said.

The speaker from NORAD erupted with shouts and cheers, but Eileen paid no attention. She was kissing Joe, and Lucy, and even Alan Stillwell, who was rank and sweaty and dirty—but she didn't care, they had done it. The earth floated on the big screen, pure and blue.

•38

Memorial Hospital, Colorado Springs

When Lucy parked her rental car the sky was beginning to lighten, although it wasn't yet five o'clock. The bulk of Pikes Peak blocked out the stars to the west, clearly visible in the light of the false dawn. Lucy lingered for a moment, breathing the clear morning air, then headed for the entrance doors to Memorial Hospital.

"Yes?" The nurse behind the emergency-room admitting desk looked tired.

"I'm looking for Detective Reed," Lucy said politely. "She should have come in here a little bit ago."

An orderly coming down the hall heard the conversation and stopped at the desk.

"Sure, Eileen," he said. "She's with a suspect. They've got police guards. Guzman," he said to the nurse. The nurse nodded back.

"They're up on the third floor, where we have the prisoners' rooms."

"Thanks," Lucy said politely.

"Waiting rooms are to the left," the orderly said helpfully as Lucy walked toward the elevators.

Moscow, Russian Republic

The room smelled of desperate and unexpected victory, stinking with sweat and bad breath and the sharp tang of vodka. In respect for the rules, Cherepovitch had allowed only one shot for each soldier. Alcohol was strictly forbidden in GRU headquarters.

"It's the size of the damn glasses that gets me," Major Paxton said to Kalashnikov, one of Cherepovitch's cigars clenched in his still trembling fingers. "You think they're such tiny little things, and the next thing you know you're singing and being dragged along the street by your friends because you can't walk anymore."

Kalashnikov laughed, but not loudly. He was still shaky from reaction. They were sitting in the upper control room, a booth where cable news played around the clock. Hours, it had been, and nothing had leaked. The biggest story was the American tour of the Polish rock band Night, now singing to sellout crowds and being likened to the Beatles, during the British invasion.

"Every new band gets compared to the Beatles," Paxton said. "When I was a kid the Bay City Rollers were compared to the Beatles, for godsake."

"Who?" asked Kalashnikov.

"So tell me, Major," Cherepovitch said casually. "Why do you think the weapon malfunctioned?"

"Could be the guidance systems were corroded somehow," Paxton mused. "Or faulty to begin with. I'm sure our entire fleet of nuclear missiles—what's left of them—are going to be overhauled starting immediately. I'm sure you'll do the same."

"You wouldn't, perhaps, have shot it down, would you?" Cherepovitch asked, taking a puff on his cigar and squinting his eyes as though he were telling a joke.

Paxton threw his head back and laughed.

"You don't get off that easy," he said. "Our missile defenses were never installed, remember? We made up Star Wars to end the arms race, not to actually build the damn thing." Paxton put his cigar in his teeth and put an

328 • BONNIE RAMTHUN

arm around Cherepovitch and his other arm around Kalashnikov. He gave them both an unexpected and very Russian bear hug.

"We were damn lucky, that's all," he said.

Memorial Hospital, Colorado Springs

Eileen was slouched in a chair in the waiting room, trying to read a magazine. Stillwell, who was grimacing and sipping at some very old coffee, looked up.

"Did you get the Pickle home safe?" Lucy asked. Stillwell had dropped her at the hotel before returning Gwen's car to the airport.

"Safe and sound," Stillwell said, grinning. Eileen snorted.

"I can't believe you got that thing to go over twenty."

"Gwen was amazed too," Stillwell said.

"Where's Joe?" Lucy asked.

"At home," Eileen said. "I took him home. He needed the sleep. And he didn't want to talk to Lowell."

"I can understand why," Lucy said. "And Blaine?"

"Safe in custody at Peterson," Stillwell said with satisfaction. "Now all we have to do is figure out why Blaine was trying to shoot Lowell."

"That's all we have to do now," Lucy said. She saw her smile answered in her new friends' faces. Even though none of them had gotten any sleep that night, they were still all on a high. Saving the world was better than sleep.

"Blaine won't talk, right?"

"Oh, he talked," Stillwell said. "He sounded like a lawyer trying to beat a speeding ticket. He kept telling me he thought Lowell was armed, he thought Lowell was threatening Eileen, blah blah blah. I don't buy it."

"I don't either," Eileen said. "Hey, is that a package of Oreo cookies?" Lucy looked down into the open mouth of her handbag.

"Hey, so they are. You want some?"

"The vending machine is out of order," Stillwell explained.

Lucy doled out the cookies and sat down with a sigh.

"Somebody give me background," she said. "Eileen, how about you?"

"Lowell should be coming around pretty soon. They said it was only a concussion," Stillwell said. "I want the story too, if you don't mind."

"I don't mind," Eileen said, crunching into an Oreo. "You told us all 'bout that Muallah creep, anyway."

"Let's just call him the Creep," Lucy winced, looking around the very unsecured waiting room. She'd told the story of Fouad Muallah and his Trumpet of Doom during the wait for Colonel Willmeth and the rest of the Schriever cavalry.

Eileen Reed would have made a great CIA analyst, Lucy decided, even if she was beautiful the way Lucy usually detested: long-limbed, straight dark reddish hair, gorgeous cheekbones. Still, she had an incredible brain behind all of those good looks.

"Well, I'm glad the Creep is dead," Eileen said with satisfaction, sipping at her coffee. "You know, it's too bad he never knew all his great plans were foiled by a woman."

"A woman?" Lucy asked in confusion. Joe Tanner wasn't a woman.

"You, Lucy Giometti, you know?" Eileen said, as though it were obvious. "We and the Russians both were alerted to the whole situation in time to stop him from getting away, if not stop him. And if you hadn't been at Schriever we couldn't have started up the system to stop"—here Eileen looked around cautiously—"it."

Lucy smiled. "I never thought of it that way," she admitted. "It's almost too bad they didn't catch him alive. I would have liked to see him realize he was beaten."

"For Sufi's sake, if no one else's," Eileen said, and Lucy nodded, feeling an enormous rush of affection for her new friend. Eileen *understood.*

"So what about Lowell and your investigation?" Stillwell asked. He hadn't showered and was still remarkably filthy, but his raccoon eyes were intent. Lucy realized that his man, Blaine, was still not quite in the bag.

"I'll fill you in up to tonight," Eileen said. "My partner should be here before I'm done. I want him to hear what happened tonight. At least, the part about Lowell and Blaine."

They all exchanged grins, and Lucy felt the laughter bubbling up inside of her again.

"Okay, I'll start with Terry Guzman. She was murdered during the War Game this week, found with a sharpened screwdriver in her back. . . ."

Rosen showed up before Eileen was finished, carrying a bag of subs and a thermos full of coffee. He delivered the subs and shook hands with Lucy and Stillwell. Economical as always, he said nothing, but sat down in a chair and unwrapped his own sub.

"I'm almost finished catching them up tonight," Eileen explained. Rosen nodded, and for a few minutes there was no talking at all.

"Ahh, better." Lucy sighed after swallowing her last bite and crumpling up her sandwich paper. "Thank you for bringing those, Detective."

Rosen nodded gravely.

"Okay, go on," Lucy said. "This is incredible. You know Terry's contact was Major Blaine?"

"That's why we have to wait for Guzman to wake up," Stillwell said. "I don't think we can get an espionage conviction from a single phone number. And unless we can prove the espionage, Major Blaine can beat the attempted murder rap in court."

"Sure, just doing his job," Rosen said gloomily from the depths of his chair.

"We thought the murderer was Blaine," Stillwell said, sipping at his coffee. "Now we know it was Lowell."

"Lowell was trying to kill Joe Tanner, at least," Lucy said thoughtfully. There was a silence among them.

Eileen looked out into the deserted hallway. The waiting room was softly lighted and tastefully decorated, but the chair arms were soiled and the magazines tattered. The signs of waiting.

"I'm hoping Lowell has something to say about Blaine," Eileen said.

The on-duty doctor appeared in the doorway and contemplated the small group of people. He was thin and elderly. He wore glasses, and his blue scrub suit was wrinkled.

"No problem with the stitches, no fractures, and your patient is waking up," the doctor said, taking off his glasses and polishing them with a handkerchief. "Four visitors?"

"Four, please," Eileen said.

"Room 309," the doctor said. "Don't stay long."

LOWELL WAS AWAKE. The face was as innocent-looking as Eileen remembered it, although it was bruised and swollen along the right side. A white bandage covered half his head. There was an IV taped to his wrist. Lowell saw Eileen first and looked away. His eyes were blurred and vague.

"First, the business," Eileen said. "You have the right to remain silent . . ."

When Eileen finished reading Lowell his Miranda rights, she asked him if he was willing to speak.

"Sure, why not?" Lowell said, not looking at Eileen. He glanced at Lucy Giometti, and turned away from her bright look of loathing. Rosen leaned against the door frame. Stillwell stuffed his hands into his grimy pockets.

"Why did you kill Terry?" Rosen spoke first, quietly.

"I don't know why she married me," Lowell said, and moved his hands on the covers. "I don't know why. She wanted—I don't know what she wanted."

"Why?" Eileen repeated patiently.

"Because she was going to lose her job. She was so obvious about her little games. I found out about her and Major Blaine—"

Lowell caught the abrupt movement from Stillwell. He looked at Stillwell, and understanding cleared the sad brown eyes for a moment.

"Ahh, you want him? He's got a habit, that's what Terry said. When I confronted her. They didn't sleep together, they just did business. You can't screw on heroin. I guess he got the habit overseas."

Lucy gave a little shudder of disgust.

"Terry, everything was easy for her, you know?" Lowell added in a blurred voice. "From the time she was a little cheerleader in high school, everything was just handed to her. Her mom and dad gave her money, a car, a college education. When things got hard in college she just went out with guys who would help her get through her classes, help her cheat. She didn't even really have a computer science degree, she had a business degree with a CS emphasis."

Lowell chuckled rustily, his eyes focused far beyond the people in the room.

"Emphasis," he said bitterly. "She couldn't code her way out of a paper bag. But ah, God, she looked so good, she smelled so good, she wanted me, and I would have done anything for her, anything. . . ." His voice trailed off and his eyes sharpened. He looked over at Eileen. "She had anything she wanted, but she always wanted more. Why is that, do you know?"

"Who did Blaine pass the information to?" Eileen asked neutrally, struggling with a desire to feel pity for the drugged man. He was pitiful, but he was a monster.

"I don't know." Lowell sighed. "Once I found out it was too late, you know. All I could do was beg her to stop, and she just laughed. I'd lose my clearance. They'd probably send me to jail, too."

"That's why Blaine tried to shoot him," Lucy said. "With Lowell dead, no one could prove that he was her contact."

Lowell turned his blurry gaze to Eileen.

"She was so wicked. Didn't you find that out? Didn't everyone tell you how evil she was?"

"She didn't deserve to die," Rosen said coldly.

"And Art?" Eileen said, tasting the brightness of revulsion in her mouth. "Was Art evil and wicked? Is Joe Tanner?"

Lowell looked puzzled. The big hands on the coverlet stirred a little, then relaxed again.

"I—don't know," he said. "I couldn't let Art find out it was me. Who would have thought you could play back those terminals? I thought I had the perfect murder planned. I worked on it for months. I even tested it one Game earlier, without raising the floor tile behind her. But Art figured it out." Lowell shook his head.

"Then Joe figured it out too, and left a message for Nelson. I—" He looked around the room, seeking understanding. "I couldn't let them figure it out. It was easy, after killing Terry. It was easy after the first time."

Lowell laid his head back on the pillows, his bruised face gray and wan.

"It was pretty easy, really," he muttered, and fell asleep.

Eileen, Lucy, Rosen, and Stillwell stood around the bed and watched Lowell Guzman sleep. They looked at each other, and as they turned to leave the room the first light of dawn began to touch the windows with pink and gold.

•39

Denver Animal Shelter

Fancy surged to her feet along with the other dogs in the kennels that lined the room. It was morning. Someone was coming in from the street entrance. The dogs barked. Debbie walked an elderly couple down the corridor. Fancy wagged her tail, trying to shove her tender nose through the chain link of the kennel gate.

A volley of barking burst from one of the kennels and the couple rushed to the door. The girl opened the door and a little white poodle came bounding out, leaping in joy around the old couple's feet.

The barking died down as the kennel keeper escorted out the old couple and their dog.

Debbie petted Fancy as she hosed out her kennel later.

"Tonight for you, Fancy. Game over. Sometimes I hate this job," the girl said to herself. She latched the door and moved to the next cage.

Peterson Air Force Base, Colorado

Major Stillwell looked at the film on the closed-circuit camera.

"What's the matter with him?" the guard asked. "He's driving me crazy in there. He keeps pacing and pacing."

"I know what the matter is," Stillwell said. "He's a junkie. And in about six hours he'll be so frantic he'll tell us everything we want."

"A junkie," the guard said, and looked with disgust at the tiny figure walking back and forth, back and forth, in the little cell.

"Be careful around him," Stillwell warned. "He might get pretty violent."

"I'll be careful," the guard said.

He'd let Blaine stew for a while longer, Stillwell thought. Time enough to go home and shower and catch a few hours of sleep. He smiled in grim satisfaction, looking into the camera.

"Hey, you're the one who crashed in that cornfield?" the guard asked suddenly. "I heard about that. What a pain in the ass that must have been, sir."

"You're telling me," Stillwell said with feeling.

"Was this guy the reason?"

"One of them," Stillwell said with an unbelieving laugh. "One of them."

For the first time, Stillwell realized that his little adventure was going to accelerate his career. Accelerate? Hell, he was the ranking military officer at the first-ever shoot-down of a nuclear missile in flight. He was going up for colonel in another year, and he had no doubt about what would happen. He might even be a general someday. For the first time in the whole endless journey from the Oklahoma cornfield to Colorado, Alan Stillwell contemplated his suddenly brilliant career.

"Well, you got your man," the guard said. "Sir. Congratulations."

"Thanks," Stillwell said. He felt great. Tired and still dirty, but no longer confused. He felt just great. "Thanks."

Village Inn Restaurant, Colorado Springs

The sunlight glittered on the clean table, the glasses of ice water, and the surface of the hot coffee in the thick china mugs. Steam curled up from the coffee.

Eileen sighed, feeling the exhaustion but not willing to surrender to it, not yet. Now was the time for a few minutes of contemplation and quiet celebration. There were people eating eggs and drinking coffee at Village Inns in Detroit, Michigan; Scranton, Pennsylvania; and Buffalo, New York. There were babies being born, old people sitting in rocking chairs, punks stealing cars and addicts getting their morning fix, and all of it was wonderful, wonderful, because the alternative was too horrible to contemplate and it had nearly happened.

"I wish he would have lived. He should have known he was beaten," Lucy said quietly, sipping her coffee and looking out the window. Pikes Peak looked as stunning as it always did. Eileen saw with affection that Lucy couldn't seem to stop looking at the mountains.

Eileen understood about Muallah. She'd met several Muallahs in her police career, men who believed women were like disposable tissues. The way Lucy tracked Muallah down and figured out what was going on was stunning. If only the CIA had listened, they might have had a team in place and the missile might never have been launched.

"I can tell you're not a cop," Eileen said. "I'm glad they shot him. If he'd lived, who knows what would have happened? He might escape, or be acquitted. Nope, I like the idea of Muallah cold and dead just fine."

"You're right," Lucy said. "I really meant to say, I wish *I* was the one who shot him." She grinned at Eileen, and Eileen grinned back. They were the same kind of woman, Eileen thought, even if Lucy was a stunning beauty and Eileen was just Eileen-looking.

"Here's breakfast, ladies," the waitress said cheerfully, and started setting down an amazing array of plates.

Later, Eileen watched as Lucy continued to tuck her enormous breakfast away. Bacon, eggs, hash browns with gravy, pancakes. Eileen had finished her pancakes long before, and was sipping her coffee contentedly.

"I'll be out of here this afternoon," Lucy said with real regret. "I have about a zillion debriefs to go through when I get home."

"I hope this helps your career," Eileen said.

"Oh, I think this will help a bit." Lucy grinned. "You're going up to NORAD today? Or tomorrow?"

"Tomorrow," Eileen said. "I need to sleep today. I have about a jillion reports to fill out, too. I've been to NORAD, anyway."

"This will be a classified visit. You're going to see things you never saw before," Lucy predicted confidently. "Besides, you're a hero. They'll roll out the red carpet."

Eileen shrugged, feeling uncomfortable.

"Not me, that would be Joe," she said. "And you."

"Hmm," Lucy said, waving a chunk of sausage on her fork. "Let's see, if you hadn't gotten out there Lowell would have gotten Joe, and Joe wouldn't have been alive to start the system, so—"

"And if you hadn't been there Blaine would have gotten both of us," Eileen shot back, smiling.

"And if Stillwell hadn't crash-landed in his cornfield and showed up at just the right time—"

"And if my mom had never met my dad," Eileen finished, laughing. "It was all a miracle, that's all. I'm glad I was there. I'm glad you were there. You know, if you ever get tired of Washington, I could get you a job out here."

"Funny, I was about to say the same." Lucy grinned.

"It was nice to work together," Eileen said wistfully. How often had she met someone like Lucy? Once, twice in her life? One of those had been Bernie, and she felt a surprisingly sharp stab of grief for her lost friend.

"Yes," Lucy said. "Thanks for the file." She gestured to her briefcase, where a copy of Doug Procell's conspiracy file lay, as yet unread.

"The least I could do." Eileen shrugged. She had a sudden idea and cleared her throat nervously. "Uh, I have a favor, maybe . . ."

"If I can do it, it's yours," Lucy said simply.

"I was wondering if you might be able to get a government file on a plane crash," Eileen said. Her voice grew harsh. "I was a friend of hers, and they'd never let me see the file. I was wondering—"

"I'll see what I can do," Lucy said. "I'll get it for you if it's out there. You've got a clearance. You'll be cleared to see it."

"Okay," Eileen said, and she felt a smile of relief spread across her face. "Her name was Bernice Ames. And the crash was an A-10. Seven years ago."

"You have an e-mail address?"

"On my card," Eileen said, and dug one out of her wallet. She wrote the information about Bernie on the back of the card, in sloppy large script. "You know, I don't know that it means so much anymore. I don't want revenge. I just want to know. If I can, I want to clear her name."

"I understand. To put the memory to rest. Ghosts die hard sometimes," Lucy said slowly.

"I suspect we'll all have bad dreams for a while," Eileen said. "I can deal with bad dreams."

"Me too," Lucy said bravely, but her eyes were sad. Her hand hovered over the swelling of her stomach. "I wish we'd never thought up the damn things. The bomb, I mean."

"If we hadn't, I wouldn't be here," Eileen said with a wry smile. "My grandfather was on a transport ship headed for the invasion of Japan when we dropped the bomb. His survival chance was less than zero, and he was only eighteen. He hadn't met my grandmother yet."

"So no Eileen Reed without the bomb," Lucy said. "So Muall—I mean the Creep—succeeds. But he doesn't have a bomb without the bomb. So maybe it would have been plague, or mustard gas. I think I'm getting a headache." But she looked more cheerful, which made Eileen feel better.

"What really matters is the end of the story," Eileen said. "The good guys won. We won."

"This time," Lucy said.

"This time," Eileen agreed.

THEY WALKED TOGETHER to Lucy's rental car. The morning was hot and cloudless, but there were hints of the eternal afternoon thunderstorms to come moving up around Pikes Peak.

"Hey, if you want to vacation out here sometime," Eileen said, "I make a great baby-sitter."

"I might take you up on that." Lucy smiled. She took Eileen's hand. "Thank you again," she said. "We Italians take loyalty seriously. If you need anything, ask me."

"Thank you," Eileen said, surprised. "I—er—well, I'm a mutt, so I guess I have to say we mutts take our loyalty seriously, too." She smiled, but her eyes were unexpectedly stinging.

They squeezed hands and let go.

"I guess we did it together, didn't we?" Lucy said. "Well, I have to get up to Denver for my flight, so I better get going."

"Why Denver? Don't you want to fly out of Colorado Springs?"

338 • BONNIE RAMTHUN

"There's something I want to do in Denver first," Lucy said. "I'll call you!"

She put her briefcase in the car and started up and drove expertly away, one narrow hand lifted in a wave. She did not look back.

"Good-bye," Eileen said, and lifted her hand to wave back. She wondered if Lucy would send her a package in the mail. She wondered what it would contain.

One way or another, she would set her memories to rest. Eileen stretched and yawned happily in the morning sunlight. There was another duty she had to perform, and that one wouldn't be a chore at all. She turned to find her car.

JOE TANNER STIRRED and woke. He was being kissed.

"Mmm?" he said sleepily.

"It's Eileen," a voice whispered to him. Joe opened his eyes with a start, and remembered everything.

"Eileen," he said, and put his arms around her neck. "You're here."

"I'm here," she said, laughing. "Move over."

He moved over, leaving a delicious warm space for her. Eileen crawled in, and Joe wrapped his arm around her. He was almost asleep again, his arm heavy and limp, his breathing slow and even. Slowly his arm hugged her close, as though he was dreaming of holding her.

"Love you," he mumbled. His breath evened out and he was gone.

"I love you back," Eileen whispered. The exhaustion she'd held at bay for the last few days washed over her like surf, carrying her away bit by bit. Her heart had known about Joe, and it had been true. She had never been happier. She lay in the curve of Joe's sleeping arm and let the waves carry her away.

● Epilogue

Denver Animal Shelter

Fancy was dozing fitfully when the door opened. The dogs all rose, howling, to their feet. Not Fancy. She knew it was her time. She lay with her head on her paws, her eyes dull.

Then the little dog pricked up her ears at the sound of two sets of footsteps instead of one.

"This is Fancy," Debbie said. "What was your name again?"

"Lucy," Lucy Giometti said, and smiled.

"Fancy, this is Lucy," Debbie said, and reached to unlatch the door. "Oh, I'm so glad! She's such a good dog, and today was going to be her last day."

"I know," Lucy said. The kennel keeper opened the door and Fancy hesitantly put her nose out to nuzzle Lucy's hands. Her tail, bedraggled after days in a concrete kennel, wagged a little bit. Then Lucy smoothed her fur and rumpled her ears, and Fancy sniffed and licked Lucy's hands and thumped her tail again and again.

"How are you with babies?" Lucy asked the dog. Debbie smiled indulgently.

"I bet she'll be great."

"Well, we better go. I've got to make arrangements with the airline to get her back home."

"Where do you live?" Debbie asked. She attached a leash to Fancy's collar, and they started toward the entrance.

"Virginia," Lucy said. She took the leash from the other woman, and Fancy fell in instantly at her side, panting happily.

"You came all the way out here to adopt a dog?" Debbie looked incredulous.

"Well, not really," Lucy smiled. "I was out here on business and I knew she was here, so I thought . . ."

Debbie nodded happily. She needed no more explanation.

"I'm so glad," she said again. She filled out the adoption form, and Lucy gave the woman her credit card. She bought the collar and leash, too. Fancy sat obediently at her side.

"Well, Fancy," Lucy said to the dog, and took up the leash. "Let's go home."

"You saved her just in time," Debbie said to Lucy. "I just want you to know that."

"I know," Lucy said. "Thank you. I was just in time for my assignment out here, too. So it all fits together just right."

Fancy trotted obediently at Lucy's side as they walked out the entrance and into the blaze of the afternoon sun. The last that Debbie saw of them was Lucy's silhouette in the doorway and, next to her, the curling plume of the dog's tail, wagging as though it would never stop.